MINECRAFT

THE ELEMENTIA CHRONICLES
BOOK 1: QUEST FOR JUSTICE

BY SEAN FAY WOLFE

TABLE OF CONTENTS

"Justice will not be served until those unaffected are as outraged as those who are."

-Benjamin Franklin

PROLOGUE

The hallway of the brick castle echoed ominously with footsteps as a man ran down the corridor. He was in an outfit that was comparable to that of a medieval English King; brown hair, red shirt , pants of elegant design, and a flowing cloak with white fur around the edges. This man was a player on the Minecraft server Elementia. His tag was Charlemange77, known informally as Charlemagne.

The hall he was running down was lined with paintings of pixel art. Torches protruded from the walls and gave light to ward off the mobs, terrifying creatures that lurked in the dark. There were arched windows that revealed an expansive metropolis beyond the outer protective walls of the castle, sprawling as far as the eye could see. All of this was made entirely of cubes, one meter long on each side, with textures that resembled brick, wood, glass and all sorts of other things.

In this game, Minecraft, the entire world was entirely made of these cubic "blocks", which were in formations and with textures that were made to resemble the trees of the forests, the water of the oceans, the green grassy hills, and the stone and minerals of the underground mines. These blocks also made up the castle and the city, textured as stone and glass. The living things were composed of blocks as well, including Charlemagne and all other people, animals, and monsters that inhabited the spacious world.

Charlemagne was running because he was late to the meeting of the Council of Operators (there were no operators on the council, despite the name). This council was of the highest level players on the server, and was lead by King_Kev, often referred to as simply the King. The meeting was to discuss a most important matter, a matter which, unbeknownst to the council, would be the downfall of the King, of Charlemagne, and of so many others. This decision would be the downfall of the luxurious life that the high-level citizens of Element City enjoyed.

The man finally reached the iron doors and pressed a button on the wall. Five note blocks above his head activated, and played the chime that functioned as a doorbell. Moments later, the doors opened, and Charlemagne stepped into the council chamber.

There was a round table in the middle of the chamber, the King's allusion to the mighty King Arthur. Around it sat six of the eight council members. The other two seats were situated at the right and left hand of King_Kev, who himself sat upon a throne, elevated eight blocks above the floor, presiding over the council. The right seat held Charlemagne's fellow advisor to the King, Caesar894, while the left was reserved for Charlemagne himself. The king looked down upon Charlemagne. He had changed his skin, Charlemagne noted. The King had, indeed, changed his appearance; King Kev now had on a baby blue shirt with navy pants and black boots, and he had even added a blood-red cape. The only thing that remained unchanged was his head; a golden crown perched upon a neat comb of blonde hair. But enough of this, thought Charlemagne, I have other things to attend to.

"Forgive my tardy arrival, your highness," said Charlemagne, bowing by looking at the floor and crouching simultaneously with his Golden Sword drawn (this sword was ceremonial only; all council members and the King had one, though it was an impractical weapon).

"Forgiven," boomed the King, pointing his golden sword at Charlemagne (which is a sign of either welcome or intent to kill). "I trust your lateness has a good reason?"

"Oh, yes, my liege," grinned Charlemagne. "My lingering amongst the low-level peasants under the disguise of leather armor" (At this, several council members cringed; this was something not many of them were willing to do.) "took longer than I had anticipated, as I took part in a conversation regarding the local attitude towards certain aspects of the last major law you have imposed."

"The Law of One Death?" asked the King.

"That's the one, my lord," Charlemagne replied. "The attitude of the common folk is mixed; some, mainly those under level ten, say that it is a good law as it gives the game a higher risk factor, while most say that it undermines the superiority of the high-level folk. With the former, I agree," added Charlemagne.

"You dare to question the reasoning of my law?" bellowed the king. "Have you no respect for my authority? I ought to have you executed at once."

"Oh, no, your highness, that is not what I am trying to say at all," exclaimed Charlemagne, although he knew the king would do no such thing. Charlemagne had enough skill to escape any attempt by the King on his life. Moreover, Charlemagne knew things about the king, dark things, and the King would be a fool to provoke Charlemagne into revealing them to the public.

"I agree with both arguments, but only to a degree. The game is now much more...er... exciting now that you can die at any minute and be forever banished from the server, as opposed to simply returning to the last place you slept in a bed as is usual in Minecraft. However," he continued, "this does mean that the game is harder for those who have worked their way to the top, such as the members of this council. We upper-level players have the best plots of land in the known server, and a bounty of well-earned supplies. If, say, I was to die, I would leave a plot of fertile land and a house full of diamonds, emeralds, gold... well, you get the point, and I would never be able to return and retrieve them. Meanwhile a player who has just spawned could waltz into my home and steal everything I own, thus making them rich by doing almost nothing! Well, you can imagine how the people in the city who have worked their way to the top feel about that."

There was a murmur of agreement around the table.

"Hmmm," said the king. "You may be right. This new law does undermine the level system that rightfully benefits our upper class ... which is ironic, given the circumstances in which the law was imposed...but what do you propose we do to fix this problem?"

It was at this point that Caesar894, dressed as his Roman namesake, stood up.

"I have an idea," suggested the King's right-hand man.

"Speak it," replied the King.

"Well, it occurs to me that, within the walls of our city, we have almost no remaining fertile land. The forest beyond the city limits on all sides will not make good farmland. If we are to keep this city to the standard we are used to, we must take multiple actions. First, we must not give away any more of this fertile land.

9

Second, we must force the lower-level citizens of this city to leave. As Sir Charlemagne pointed out, they are likely to steal from us if we die, or, even more likely, rise against us and murder us in our sleep just to take our supplies!

"The lower-level citizens of this city outnumber us two to one," Caesar continued, "and if they should ever realize this, we would have a serious problem on our hands. We must force them to move from the city. If they do that, this city will have more land to be taken by those who deserve it.

"The Adorian Village can take on most of the outcasts, and there must be a fertile tract of land out there somewhere beyond the Ender Desert, even if our cartographers haven't mapped it yet. Some of the refugees can settle there. One thing remains certain, however; the lower-levels must go."

As he finished his speech, the council members clapped their blocky hands in approval. The king stood up.

"Very well. The law proposed shall state the following: Any citizens of Element City with a level under that of fifteen are required to leave Element City within one week of today's date. After that date, any players under level fifteen found in the city shall be killed, their houses destroyed. Those in favor of this law?"

Ten geometrically shaped hands raised into the air.

These ten players on the Minecraft server Elementia had no idea what they had just done. They had no idea just how people would react to this law. And they had no idea at all what this simple action would do to their way of life, to their citizens' lives, and to the game of Minecraft itself. But still the King spoke.

"Motion carried. The law shall be put into place at the next Proclamation Day. It is time for the elite of this city to take back their kingdom!"

At that very moment, a player called Stan2012 appeared on Spawnpoint Hill.

PART I: WELCOME TO MINECRAFT

CHAPTER 1: WELCOME TO MINECRAFT

It was dark in the Great Wood. Visibility between the tall trees surrounding the flowery hill was limited; who knew what was lurking in the shadows? The stars were still out, but the white square that was the sun had begun to peak over the horizon, giving the starry sky a faint pink and orange glow. The haunting howl of an Enderman pierced the peaceful dawn. It was this striking scene that was the first impression of the Minecraft server Elementia, to a new player that had appeared on Spawnpoint hill.

This player was clearly new; he held nothing in his rectangular hand, and was gazing in wonder at the infinite cubes of dirt, grass, and oak wood that composed the meadow hill and forest that surrounded him now. He had dark brown hair, a turquoise shirt, and blue pants, the standard look for a Minecraft player who had not yet changed his skin, or appearance. This player had never played Minecraft before. Unbeknownst to him, he couldn't have picked a worse time to join this server. His name was Stan2012.

Wow, Stan thought, as he gazed around at the dimly lit morning. This is awesome! Everything's made out of cubes! The dirt on the ground, the trees, even the leaves! And look at that stream over there. Even the water is perfect cubes! You can pick up these... blocks, and build stuff out of them? But there are blocks everywhere! Awesome! Oh, wow!

Stan looked around. The place he was standing in had clearly seen other players before, though he saw none now. He was surrounded by pixilated torches sticking up out of the ground, and there were signs and what looked like chests. One of the signs told him not to steal any of the torches, and another told him that he was standing on Spawnpoint Hill, where all new players enter the server. But it was one particular sign that caught his attention. The sign, which was located next to a chest, read: IF YOU HAVE NEVER PLAYED BEFORE, TAKE A BOOK FROM CHEST.

Stan walked over to the chest and opened it. It was sectioned off into compartments. One was full of loaves of bread, another with what appeared to be swords constructed out of wood, and in yet another, books. Stan took one of these books, and walked down the hill with it. He sat down on the side of the stream, dangled his feet in the water, and was about to begin to read when he heard a shout from behind him.

"Hey, wait up!"

Silhouetted against the brightening blue sky was a figure that appeared to be another player. As he walked down the blocky hill, Stan could see that this player was wearing a simple white tunic and white pants, with dark brown boots. He looked like one who might make his home in the desert. The player walked down the hill and stood over Stan.

"Hi," he said. "My name's KingCharles_XIV, but you can just call me Charlie. I've never played this game before and I have no clue what to do. Could you help me?"

"Maybe. My name's Stan2012, but you can call me Stan," Stan replied. "I've never played before either, I just heard that it was a fun game, and that this server is a great place to learn to play.

The sign up there said that this book would tell us how to play." He held up the book.

"Well then, let's read it," said Charlie. He sat down next to Stan and looked on as Stan read aloud.

INTRODUCTION

Welcome to Minecraft, new player. This is a very fun game with no particular goal. You can see that the world around you is made out of blocks. You can destroy these blocks with certain tools and place them elsewhere. After you have established a place to take refuge from the monsters of the night, you may work by day to arrange these blocks into fantastic structures. You are now standing on Spawnpoint Hill, where new players such as yourself enter the game. Before you can start building crazy inventions, you are going to want to join a community.

The suggested thing to do would be to follow the path you can see. It will take you to the Adorian Village, a community dedicated to the training of new players. It is a day's journey away, so take one wooden sword and two pieces of bread from the chest.. The bread will keep you fed until you reach the village, and the sword can be used to fight off the monsters of the night. If you have not reached the village by dusk, take some blocks from around you and build a wall around yourself to keep out the monsters. If you need to know anything immediately, this book is full of information about blocks, crafting, and monsters. Good luck, and see you in the village!

Stan flipped the page. That was the end of the introduction. On the following pages were information about the different blocks and their properties, instructions for crafting various tools, and descriptions of a bunch of different monsters. Stan looked at Charlie.

"Did you know that there were monsters in this game?" he asked.

"Well, I heard rumors about this thing called a Creepy or something like that, but I didn't think that it was actually real."

"Well, let's hope we don't run into any of those, or anything else. Now, do you see that road anywhere? Cause I kind of like the sound of this Adorian Village."

"Yeah, we should try to find it. But where is the road? I don't see it anywhere."

They glanced around. They didn't see a road, but Stan noticed something else. In the shadows of the trees was what looked like another player. The figure was the right height and had the right figure, but Stan couldn't see his face.

"Hey Charlie, look down there! Do you think he knows where the road is?"

"Maybe. Let's go find out."

The two walked down the hill and towards the figure. It was dark; the green foliage above provided shade from the sun. As they got closer to the figure, he suddenly turned and walked towards them, arms outstretched.

"Great, he sees us! Maybe he'll give us directions!"

"Yeah..."

But something didn't feel right to Stan... the player completely ignoring them until they got close, the walking straight towards them, the outstretched arms...

"Charlie, look out!"

"Stan? What's your prob.. OH MY GOD!"

The figure walking towards them had just walked under a patch of light. It was dressed like Stan was but it had rotten green flesh, and empty eye sockets. It smelled like death, and it was making soft moaning noises. The figure was still walking towards Charlie, who was immobile and wide-eyed with panic. Stan charged at the monster and did the only thing that he could think of.

He clubbed it over the head with his book.

The monster stumbled backwards a few feet, but landed upright, and again began to walk, this time straight at Stan. He started to run, but the monster was right behind him. He ran out of the woods, across the field, and suddenly stopped. He was standing in front of a ravine that he hadn't noticed before, which cut straight through the field. It was deep; he couldn't make out the bottom. He was trapped, with a fall to his death in front of him and the monster behind him. Afraid that he was about to die before he had even started playing the game, Stan balled his fists and turned towards the monster, ready to fight. Then he stared.

The monster had stopped chasing him. It was running back towards the woods, away from him and not towards Charlie. But the strangest part was that smoke was rising up off it's skin; Stan caught the putrid stench of burning flesh. The monster was making loud moaning noises, and Stan was sure that it would be screaming if it could. Suddenly, the monster keeled over, and burst into flames. It writhed on the ground until it had burned out of existence, leaving nothing but a small piece of rotten flesh in its place.

Charlie walked out of the woods, staring with a look of shock at the small piece of flesh on the ground. Stan wore a look of equal bewilderment. Charlie turned to Stan.

"What WAS that thing?"

"I don't know man, but it definitely was not a player."

"Maybe it was one of those monsters that were mentioned in the book. Maybe it was a Creepy, or whatever you call it."

"Let me look in the book."

Stan flipped open to the section of the book describing monsters, and on the first page he found what he was looking for. He found a description written next to an illustration of the monster they had just encountered.

ZOMBIES

Zombies are hostile mobs, or creatures, that spawn at night or in dark areas. They are the easiest hostile mob to defeat as their attack pattern consists of simply walking towards the player, trying to attack them. They will burn when exposed to direct sunlight. They are also able to break down doors, and are the main attackers during a siege on an NPC Village. They drop rotten flesh when killed.

As Stan finished the passage, Charlie said, "So that was a Zombie? And those things are supposed to be really EASY to kill?"

"Apparently so," replied Stan. He picked up the flesh off the ground. "Do you think this stuff is safe to eat?"

"I doubt it," frowned Charlie, staring at the rancid lump of green and tan meat. "Check the book."

After a little searching in the items section, Stan found the page describing the item.

ROTTEN FLESH

Rotten flesh is an item dropped by Zombies and Zombie Pigmen, and found in Temples. It can be eaten, but it is inadvisable to do so as it has a high chance of giving you food poisoning. It is not, however, poisonous to dogs.

"So, I guess we shouldn't eat it unless we're really, REALLY desperate," said Charlie.

"Yeah, you're right," agreed Stan. "Besides, we each get two pieces of bread from that chest up there, plus a sword. That sword should be helpful for fighting off any more monsters that turn up."

"Agreed. So let's get the stuff and GO! It's still morning; we've got an entire day to get to this Adorian Village before more monsters come out tonight."

The two players walked up the hill and each took two pieces of bread and a wooden sword. They then went to the top of the hill and looked around until Charlie spied the path. Bread in their inventories and swords in hand, Charlie and Stan started on the road to the Adorian Village.

CHAPTER 2: THE FIRST NIGHT

The trees around the pathway had been cleared out, so there was light shining down on the two players as they walked down the road to the village. There were no monsters on the path, but they spotted a few in the woods. Zombies seemed to be the most common, as they were all over the place, but the players noticed a few others, too. Charlie pointed out, deep in the woods, what appeared to be a zombie but thinner and less substantial, and Stan could have sworn that, from what he could see in the dim light, it was holding a bow and had a quiver of arrows on its back. Once, when Stan looked up into the trees at the sides of the road, he saw a flash of blood-red eyes contemplating him from one of the higher limbs. None of these mysterious creatures, thankfully, noticed the players.

"We'd better hurry and get to that village," said a nervous-looking Charlie. "I don't want it to be out here when it gets dark enough for those things to come out and hunt."

Stan nodded in agreement, but things did not go well from that point on. The path became less clear as they went deeper into the woods, and a few times they found themselves accidentally straying onto side trails that lead into dead ends. One of these paths turned out to have a Zombie at the end of it; Stan and Charlie barely managed to outrun it before it lost interest in them.

The sky began to turn a shade of beautiful pink, but the two players were unable to appreciate it as they made their way back onto the main road after their fifth detour and saw no sign of a village when they looked ahead.

"I think we'd better make a shelter for the night," said Stan. "We'd better make a wall two blocks high so that we have at least some type of barrier that the monsters won't be able to get over easily."

"You're right," said Charlie. "I'll go get some dirt blocks. You try to get some wood from these trees. Meet back here once you've got the stuff."

Stan nodded and the two set off in opposite directions.

Gathering the dirt was faster than Charlie had expected; after being hit a few times the blocks of dirt were lose, ready to be picked up and added to Charlie's inventory. He had amassed a whole stack of blocks of dirt by the time he went back to meet Stan.

Stan did not have nearly as easy a time; he had to punch the sections of the tree trunks a ton of times to get them to break off. It hurt, too. "What... I... wouldn't... do... for... a... chain... saw..." Stan growled through gritted teeth as he punched down a ton of tree trunks, leaving the leaves suspended in midair (Stan was quickly realizing that Minecraft doesn't always follow the laws of physics).

After about an hour the players met back on the road, and by the time night had fallen they had constructed a small rectangular box out of dirt and wood, two blocks high on all sides, with no roof.. They ate their first pieces of bread, and then bunkered down in their fort.

"Brace yourself," said Stan. "The attacks should start any minute now." Charlie gulped and pulled out his sword.

But to their surprise, nothing happened for quite some time. They just sat in their shelter, hoping no monsters would show. They popped their head up over the wall every now and then to make sure that there was nothing, and in fact, nothing was what they saw every time. When the half moon was at its highest point in the sky, Stan was about to say that there were no monsters around, and that they should just break camp and continue, when an arrow whizzed past him, grazing his shirt sleeve.

"INCOMING!!!" he yelled to Charlie as a firestorm of arrows began to fly over their heads. Charlie ducked; he looked through a small gap in the wall and saw about four animated skeletons, all standing a distance from their shelter, and raining arrows down on them. He stared at them, but he jumped back from the hole a second later as his view was obscured by the head of a Zombie.

"Zombies!" Charlie yelled to Stan, "And Skeletons, too! There's a ton of them, and," he as he looked through a few other cracks in the sides of their shelter, "they're swarming the wall!"

And he was right. From all sides, the four Skeletons were firing arrows at the players, and about six Zombies were forming a rabble around their fort, trying to walk straight through the wall. But the horror didn't stop there.

"TSSSSSKEEEEH!!!"

Something large had fallen down from the trees and landed right behind a cowering Stan. Without thinking, Stan whipped around and slashed his sword as hard as he could. He made contact; the monster was knocked back and he sliced at it many more times before it finally died. Then he got his first good look at it, and his heart gave a terrified jolt.

Stan was staring at the dead body of the largest spider he had ever seen. It had a whole mess of glowing red eyes on its head; the rest of its hairy body was dark grey. Stan knew then that this was what he had seen up in the trees during the day. The spider's body vanished, leaving a thread of fine string in its place.

More Spiders began dropping from the trees. "Charlie! Help me!" cried Stan as he tried to beat back the hoard of Spiders with his wooden sword. Charlie yelled in horror as he saw the Spiders rushing his friend, and he used his sword to get the attention of a few of the spiders as they attacked the players. In the midst of the attack, Stan managed to cut away the tree limb above them that the Spiders were climbing along to drop into their shelter, effectively cutting off the flow of arachnids from above.

"We won't have to worry about *them* anymore," sighed Stan.

However, he turned out to be quite wrong; the spiders, as it turned out, were able to climb *over* their wall to attack them. The players resigned themselves to the fact that they would battle the spiders all night long, and they put their backs to each other and drew their swords.

It was a long, hard night; the supply of spiders was seemingly endless, and they couldn't lift their heads up too high thanks to the barrage of arrows flying overhead. Miraculously, neither of the players lost any health that first night; the spiders attacked them, but Stan and Charlie managed to keep the giant bugs at bay and killed them with wild, frenzied sword slashes.

After a few hours, the sky began to turn pink, and then blue. The storm of arrows stopped. Spiders stopped climbing the walls. The players were safe.

"That," mumbled Charlie wearily, "was a very long night," and he slid back against the wall.

"Yeah, I wanna sleep too, but we have to go," said Stan through a poorly stifled yawn. "We have to make it to the Adorian village before nightfall, or we'll have to put up with all those spiders again."

"You're right. I guess we should go." Charlie stood up, but then he screeched and quickly crouched back down.

"What is it?" asked Stan.

"Don't look over the wall. Just don't." whimpered Charlie. He sounded petrified.

Stan looked over the wall. What he saw made his stomach flip.

The road ahead of them was covered with spiders. They were everywhere, crawling around and getting into fights with one another. There were no Zombies or Skeletons left, but there were so many spiders that Stan's knees failed him and he sank down next to Charlie.

"Why aren't they dead?" asked Stan. "I thought that monsters burned in the sunlight."

"Well, apparently the Spiders don't. What do we do? Fight them all?" He looked at his and Stan's swords. They were covered with spider guts from the previous night, but through the gore Charlie could see that they didn't have much more left in them. A few more hits and the swords would break apart.

"No, that's a bad idea," said Stan. Then something occurred to him. "Hey, Charlie. If these spiders are still here, then why aren't they climbing over the wall to attack us like they did last night?"

Charlie thought about it. "That's a fair point. Do you think that Spiders only attack at night?"

Stan saw what he had to do. "I guess there's only one way to find out." He started to walk towards the wall.

"Hey, where are you going?" yelled Charlie.

"I'm going to see if these Spiders are going to attack me if I'm outside the wall."

"But what if they do?"

"Then I'm screwed."

"Dude, no you can't..."

"Do you have a better idea?"

"Well... um..."

"I didn't think so." Stan began to climb over the wall again.

"Wait," said Charlie. He handed Stan his sword. "Take this," he said. "Yours is about to break, and if you have to fight off all those spiders, you need a sword."

"Thanks. Wish me luck," said Stan with a nervous catch in his voice, and he jumped over the wall and closed his eyes.

Nothing happened. Stan opened his eyes. The spiders were still minding their own business, as if Stan had never scaled the wall. As Stan tiptoed tentatively among the spiders, none of them even acknowledged his existence. He did this as hastily he could (he did not want to take chances) and he didn't stop until he came to a portion of the road not littered with spiders.

"It's okay, Charlie, they're not hostile. You can come over now.

Charlie was petrified, and his blocky hands were shaking as he collected the string from the dead spiders within their fort, scaled the wall, and sprinted through the pack of nonchalant spiders to join his friend.

"Well," sighed Charlie. "I'm glad that's over."

Stan nodded. "Amen to that… hey, look!"

He walked over to a pile of bones and arrows. He picked up one of the bones.

"One of those Skeletons must have dropped this when it died." He handed the bone to Charlie. "Do you think it could be useful?"

"Check the book," he replied, now examining the arrows. "Look up Bones and Arrows in there."

Stan opened the book to the Items section and read aloud:

BONES

Bones are items dropped by skeletons when killed. Bones have two main uses. One can craft a bone into Bone Meal or use the bone to tame a wild wolf into a dog (this may take multiple bones).

ARROWS

Arrows are items that can be either found when dropped by a dead skeleton or crafted from flint, sticks, and feathers. Arrows can be fired as projectiles out of either a bow or a Redstone Dispenser. They are also shot by skeletons.

Stan closed the book. "Looks like the bones will come in handy if we run into a wolf. And we'd better get a bow so we can use these arrows."

Charlie agreed, and the two broke their shelter back down, saving the materials for later use. They began walking back down the path, en route for the Adorian Village, with plenty of daylight and the prospect of a day of smooth sailing ahead of them. They had just taken a stop to eat their last pieces of bread when something jumped out of the woods.

It was a player holding a sword, made out of what looked like stone, pointing right at Stan's heart.

CHAPTER 3: MINES AND CREEPERS

This player had the same body as Stan and Charlie, but Stan could tell by the appearance of this player that she was a girl. She had blonde hair which extended beyond her blocky head to create a ponytail behind her. She was wearing a leather tunic, neon pink shorts, and blue shoes.

Stan then thought, why am I thinking this? She's pointing a sword at my chest!

"Give me all your materials," said the girl in a monotone, "or your friend gets a blade through his chest."

Charlie, who had been paralyzed with fear up until now, quickly scrambled to get out all of their materials. He laid them on the ground: his own damaged wooden sword, a piece of bread, a pile of dirt, a piece of rotten flesh, a bone, five arrows, some wood, and a whole mess of string. The girl looked at them with a distasteful eye.

"I should have known. You two don't have anything good, do you." It was a statement, not a question. She knew that they didn't have anything.

"I don't know. I have… THIS!!!" and Stan, who had remained perfectly still up until this time, suddenly whipped out his wooden sword and, taking advantage of her diverted focus, cut her across the chest, knocking her backward. She fell to the ground and cringed; the cut had not actually hurt her, but the leather armor on her chest fell off, revealing an orange T-shirt with a heart in the middle, the same neon pink as her shorts.

Stan stood over her, his wooden sword now pointed at her, and he was quickly joined by Charlie, his quivering hand pointing his sword at her also. Stan, sounding much braver than he felt, said, "I wouldn't try anything, if I were you. There's two of us, and only one of you."

She pulled herself up and, to Stan's surprise, looked almost bored as she said, "Don't worry, I'm not gonna try. There's no point. Killing you two, which I could easily do, would accomplish nothing. You're just a couple of noobs. Let me know if you decide to attack me, or let me go, or whatever. I'll just sit here." And with that, she sat on a nearby tree stump, put her hands behind her head, crossed her legs, and closed her eyes, as if she were lounging on a beach chair by the sea rather than being held at sword point. Stan felt himself flush.

"How do you know that we're new at this?" asked Charlie defiantly, his hand still shaking as he pointed his sword towards her heart.

"Yeah, what if we're, like, complete masters at this game who are just carrying around bad stuff to fool people like you?" spat Stan bitterly.

She opened her eyes and looked at Stan.

"Well, for one, you're on the road to the Adorian Village, which is for players under level five; and for two, any smart player would carry around any weapons he had for self-defense, now that the King passed that new law."

She closed her eyes again.

"What new law?" wondered Charlie.

She opened her eyes again.

"And for three, anyone who hasn't joined very recently knows about the law that bans you from this server after you die once, instead of just losing all your stuff and going back to the spawn point like you usually do in Minecraft."

She closed her eyes again.

"Hang on a second," said Stan. "If you *aren't* new, than why are you carrying around a stone sword? If I had to guess, I'd say stone is pretty common around here."

She opened her eyes and got a bitter look on her face.

"Oh that. It's, like, the *stupidest* thing *EVER.* I was on this server called Johnstantinople once, run by a guy named John (go figure), and I was doing really well. I found an abandoned NPC village with an iron sword and a bunch of apples in the forge chest, and I was going around killing monsters, when this griefer comes up from behind me, and *kills* me! I went back to the Spawnpoint, I killed a bunch of Creepers and I got sand and crafted a ton of TNT, and I traded a golden apple for some fire charges that this guy got from the Nether, and I griefed the house of the guy who killed me by blowing his house up! Unfortunately, turns out that that guy was John, who ran the server, and he banned me.

"It is *so* unfair! So now I had to join THIS stupid server and there's no NPC Villages anywhere, so I had to kill this sleeping guy, take this lame stone sword, and... you're not following anything I'm saying, are you."

Again, it was a statement, not a question, and again it was true. The boys stood there with a look of bewilderment on their faces; they had not followed any of her rant from the mention of PCD Towns or whatever she said. They were utterly confused, so the girl just got up and walked away.

"Hey! Where do you think you're going?" yelled Charlie.

"I'm going to find some people with stuff that I actually want," she replied, heading for the woods.

"Wait up!" Stan yelled, walking after her. "Why don't you come with us?"

She whipped around to face him, as did Charlie.

"WHAT!!?" they both yelled at the same time.

"You can't be serious, Stan, she just tried to kill us!"

"You expect me to come with you noobs?"

"She'll turn on us as soon as we fall asleep!"

"If you think I'll protect you, then you've got another thing coming!"

"SHUT UP!!!!!" yelled Stan, so loudly that Charlie and the girl did.

"If you attack people with better weapons than yourself, than you're going to get slaughtered. Come with us to the Adorian Village. They'll help you get a new iron sword, and then we can go our separate ways."

The girl thought about it while Charlie stammered weak protests, which Stan ignored.

"Fine," said the girl. "I'll come with you, but JUST until we get to the Adorian Village. After that, I'm going to leave you two to fend for yourselves."

"Good," said Stan. Charlie looked at him incredulously, but he could see that Stan had made his mind up, and he doubted that he could change it.

"Come on," said Stan. "The path leads this way." He walked down the path. The others walked after him.

"By the way, my name's KitKat783," said the girl, "but you can call me Kat."

"My name's Stan, and this is Charlie," said Stan, gesturing to Charlie, who feebly raised a blocky hand. With no further words, Stan walked off, followed by the smirking Kat and the scowling Charlie.

* * * * *

They walked along the path in silence. Stan walked first, followed by Kat, with Charlie taking up the rear ("I don't trust her behind my back," he whispered to Stan). They kept walking until about noon, when Stan spotted something on the side of the road. He pointed it out to the others. It appeared to be a large hole in the ground, lined by stone, with darkness inside that extended deep underground. He noticed black specs on a few of the stones that he could see.

"That's a mine!" cried Kat excitedly. "There are minerals inside it if you mine them out! Let's go in there!"

"Are you crazy?" snapped Charlie, still upset that Kat had come with them. "It's all dark in there. There's bound to be monsters."

"Eh, don't be a baby," smirked Kat. "See that black stuff?" She gestured to the stone flecked with black. "That's coal ore, we can make torches out of the coal to see in the dark and ward off the monsters at night. Besides, even if there are monsters in there, we can fight them off, we've all got swords. We're all big boys here, except for me, and ironically, I'm probably the least scared to go in there."

Nobody argued with her. Stan was a little unnerved at the prospect of heading into a dark mine after the episode with the spiders. He did need to make a new weapon soon, though, and it would be nice to have a sword made out of stone rather than wood (though he had no idea how to make one). He also wondered what other kinds of minerals were in there. His desires and curiosity overpowered his fear, and he said, "Alright, Kat. I'll go into the mine."

"I don't care what either of you say, I'm not going in there," Charlie retorted. "I remember the spiders. I'm going to stay right here, thank you very much." And with that he walked to the middle of the path, plopped down a piece of wood from his inventory, sat on it, crossed his arms over his chest, and stared at Stan and Kat defiantly.

"Fine," said Stan. "You stay out here. See if you can find any more food, we're almost out. Kat and I will grab some coal and stone and stuff." And with that, Stan turned and walked towards the mine.

"Hold on," Kat said, and she threw him something which he caught and examined: a pickaxe, made of stone. She held up an identical one.

"It hurts your hand and takes forever to punch through rock, and you don't get anything from it. You'd best mine stuff with a pickaxe."

Feeling a little bit stupid for his ignorance, Stan set into the mine, pickaxe in hand, tailed closely by Kat.

His first stop was the coal ore he'd seen. He took his pickaxe, and had mined a good-sized lump of coal in a matter of a minute. He saw that the coal ran in a vein, and before long he had collected about ten lumps of coal. He brought them over to Kat, who was hacking away at a stone wall.

"Good," she said. "Let me see those." He handed her the lumps. She pulled some sticks of her inventory, and fastened them to the coal. Each lump of coal yielded four torches, so they had forty in all.

"Now we can go deeper into the mine, where there isn't any natural light," she explained. They went deeper into the mine, placing torches along the wall as they went. Stan noticed that the torches ignited the second Kat attached them to the wall, with no matches or lighter or anything. Strange...

"Hey, look over here!" Stan ran over to a spot on the ground flecked with black. More coal! "I'm going to dig this out," he said. "Could you get me some stone for a new sword? And get some for Charlie, too."

"Whatever," she said. She started hacking into the wall at a new location, gathering up tremendous amounts of stone chunks.

Stan dug into the coal vein. He was about to dig into the eighth piece of coal when Kat said, "Hey, Stan! Come check this out!"

Stan walked over to her. She had made quite a dent in the wall, and she was staring at a block different from the stone all around her. This block was flecked with little spots that looked similar to the coal ore, but with light brown spots instead of black ones. Kat stepped back.

"I've never seen that before. Do you think it could be gold?"

"It might. Hang on, put a torch up," Stan said. Kat obliged. Stan pulled out his book and turned to the section on blocks. He found a page describing gold ore. He showed it to Kat.

"No," she said. "It doesn't match the color. Gold ore has yellow flecks, these flecks are tan. Check out the other pages."

Stan turned to the previous page. He held that illustration up for Kat.

"That's it!" she exclaimed. "What is it?"

Stan read from the book.

IRON ORE

Iron ore is an ore block typically found in mines or mountainous regions. When smelted, it produced one Iron Ingot.

Stan looked up.

"Do you know what an iron ingot is?" he asked.

Kat shrugged her shoulders. "Look it up," she said.

He did.

IRON INGOT

An Iron Ingot is a crafting item. It is most commonly obtained by smelting Iron Ore, but can also be found in the chest of Dungeons, Strongholds, Abandoned Mine Shafts, Temples and NPC Villages, or by killing Iron Golems and (rarely) Zombies. The Iron Ingot is an essential crafting item for a wide variety of things, including iron swords, iron armor, iron tools, buckets, shears, iron bars, tripwire hooks and many other things. Tools and armor made from iron are of a higher quality than stone or leather, respectively, but of a lower quality than diamond.

Of this entire passage, one small section of it caught Kat's attention.

"Iron sword?" she exclaimed. "So if I smelt this stuff, whatever that means, I can get an iron sword?"

"Apparently," said Stan.

"Sweet!" shouted Kat gleefully, and she began hacking away at the wall of ore. The two players hacked at the wall and managed to get out four blocks of iron ore before they hit stone again.

"Let's look around here, maybe there'll be some more!" She was about to take her pickaxe to the adjacent section of the wall when she heard a bloodcurdling cry echoing from the top of the cave.

"AAAAAAAAAAAUUUUUUUUGHHHHHHH!!! STAN! HEEEEEEEEELLLLLLLLLPPPP!"

"Come on!" Stan shouted to Kat, and the two raced up the mine and into the light.

* * * * *

After Kat and Stan had vanished into the mine, Charlie had stood up and walked around, a scowl on his face.

Stupid girl, he thought, looking around and spying a patch of wheat next to a sign that said TAKE WHAT YOU NEED, BUT REPLANT. Why should she get to be in our group? She nearly killed us! What does Stan see in her? It was true; he thought as he harvested the wheat, that the girl did seem to know her way with a sword... ah, what am I talking about? I don't know that, I didn't see her actually fight! For all I know, she's never killed anything in her life. I'm ditching her first chance I get, the arrogant brat.

And now look what she's done, he thought as he began to break the leaf blocks on the trees (he had read in Stan's book that every now and then an apple would drop from a leaf block if you broke it). She's gone with him into a mine, delaying us from getting to the Adorian vill... wait a second, he thought, not noticing the apple dropping from the block he just broke.

What if it's a trap? What if she's just lured Stan down there to kill him, and she's going to come back and finish off me? I have to go find them! He quickly picked up his sword, and was about to dash into the mine to save his friend, when something stopped him.

A little ways into the darkness of the mine, he saw a figure. It looked like a monster of some sort. He was about to run away, but his curiosity got the better of him, because it was the most bizarre thing he had ever seen. He edged slightly forward to get a better look. It was as tall as he was, two blocks high, but it didn't have any arms, and it stood upright on four stubby legs. He couldn't see well, but he could have sworn that its body was flecked with different shades of green, with some white in there, too. He edged a little closer. This turned out to be a huge mistake.

The creature suddenly turned towards him. He had gotten too close. It stared at him, and he had never seen such a terrifying face in his life. It looked like a morbid, green-speckled jack-o-lantern; it had empty black eye sockets, and a gaping hole of a mouth that was open in a horrible upside down grin.

He swung with his sword, and the monster was knocked back, but his wooden sword had reached the end of its life. The spent blade splintered into a thousand pieces, and Charlie threw the useless handle aside as he screamed into the mine for his friends to help him.

This creature was fast, but silent as well. The zombies made moaning sounds, the spiders made that clicking sound, and you could hear the rattling of a skeleton's bones as it moved. But this thing was absolutely silent; as it chased after Charlie, he could barely hear the sound of its footsteps. Also, the zombies and skeletons burned up in the sunlight, and the spiders hadn't paid him or Stan any attention. But Charlie was running around in the path in direct sunlight and the thing kept following him, not slowing down or taking any damage. Charlie did NOT want to know what would happen when the thing finally caught up to him.

Kat and Stan burst out of the mine just as Charlie was running back towards it, still being followed by the monster.

"Guys, thank God! I'm so glad that you're…"

"GET DOWN!!!!!"

The monster was upon them, and it was starting to hiss and swell like an overinflated balloon. Kat pushed Stan, who fell backwards into the mine, and she tackled Charlie out of the way just in the nick of time; there was an earsplitting explosion, and a cloud of dust rose over the road. Then, all was quiet.

As the dust cleared, Stan got up and came out of the mine. The monster was gone, and in its place was a huge crater, blown right into the middle of the dirt path. Stan stared at it and Charlie and Kat got up. Kat turned on Charlie.

"How the hell did you get a Creeper on your tail? I thought you were staying out of the mine!" she yelled at him.

"Wait... THAT was a Creeper?" asked Stan.

"Yes, that was a Creeper! Why did it start following you?"

"So that's the thing that everyone talks about?" asked Charlie, wide-eyed with shock and horror. "I've seen the posters online... but I always assumed that they, like, broke into your house and stole your stuff or something! They BLOW UP!!!???"

"Yes... now for the last time, Charlie, HOW DID IT GET ON YOUR TAIL!?"

"I went down into the mine..."

"Why?" Kat demanded.

"I... uh..." Charlie thought that it would be a little bit moot to tell Kat that he'd gone in the mine to stop her from betraying Stan and him after she had just saved both of their lives from the Creeper.

"I, uh, wanted to help you guys. I wasn't finding any food, and I didn't want to be useless so I, uh, went in after you guys. Followed the line of torches ... Yeah! And, uh, then a saw that thing and tried to fight it off but my sword broke, so I called you guys for help because I knew you had swords that were... uh... un-broken?" he finished lamely. Kat was staring at him with a look of half exasperation and half amusement.

39

"Uh huh," she said in a teasing voice. "Well, we'd better get going. We should really get you an 'unbroken' sword, and I don't know how to make one. So you didn't find any food at all?

"Well," replied Charlie, "I found some wheat and a few apples. I don't if we can do anything with the wheat, but the apples are edible."

"Well, that'll have to do," replied Kat. "Let's go."

As the three players continued on the road to the Adorian Village, Charlie sighed, resigning himself to the fact that he could never abandon this girl who had saved his life.

* * * * *

They still had plenty of daylight left. The path was going in a straight line, and they were beginning to see hovering chunks of leaves with no trunks on the side of the road. This meant that they were definitely close to civilization.

"Excellent," commented Stan as they passed a watermelon farm with a sign that was identical to the one at the wheat field. "We can get some food from this field. Just don't destroy any of the vines."

Each player picked a watermelon and destroyed it. There were multiple watermelon slices yielded from each destroyed watermelon, and the players ate all of the juicy watermelon to completely assuage their mounting hunger. Kat, who was particularly hungry, even ate the two raw pork chops that she had in her inventory.

"Hey," she said through a mouth full of watermelon and uncooked pork chop to the two disgusted-looking boys, "ih mayna

40

be preddy, butet getsa zhob bun." When their faces then changed to confusion, she swallowed and said, "Hey, it may not be pretty, but it gets the job done."

Charlie rolled his eyes at her. Stan was about to crack a joke when, for the second time that day, a player burst from the woods with a sword in his hands.

This time there was no hesitation. Within seconds all three players were on their feet. Kat held her stone sword in front of her in a guard stance, and standing behind her were Stan, who was clutching his heavily damaged wooden sword in shaking hands, and Charlie, who had balled up his fists and was getting ready to fight, bouncing back and forth on the balls of his feet.

This player was dressed like a secret service agent. He had on a black tuxedo, black hair, and black shades covering the eyes on his olive face. He was holding a golden sword in an attack stance, ready to kill the first one to make a move.

Kat spoke first. "What do you want?" she asked.

The player's eyebrows creased he pointed his sword at her. "What I want? Well, there are a lot of things that I want. I want my old life back, for one. Everything was perfect..."

"Yeah, yeah, we couldn't care less about your 'oh, woe is me' story. Get away before you do something that you'll regret. There's three of us and only one of you, and two of us have swords. I suggest that you just crawl back into those woods that you came from."

The player looked mortally offended. He pointed his sword at Kat.

"I will not have you telling me what to do! You are all noobs, armed with primitive weapons of wood and stone, while I, I am the most honorable Mr. A, the most powerful warrior this server has ever known! If you knew only half the reasons that I want new players like yourselves dead…"

"Oh, just *shut up!*" Stan interjected. "There is no way you're going to win against us, *honorable* Mr. A! Besides, if you really were honorable, you wouldn't attack players armed with 'primitive weapons' through ambush, that's just a low thing to do. I don't care what you were; it's obvious that you're nothing special now! Just leave us alone! We haven't done anything wrong! You're just being a… a… a griefer, that's what you are!" He didn't know exactly what the term meant, but it had the effect that he'd intended.

Mr. A charged the trio; Stan was glad for an excuse to fight, he was getting heated. As Mr. A's sword was about to come down on Stan's head, Stan raised his own sword in a counterstrike. Both swords shattered; the wooden blade shattered just as Charlie's had, and the golden blade bend back in on itself and fell off the handle. Furious that his sword had been broken, Mr. A flew at Stan with his fist. Stan raised his arms to brace himself for the blow when, at the same time, Kat sliced Mr. A's leg on one side and Charlie punched the side of his head on the other. The griefer went tumbling head over heels and slammed hard onto the ground. He immediately got back up, but he held his side with his hand, his face in a grimace.

"Fine! You win! But don't think for a minute that this is over! I will find you again, and when I do, you are worse than dead! Now, good luck getting out of THIS!" and Mr. A whipped out a bow and fired an arrow; he wasn't aiming for the players, but at something in the woods. Stan, Charlie and Kat watched the arrow fly into the brush as Mr. A sprinted into the woods on the other side of the path.

They heard a pained yelping noise as the arrow connected with its target, and a moment later, a white beast with glowing red eyes jumped out of the woods. It was a wolf, provoked by Mr. A's arrow, which had set its sights on the nearest target: Stan.

Stan was unarmed. It was all he could do to try and outrun the wolf, but it was swift as it ran, faster than the Creeper, faster than Stan could sprint. The wolf pounced upon him, pinning him to the ground. The beast growled, its evil red eyes glowing, and it was about to tear into Stan's throat when there was a whistling noise from behind him. The animal's head whipped around.

Kat was standing, not too far from Stan and the wolf, holding out the bone that she had just snatched from Charlie's inventory. The boys watched in awe as the wolf's eyes stopped glowing red; they became a sad, black color. The wolf cocked it s head slightly to the left, paused, and walked slowly towards Kat. It came to a stop in front of her, and she gave the wolf the bone.

The wolf wasn't on the attack anymore. It sat down in front of Kat with its tongue out and its tail wagging. Kat grabbed a red collar from her inventory and fastened it around the wolf's neck. The wolf had been tamed by the bone.

"That's twice I've saved your life now," Kat said smugly to Stan as she petted her new dog on the head. "I think I'm going to call him Rex."

"Oh, imagine that, a dog named Rex, how creative," mumbled Charlie under his breath, but Kat didn't hear.

"Stan, could you look up dogs in that book of yours? I want to know how to take care of this little guy."

Stan obliged, mouth still hanging open at the way she had tamed the wolf. He opened his book and flipped through the pages of animals and monsters but he didn't find anything about dogs.

"Try wolfs," she suggested.

He looked up wolfs, and there was a page on them.

WOLF

A wolf is a neutral mob found in forest regions that usually travels in packs. A wolf is usually not harmful towards a player, but if attacked a wolf will become hostile and attack with similar speed and jumping ability to that of a Spider. When a wolf is attacked, all other wolfs in its pack will also join in attacking the wolf's attacker. A wolf can be tamed by feeding it bones dropped by Skeletons. A tamed wolf can be made to sit still, or to follow the player around. When the player attacks or is attacked by a mob, the player's wolves will join the player's attack. A wolf's health is indicated by the angle of its tail. The lower the tail droops, the lower the animal's health is. The wolf can be healed by feeding it any kind of meat; it will not contract food poisoning from Rotten Flesh or Raw Chicken as a player might.

Kat glanced at Rex's tail; though it was still wagging, it was drooping almost to the ground.

"Looks like he took a lot of damage from that arrow, and he must've been separated from his pack. Poor little guy," said Kat with a look of pity on her face (Stan looked baffled at her as he massaged the scratches Rex's paws had left on his neck). "Charlie, let me see that rotten flesh you have." He handed it to her, and Rex started eating it out of her hand. Instantly, his tail shot up.

"Well, looks like we've got a dog!" she said to Stan and Charlie.

"Wait," said Stan. "What do you mean, we? I thought you were ditching us as soon as you got that sword of yours."

"Are you kidding?" she said with a grin. "If it weren't for me, you would be torn to pieces by Rex here," she said, gesturing to Stan, "and both of you would he lying in pieces around that mine thanks to that Creeper. Without me, you two would both die, and, let's face it, that would just be a lot of tedious paperwork for the ops of this server. Now come on," she chirped, blind and deaf to Stan and Charlie's indignant faces and stammers of protest. "Let's get to that village. I need a sword!"

And they continued on the path, munching on Charlie's apples, the boys still fuming, the girl still laughing. And by the time the sun had started to sink in the sky, the sight of two towers came into sight, and the three players heard someone yell.

"New players! New players incoming! Welcome to the Adorian Village, new players!"

CHAPTER 4: THE ADORIAN VILLAGE

The Adorian Village was unlike anything Stan had seen in Minecraft. The only man-made objects that he had seen up to that point were signs, chests, and torches. In this village, everything appeared to be made of manufactured blocks.

The buildings were mainly made out of three materials; there were wooden planks stacked on top of each other, glass panes in the windows, and stone that wasn't as natural as the stone in the mine, but rather, put together in chunks, like a cobblestone street. Torches were everywhere, and the road was paved with gravel.

As the three players entered the village through a tall wooden gate between the two watchtowers, they saw a player walking towards them. He had brown hair, and he was wearing a red jacket over a white shirt, with blue jeans. As he met the players, he introduced himself as Jayden10, and told the players to come with him to meet the mayor of the town. He then walked down the gravel street towards a large brick building; Stan, Charlie and Kat followed.

Going down the street, Stan saw players everywhere in the village. One player appeared to be exchanging two apples with another player for a piece of flint and a metal ring. Through a large window, Stan saw a whole group of players sitting around tables that had tools dangling from them. One of these players gave a final strike with a hammer to the object on his table and held it up for examination; it was a shiny metal pickaxe. To the right of the brick building was a large wooden building with a vast expanse of land behind it that held multiple types of animals as well as fields of wheat, pumpkins and watermelons. Stan had never seen anything like what these players were doing in Minecraft before; he was getting excited. The players appeared to be friendly; they waved to Stan and one of them even yelled "nice dog" to Kat.

"Here we are," said Jayden, gesturing to the immense brick building, "Town Hall. Our mayor Adoria lives here. She is the founder of this village, and one of the highest level people here. Come inside, she likes to meet all new arrivals." And he walked inside.

The three players exchanged quick glances with each other, and went in after Jayden, leaving Rex sitting outside.

Stan was impressed; the corridor that they were in had a red carpet, and it was lined with electric lamp blocks that surely would have been on if the sun weren't streaming in through a magnificent glass roof. The places not covered by lamps on the wall had different paintings; a small one had a sunrise on it, a wide one (Charlie jumped when he saw it) had a Creeper's face, and one painting depicting a game of Donkey Kong took up the whole wall. All of these paintings were heavily pixilated.

Jayden pushed a button at the end of the hall and an iron door swung open. Inside, Stan could see a player, a girl judging by the plait of her black hair, sitting at a desk, writing in a book. She looked up at the sound of the opening door.

"Hello, Jayden. These are the new players, I assume?" her voice was kind; it reminded Stan of his mother.

"Yes, Adoria ma'am," Jayden replied respectfully.

Adoria stood up. Stan saw that she was wearing a pink blouse and a red skirt.

"Well, then, welcome to the Adorian Village, new players. I am Adoria1, founder and mayor of this community. But please, call me Adoria. What are your names?"

Stan spoke up. "My name is Stan2012, but you can just call me Stan. This is KingCharles_XIV, or Charlie," at this Charlie gave a polite nod of the head to Adoria, and Stan continued, "and this is KitKat783, or Kat." Kat said, "Pleased to meet you, ma'am."

"Pleased to meet you too, players. Tell me, have you ever played Minecraft before?" inquired Adoria.

Stan and Charlie shook their heads, while Kat said, "I have, but on a different server, and I wasn't there for long. I'm not much more experienced at this game than these two." Stan and Charlie shot her incredulous looks but they backed down as they caught her eye.

Adoria nodded her head. "I understand. In that case, we in this village will be more than glad to help you learn how to play this game. We have a program here that teaches you everything that you need to know about Minecraft in five days. Do you think you would be interested in that? The deal includes a temporary place to stay, and food."

Stan said, "It sounds good to me."

"I'm game," said Kat excitedly.

"Count the three of us in, then," said Charlie. "But what kind of things are you going to be showing us?"

"We have a group of people in this village dedicated to training new players. Each have different strengths that they will pass on to you. They will show you how to fight, craft, create, and other such things."

"So, it's your job to train new players to prepare them for the server?" asked Kat.

"That's right," replied Jayden. "Almost every new player on this server came through our program first, including most of the population of Element City."

"What's Element City?" asked Stan.

"The server's capitol," said Adoria. "Element City is where most people go after they go through our program. It's situated on a huge open plain, surrounded by forest on all sides, and it has the greatest population of any settlement on this server. That's where people build their houses and a bunch of crazy contraptions and structures and all of that. At the center of the city is Element Castle, where the King of this server presides over a council that makes the laws of the land."

"Sounds like an interesting place. Do you think we should go there after we finish your program?" asked Charlie.

"Um... yes, I don't see why not," replied Adoria. But her hesitation was not lost on Stan, and she didn't meet Charlie's eyes when she said this. Stan wondered what was wrong with Element City.

"So, is there a place for us to sleep?" asked Charlie, yawning. "I'm bushed; we haven't slept yet and we've been on the server for almost two days now!"

"Oh, by all means, go ahead!" said Adoria with a warm smile. "You'll find some things for you in your rooms at the motel. Jayden, show these players to their rooms please."

"Yes, ma'am," replied Jayden. "Follow me," and he left the room. Stan, Charlie and Kat followed them, ordering Rex to follow.

"So," said Jayden as they left the building, "what kind of materials do you guys have so far?"

"Not much," replied Charlie, looking in his inventory as he walked. "Jus ... a stack of dirt, five arrows, some string, and some wood. You guys got anything else?" he asked as he looked to Kat and Stan.

"I've got a stone sword and pickaxe, some cobblestone, and a few torches," replied Kat. "Stan?"

"Oh, I've just got some coal, the pickaxe you gave me and the book."

"Come on, you guys! To survive in this game you're gonna need better crap than that!" Stan could tell that Jayden wasn't being condescending, he was just ribbing them. Stan laughed with Jayden.

"I guess Stan and I owe you a thank-you," said Charlie. "Without those swords and the bread, and the book, we definitely wouldn't have even come close to here. We wouldn't have even survived the first night with those spiders!"

"Yeah ... thanks a million," agreed Stan, shuddering as he remembered fighting off the Spiders.

"Ah, don't mention it," replied Jayden with a shrug. "Besides, it wasn't me who put those out there, it was my friend

Sally. She's the one that goes out there and replenishes the stocks at the Spawn Point every week. Speaking of which, why did it take you guys two days to get here, anyways? It's only a day's journey."

So Stan and Charlie told Jayden about the time that they had getting to the village, about getting lost, and the spiders, and running into Kat (who added to the story from that point on), and the mine, and the Creeper, and Mr. A. Jayden seemed taken aback by the story of Mr. A.

"You guys ran into a griefer?" he asked skeptically. "But none of you are even level four yet! The best weapon you have is a moderately used stone sword! Why would anyone want to attack you?"

"Well, he was about to tell us in a melodramatic monologue, but I believe that that was the point when Kat told him, and I quote, 'we couldn't care less about your oh, woe is me story,'" replied Charlie, grinning at her.

"I regret nothing," smirked Kat. "So, Jayden, what do you do around here? It must get pretty boring."

Jayden shook his head. "No, not really, it's fun to teach the new guys, like you. At the school, I teach axe fighting and I help my brother on his farm. Plus, Adoria sends me on missions; I actually just got back from one a little while before you guys got here," he added as the four finally arrived at the motel, a sprawling four story complex made of mainly wood planks. Stan saw a hole in the side of the building that was closest to him, next to several chests and a sign that said, "CONSTRUCTION IN PROGRESS."

"Well, here we are, home sweet home," announced Jayden, gesturing to the building. "You guys are lucky; you'll be bunking with me and my friends tonight. You'd ordinarily get your own rooms, but we've been so swamped with new players lately that there isn't any room left for you guys in the main wing, and the expansion isn't done yet. So, come with me," and he started to climb a ladder up to the roof.

"Wait!" cried Kat. "What about Rex?"

Jayden paused. "What? Oh, your dog. Just leave him there, but don't tell him to sit. I think he'll find his way up on his own," and he continued to climb.

Shrugging, Kat gave Rex a quick scratch between the ears and went up after Jayden, followed by Charlie, and then Stan.

Jayden's room was situated on top of the fourth floor roof. It was a large room, big enough to comfortably hold eight players. Jayden flipped open the wooden door and was greeted by two distinct voices. The other three followed him in.

There were four beds sitting on the floor, two of them occupied with people. The room was lit by torches not unlike the rest of the town, and there was a table with tools hanging from it like the one Stan saw in the building in the village. Next to the table stood a stone oven, with a fire lit in it. The walls were lined with paintings, and there was a large chest next to each bed. Next to the door was a box with a slot on top.

The two players in the beds looked unlike anybody Stan had seen in the game so far. One of them was dressed like the skeletons that had made Stan's first night in Minecraft so difficult; Stan would have panicked if it weren't for the red hair on the top of his head that distinguished him from a monster. The other player on the other bed looked exactly like Stan did (the standard look for Minecraft), except that he was entirely gold. His hair, skin, arms, body, and legs were completely golden. The only thing that told them that he wasn't some sort of statue was his green eyes.

"Yo Jay! Good to have you back!" boomed the skeleton; he had an unexpectedly deep voice.

"Good to be back, Archie! I tell you, that trip was hell!"

"No," said the gold one, in a disconnected voice. "Hell is being trapped in a pit of burning Netherack that was set as a monster trap in the middle of Ender Desert, and only getting out because some guy happens to..."

"Enough, G, you've told us the story like a hundred times!" whined the skeleton in an exasperated voice.

"Still, what could you have possibly done that's worse than that?" the gold guy asked, now in a regular voice.

"Dude, didn't you hear Adoria give me the assignment? I had to go to the nearest Mushroom Island and take back samples of the mushrooms there, and I also had to learn how to farm them from the tribe living there. She also made me lure two Mooshrooms away from the island and *across the ocean* using wheat and bring them all the way back here."

"Ouch!" yelled the gold one. "That is pretty bad!"

"You're telling me. The worst part was trading with the tribe there; I tell you, to be iffy about trading two Mooshrooms for four trees and bone meal when you don't even have trees on your island! Still, you can't say you've lived until you've killed a Spider Jockey while keeping two Mooshrooms interested in you with wheat. So where's Sally? She back yet?"

"Oh, she tried a new shortcut to get to the hill, she said that it would take her anywhere from half to double the normal time, she's not sure. She said not to worry if she was late."

"So Jay, who are these guys anyway?" asked the skeleton, pointing at Stan, Charlie and Kat, who had entered the room and were listening to the conversation with a mixture of confusion and admiration at these players that had clearly seen so much of the game.

"These are new players. The motel's full today so they're staying in here."

"Excellent. I just love a good slumber party," said a girl's voice from behind them. They all turned around.

A girl was leaning against the door frame. A plait of black hair ran down her back. She was wearing a green tank top and a black skirt. She was holding an iron sword with spider guts fresh on the blade.

"Look what the ocelot dragged in! Sally's back!"

"Glad you're not dead, Sal."

"What took you so long, girl?"

Sally gave a tired grin that suggested that she was dealing with little siblings who were entirely too happy to see her after a long day. "Do you remember when we used to greet each other with a nice 'Hello'?" she asked.

"I'm sorry," said the skeleton. "Would you prefer that?"

"Course not!" laughed Sally. "I'm just reminiscing. So, you gonna introduce me to these noobs?"

Jayden said, "If you insist. You're lucky I hadn't already introduced them to Archie and G, or I wouldn't have wasted my breath on you," he added good-naturedly. "This is Kat, Stan, and Charlie," he introduced them, pointing them each out in turn. "New guys, this is Archie," the skeleton nodded, "Goldman, aka G," the golden guy nodded, "and Sally." The girl nodded.

"Sup, guys," said G. "Cool dog, Kat."

"What are you talking... what ... !?" Kat's eyes widened as she looked behind her. For Rex had just walked in the door and was walking over to Kat, who pet the dog with her hand, still looking amazed.

"How did Rex manage to get up the ladder?" she asked.

"Nobody knows..." replied Archie ominously.

They all stared at the sitting dog for a moment, then looked away; none of them made eye contact with Rex for the rest of the night.

"So anyways, why are these noobs staying in here?" asked Sally, frowning as she leaned against the door frame.

"Could you please stop calling us noobs?" asked Stan. "It gets really annoying after a while."

"Sorry buddy, I paid my dues. I was a noob like you once, but then I took an arrow to the... heh heh heh , just kidding. My point is, people are gonna call you that until you pass, say, level ten. But until then, you're just gonna have to put up with it. We all did," she said, gesturing to herself, Jayden, G and Archie.

"Fine, I can accept other people calling me that," said Stan, "but could *you guys* not, seeing as I have to *live* with you for a few days?"

"Hhhhmmm…" said Sally, pretending to think. "Uh, yeah, no, I think I will call you that. I probably wouldn't if it didn't annoy you so much though." She shrugged.

Stan sighed. "Is she always like this?" he asked, turning to Archie.

He laughed. "Of course not! Sally is an absolute pleasure to live with, she's not aggravating, obnoxious, and condescending to us guys, whatever would give you that idea?"

Sally rolled her eyes. "Are you finished?"

Archie replied, "Well, as I glance at that sword in your hand, I think I'll say yes?"

They all laughed.

"So, you guys starting the program tomorrow?" asked G as Sally went to the chest next to one of the beds and put in a sword and some watermelon.

"Apparently so, Jayden mentioned that you four teach the classes. Is that right?"

"Yep," replied Sally as she sat down on her bed with her legs crossed. "I'm gonna teach you guys sword fighting and crafting 101."

"Yes, and when she says everything, that includes the how-to of disemboweling a spider," added G, and they all laughed again.

"Anyways, I'll teach you how to fight using a pickaxe, and everything you need to know about mining."

"I myself," boomed Archie, "will be instructing you on the precision art and skill of the launched projectile forged from the stone of gravel, the spindle of a tree, and the coat of a bird. In other words, I'm teaching archery. Go figure," he said, gesturing to his skeleton costume.

"I'm teaching axe fighting and farming technique," said Jayden. He reached into the chest next to his bed and pulled out an axe, but this wasn't just any axe. This axe was created from diamond, and, though the wooden handle was worn, the diamond still glinted in the light of the torches, sharp, and deadly. Stan stared at it; it was the most impressive thing he had seen in the game so far.

"This is my most prized possession," he said. "My brother gave it to me when I left his farm."

"Stop showing off," moaned G. "We can't all have diamond tools," and he opened his chest to get some food.

"Hold up! What's that!" interjected Charlie, pointing to something in G's chest.

"What, this thing?" he asked, and he pulled out something just as impressive as the diamond axe; a pickaxe, forged from solid gold.

"How can you say you have bad tools when you have that thing?" asked Kat, and Charlie and Stan nodded in agreement.

"What? Oh! That's right, you don't know, do you?" G laughed. "Well, it may look cool, but golden tools aren't very practical at all. They break absurdly fast. They actually break faster than stuff made out of wood. The only upside to them is that they break stuff quickly, and even then a golden pickaxe can only break cobblestone and coal ore. I mostly just carry mine around for show, to go with my image," and G gestured to his golden body. As G sniggered at his own whimsy, Stan noticed Kat raise an eyebrow and give an amused chuckle.

"Well, I'm exhausted," said Jayden, yawning. "That mission was exhausting, and I'm sure that you guys must be spent after all that you went through to get here." The three new players nodded gratefully. "G, Sal, pull out the extra beds. Charlie, Kat, Stan, you guys should eat something before you go to bed. Try this."

Jayden reached into his chest and pulled out two cooked steaks and a cooked pork chop. He handed a steak to Stan and Charlie, and a cooked pork chop to Kat.

"Mmm," said Kat, licking her lips when she'd finished, "that was SO much better than the raw one." Charlie rolled his eyes.

All fed, the seven players climbed into their beds, and five of them were out cold almost immediately. Stan was just about to fall asleep when he heard a voice from behind him.

"You asleep, noob?"

Stan flipped over in his bed to face the one talking. Sally was crouching down next to his bed. "I'll take that as a no, then," she said.

Stan sat up. "Can I help you?" he asked.

Sally sat down next to him. "Yeah, you can," she asked. "Is this your first time on Minecraft?"

Stan nodded.

"Have you ever played a game like it before?"

Stan looked at her. "How many games like Minecraft are there?" he asked.

"Not important," she shrugged. "I guess my question is... do you feel like you're something special?"

"Why, yes. I mean, that's what my mommy tells me every night," said Stan sardonically. "'Stan, no matter what those mean boys tell you, you just remember that you'll always be special to me.' Is that what you mean?"

Sally giggled, which seemed oddly out of character to Stan. "You're funny," she said.

"Am I?" asked Stan, getting aggravated again. "Is that why you woke me up? So I could make you laugh? I'm exhausted, please just let me sleep!"

And with that he flopped back down on his bed. Unfortunately, he had misjudged the exact position of the pillow and he ended up with his head on the floor, a painful throbbing in his head from the impact.

As he sat up he could see Sally, not even trying to keep a straight face, just holding her mouth, trying not to burst out laughing and wake up the others. Stan frankly couldn't blame her; it must have looked fairly ridiculous. "Not a word," he said as he sat back up. "So what did you want to talk me about?"

Sally eventually calmed down, and when she did, she rolled her eyes and said, "We'll talk about it later. You need some sleep. G'night, noob." And she stood up and lay down in her own bed.

Nice girl, thought Stan as he drifted into sleep. Annoying though.

CHAPTER 5: THE PROGRAM

"GOOOOOOOOOOOOOOOD MOOOOOOOOORNING, FREEEEEEEEEEEEEEESH MEAT!!!!!!"

Stan sprang up and out of bed, startled by the deafening noise. He looked wildly around, and saw Kat and Charlie still in their beds, Kat swinging her sword (which she had apparently slept with in her hand) around yelling "DIE DIE DIE DIE DIE!!!" Charlie sat bolt upright, his hand clutching his chest. Archie was standing on top of the table with the tools on it, his hands cupped; clearly, it had been him who had yelled. G and Jayden were behind him, laughing hard at their reactions.

"Oh God, you three... you three should have seen the looks... the looks on your faces!" Jayden managed to get out between laughs.

"We've had some pretty... some pretty good reac... reactions," wheezed G, clutching his sides, "but you guys... that was so over the top! Especially you Kat! 'DIE DIE DIE DIE DIE!'" he said, renewing the uproarious laughter.

Kat stood up, walked over to G, put her hands on her hips, and stared at him in his eye.

"That was not funny! What if I had hit someone! Someone could have died!"

"I'm sorry, but why were you sleeping with a sword anyway, Kat?" asked Archie.

"Aw, did da wittle girl have a bad dweam about da cweepas comin to get her?" said G in a mock-baby voice, to another round of hysterics.

Kat pocketed her sword, walked up to G, who was now cramping with laughter, and punched him in the chest with her hand.

"Ouch!" G yelled, doubling over. "Dammit Kat, that actually hurt! Should I punch you now? Huh?"

Kat smirked. "Even in a game, I doubt that you would hit a girl, unless she was armed and trying to kill you."

"Huh, what was that about girls trying to kill people?"

Sally had just walked into the room. She said, "Kat, if you want to kill these five, I'm more than happy to help you."

"I'd like to take that offer, please," Kat replied, rubbing her eyes, "because they just woke me up by yelling at me."

"It was hilarious!" laughed G. "She started freaking out with her sword, which she SLEPT with..." and the three boys fell to the ground in fits of laughter.

"You three are so immature," she said arrogantly. "Any ways, get off the crafting table, Archie, I'm crafting us some breakfast." He complied, still snickering.

"Where'd you go this morning anyway, Sal?" Jayden asked inquisitively.

"Yeah, we had to pull the prank without 'ya," added G.

"Pardon me, boys, but I think you'll be happy when you see what I have planned." Sally reached into her inventory and pulled out three buckets of milk, an egg, some sugar, and some wheat.

"Oh boy, Sal, are you making what I think you're making?" Archie boomed eagerly.

"Well, when it's my turn to make breakfast, I prefer to do it right," she said as she started a complex series of crafts with the food items, "especially when we have guests." And Stan could have sworn that she caught his eye.

"Here we go," she said after a minute of waiting," and she held up a square cake; from what Stan could see, it was strawberry shortcake (which he didn't understand, as Sally had added neither strawberries nor frosting). "Dig in."

There were six equal pieces of cake; everybody was allocated a slice except for Sally. Stan was about to eat his piece when he looked at Sally. She was glancing at him in an expectant way. Stan had a feeling he knew why.

"Uh, Sally? Do you, uh, wanna have some of my cake?"

"Why, thank you, Stan, I would like that very much." She grabbed a knife from the table with the tools, and she cut Stan's piece down the middle. She took half of it and ate it in one bite, giving a loud burp afterwards. G and Archie snickered, but Stan wasn't sure if it was at Sally belching, or him sharing his cake. After they were finished eating, Jayden stood up.

"Alrighty then, thank you Sally, for the excellent breakfast," there were murmurs of consent, "if anyone is still hungry, we'll stop by my brother's farm on the way to the school for watermelons.

New inductees, put all of your things in the extra chest in the corner over there, and follow me."

After they had put their things away, the players left the building and went down the ladder, leaving Rex sitting in the room. As they walked down the main road of the village, they stopped just before the Town Hall and turned into the farm to the right of the Hall.

"This is where my brother lives," explained Jayden, as they walked under the hedge that marked the entrance to the farm. "He's the most productive farmer in this entire village, and the only one who is a higher level than Adoria; he's level fifty-four, five higher than she is. The only problem is that he's..."

"Hey, Jay!"

A man with wild gray hair and farmer's clothing was running up to them, holding what appeared to be an iron hoe.

"Hey, hey, you guys! Hey, you guys are new?" he asked in a jittery fashion to Stan, Kat and Charlie. "Ya' look new, carryin' around all that stone crap, you know, hey! Hey! You want some Lightnin'? Cause I know dis great place where..."

"Steve, again!? Really!!? I thought that we agreed that you wouldn't be QPOed on duty!" Jayden cried in an exasperated voice.

"I ain't QPOed, whadevah'd give yah dat ideeeeee-ooooooooooooooohhhh....." and then the crazed man, Steve, Jayden had called him, slunk down the ground, passed out.

"Oh, for the love of God," moaned Jayden.

"What the... what... what just happened?" asked Kat, looking repulsed at the comatose body on the ground.

64

"Is he gonna be okay?" asked Charlie.

"Well Charlie, yes he is, but I'm getting awfully sick of detoxing him," sighed Jayden as he pulled an apple out of his bag. This apple was shimmering golden in the sunlight, and Jayden bent over and stuffed it into the man's mouth. Jayden stood up.

"To answer your question, Kat, he was high on a potion called the Potion of Swiftness, also called QPO or Lightning. It's a potion that'll give you a quick burst of energy, but it will make you weak for a short while afterward. Steve here overdosed on QPO one night at a Spleef match, and he hasn't been able to drink it without passing out afterwards ever since. It's a shame; it really did help him run this farm more productively."

"Hold on," said Stan. "He runs the farm? THAT'S your brother?" (He decided to save the question of what Spleef was for a later day.)

"Yep," said Jayden grimly. "You see, the only way to detox him is to give him a golden apple, which would normally heal you. The problem is, apples are really rare, and gold isn't that common either, and that's what you use to craft the golden apples."

Steve had begun to stir. As he came to, Stan took an opportunity to look at the farm.

It was gigantic; it must have taken up a quarter of the entire Adorian village. There were fields and fields covered in wheat, pumpkins, watermelon, and tall stalks that Stan couldn't identify. Irrigation ditches ran between the plants. Cocoa bean pods grew on logs that looked like they came from a jungle. There were also pastures; there was a whole herd of cows and a group of pigs. Stan saw some sheep with white, black and brown colored wool, and some with no wool.

Stan looked around and also saw chickens, a pool filled with squid, some wolves, and some things that looked like wild cats. But the most peculiar thing was a thing that resembled a cow, but it was red and white, and it was covered with mushrooms actually growing out of its back. While there were herds of the other animals, there were only three red cows; two large ones, and one small one. Stan guessed that these things were the things that Jayden had just lead from the Mushroom Island, what did he call them? Oh, yeah, Mooshrooms. Funny name...

Steve had come back around and was beginning to stand up. He put his blocky hand to his head and moaned.

"Oh, God... oh, what happened?"

"Don't give me that crap!" fumed Jayden. "You know perfectly well what happened. You know that you can't be QPOed on the job! I'm running out of golden apples to detox you with, apples don't just grow on trees! Well, not in this game, anyways... but the point is, you've gotta be more responsible Steve!"

"Hey, who are those guys?" asked Steve, who had not been listening to Jayden, and was now looking distractedly at Stan and his friends.

Jayden looked furious and was about to yell at Steve again when G said "Don't Jay, there's no point. Steve, this is Stan, Charlie, and Kat. Guys, this is CrazySteve1026, aka Steve."

"Hey, noobs," said Steve, disregarding the exasperated sigh of Stan and the smirk of Sally. "About to start the program, I assume? Yes? Alrighty then, what can I help you with, little brother?" asked Steve, looking at Jayden.

"We just need some watermelons," said Jayden. "Sal made some cake for breakfast but some of us are still…"

"Say no more, Jay," said Steve. He then proceeded to walk over to the watermelon field nearby and bring his hoe down into two watermelons. They burst open, leaving a mess of watermelon slices in their places. He picked them up and walked over to the group of players, handing two slices to each of them.

"Man, dis shtuff ish good," mumbled G.

"Yeah, you should make a watermelon cake next time, Sal," boomed Archie.

"You're welcome," spat an annoyed Sally.

Once they finished their watermelon, Steve said, "Alrighty then, all fed? Good, then off you kids go, have fun at your little program. Be careful, any more deaths and the King might shut the program down."

Charlie spat out his watermelon. "What?" he sputtered. "What'd you just say?" But Steve just laughed manically and went back to the farm to feed some wheat to the Mooshrooms, and the seven players walked out of the farm feeling excited and, in Charlie's case, petrified.

* * * * *

Stan, Kat and Charlie weren't the only ones starting the program. There were also five other people there, all boys under level five, all determined to learn how to play Minecraft. After a brief introduction to the other five the group was divided in half; four of the other players went with G to learn about mining and pick fighting, and Stan, Kat, Charlie, and one other boy who looked exactly like Stan but with darker clothing, went with Archie to learn archery.

Archie took them to the firing range; it was a long clearing located a ways into the woods, away from people. Archie explained the proper technique of handling the bow. Stan and his friends listened intently, but the fourth player couldn't focus; he just kept staring at Kat with his mouth open. It was apparent that he hadn't expected to find any girls in Minecraft.

After the explanation of the theory, they started target practice. There were lamps located on the range at different distances and heights. Archie stood to the side as he flipped switches to turn the lamps on and off. The goal was to hit the lamp that was on. The only one who was okay at the archery was Kat; she managed to hit one lamp twice before it switched off. Stan hit one of the lamps every time he shot, but it took him time to think about the trajectory of the arrow and he hardly ever got a hit on a lit lamp because the lamp changed before he could fire his shot.

Charlie was abysmal; he only hit the lamp one time, though it was he who shot the most arrows. His arrows usually landed a good distance away from the target. One time his arrow came dangerously close to impaling Archie in the chest, though he whipped out his sword and deflected it. The other boy on the range may have been a good archer, but he didn't do anything because he still couldn't stop staring at Kat.

After target practice, it was around three in the afternoon judging by Archie's clock, and he said that it was time for the last activity of the day: sparring. The fighters were given diamond armor that Archie told them had been enchanted to take all damage from the arrow fire without damaging the players themselves; Archie called the armor "training suits". They also were given a bow and a stack of arrows, and told that the first one to score three hits with the arrows won.

The first match was Kat versus Stan. Stan knew who was going to win, and though he tried to fire as quickly as he could, Kat had won before he managed to sink a single arrow into her armor. The match had lasted five minutes, and, though he was hiding it well, they could tell that Archie was impatient by the time it was over.

The match between Charlie and the other boy was over in ten seconds, but that was mainly due to the fact that the boy couldn't stop gaping at Kat for long enough to stop Charlie from actually walking to within one block of him, and firing the three arrows into his chestplate at point-blank range. Archie proceeded to slap his face with his blocky hand at this.

The match between Kat and Charlie lasted longer than the one Stan had had with her, but that was mainly due to that fact that Charlie's strategy consisted of running in an unpredictable pattern, not trying to shoot at all. The match stopped after Kat ran out of arrows. Archie then rolled his eyes, stood up, whipped out his bow, and preceded to fire three arrows at the still-moving Charlie in a matter of seconds. All three arrows sunk themselves into Charlie's headgear.

Archie stood up, sighed, and said, "Let's go." It was clear from the tone of his voice that he didn't think that any of them had a knack for archery. They all walked back to the motel to go to bed feeling slightly disappointed.

As everyone was getting ready for bed, Sally asked Stan as she pulled off her armor, "So, what did you think of your first day of training?"

"Well," said Stan, "let's just say I hope tomorrow is better, A LOT better." And they both laughed.

* * * * *

The next day *was* considerably more enjoyable by all accounts.

After a breakfast of bread, they followed G to the outskirts of the village and took a ride in some mine carts to the entrance of a large mine.

The upper mine was illuminated by torchlight, but Stan still couldn't make out the sides; it was enormous. As they went further down, there were fewer torches, but more players hacking away at the sides with pickaxes. Stan guessed that this was where all of the good materials were.

The mine carts took them past several stops at different levels, and all the way down to the bottom of the mine. Down there, Stan saw a room constructed out of cobblestone, with torchlight inside. The four new players and G walked into the room, and G explained Mining 101 to them; he showed how to distinguish the seven different types of ore (coal, iron, redstone, gold, lapis lazuli, emerald and diamond), which pickaxes were good for mining what, and some basic mining safety tips (don't dig straight down, watch out around gravel and sand, etc).

Once they were done, G took them outside, gave out stone pickaxes and taught them the theory of how to fight with them. Once again the training suits were put on, and there was another tournament. To everyone's surprise, the one who excelled fastest at pick fighting was Charlie. You had to get three hits in on your opponent, and Charlie beat Stan in the first round and then Kat in the second round (needless to say, Kat obliterated the other boy).

70

The best moment was during Charlie's fight against Kat. He was up by two points when Kat took a lunge at him; he fell back and threw his pickaxe through the air, knocking off her helmet.

They then started to mine. Stan did alright, he only had some gravel fall onto him once, and he got out of it pretty quickly. He also found some coal and iron ore, and even two blocks of lapis lazuli ore, which G said was a rare block used to make blue dye. Kat did about the same as him, not having any gravel fall on her, but not finding any lapis lazuli either. Charlie, however, excelled once again; he seemed to have a sixth sense that told him which way to dig to find the best materials. He brought up much more iron than either of the others, and he also found five lapis lazuli ore blocks and even some gold ore, which G said was very rare. It was a shame, said G, that all materials found during the program went to the stores of the village.

"But don't worry, I'm sure that you'll find really good stuff mining on your own, Charlie," said G with a smile. "You have the best mining instincts of anyone I've ever taught."

The three went home feeling content that they had done better at mining than they had at archery, with Charlie absolutely beaming at his newfound prowess.

They had a dinner of watermelon and some more bread, and they were going to bed when Sally spoke to Stan yet again.

"Tomorrow you guys are with me," she said to him. "I'm teaching you sword fighting and crafting."

"Is that so," said Stan. "Well, I look forward to it."

"Just know," said Sally, "I have high expectations for you."

Stan's stomach flipped. "In what? Sword fighting or crafting?" he asked. Immediately afterwards, he felt like an idiot. What kind of question was that?

She looked him in the eyes, and smiled. "Both," she said, and she went off to bed.

* * * * *

The following day was the day of sword fighting and crafting. After bowls of mushroom stew for breakfast, they headed into the dojo above the crafting building to train.

Stan was nervous; before the archery and mining lessons he had felt excited, yes, but not nervous. He remembered the exchange between Sally and himself last night. She had expectations for him; he couldn't let himself mess this up.

Stan, Kat and Charlie sat down across from Sally, the other boy that had been with them having been moved to the class with his other friends after a not-so-subtle request by G and Archie. Stan listened intently as Sally explained that the most important aspect of sword fighting in Minecraft is to not think too much, and to basically just to do what feels natural.

After she explained and demonstrated some different techniques, she pulled three training suits out of her inventory.

"Stan, Charlie, Kat, please come up here."

They did as she said, not knowing what would happen next; G and Archie had called them up two at a time to fight, not three.

"Put these on," she commanded; they obliged. As Stan was pulling on the diamond pants, he saw Sally pull two stone swords and one iron sword out of her inventory.

"Kat, Charlie, come stand over here," she said. They walked to where she was standing. She threw Charlie and Kat the stone swords. "Stan, just stand there," and she threw him the iron sword.

"Kat, Charlie, when I say go, you are going to attack Stan with everything you've got. Stan, you have to defend against both of them. As usual, you are out after three hits."

Stan was dismayed; he had never really fought another player with a sword in his life! He knew that Charlie wasn't any better than he was, but Kat had supposedly done all that stuff on the other servers! She had killed a player and taken his sword and pickaxes! How was he going to beat her?

"Sally, can't I get some advantage or something? Like I have four hits and they have two? Wouldn't that be fair?"

Sally sniggered. "Stan, imagine if a group of about twenty players armed with loaded bows and diamond swords jumped out of the woods and ambushed you. Would that be fair? No, but you'd STILL have to fight, right? You would, cause you know what? Sometimes life isn't fair. I was nice, you HAVE an advantage, you have an iron sword and they both have stone, so don't be a wimp, noob! Now take your positions!"

Up until this point, Kat had been smirking and Charlie had been looking confused, but now they both dropped into fighting stances, swords raised. Kat wore an expression of aggression, while Charlie wore one of apprehension over attacking his friend. Stan was petrified, but he could see Sally's mind wasn't changing, so he readied himself to fight.

Sally sat down in a wooden chair with her legs crossed. "Okay then... FIGHT!"

Stan was caught totally off-guard, but both Charlie and Kat rushed him at the same time. Charlie gave an uppercut to Stan's right arm, and Stan dodged him by sidestepping left. However, he forgot about Kat, who brought her stone sword down onto his helmet with an almighty clang that reverberated in his skull.

Sally yelled out "POINT to Kat and Charlie! Stan, two hits left... Charlie, three... Kat, three. Back to positions." They walked back to their original positions and dropped into fighting stances once again. "Ready? And... FIGHT!"

This time Stan was ready. Charlie rushed first and tried the same uppercut attack, and again Stan dodged, but when Kat swung her sword to his left side he spun his iron sword and blocked Kat's attack. The two players pressed into each others' weapons; Kat was stronger than Stan, but Stan had better leverage. Stan was about to overpower her when he felt a dull pain his right rib cage; Charlie had spun back around and hit him hard on the right side of his body armor. It had hurt, too.

Again, Sally called out, "POINT to Kat and Charlie! Stan, one hit left... Charlie, three... Kat, three." But instead of calling out "ready", she walked over to Stan. She stood behind him, put her hands on his shoulders, and whispered in his ear.

"Stan, you aren't going to win if you put all your energy into fighting one of them. When one of them strikes you, dodge it, and use the opening to come back in and deliver a strike. And better yet, use their own energy against them if you can. Also remember, go for the weakest link first." With that, she went back to sitting in her chair. Stan felt light-hearted as she was so close to him, but immediately got back into his fighting stance, knowing what he would do next.

Sally announced, "Match Point! Ready? And... FIGHT!"

Stan moved instantly; he cut hard to the right, towards Charlie's side. Kat couldn't attack him, because Charlie was in between them. Charlie took a slash with his sword at Stan, but Stan feinted backwards, and at the first opportunity he rushed forward and thrust his sword with all his might at Charlie's stomach. The direct blow glanced off his training suit, but Charlie still doubled over, the wind knocked out of him.

"POINT to Stan! Stan, one hit left... Charlie, two... Kat, three." As they reset, Stan caught Sally's eye. She smiled, and instantly another plan, more brilliant than the last, popped into his head.

"Match point! Ready? And... FIGHT!"

Stan stood still, and Charlie rushed into Stan. Knowing what they were trying to do, Stan feinted right and slammed his sword into Charlie's back, forcing Charlie to the spot where Stan had just stood. Just like Stan had expected, Kat jumped up; not aware of Charlie's new position, Kat brought her sword down on where Stan had just been standing, but instead of hitting him on the head, she clubbed her partner. His helmet flew off, and Charlie hit floor like a ton of bricks.

Sally yelled "POINT to Stan! Stan, one hit left... Charlie, zero... Kat, three! Charlie is out!" but Kat and Stan didn't notice as they were both checking to see if Charlie was okay, and even as she said it, Sally was standing up to join them.

"Charlie, are you all right?" cried Stan, his voice hoarse with worry.

"Oh God, Charlie, I am SO sorry!" yelled Kat, tears in her eyes.

"Charlie? Charlie, can you hear me?" said Sally, bending over Charlie's unconscious form. Stan noticed a trickle of blood running down Charlie's forehead from the slash on his head, and his stomach felt like it dissolved. Charlie couldn't be... no, he refused to let himself think it. Sally waved her blocky hand over his closed eyes. When there was no response, she reached into her inventory and pulled out something. It was a golden apple, like the one that Stan had seen Jayden issue to his unconscious brother. The second Charlie had swallowed the shiny fruit, the wound and blood on his head disappeared, and he sat upright, holding his head.

"Well, that was unpleasant," he said with a dark smile.

Kat gave a shout of relief while Stan yelled out "Thank God you're alive, man! What happened?" he asked, turning to Sally. "I thought you said that the armor absorbed all damage!"

"It's supposed to," Kat said, frowning. "Let me see Charlie's helmet, Stan." Stan picked up the helmet from the floor and handed it to her. She examined it. "Well, it looks like somebody didn't enchant this helmet correctly. It appears to have been given Blast Protection instead of just normal Protection, so you wouldn't get hurt by an explosion, but you would by a sword... how did we not catch this in review?" she wondered out loud.

"Well, I guess it doesn't matter, we can fix It." she said. "And may I say, that was an excellent move, Stan, if Charlie was in any condition to fight right now, he would have lost the match due to taking damage from both you and Kat. And Kat! To produce a strike with a stone sword that does that much damage to someone wearing a diamond helmet! Very impressive, both of you!"

76

Stan tried not to look to proud of himself seeing as he had just injured his best friend. Kat, meanwhile, was trying to hide the fact that she was blushing.

"Well Charlie, you'd better not fight anymore seeing as you don't have a helmet, but we still have to finish this fight. Kat, where's your sword?"

"Over there," she said sheepishly, gesturing to a handle and several chunks of stone; the impact with Charlie's helmet had reduced her weapon to rubble.

"Damn, girl, you are GOOD at this!" laughed Sally as she picked up the remains of Kat's sword from the floor. "It must have taken a ton of power to shatter a stone sword in one blow. Here," she said, picking Charlie's sword up of the ground and tossing it to her. "Match point! Ready? And… FIGHT!"

This time there was no contest; Kat was simply more talented with a sword than Stan was, and she had delivered a blow to his leg and won the match in a matter of seconds.

"POINT to Kat! Stan, 0… Kat, 3. KAT WINS! Now come on, I still have crafting to show you guys."

The three friends stripped off the training suits with pleasure; they were really quite uncomfortable after a while. They followed Sally down the ladder and into the crafting room below them.

Sally explained to them that the tables with tools on them were called "crafting tables", and that they used these to create a wide variety of different items. Sally handed them each a copy of a book that was exactly like the one Stan had gotten out of the chest that first day in Elementia.

Sally gave Stan, Kat and Charlie instructions to craft certain items, and she said to use anything in the chests to do so. They all proved to be quite capable of crafting. They crafted their own wooden planks and then crafting tables, and then some sticks, a stone sword, a stone axe, a bow, some arrows, and leather armor.

After they had learned how to craft sufficiently, and Sally had explained how to smelt (changing the properties of certain blocks by putting them in a furnace), they headed back to the room, with a long, hard, successful day behind them. Sally once again came to talk to Stan. He was waiting; it was becoming a thing that they did. She sat down.

"You're really good with a sword," she said.

"No I'm not! Kat was better!" he said, wondering why she would say this.

"Yes, she is better with a sword than you are. But you were innovative. Once you realized what you were doing, you managed to score three points with two people going against you. That's not something just anybody could do."

"Thanks," he said, smiling at her. "I had a good teacher."

She smiled back at him. "You'd better get to bed, noob. Tomorrows your day with Jayden, and you can't expect him to be as nice as me. Get some rest. You'll need it." And with that she went to her own bed.

CHAPTER 6: STAN AND STEVE

Stan woke up the next morning to a hissing sound.

"Very funny guys," he mumbled. "That actually sounds a lot like a real Creep... AAAAUUUUUGGGHHHHH!"

This was no prank. An actual Creeper was standing right next to Stan, and he was staring right into its horrible, empty face. The monster was beginning to swell, and in the split second before the inevitable explosion, Stan flew at the monster and punched it in the face.

To Stan's amazement, instead of exploding, the Creeper flew backwards. As it walked back towards him, it suddenly keeled over sideways, an arrow protruding from the side of its head. Everyone woke up to the sound of Stan's yell. Rex started barking up a storm. Archie still stood with his bow in hand, aiming exactly where the monster's head had been. The body disappeared, leaving a small mess of gray powder beneath it.

"What the hell?" yelled Kat, holding her sword up.

"Yeah, what's with all the noise?" whined G. "I'm trying to sleep here!"

"A Creeper got in," said Stan.

"WHAT?" said Sally, looking disheveled, not at all like her usual self. "How did a Creeper get in... hang on. Why is it so dark in here? Where are the torches?"

She was right. The windows around the edges of the building provided the only source of light; besides that it was dark.

"Yeah, where are the torches?" asked Jayden, who was still breathing heavily. "Did someone steal them?"

"I guess so," said Charlie, looking around. "But why? Why would somebody break in here just to steal the torches? And the door?" For he had just noticed that the door, too, was missing.

"It was probably just some random griefer; you know, a player that likes giving other players crap for no reason," said Archie, putting his bow back into his inventory. "Felt like having a laugh by making it so that monsters could just come in here in the night."

"Yeah," said Stan as he remembered how Mr. A had attacked them for no apparent reason, "Yeah, a griefer would do something like that.

"Well, good thing that that thing woke us up actually, I was about to oversleep," said Jayden. "It's my turn to make breakfast, so I'll go get some stuff for that. Sally, you go down to the storehouse and craft us a new door and some torches." Sally nodded and ran out the hole where the door used to be, followed closely by Jayden.

Sally came back soon after, and she put new torches on the walls and fixed the new door in the frame. Jayden arrived not long after, holding some wheat and a brown powder. He put it on the crafting table, and before long he had created a batch of cookies. Everyone had some; they were chocolate chip, and they tasted delicious.

"Okay," said Jayden after they had all finished, and Kat had calmed the still-barking Rex by feeding him some rotten flesh. "Come with me, you three. We have axe training and farming today."

Kat and Charlie filed out the door, with Stan in the rear, feeling sure that he would not be very good at axe fighting. Frankly, he had always been slightly awkward, and he did not imagine that swinging a long stick with a hunk of metal on the end would be his forte. As he realized this, Stan felt suddenly sullen; Charlie had proven to be exceptional with a pickaxe, and the same with Kat and her sword. If he couldn't master axe fighting, what would he have to fight with? But as Stan left the room, he could have sworn he heard Sally whisper, "Good luck, noob" in his ear as he walked out of the door, and instantly, he felt more confident.

They followed Jayden down the road and they were surprised when they entered Crazy Steve's farm.

"What are we doing here?" asked Stan.

"Well, what better place to learn about axe use than at a farm?" asked Jayden. "As part of the program, you'll be doing some volunteer work here, helping my brother with the farming."

This made sense, and the four players walked into an empty yard enclosed by fences. In the adjacent pumpkin field, Crazy Steve was tilling some new land with his hoe. Stan was relieved to see that, based on his calm and methodic demeanor, he was not QPOed.

"Hey, bro," the farmer said, and he tipped his straw hat as the teacher and three students entered through the fence gate. "You three gonna help an old farmer with his work today? Those

Mooshrooms are giving me quite a hard time, and I could use the extra hands."

"You'll get your help, Steve," replied Jayden. "We have axe fighting to do first."

Stan's stomach did another flip as he thought of the pressure surrounding his mastery of the axe, which Jayden pulled out of a chest in the enclosure.

"The key," said Jayden, holding up the axe and demonstrating proper form, "is to let the axe guide you. It knows what to do. You are not the master of the axe; you are simply its modest guide."

"Oh, brother," grumbled Kat under her breath. Jayden proceeded to explain the basic mechanics of axe fighting, which Stan understood surprisingly well.

"To help you appreciate the art, each of you must pass a challenge." He called out, "Yo, Steve! Toss me four pumpkins, stat!"

Crazy Steve may have been old, but he was *strong*. He picked up four pumpkins growing in the field and tossed them all to Jayden in two throws. Jayden put three of the pumpkins in the chest, and then pulled out something Stan had never seen before. It appeared to be a large block made out of snow. Jayden took out another. He put one snow block down towards the back of the empty lot, and put the other on top of it. He turned to Stan, Charlie and Kat.

"Your goal in this exercise is to get across this red line," and he gestured to line of red dust behind the pile of snow that Stan hadn't noticed before. "You also must kill the enemy that I am about to create."

The three new players started all talking at once.

"What do you mean, create?"

"Why isn't the snow melting?"

"Are you going to make a Creeper or something?"

"How does that work?"

"Why isn't the snow melting?"

"How are we supposed to survive without armor?"

"This honestly can't be safe!"

"Why isn't the snow melting?!"

Jayden waited for the questions to die down before he continued. "I'll demonstrate, and all your questions will be answered. Charlie, could you come here, please?"

Looking scared stiff, and with good reason, Charlie walked over to the tall pile of snow. Jayden tossed him a pumpkin and said, "Now Charlie, when I say go, put that pumpkin on top of the snow pile. Got it?" Charlie nodded, looking confused. Stan shared this puzzlement; he had no idea what Jayden was about to do.

Jayden stood at the opposite end of the enclosure from the red line and pile of snow, and he pulled an iron axe out of the trunk. He stood with the axe at his side, got in a fighting stance, and said, "Ready Charlie? And ... GO!"

Charlie placed the pumpkin on the snow pile, and immediately fell backwards screaming, a look of horror and amazement on his face. For the pile of snow with the pumpkin had turned into some type of animated snowman. Sticks had sprouted out of its sides, and it was hurling snowballs that it seemed to procure from nowhere rapid fire at Jayden, who was running towards the snowman. Jayden was agile; not one of the snowballs hit him as he charged the snowy beast.

Then, as Jayden reached the snowman, he jumped in the air and did sort of midair twirl, just dodging one of the snowballs, and his axe sliced through the bottom chunk of the snowman. Another twirl saw the middle section cleaved in two, and another jumping spin and the axe sliced clear through the pumpkin on the snowman's head. The snowman was seriously damaged, not throwing snowballs anymore, and it seemed to be struggling just to keep upright. Jayden was ruthless, though, and with one last jump into the air, he delivered an almighty blow with the axe straight down on the snowman's head. The entire pile of pumpkin and snow fell to two sides; snowballs rained onto the ground, and the pumpkin burst apart and split into nothing but seeds and a few pieces of orange flesh.

Completely ignoring the gaping mouths of his three students, Jayden wiped the snow and pumpkin guts off his axe and calmly walked across the red line.

Stan, Charlie and Kat exploded into cheers. None of them were entirely sure what they had just seen, but it was certainly spectacular. "That was amazing!" Stan yelled.

"Yeah, it was! And what exactly was that thing you just killed?" asked Kat.

"Oh, that was just a Snow Golem," explained Jayden. "They use snowballs to keep away monsters and unwanted guests. So, which of you wants to try first?"

The smile fell from Stan's face. He had forgotten that *he* would have to do what Jayden just did. He had made it look so easy! What if I just end up looking like an idiot? Stan thought.

"I'll take the bullet," Charlie said meekly, stepping forward. The others looked surprised, even Jayden, though he still tossed Charlie the axe. Charlie never volunteered to go first.

"Well, snowballs don't hurt, do they?" said Charlie, taking his stance as Jayden readied the Golem. "What's the worst that can happen?"

Huh. Famous last words, thought Stan.

And he turned out to be right, as Charlie's trial was a bona fide disaster. The second Jayden yelled go, Charlie dashed forward, but he instantly fell back on his butt, still grabbing the handle of the axe; he had clearly underestimated its weight. With Charlie on the ground, the Snow Golem had a clear shot at Charlie with the snowballs. Each snowball knocked Charlie into the air a little, but he was so bad at dodging the snowballs that he was actually blasted into the air by the rapid-fire stream of snow. It was only a hoe thrown spear-style by Crazy Steve which impaled itself in the Golem's face that stopped Charlie from being lifted to a fatal height. Still, Charlie was pretty badly hurt when he fell back down, and a disgruntled Jayden had to pull out another golden apple to fix Charlie's leg.

Kat's trial was almost as bad. She decided to throw the axe with all of her considerable strength towards the Golem's head. It would have worked had her aim been better; the flying axe ended up hitting and killing a cow in the adjacent field. From there, it was all Kat could do to keep from being lifted into the air as Charlie had. She was better at dodging than him, but she had no weapons, and she only dodged about half of the rapid-fire snowballs. Jayden had to pull out a bow and arrows from the chest and fire three shots into the Snow Golem's pumpkin head to finally silence it.

Finally, Stan took the axe, and dropped into a fighting stance with a nervous pit in his stomach. He hoped he wouldn't just drop the axe like Charlie, or do something else to make him look stupid. Jayden placed on the pumpkin head, the Snow Golem became animated, and Stan took off.

The first thing he noticed was that the axe wasn't as heavy as he thought. It felt rather light in his hand as he ran with it trailing behind him. The second thing he noticed was how easy it was to dodge; he simply knew when to duck and weave around the snowballs, and within no time, Stan had reached the Snow Golem. What happened next was so incredible that even Jayden didn't believe his eyes.

As he neared the Snow Golem, Stan had a brilliant idea. Instead of doing what Jayden had done and doing a triple spin, Stan launched himself forward and into the air and spun with all his might, axe stretched in front of him. He slammed into the Snow Golem with such speed and such incredible revolution that the Golem was cut into dust as if it was in a blender set to "liquefy".

Stan landed with one hand and two feet on the ground, well past the red line, breathing hard, his axe held in the remaining hand, and there was no evidence that there had ever been an enemy there. Nobody could even see any pieces of the pumpkin. The only evidence of the snow was the light dust hanging in the air, creating a rainbow in the light from the square sun.

There was an absolute explosion of cheers from Charlie and Kat, and Jayden looked just amazed. Stan's smile filled his face; the move had seemed so natural, so easy! Then he noticed Crazy Steve's face, and his smile faltered.

The look was a shrewd, calculating look. It was as if the old-timer was seeing Stan for the first time, and was now trying to figure something out about him, as if there were something hidden in Stan's pixilated body that he was trying to decipher. But his friends came over, and Stan soon forgot about the old farmer.

"That was *amazing!*" cried Kat.

"Wow! Awesome, man!" exclaimed Charlie.

"How did you DO that!?" asked Jayden, eyes wide.

Stan shrugged, unable to stop grinning. "I don't know. It just kind of happened."

"Well it was amazing!" Kat said again, and Charlie nodded enthusiastically in agreement.

"I think we may have just found your talent!" said a smiling Jayden, and Stan's heart leapt. And as the training commenced, it seemed that Stan had indeed discovered something that he could do without trying. Like Charlie with the pickaxe and Kat with the sword, Stan blew away all of the others in the sparring ring. He even managed to just beat out Jayden. Now Jayden was even more impressed, not to mention slightly jealous.

After a farming lesson that was no problem at all (though none of them particularly liked farming, they were all capable of it with ease, and Steve really appreciated the help convincing the stubborn Mooshrooms to breed), they put away their axes and hoes and headed out. Jayden was just about to exit under the hedge when a hand grabbed his shoulder.

"Yo Jay!" Stan turned around and saw Crazy Steve yelling to Jayden. Jay turned. "Could I talk tuh Stan here for a few minutes?" Jay nodded and walked off, the others following behind him.

"Come on, noob," said Steve as he walked back into the farm. Stan was apprehensive; he had had misgivings of Crazy Steve since the episode with the QPO and was not keen on talking with him one on one. When they got to the cow fence, Crazy Steve sat down on a stretch of fence and looked Stan straight in the eye.

"Look kid," said Crazy Steve, "I realize dat ya may not think much'a me since that whole QPO thing, but I've been on dis server a real long time. I'm level fifty four, da highest in da village. I've got a whole lotta' knowledge worked up about the server, who runs it, and how it works. Do me a favor and remember that as I talk tuh ya, okay?" Stan nodded, unsure of where this was going.

"Like I said, I've been here a real long time, and frankly, the servers neva' been in worse shape than it is right now. Don interrupt," he added as Stan opened his mouth to ask what Crazy Steve was talking about. "Dem in Element City, that run da government, dey don't like people like you. Freshies. Beginners. Noobs. You get it, don'cha?"

Stan nodded, his gut knotting at this revelation, and asked, "But why? Why do they not like us? And what does this have to do with me?"

Crazy Steve's reply was cut off when an arrow sunk into his temple.

Stan's immediate shock was cut off when he heard the twang of another arrow being fired. He rolled off the fence and grabbed the iron hoe that Crazy Steve had dropped, and he threw it in the direction of the arrow. The hoe connected, and Stan saw a player with a black ski mask, bare muscular chest, and black pants and shoes stumble backwards, holding his face.

Stan used his attacker's recovery to look at the player besides him. Crazy Steve had fallen to the ground, and now lay unmoving, bleeding from the arrow in his head. All of the items that he carried were strewn on the ground about him. There was no doubt about it; he was dead.

Stan's brain did not have time to process this horrific turn of events. He grabbed Crazy Steve's iron axe and looked at the murderer just in time as he sent another arrow flying towards Stan's head. He deflected it with the axe, and then charged his assailant.

The murderer was now on the run. He had pulled out a piece of flint and an iron ring, and he was striking them together to create showers of sparks, setting fire to anything in his reach. The melons, the fence around the pig pen, and the logs of cocoa beans were instantly set ablaze and the fire was spreading fast, quickly blocking off Stan's pursuit of the murderer.

Stan's brain went into emergency mode. Without hesitating, he shoved all of Crazy Steve's items into his own inventory, grabbed the old farmer's body, and bolted towards the exit, yelling for Jayden. Stan burst through the hedge archway, which was already burning, and he saw Jayden running back, a look of horror on his face, closely tailed by Kat and Charlie.

The second Jayden saw the burning farm, his eyes bulged, but it was the sight of his dead brother that made him go completely berserk. He grabbed Stan by the shoulders, and shook him back and forth, yelling, "WHAT THE HELL HAPPENED HERE?"

"A player with a ski mask killed Steve, tried to kill me, and then set the farm on fire!" choked Stan, for he found it hard to breathe due to the smoke and his horror at Crazy Steve's untimely demise.

A flash of recognition showed momentarily in Jayden's eyes, and he could tell that this... this... griefer, with the ski mask, had struck before. "DAMN YOU!" Jayden yelled at the top of his lungs at the sky, cursing out the griefer, his eyes and veins bulging. Stan, Kat, and Charlie stood there, looking terrified.

Stan stood there numb for the longest time. He was vaguely aware of Jayden breaking down sobbing next to him, of Adoria's voice yelling, of people running past him with water buckets. He realized that the inferno was gradually dying down. Before long, there was no fire to brighten the dark night that had fallen in the midst of the firefight.

Stan snapped out of his trance when he heard Sally's voice next to him. "You all right, noob?" she asked gently.

Stan looked at her. He wanted to tell her that he wasn't all right, and that Crazy Steve could never return to the server due to his banishment, and that he couldn't understand why someone would kill another player if they knew that eternal banishment was the consequence... but instead he looked her in the eye and said, "I'll be alright." Her eyes were full of tears too, and he didn't want to seem weak to her, not after she had believed in him.

"Sally, we have a big problem," Adoria exclaimed as she rushed over to them, panic in her voice. "I think that there's a possibility that this attack may not be isolated. We need to get all of the lower-levels into the mine, but there won't be room for all of them down there. The mine wasn't meant to hold the number of people we have now, any more than two thirds of the current population would make it too susceptible to accidents. I'm out of ideas, Jayden's still distraught, and Archie and G are still busy preparing to evacuate the lower-levels. What do you think we should do?"

The panic in her voice led Stan to speak.

"We'll leave," he said. Sally and Adoria both stared at him. "We'll leave, Charlie, Kat, and I. If there's any chance at all that there are more griefers coming, we'd stand the best chance of survival, we've finished the program. Send us out, ask for other volunteers to leave, and you can stay and defend everyone left in the village."

Adoria opened her mouth to protest, but Sally cut her off. "That's actually not bad thinking. Those who've completed the program will have the best shot at surviving, and we upper-levels will have to stay here and defend the village. We can send off volunteers who have completed the program into the forest, towards the city."

Adoria protested, "But what if they run into griefers along the way?"

"They won't," Sally responded. "The griefers avoid the main road in case they come across well-armed travelers. They're cowards, all of them. And besides," she added, smiling at Stan, "that griefer didn't run away for no reason. Am I right in thinking that you fought him off?" asked Sally, to which Stan nodded.

"Okay," Adoria said, and she ran off towards the mine, skirt billowing in the wind, to make the announcement.

Stan looked at Sally, and said, "Sally, I..." but he was cut off by Sally kissing him on the mouth. "Come back and visit someday," she said when they broke apart, and she ran off to join Adoria. "Oh, and take some weapons and food from the storehouse!" she called back to him.

CHAPTER 7: THE THUNDERSTORM

I knew it! I knew it! I knew she likes me! Oh man, I am *definitely* coming back to this village as soon as I can! Wow, I don't know what I expected from this game, but THAT was not at the top of my list! Wow...

These were the thoughts that filled Stan's head as he sprinted out of the Adorian Village, tailed by Kat and Charlie, as the rain started to fall. They were not thrilled when he told them that they had to leave, but they were very excited at the prospect of new weapons.

Kat now ran right behind Stan with a bow slung over her back, a quiver of twelve arrows and a gleaming iron sword dangling at her side. Rex was dashing along at her heels. Charlie was close behind the dog, with an iron pickaxe in his hand, and a whole mess of watermelons in his inventory; he held the group's food. Stan was in the lead, holding an iron axe in his hand, and a crafting table, furnace, and some coal in his inventory. They were well trained and on the move; any enemies that they encountered out here, in the light rain that had started, were dead meat in their minds.

In due time, they stopped to take a breather. While they caught their breath, Charlie said, "Wow, what a day, right?"

"Yeah," replied Kat. They certainly were in no mood for laughter, but they had recovered from the initial shock of Crazy Steve's death.

"I still don't get it, though," she said. "Why did that guy pick Crazy Steve out as a target? He was a farmer! He *helped* lower-levels!"

Something connected in Stan's mind as she said this. Crazy Steve's last words came back to him. *Dem in Element City, that run da government, dey don't like people like you. Freshies. Beginners. Noobs.*

"You don't think that the assassin was with the government, do you?" asked Stan.

Charlie and Kat looked at him in shock. "Why would the *government* send out assassins to kill people that gave food to their lower-leveled citizens?" Kat asked skeptically.

"That's just it though," said Stan, standing up. "He gave food to lower-level citizens." He explained to them about his conversation with Crazy Steve, and what the old farmer had said about the government. This left Kat looking bewildered, and Charlie asked, "Why? How does that make *any* sense?"

"I don't know," Stan replied. "Crazy Steve was just about to tell me when…" He sighed, and looked away from the other two and sighed again. They got the message.

"It's certainly a weird theory," said Kat, also standing, "But we'll think about it later. We need to get going!" she had to yell to be heard over the sound of the rain, which was falling hard now. Stan saw a lightning strike in the distance, which Rex barked at. In the illumination from the lightning, he noticed a tower in the distance, right in the middle of the path.

"What's that?" he asked, and he gestured to it.

"What's what?" yelled Kat.

"That, the tower up there!" he yelled back, and another lightning strike illuminated the sky, letting Kat and Charlie see the tower as well.

"Maybe it's a shelter! Or another player's house!" yelled Charlie.

"Maybe! Let's go there, because we need to get out of this storm! This lightning is getting dangerous!" screamed Kat over the whistling wind and pounding rain.

The thunderstorm was beginning to get dangerous, with the bolts extremely frequent now. Once, lightning struck a tree right next to Kat and it caught fire, causing her to give a screech of surprise. Fortunately it was immediately extinguished by the rain.

As they approached the tower, they noticed that it was actually a pyramid, and that it covered the entire road. Stan was suspicious; something felt wrong. As he walked closer, his suspicions were confirmed; the entire pyramid was made of stacked blocks of TNT.

"Why would someone put this here?" asked Kat?

"I don't know, but I don't feel safe near it," replied Stan.

"Why?" asked Charlie, walking up to the pyramid. "What's the worst that can happen?"

As if on cue, the worst thing did happen. Lightning struck the top of the pyramid and the powder in the block was ignited. It began to flash dangerously.

"RUN!" screamed Stan as the block exploded. As the three players and dog ran for it, the entire tower exploded from the top down, with each explosion sending lit TNT blocks flying everywhere like lava spewing from a volcano. Luckily, they escaped the range of the explosions with top-speed sprinting. As they gazed at the exploding pyramid it became clear that the explosives were underground, too; they could hear the explosions continue on for about sixty seconds before the tumult finally stopped.

The rain had died down, so they could talk in normal voices again. There was dust in the air now from the explosion, just like the Creeper explosion in the mine on the way to the Adorian Village. But this explosion was much larger than the creeper explosion, and it had blown a huge fissure in the middle of the road. They were cut off from the other side.

"The woods, then?" Stan said in an unnaturally high voice. They looked at each other. They remembered what Sally had said. *The griefers avoid the main road in case they come across well-armed travelers.* Straying off of the road would lead them directly into enemy territory.

"Oh, don't be ridiculous, we don't…" started Charlie, but he was cut off by Kat.

"Don't kid yourself, Charlie. Stan's right." You could tell from her trembling lip that Kat was making a determined effort to keep her cool. "Come on," and she started into the woods, Rex at her heels, growling a low-tone growl. Charlie made a high pitched squeal, but forced himself to follow Stan into the forest.

It was dark; Stan could barely make out the neon orange of Kat's shirt. Every now and then, there was another flash of lightning, and Stan could make out a spider web, a tree trunk, a zombie lumbering in the distance.

Suddenly, there was a rustling to his right. There was something in the underbrush, and it was running straight towards him. "Run!" he yelled, and he started running, hacking branches out of the way with his axe. Kat and Charlie looked confused for a second, but when they heard the rustling they followed in suit.

Stan burst out of the forest and into the light, now on the other side of the giant crater. Kat burst out right after him, closely followed by Rex and Charlie. Stan whipped out his axe and raised it above his head, Kat drew her sword and dropped in a fighting stance, and Charlie held his pickaxe in trembling hands. Then, the thing that had been chasing them burst into the clearing.

"Are you kidding me? You were scared of this little guy?" laughed Kat as she walked up to the pig and stroked it behind the ears, which it seemed to like. Rex came up to the pig and started sniffing it.

"Honestly, Stan, don't DO that!" said Charlie, his eyes wide, holding his chest. "You almost gave me a heart attack!"

"I'm sorry, alright?" said Stan, but he was smiling; it was a cute little pig. "Kat, get Rex away from that pig, I could use some meat." At Kat's command Rex left the pig alone and sat at her feet. "Bye bye, little guy," said Stan, and he raised his axe, and brought it down on the pig, just as the lightning struck.

His axe was countered by a golden sword.

Kat's jaw dropped, Charlie gave a yelp, and Stan nearly fell back, eyes wide, at the monster that the pig had transformed into upon being struck by lightning.

It was humanoid in form, and it had the general color of a pig, but the flesh was rotting off all over its body, and part of its skull was showing through the side of its head. Its ribs stuck out of its stomach. It wore a brown loincloth, and in its hand was a golden sword that was locked against the steel of Stan's axe. The pig-zombie looked mad.

The pig-zombie pressed the attack. It swung its sword in complicated patterns and drove Stan backward. Stan tried to counter with his axe, but the attempts were futile. The pig-zombie's golden blade dodged an axe blow and severed the axe's blade from the handle. Stan's weapon was destroyed.

Stan danced backwards, out of range of the slashes, trying to avoid the sword slices, when a pickaxe flew through the air and embedded itself in the pig-zombie's exposed skull. The attack did no damage whatsoever, but it had the intended effect; the pig-zombie turned his attention from Stan and now had its sight set on Charlie.

Charlie might have thought the desperate attack through a little better, though. The pig-zombie was faster than he thought, and Stan watched in helpless horror as the undead warrior rushed in and slashed Charlie's leg and forehead. Charlie yelled out in pain, falling to the ground and grabbed his damaged limb and temple. The golden sword again rose for the deathblow, but before the inevitable strike, a white blur connected with the pig-zombie and it was knocked to the ground.

Rex, at Kat's command, had tackled the pig-zombie. There was a moment when the two animals wrestled with one another, attempting to tear out the other's throat, when Rex was finally overpowered. The dog was thrown to the edge of the crater, and whimpered, unable to get up.

Upon seeing Charlie and her dog in such pain, Kat's eyes blazed with fury, and she rushed the pig-zombie. The iron and golden blades clashed, and the two warriors began to fight. Kat's skill was incredible, but was matched equally by the pig-zombie. Kat was at an obvious disadvantage; she managed to slash the pig-zombie across the stomach once, but all that it did was make some of its flesh fall off, not slowing it down in the least.

Stan was feeling hopeless. His axe was broken, Charlie was on the verge of death, and Kat was beginning to wear out fighting the pig-zombie. It was clear that it would take an incredibly powerful attack to finish off the pig-zombie, like an explosion of some sorts, like…

Stan suddenly felt something, like the air was static. He looked towards the source. A little ways down the road, a figure was emerging from the forest. It was as tall as he was, but with four squat legs. A Creeper. But there was something different about this one. It had little lines of electricity dancing around its body, and it was giving off electricity that Stan could feel even from such a distance. It was as if the Creeper had been struck by lightning. Stan could sense that an explosion from a Creeper that charged with electricity could be… *fatal.*

He knew what he had to do. He yelled, "KAT! Toss me the bow and arrows!"

Kat was tired from fighting the pig-zombie, and she knew that it would overpower her soon. As the zombie slashed, she feinted back, and gave the pig-zombie an almighty attack with her sword, as if she were brandishing a baseball bat. The undead being flew backwards and slammed into a tree. She threw the bow and arrows to Stan, and took the opportunity to catch her breath.

Stan took the bow, positioned the arrow, took aim, and fired.

He hit his target. The arrow sunk deep into the Creeper's head.

The Creeper looked at Stan. It's eyes glowed red, and the electric activity around it's body increased significantly. Then, the monster charged, full speed, towards them.

"WHAT THE HELL DO YOU THINK YOU'RE DOING!!!???" yelled Kat, but she should have kept her eyes on her own fight. The pig-zombie was back on its feet, and it gave her a cut across the back that sent her tumbling away. Her sword flew high into the air.

Stan didn't allow himself to think of his two fallen friends until he completed the task at hand. He caught the iron sword and rushed into the pig-zombie. The swords collided, and the two struggled to overpower the other. Stan stared into the eye and eye socket, and he saw out of the corner of his right eye that the Creeper was almost upon him. Stan feinted back, and used all of his remaining strength to thrust the sword into the pig-zombie's stomach. Before the undead fiend had time to react, Stan flung the pig-zombie over his head, and it collided with the hissing Creeper. Stan dove out of the way just as he heard the tremendous explosion behind him.

Stan was badly rattled from the blast, and he knew that his innards had been damaged during the fight, but he forced himself to get up and survey the scene around him. Charlie was laying on the side of the road, the cuts on his head and leg bleeding. Rex lay on the edge of the crater, whimpering. Kat was nowhere to be found. In the place where the two monsters collided, there was a crater, three times bigger than a normal Creeper explosion crater.

The pig-zombie was gone, and all that remained was a pile of rotting meat and a bloodstained gold sword.

Wasting no time, Stan started to walk to the crater. Each step was excruciating, but he had to save his friends. He scooped up the golden sword and put both his swords into his inventory, and held the rotten flesh in his hands. This he fed to Rex, whose tail instantly shot up, and he became the same dog again, licking Stan's hand.

This being done, Stan hobbled over to Charlie. He wasn't moving at all, and his wounds looked worse up close. Fearing the worst, Stan reached into Charlie's inventory and pulled out a watermelon slice. He stuffed it into Charlie's mouth, hoping for a sign of life. To his relief, Charlie slowly started to chew the watermelon, and then give a sigh. Stan sighed too, now sure that Charlie would be alright if he could find the right treatment quick enough.

That left Kat. He had no idea where she was; he couldn't see her anywhere. He was just starting to panic when he heard a raspy, female voice calling his name from within the crater made by the pyramid explosion. He looked into it and saw Kat, laying spread-eagle in a shallow pool of blood, on a ledge about five blocks down. She seemed unable to speak. As Stan punched his way through the dirt to get down to help her, it became clear that Kat had had the wind knocked out of her, and her breathing was shallow and raspy.

With great difficulty, Stan and Kat made their way out of the colossal crater and then, without a word, both fell on the ground, passed out.

* * * * *

Stan woke up to the feel of Rex licking his face. Judging by the fact that it was early morning, and the sky was no longer gray, they had been passed out for a while. Stan sat up, and woke Kat up. By now she had re-caught her breath.

"It's funny," she said with a grimace. "Each day I think this game couldn't get any more dangerous."

Stan nodded; he understood what she meant. "Well, let's hurry. We have to get Charlie some help as soon as possible, and I have a hunch that we'll find that in Element City." Kat nodded, and stood up. Stan saw that the backs of her shirt, shorts, and thighs were coated with dried blood. Looking at himself, he was covered in dust and debris from the explosion. "We'd both better jump in the water when we get a chance, too," said Stan. "We're a mess!"

Kat didn't say anything, but got up and walked slowly, painfully, over to Charlie. Stan followed right behind her. Together, with extreme difficulty, they slung the unconscious Charlie onto their shoulders, and started limping down the path once again.

It was agony. The Creeper's explosion had damaged something within Stan, and every breath he took felt detached, like it was hurting rather than helping him. Kat, on the other hand, had that huge slash on her back battling the pig-zombie, and she may have also suffered internal damage from being thrown into the crater. Charlie wasn't capable of doing anything to help; the wounds to his head and leg were severe, and it was the thought of these wounds not healing that was the only thing pushing Kat and Stan to continue on the path.

After what seemed like an entire day (though, in reality, the sun was high in the sky, and it was only about noon), a wall came into view. It was a huge wall, and the only things that Stan could see over the wall were the tall towers of what looked like a castle. Stan was just noticing the guards pacing back and forth on top of the wall, armed with bows, when something inside him gave an awful lurch, and he found himself falling, blacking out before he had even hit the ground.

CHAPTER 8: PROCLAMATION DAY

When Stan woke up, he found himself lying on the ground. There were dirt and weeds beneath him, and two brick walls rose on both sides of him. He had just noticed this when he saw Kat squatting down next to him, stuffing a golden apple into the unconscious Charlie's mouth. Stan noticed that the cut on her back had vanished; she must have eaten a golden apple as well.

"Oh, Kat... what happened?" Stan asked, his hand to his head, as Charlie began to stir, his cuts already completely vanished.

"You passed out," Kat said, "right outside the gate. You and Charlie were both down, and I knew that I needed Golden Apples. None of the guards would even talk to me, and I had to look through about three shops before I found one that was willing to trade for three Golden Apples. I gave him the crafting table, the furnace and coal, the bow, the eleven arrows, the iron and golden swords, and most of the watermelon, and he STILL seemed to think that I it was almost a steal, me taking the apples from him."

"Wait," said Stan, trying to process what she had said. "Questions. What do you mean, shops?"

"Oh, well, we made it to Element City, apparently, that's what that wall was," and Stan noticed a row of buildings with players swarming in the streets, "and right at the entrance is the merchant's area. They barter from inside their shops."

"Okay," Stan said. "Where are we now?"

"Oh, I just dragged you two into the nearest convenient alleyway, then got the golden apples."

"Okay so… wait a minute… crafting table… furnace, coal… bow, arrows… two swords… watermel… YOU GAVE HIM *ALL OF OUR STUFF!!??*" Charlie said, for he had sat up and was listening, too.

"And he STILL thought I was ripping him off, even though I was still bleeding really bad," said Kat, shaking her head. "I tell you, these people here are total jerks compared to the Adorian village."

Stan remembered how Adoria had hesitated before telling them that going to Element City was a good idea. This must be what she meant, he thought.

"I'll say, though," said Kat, "the guy seemed really surprised when I said that the wounds were from a Zombie Pigman. Apparently they…"

"Wait, what's a Zombie Pigman?" asked Charlie.

The other two stared at him for a minute.

Then Kat said, "Charlie, are you dense?"

Charlie looked confused.

"Dude, what did we JUST fight? What gave you cuts on the head and leg?"

Charlie concentrated for a second, then his face lit up. "Oh, I get it! Cause it's a zombie but it looks like a pig and has the body shape of a man!"

Kat and Stan glanced at each other.

"Let's hope that's just a side effect of the apple," said Kat dismissively. "Anyways, we're here now, and Goldman told me that the thing that you want to do once you get here is get a job. They offer you lodging and food, and you work for them. Sometimes, they'll offer you a more tedious task, and they'll pay you in materials. Those materials you can trade for other things that you need, and eventually you'll be able to open your own house that you buy on the real estate market, and open your own business beneath it."

As she finished her monologue, Stan and Charlie looked at her with raised eyebrows.

"When did you spend so much time talking to G?"

"And why did you call him 'Goldman'?"

Kat rolled her eyes. "I talked to him at night after training. It's nice to talk to someone who knows what he's talking about. And for the record, he *prefers* to be called Goldman, but he lets people call him G because Goldman is kind of a mouthful. I don't mind, though," she added, as Charlie and Stan snickered. "Let's go find jobs."

And with that, the trio stood up, ate the last three watermelon slices, and, with nothing left to their names, walked out of the alley and into the street.

The city was, by all accounts, breathtaking. The cobblestone streets were overflowing with people, walking down the blocks. Above their heads, a monorail-like system of railroad tracks ran above the houses. And the houses were everywhere. The ground floors of the houses were various stores and shops, with the living quarters above.

Overlooking this metropolis were skyscrapers. This was clearly the merchant's district, but there were clearly other zones of the city, and one of them was filled with skyscrapers. The tallest towers were three towers, all of which were connected by bridges at various points in the height, the middle of which had a slender spire on top. However, the main building of this city was clearly the castle.

Raised up significantly higher than the skyscrapers, this building was in the clouds at its peak. The tallest towers of the castle, the ones that could be seen from outside over the high wall, must have literally been able to touch the sky. And the castle was wide, too; it stretched halfway across the city. Even from this distance, they could clearly make out the flag flying from the castle's bridge. It was emblazoned with a design of three beings: a Creeper, a Cow, and a man with pale skin, blond hair, and a gold crown who Stan guessed must be the King.

Kat let the boys marvel at the city for a few minutes, but then she forced them to start walking around and asking for work. They went door to door, asking if there were three jobs available. Stan noticed a pattern throughout the process. Whenever they asked for jobs, the first question that was asked was what level they were. Every time they said that Kat was level eight, Stan was level six, and Charlie was level five, they were turned down without further questioning.

After their twelfth rejection, Kat was looking exasperated, and Charlie was looking outright irritated. Stan was about to say that they call it quits and tough it out in the alley for the night when he heard a noise behind him.

"Psst!"

His immediate thought was 'Creeper!' (Being the target of three Creeper attacks will do that to you.) He whipped around and made to draw his axe (which, as he had forgotten, he no longer had), but he realized that it was not a Creeper, but a man that was gesturing to them from a store across the street. This man had on the most bizarre getup they had ever seen. He appeared to be dressed as a black crow, complete with a yellow beak down his face.

"Psst! Come here, you three!" he whispered, which Stan didn't get, seeing as all of the other stores were closing for the night. And besides, why would he want to keep their visit secret from the neighbors? It all seemed a little sketchy to Stan.

The lights turned on as Stan entered the man's store. He saw shelves and shelves stocked with rotten flesh, bones, string, spider eyes, and other things that were taken from the monsters of Minecraft. He also noticed the weapons; swords of various materials lain out on tables, axes hanging from hooks on the ceiling, an entire wall completely covered with hanging bows. There were also mannequins dressed in full sets of leather, iron, and diamond armor. Stan was impressed; he had a feeling that if this man wanted to hire them, he would like the job quite a lot.

They climbed up a ladder in the back of the shop, and into the man's house. It was very simplistic; torches, a bed, two chairs, a sapling tree on a block of dirt, some chests, a crafting table, a furnace, and a counter with a machine with a button on it.

"Sit," he said, and while Charlie and Kat sat on the chairs, and Stan on the floor, they saw the man walk over to the machine and pressed the button four times. Four loaves of bread popped out of a hole in the front of the machine. He handed three of these to his guests, and kept the fourth for himself. He sat down on the bed.

"Am I correct in thinking that you three are looking for jobs?" the man asked.

"Yes," Kat said. "We're new here..."

"Sh, sh, shhh!" said the player, looking nervous; for whatever reason, he clearly didn't wish to be heard. "Not so loud! Anyway, my name is Blackraven100 and I'm looking for some helping hands in my hunting business."

"What do you mean, hunting business? Hunting what?" asked Charlie.

"Oh, right, I keep forgetting that you three are... *lower-level players,*" he whispered as if it were an awful swearword. "You see, some rich players like to go hunting for Zombies and other mobs for sport. It's great fun if you're well prepared, and you can get some pretty valuable loot. I used to be one of those hunters, but ever since I passed level fifty, I don't find it as fun as I used to. Now, I sell all of the loot that I collected over the years, and I plan to buy an unsettled plot of land that I can build on.

"Unfortunately, my supply has begun to dwindle, and now I need some help with my hunting while I tend the shop. I need players to go into the woods, kill all of the monsters that they can find, and bring the loot back to me. The pay will be high. So what do you say? Obviously I would be happy to lodge and feed you."

He looked at them expectantly. Stan, Kat and Charlie looked at each other. Stan was nodding, and Charlie was shrugging with a smile, so Kat said, "That sounds good. Thank you for hiring us, nobody else would. By the way, why wouldn't any of the others hire us? We're very grateful that you hired us," she quickly added, to which Stan and Charlie nodded, "but I'd still like to know."

109

Blackraven closed his eyes for a moment, then opened them again. "Oh, some of the higher-level players here have a prejudice against anyone under, say, level fourteen or fifteen. It's stupid, really, they say the upper-levels have been on the server longer and have had to fight their way to the top, and the lower-levels today don't have to work as hard because they are building off of what the upper-levels have done."

Kat's and Stan's mouths dropped open, and Charlie actually said loudly, "That's the stupidest thing I've ever heard! Do you know what we've been through since..."

"*SSSSSHHHHHHHH!!!*" said Blackraven, cutting Charlie off. "The people around here aren't fond of upper-level players who treat lower-levels kindly. Personally, I think that the whole thing is utter nonsense, but I can't afford to voice the opinion when so many around me think that it isn't.

"Now, let's go to bed," he said. He walked to the chest and pulled out some wool and wood. He walked over to the crafting table, and within minutes there were four beds lined up around the room, all occupied by a player.

As he lay in bed, Stan wondered if this unjust prejudice against lower-level players was the motive of the griefer that killed Crazy Steve, or even... yes, yes that would make perfect sense, if that same motivation drove Mr. A, the griefer that had tried to kill them so many days ago. Perhaps a lower-level player had once robbed him of his items, and he was struggling to get back what he had once had. Yes, that would make perfect sense, thought Stan, as he drifted into sleep.

* * * * *

110

The next day, Stan, Kat, and Charlie set out, laden with gear, to go hunting on their first day under the employ of Blackraven100. Each player was wearing an iron chestplate and helmet. Kat walked in front, holding an iron sword at her side, and a bow and quiver of arrows slung across her back. Rex walked behind her, followed by Stan. Stan was holding an iron axe that glinted in the sunlight, and he was also carrying six loaves of bread. Charlie walked next to Stan, and he was holding a pickaxe and their two most important items; a compass and a clock. The compass would help them if they got lost, and the clock told them the time of day in the dark forest.

"Be sure you get back by noon," Blackraven had said, "so you don't miss the King's proclamation. You can go back out after that."

"Proclamation? What's that?" asked Stan.

"Oh, every now and then the King of Element City makes an announcement that there will be a major law change or something of that sort. You're citizens of the city now, so you should be there."

With this in mind, the three players and dog went out of the big city gates and into the forest to start to hunt.

It was odd; they had run into so many monsters in that dark forest before, but now they ran into virtually none at all. The only monsters that they were able to find and kill were a Zombie (killed by a pickaxe to the head from Charlie), two Skeletons (shot from afar by Kat), and a Creeper (felled by Stan's axe).The Creeper was actually pretty impressive, as it was the first Creeper that any of them had actually personally killed. Still, they were upset by the fact that, when the clock showed that it was nearing midday, they walked back into the city almost empty handed, holding just a piece of rotten flesh, three bones, two arrows, and a handful of gunpowder from the Creeper.

The moment they stepped through the gates Stan could tell that something was wrong. The people on the streets were unusually quiet, and Stan occasionally caught whispers, such as "Did you hear about that merchant whose store was vandalized?" or "Yes, I heard that he was offering jobs to noobs. The thought!" This particular comment heightened Stan's panic, and he started to actually hyperventilate when he saw the smoke rising from the area of Blackraven's store, and heard the angry shouts from that direction.

The trio turned the corner, and their eyes bulged in horror; even the dog whimpered as the awful scene before them.

Blackraven's store had been set on fire. Flames blazed out of his upstairs bedroom, and the downstairs was gleaming with the rising blues, yellows, reds, and blacks of burning charcoal. There was a mob outside, and they were yelling in fury, but not at the scene of destruction. Stan heard yells of, "How do you like being forced out of house and home?" and "That's what you get for sheltering noobs!" Stan watched in terror as the people threw bricks, shattering the upstairs windows. Stan was petrified. The three of them had brought this on! What if Blackraven was still in there?

Then, the unimaginable happened; in a shower of sparks, the support beams of the store gave in, and the entire store and house folded in on itself until nothing remained but a smoldering pile of charcoal, flames, and scorched brick. Only one thought filled Stan's mind: Blackraven100 was almost certainly dead.

As the crowd cheered as the collapse of the store, Stan drew out his axe, his eyes blazing in fury. The rage he felt here consumed him, unlike anything that he had ever felt before; what he had felt at Crazy Steve's death was nothing compared to this. He raised his axe over his head, and was about to charge the cheering mob when a force unseen pulled him backwards by the back of his collar, and he fell on his butt.

Kat had grabbed him, sensing what he was about to do. Stan, unreasonable with apoplectic rage, pushed Kat down and leapt back to his feet, ready to charge the mob again, but this time it was Charlie who caught him in the front and prevented him from making progress. This gave Kat the chance to bear-hug Stan from behind; she was much stronger than him, but he continued to struggle as Kat and Charlie dragged their furious friend back into an alley, where it took the combined effort of Kat and Charlie to force Stan onto the ground.

"STAN! SNAP OUT OF IT!" cried Charlie hysterically, tears streaming down his face, and it was the pain in his voice that made Stan finally stop fighting Kat. "We're all upset! And it's not our fault!" he yelled, reading Stan's thoughts. "He did the right thing, you hear me? The RIGHT THING! If I could, I would run out there and kill all of those bigots myself, but what's the point?" His voice wasn't hysterical anymore, but shaky, and most certainly pained. "They would turn on us. They hate us, remember? That would just cause more senseless deaths. Just more senseless, senseless deaths." And he no longer sounded pained, but disgusted.

Kat, on the other hand, still had streams of tears on her cheeks. She took her body weight off of Stan's body and gave a sniffle. "Come on, you guys," she said, her voice shakier than Charlie's. "Let's go to this Proclamation Day thing, and we'll work out what to do from there." She stood up, and Charlie along with her. They looked down at Stan, still lying on the ground.

Stan no longer felt his anger and grief choking him. He felt nothing but repugnance at the mob that had killed his friend, which was going wild in their ecstasy, making the fire bigger and bigger. He wanted nothing more right now than to get out of this alley, away from this street, and away from the injustice, and never to come back again.

Stan stood up slowly. "Yeah," he said, looking at his friends. "Let's go to the proclamation."

* * * * *

The sun was high in the sky, and the crowds were already thronging onto the grounds of the castle. The mechanical doors in front of the castle swung open, and the King walked out, onto the bridge. It was from the bridge, which straddled the two front towers of the gigantic castle that the King gave all of his proclamations.

As the King walked into view, the crowd burst into cheers. It was a huge crowd, the entire population of the city.

The King did his best to make the area nice for these guests; the grounds were well kept, and there were topiary bushes of players and animals. The King's personal favorite part of his lawn was the moat of lava that surrounded his castle. Never a bad defense against attackers, and it gave the castle a majestic glow at night.

The King was content with the council's decision; he realized that his new law would outrage the city's lower-level citizens, but the upper-level citizens, who made up a good third of the city's population of just over one thousand players, would be overjoyed at the announcement.

The King's right-hand man, Caesar, who was standing to the right and behind the king, handed him a microphone. Downstairs, they were broadcasting the sound through the speakers around the grounds. The King cleared his throat.

"Greetings, citizens of Element City!"

He had a deep, booming voice, and the townspeople cheered and created a wild tumult at his greeting.

"I have called you here before your King for a reason," the King continued. "I am sure that you will all remember the last time I called for a Day of Proclamation. At that time, due to a player's increasing negative influence on the Council of the Operators, it was decided that a new law would be passed, that banned a player from the server after his first death."

There was a dissatisfied murmur at this; many of the citizens were not fond of this law.

"I am aware that many of you were opposed to this new law. A petition from those who felt this way the strongest brought out a compromise; I would give up my operating powers, and the law would remain unchanged.

"I am an honorable man, and I always keep my word. Since then, I have given up my operating powers, and I am now as mortal as the rest of you. However, the dissatisfaction at this law did not cease. A new point was brought up.

"In recent months there has been an influx in the amount of new players joining the server. This causes great dissatisfaction to the upper-level citizens of Element City, who have lived here longer, and have rightfully earned the land on which they now live. These lower-level players have made life much more difficult for the upper-level players, causing shortages in jobs, in food, and in land."

At this point the crowd was in frenzy. The upper-level players were cheering the King's praises, and the lower-level players were shouting in fury. The King had to shout to make himself heard.

"Here is the proclamation that you have all assembled here for: Any citizens of Element City with a level under that of fifteen are required to leave Element City within one week of today's date. After that date, any players under level fifteen found in the city shall be killed, their houses..."

And that was when the arrow hit the King.

Luckily the one who shot the arrow was not a better shot, or the King would have been impaled through the skull and killed, but the arrow instead bounced off of his crown, knocking it off and knocking the King to the ground.

The crowd, which had just gone wild with cheers and outrage at the King's proclamation, was now silent.

The King quickly got up and looked over the railing of the bridge to see who had tried to assassinate him. It didn't take long for the King to see a clearing towards the back of the lawn; everybody had backed away from the three players standing in the clearing.

One of the three in the clearing was a girl with blonde hair, an orange t-shirt with a heart on it, and pink shorts. A dog was sitting at her side. The second player looked like a desert nomad. Both looked absolutely shocked.

But the third player, who had the Standard look, had the bow still raised, pointing at the King; even at the far distance, the King could see the hatred etched in every line of his face, and the red fury of his eyes.

PART II: BIRTH OF THE REBELLION

CHAPTER 9: THE SHOT HEARD ROUND THE WORLD

There was a moment of stunned silence, as the King, his officials, the crowd, and even the players by his side took in the enormity of the player's attempt on the King's life. Then, all hell broke loose.

The player turned around and dashed towards the gate, and he was quickly followed by the two players and dog that had been next to him. The King was still too shocked to be angry, but he was sure that the players would never escape alive, that the King's loyal subjects would destroy the player that had attempted to assassinate their beloved leader...

But alas, the King was only half correct. For at the exact same moment that the players turned and ran, a path through the people opened for them to escape through. It seemed while the upper level players were indeed trying to kill the three players, the lower-level players were defending the three players, fending off the upper-levels. This was a revolt.

Over his shock now, the King was insane with fury at this player that had not only tried to kill him, but also had turned the lower-levels of the city against their superiors. Screaming like a mad animal, he ordered that the gates be locked immediately, and that the riot control be sent in, effective immediately.

They weren't quick enough though; the three players escaped just as the gates slid closed behind them. The King gave a bellow of rage, and ordered that police forces be sent out into the city, attempting to find and kill the boy, the other two players, the dog, and any accomplices that they might have in the city.

Meanwhile, the riot control had reached the mob. The crowd was still fighting amongst itself, sending players of all levels toppling like tipped cows. The riot control mainly fired arrows into the crowd, trying to subdue the lower-levels, but the leader of the control force had other ideas.

Minotaurus was a player who had, through modding, become twice the size of a normal player, and looked just like a real Minotaur, horns and all, and carried around a double-bladed diamond battle-axe that never wore out.

Normally, the King would not allow a modified player on the server, but Minotaurus had shown a wicked taste for massacre. He had been deemed worthy by the King when the King had ordered Minotaurus to prove himself and kill his own brother and two sisters on the server. He had done it without batting an eye. He was absolutely ruthless… and the King loved it.

The King prized loyalty, and he had made Minotaurus the head of riot control. He could slice through men like butter with that battle-axe, and he could effectively and quickly end riots, which were common in the city. Why, no more than an hour before the Proclamation, the King had sent Minotaurus and his men out to stop an angry mob that had killed a man and set his house on fire.

The King had no sympathy for the man they killed… he was sheltering lower-levels… but the fire was starting to spread, and the gang had kept making it bigger. Within sixty seconds of Minotaurus's arrival, all the rioters were either dead or retreating.

This player, Minotaurus, was the one who led the charge on the rioters. He killed without mercy, slicing through everybody in his way with that giant battle-axe. Within a matter of minutes, the riot had stopped, but Minotaurus was still killing. It took five Slowness Potions thrown by his own men to finally subdue him.

The King smiled. He was still here, and as long as he had Minotaurus and riot control, there wouldn't be any more riots of this magnitude. He did have to do something about the assassin, though... The last thing he needed was an uprising on his hands, and if there was any player that held a high risk of creating an uprising, it was the assassin... but if so, where would he get the men? The King would make sure that the lower-levels here were closely monitored by the authorities so that they wouldn't rebel, but the assassin must have known that he would do that. And the only other place where there were enough lower-levels to start an uprising would be...

The King knew what he had to do. He took the liberty of personally walking down to the riot control office. Minotaurus was waiting, having been informed of the King's coming.

"I have a job for you," the King said.

"What kind of job?" Minotaurus asked in his baritone voice.

The King watched Minotaurus's eyes grow wide with pleasure at the assignment. That kind of thing was right up his alley.

"Take half of your men with you," the King said, "Leave half here in case they riot again. Destroy everything. Leave no survivors. Make sure that there is no way that civilization can continue on that spot. Take what you need from the armory. I suggest fire and TNT. Do me proud, Minotaurus."

The giant bull-man sprang to a salute. "Yes sir. We won't let you down, sir!"

Then, glowing with excitement, Minotaurus and half of his team ran down the hall to the armory.

* * * * *

Stan was running. Charlie, Kat and Rex were running behind them. They didn't stop to walk. They didn't take breaks. They kept running until they were out of the castle grounds, out of Element City, into the forest, around the crater, and down the path. They finally stopped when they were back at the Adorian Village.

The thoughts in Stan's head were amazing. He had just tried to kill the most powerful man in Elementia and sprinted an incredible distance back to the Adorian Village. Yet the only thing that filled Stan's mind was his astonishment that he had been able to shoot so accurately. He could only remember that he had been deemed hopeless by Archie, and that he had only hit the target once. That being said, he *had* had time to aim this time.

Stan saw Sally and Jayden running up to them. They initially looked happy to see them, but the smiles dropped when they saw the looks on their faces. Jayden addressed them.

"What happened guys? You look like you've…" but he was cut off by Charlie, still out of breath, sputtering out, "Stan… Proclamation… arrow… King… riot…"

"What the HELL are you *talking* about?" asked Sally incredulously.

"Stan tried to kill the King with an arrow," Kat said gravely.

There was nothing but stunned silence from Sally, Jayden, and Adoria, who had just walked up and heard Kat's announcement.

"You tried to… WHAT?" she yelled, a look of terror on her face.

"What possessed you to try and kill the King?" screamed Jayden, his eyes bulging. Sally looked like death had warmed her over.

"That's a fair point, Stan," said a Charlie who was on the verge of tears of fear, "Why?"

"I… just…" said Stan, and he sputtered for a minute, the rage building in him again, the rage at their mistreatment, about Blackraven's death, about the Proclamation, and after a minute of him sputtering and the others questioning, he blurted out, "He deserved it!" He told them all about what had happened after their departure from the Adorian Village. It was the news of the new Proclamation that stunned everyone the most.

"The King's going to kick all of the lower-levels out of Element City?" said Sally disbelievingly. "How can he do that? They make up two thirds of the population now!" said Adoria, and Charlie explained about the shortages.

"So he gets more land!" yelled Jayden. "He orders trees cleared, which opens new land, which would create new jobs! He's the *KING*; he has *the entire city* at his command! He can do *anything*!!!!!"

"Oh, it's more complicated than that," added Adoria. "He thinks that the groundwork laid by the upper-levels makes life easier for lower-levels, and the upper-levels resent that. When you think that the city's council is made of all upper-level players, it's not surprising that they would pass a law that selfish."

"This is all well and good, but the fact remains," said Kat, who had kept quiet ever since she told them of Stan's actions, but who now spoke in tones of quiet fury, "that Stan tried to kill the King of this server, and if you think that there won't be retribution…"

And she was cut off by the flaming arrow hitting the side of the building next to her. Too late, Stan thought, a pit opening in his stomach.

As was inevitable, more arrows flew out of the woods like a swarm of hornets. The six players ran for it as the buildings began to catch fire. Then came the swarm of men in white uniforms, the riot control office, pouring into the village.

The six players ducked behind the brick Town Hall, out of sight for a moment. Then Adoria said to Stan, "You have to go. All three of you."

"What?" Stan said. There were many things that she had expected he would say to him, but this was not one of them. "Why? We want to help fight them off!" Charlie and Kat nodded in agreement. "I got you into this mess, and I want to help you get out!"

"No! It will only make matters worse," Adoria replied quickly; they were running out of time. "Maybe if they find that you three are not here, they won't destroy any more. Now I'm going to go talk to them. You all get out of here, quickly!" And before they could argue, she stepped into the clearing, and began to speak.

"My name is Adoria, and I am the mayor of this village. I know why you are here. You have come to find and destroy the one who has tried to assassinate the King of Elementia. I tell you that he is not here, and that we will not harbor him. If you do not believe me, I will be happy to comply with a full search of the village. Please, do not destroy anything else. We will cooperate in peace."

There was a moment of silence greeting this proposal. Then, a double ended diamond axe flew through the air, straight towards Adoria.

It buried in her head and stomach, and she fell to the street. Dead.

Stan, Kat, Charlie, Jayden, and Sally were too stunned to speak, move, or in Stan's case, think. A player, twice the size of a normal player, who was dressed just like a bull, walked up to Adoria's disfigured corpse, and pulled out the axe, haphazardly brushing the body to the side.

This heinous act pushed Jayden and Sally over the edge. They both leapt out into the clearing, crying like Spartans, terrifying looks on both their faces. Jayden whipped out his diamond axe, and Sally drew out two iron swords, holding one in both hands. Then, still issuing their warrior yell, they battled with the giant man.

Stan didn't yet feel any sadness at the loss of Adoria, his brain still unable to process what he had just seen. He just blindly followed commands from his brain to follow Kat, Charlie and Rex, and run into the woods.

At the edge of the woods, he looked back at the Adorian Village.

It was like Blackraven's house a thousand fold. Fire was everywhere. The houses were a blazing inferno, all of them starting to crumble already. Stan looked at the brick Town Hall, and saw it explode from the inside out, making bricks fly everywhere. But the worst was the people. Everywhere, new players burst out of their burning houses, wooden and stone swords drawn, but most of them were immediately felled by a flaming arrow from the bows of riot control.

Stan looked in one street and saw a girl with a pink blouse, blue skirt and white knee socks kill a riot control man from behind with her wooden sword, but then the giant Minotaur-man came up from behind her and raised his axe. Stan looked away as he heard the swish and thud of the diamond blade.

Stan was sickened by the whole thing more than anything. Sad, yes. Angry, yes. But sickened most of all. Why would they burn down the village anyways, even after Adoria had tried to reason with them? All of those lower-level players. Gone...

Stan keeled over on his side, threw up on the ground, and cried.

CHAPTER 10: FLIGHT TO THE JUNGLE

The King was not happy.

The Chief of Police had searched the entire city with his force, and they had found no sign of any of the three assassins. They had, however, found records of the players from the front gates. Their names were Stan2012, KitKat783, and KingCharles_XIV. All of them were under level fifteen. They must have come from the Adorian Village, to be such a good shot. It was a relief that Minotaurus was finally destroying the loathsome place.

The doorbell rung and the King pressed a button to open the door. Caesar and his partner, Charlemagne, walked in and bowed. The King absentmindedly pointed his sword at them, and they all stood up.

"What is it, my liege?" asked Charlemagne.

"Have you captured the assassin, sir?" asked Caesar.

The King looked at his two highest generals and said slowly, "No. No, as a matter of fact I did *not* capture them. They are not in the city at all. *That* is why I called you two down here. I need your advice."

"But why just us, sir?" Charlemagne asked.

"Because this mustn't be voted on. I would like to discuss it with my two most trusted men, and then I personally will decide what shall be done. I am suspending the Council due to the present state of emergency. I can only trust you two."

"What state of emergency, sir?" asked Caesar. "I know that somebody tried to kill you, which is awful and treacherous, but with the whole server looking for them, won't they be dead by the end of the week?"

The King slowly turned his head towards Caesar. "That's just the thing, Caesar. *Not* everybody will want him dead. I accept the fact that the lower-level citizens of the server hate me, it is necessary to maintain the lifestyle of the upper class which is so near and dear to my heart, but up until now the lower class have not had the courage to do anything about it.

"Now, one of them has broken that barrier. He tried to assassinate me right in front of my own people. What is to stop others from thinking that they can do the same? If that is their mindset, there may be a rebellion on our hands. That is why the situation is so fragile right now. Our top priority must be to find and kill that player, so that the lower-levels know what happens to a player that betrays his king."

Caesar and Charlemagne shot a sideways glance at each other. They very much enjoyed their way of life as upper-level citizens, and they had no desire to have that way of life destroyed by a lower-level rebellion.

"Yes, sir, you're quite right," said Charlemagne.

"I suggest," said Caesar, "that we not only put the entire server up to the task of finding them, but we span our forces out far and wide. If the players did intend to start a rebellion, they'll plan it abroad and not near Element City or the Adorian Village."

The King nodded, "You're right, but I had a thought, and your thoughts on this idea are the main reason I wished to speak to you two. My thought was to send RAT1 out to find them."

The King's generals were taken aback by this radical idea. Charlemagne said slowly, "Sir, are you sure that… that… that team is *competent* enough to handle a task of this magnitude?"

"Sir, do you remember the *last* time that you sent them on a mission?" added Caesar skeptically. "I mean, they may have found the target, but…"

"I remember, I remember!" said the King irritably, banishing the unpleasant incident from his mind. "However, they are by far the most talented group of assassins I have at my disposal. They did fail miserably last time, but they have not failed at any other mission that I have *ever* assigned to them. And after all, a second failure would give me motive to have the lot of them executed."

Caesar and Charlemagne mulled this over for a minute. Then Charlemagne said, "Yes, yes my lord, that is a good idea, when you put it that way. I support it."

Caesar nodded. "As do I. And also, as it happens, I just had an idea. Why don't Charlemagne and I both assemble some of your forces and comb the kingdom, looking for conspirators? Maybe make a few… how should I put it… *hasty judgment calls*?" An evil smile broke over Caesar's face. "That would certainly lower rebel morale."

The King nodded. "Yes, that is a wise idea, Caesar. I will give you each twenty soldiers to comb over the entire country. You leave tomorrow. Dismissed."

Charlemagne and Caesar left the room, and the King smiled. Maybe this won't turn out so bad after all, he thought as he ordered RAT1 to the room.

* * * * *

Stan was unsure of how long he lay crying in the pool of his own vomit. All he knew was that at some point, he heard Kat's gruff voice telling him that they had to run, that riot control was about to start to search the woods. Stan didn't care, he wanted to just lie there forever, but he still went through the robotic movements of following the neon orange back of Kat's shirt into the woods.

Stan was dead to the world. His brain was numb and dumb from the destruction and death that he had just witnessed. He was unaware of the fact they walked for hours, that the heavy woods eventually thinned out into a wooded plain, but soon thickened again into a dense jungle.

He was vaguely aware of Charlie and Kat trying to decide what to do next, and that they eventually decided to climb one of the hundred-foot-high trees. They scaled the vines growing up the sides and ended up on a branch.

Stan was still sickened by the senseless murder and destruction that he had seen back in the Adorian Village, but he couldn't help but wonder why the government had attacked the virtually unarmed village. He understood now that they irrationally despised lower-level players, but was the government so corrupt that they would attack innocent civilians out of prejudice? Despite how little he thought of the King and the Elementian government, he still found himself shocked that they would murder lower-levels for no reason other than spite.

He looked up at Kat and Charlie. Neither of them looked good. Charlie had pulled his knees to his chest and was staring at the ground, a compassionate frown on his face. Kat was staring out into the starry sky, absentmindedly stroking the ears of the dog that had somehow joined them up on the tree branch.

Suddenly he knew what to do. He looked at his friends and spoke his first words since Adoria's death.

"So, how would you two like to overthrow the King with me?"

Kat and Charlie turned their heads and stared at him. Charlie wore a look of confusion, like he must have heard Stan wrong. Kat looked incredulous. Stan, on the other hand, wore a disturbingly cheerful smile on his face.

"You're kidding, right?" said Kat.

"No," replied Stan.

The boy and girl held their gaze for a long time, and Kat saw that Stan was not joking. Then, it was as if Kat was trying to look past Stan's eyes and into his head, as if to try and see exactly which screw had come loose.

"Are... you... *insane*?" she finally said.

"No," said Stan, still wearing that maddening smile. Perhaps he *had* gone insane. He was feeling unnaturally excited, and he had absolutely no reason to be smiling, and what he was saying was, in fact, insane, but he sure did want to overthrow the King.

"I'm not joking," he said as Kat opened her mouth again. His face shifted to serious. "The King just had the entire Adorian village burned down for no reason. Because of the government, Crazy

131

Steve, Blackraven, and Adoria are all dead. Do you honestly want to stay on this server under the King's rule? We need a new government."

"I agree," said Charlie.

Both Kat and Stan looked at him. He had not spoken since they had decided to climb the tree, and he still looked at the ground as he spoke. Kat couldn't believe that he was going along with Stan's crazy idea, and Stan was just as surprised that Charlie was agreeing with him.

"Really?" asked Stan in quiet disbelief.

"Yes. The government is biased and prejudiced, and their leader is a tyrant. He needs to be brought down."

"Oh, what noble thoughts," sneered a sarcastic voice from behind them.

Stan recognized that voice. The last time he had heard it, a wolf had nearly ripped his throat out. He instinctively turned around and whipped out his axe to counter the diamond blade of Mr. A's sword. He looked much better now, no longer beaten up, but full of energy and ready to kill. The diamond sword he was holding in his hands was not new but bloodstained, and he could tell that it had claimed many lives.

The others were on their feet, too. Charlie stood with a determined yet scared look on his face, holding the iron pickaxe in his slightly trembling hand. Kat was right behind him, sword poised to strike at a moment's notice. Rex's hair was on end, his eyes glowed red, and he snarled at the griefer that was now engaging in battle with Stan; it appeared that the dog had not forgotten his last encounter with Mr. A.

The battle was intense; there was no doubt that both players were incredibly gifted with their respective weapons. Kat and Charlie were ready to strike if need be, but they stood far back to avoid being slashed by the axe or impaled by the sword. Mr. A's sword moved like lightning, blocking each swing of Stan's axe without effort; it appeared that he was only toying with Stan.

"By the way," said Mr. A coolly between strikes, not even breathing hard from the battle, "How did you like my presents, Stan? You know, back at the village, the Creeper in your bedroom, and Charlie's defective helmet during the sword fight... did those gifts make you think of me?"

An intense surge of hatred bubbled up from within Stan, and without thinking he gave his axe an unnecessarily strong swing. Mr. A fluidly sidestepped the frenzied attack, and before Stan could react, the griefer's sword struck him across the head. If it weren't for his helmet, Stan's forehead would have been slashed open, but instead he was knocked backwards. His helmet flew off and dropped a hundred feet into the jungle below, while Stan was grabbed by Charlie before he suffered a similar fate. Charlie gritted his teeth and used all of his strength to pull Stan back up onto the tree branch. Stan was not hurt, just a little dazed, and as the boys caught their breath, Kat rushed into engage Mr. A.

She was talented with the sword, but he outstripped her in skill. They fought for about a minute before Kat was finally disarmed, her sword sent sliding down the branch. She was knocked to the ground. Mr. A was just about to deliver the killing strike when Rex flew from over her and knocked Mr. A into the thick tree trunk. His diamond sword spiraled off of the branch and into the jungle far below, and he looked stunned as the dog glared into his eyes, growling.

Stan did not want to kill, but he jumped up and held his axe over his head, ready to strike if Mr. A tried anything funny. Charlie had his pickaxe at the ready behind him, and they were quickly joined by Kat after she retrieved her sword.

The three players looked down at their adversary. He looked furious, but there was another emotion on his face to. Stan couldn't tell, but he thought that it might have been amusement.

"You really think that you're gonna overthrow the King?"

Stan raised his eyebrows. He shot a quick glance back at the others, who looked a little unnerved at Mr. A's question.

"I hate all three of you, but you don't know what you're talking about. I hate the King more than anybody on this server, but the citizens, upper and lower-level, are just as bad as he is. Mark my words, try anything, and you'll get screwed over. You have my caution."

Without another word, he whipped something from his inventory: a small black ball flecked with orange, and he threw it to the ground. There was a small, hot explosion, and Stan was knocked back, with Charlie, Kat and Rex landing on the branch beside him. He looked up and saw a cloud of grey smoke. He held his axe at the ready, prepared to defend himself, but when the smoke cleared, Mr. A was gone.

Stan brushed himself off and looked around. There was no sign of the griefer anywhere.

"Fire charge," coughed Kat through the grey smoke. "Great for quick escapes," she added as she hurriedly punched out the small fire that the charge had left on the branch.

"What do you think he meant when he said the citizens are just as bad as the king?" asked Stan, pondering the words of Mr. A.

"He was just trying to unnerve you," said Kat. "But I'll tell you one thing: If he thinks that overthrowing the King is a bad idea, then I think that it's a good one. I'm in on your plan."

Stan smiled at his two friends, that his friends would always be there for him, and support him no matter what. Then he noticed that Rex was chewing on something.

"Hey Kat, what's that your dog has?" he asked.

She took the item out of the dog's mouth and saw that it was an uncooked fish, with the tail fin ripped by the dog's teeth. "How'd this get up here?" she wondered.

"Mr. A must have dropped it," said Charlie. He was staring at the fish intently, as if trying to decide something. "Kat, let me see that, I want to try a trick I read about." She handed him the fish and he whistled two notes, one high and one low.

There was a rustling in the leaves just above them. Kat and Stan instinctively whipped out their weapons, ready to attack, but Charlie quickly yelled, "Wait! Hold on a second! And don't make any sudden movements." Seconds later, a yellow animal dropped from the branch above and looked up at Charlie.

It appeared to be some sort of wild cat, with a golden, streamlined body, black spots, and deep green eyes. It looked quizzically up at Charlie, and then at the dead fish he was holding in his hand.

"What is that?" Kat asked in amazement.

"An ocelot," replied Charlie, eyes still fixated on the cat. "Don't make any sudden movements," he repeated, "or you'll scare him away."

Kat and Stan watched in amazement as the cat slowly approached Charlie, gave him a look of pondering, and began to slowly eat the fish out of his hand. Then, the cat's fur began to change; the black spots began to vanish, to be replaced with orange stripes slightly darker than the golden fur. The ocelot had changed to take on the appearance of a tabby cat.

"Where did you learn to do that?" asked Kat.

"You two should really read that book more," replied Charlie, stroking behind the cat's ears. "Now he'll follow us around like Rex does, and he'll scare Creepers away."

"Excellent!" said Kat. Then she hesitated. "But wait, he won't get into fights with Rex, will he?"

"He shouldn't," said Charlie, and as if in response the cat walked over to the sitting Rex and curled up into him. Rex started to lick the cat's ears.

"Aw, that's cute," said Stan. "What are you going to call him, Charlie?"

"Lemon," said Charlie, as if he had been thinking about it for his entire life. "Now come on, we should try to get at least a little sleep before we try and start a revolution tomorrow."

It sounded weird when he said it like that, thought Stan. He lay down with a tuft of leaves as his pillow and, with Lemon and Rex as their guards the three players drifted out of the awful day and into dreamless sleep.

CHAPTER 11: THE APOTHECARY

It was the scream that woke Stan. Actually, it wasn't as much as a scream as it was a howl, or shriek, that sounded far off in the distance. It was a high-pitched, ominous, other-worldly sound that brought about a sense of foreboding, comparable a noise that that a small bird might make upon freezing to death in the Arctic.

Stan opened his eyes and found himself staring straight into the sun. It took his eyes time to adjust for a moment before he fully saw the impressive skyline of jungle trees that were silhouetted against the sunlight. Suddenly, he heard the shriek again, and this time he followed the sound, and his gaze met a figure perched upon the highest tree.

This figure was tall, with a slender body, and long, spindly arms and legs. It appeared to be holding something in its hand: a block, although Stan could not tell what. The creature had purple glowing slits for eyes, and it appeared to be looking right back at Stan.

Stan did a double take and looked back out to the trees, and the figure was gone. Stan shook himself and dismissed the form as a fatigue-induced hallucination. However, even as the others woke up, and they broke camp and climbed back down the vines, Stan couldn't shake the feeling of uneasiness that the haunting cry had sent down his spine.

They went back down the tree, and they did an inventory of all of their items.

"Two iron helmets, three iron chestplates, an iron sword, an iron axe, an iron pickaxe, a compass, a clock, a book, a bow, and twelve arrows," counted Kat as they lay all their items on the ground in front of them. "And we're going to overthrow the king."

Stan realized that they did have a very limited amount of supplies, exactly three people devoted to their cause, and no food at all. They had a lot of work to do and he knew it.

"Well, let's get back to the basics, I guess," he said. "We've got to start somewhere, so let's establish a house out here. There are plenty of resources around this jungle, so let's gather some materials today, and tonight we can discuss how we're gonna do this thing."

Kat nodded, and Charlie said, "Good idea Stan. You go into the woods and gather some wood with your axe. I saw a mine a little while back; I'll take my pickaxe and go see what I can find down there. Kat, you go find some food, and see if you can build a house around here that we can use until we get a permanent base."

"Okay," Kat agreed. "I'll make it underground, so if the King's men come looking for us, we'll have a little bit of concealment."

"Good thinking. Okay guys, let's fall out," ordered Stan, and with that, they put their armor back on, and Charlie and Lemon walked back the way they had come the previous day. Kat drew her sword and ran towards some wandering chickens, Rex at her heels, and Stan pulled out his axe and skirted around the edge of the lake, towards the woods.

As Stan walked at the water's edge, he noticed a type of plant growing in front of him that he had never seen before, except from a distance on Crazy Steve's farm. It appeared to be some kind of cane, and it only grew on the sand and dirt directly adjacent to the lake. Stan, curious, brought his axe down on the base of one of the plants, and several pieces of the stalks fell to the ground, which Stan picked up and put in his inventory. He did this to another plant, and was about to do it again when he heard a stretching sound behind him, then a twang and a whizzing sound.

Stan knew that sound quite well from his first night in Minecraft. He spun around and flipped his axe over, the metal blade just stopping the flying arrow from entering his chest. He dodged another arrow and looked up, expecting to see a Skeleton firing at him from the shade of the woods. Instead, he saw another player standing in the bushes, who was drawing another arrow. He was mostly obscured by the bushes and the leather tunic and cap he was wearing, but Stan could see a neat white beard on his face.

Stan rushed the player, axe raised, deflecting two more arrows as he went. The old man was about to draw the stone sword at his belt to fight Stan weapon to weapon, but Stan was too quick. His iron blade shattered the stone blade in two before it was drawn. For good measure, Stan also spun around and cut the string of the bow, and he kicked the old man, who was also wearing leather pants and shoes, to the ground. Stan stood over the player, axe raised.

The old man, without hesitation, ripped off the leather tunic to reveal two black sashes across his chest, each with various bottles of colored liquid attached to them. He yanked a green one from one of the sashes and proceeded to throw it at Stan before he had even realized what had happened. The bottle shattered on

Stan's chestplate, and a foul-smelling green gas seeped from the jade liquid that had splattered all over Stan. The stench overpowered Stan, and he blacked out, falling right besides the old man.

* * * * *

When Stan came to, he was in a grey cobblestone room. Torches lined the walls, and Stan became aware that there were twelve machines surrounding him, six on each side. Each was a block in size, and had a hole on the front of it.

"Don't move," said a voice, and Stan realized that the old man was standing next to the wall, away from the machines. His hand was on a button. "Cooperate with me, and you won't get hurt. Try to run away, kill me, or even move, and I press this button and you get shot to death with arrows by my machine. Why were you destroying those plants?"

"I don't know" was the first response that came out of Stan's mouth, and he had a feeling in retrospect that it was the wrong one. The old man sneered.

"I've been away from that damn Element City for a whole year now," replied the old man in his ancient yet powerful voice. "They banished me, so I was just looking for a little peace out here. I don't need juvenile delinquents like you destroying my beautiful sugar cane farm like that."

Stan was confused for a moment, then he understood. "Oh, those were your plants?" he asked as he pulled the sugar cane from his inventory. "I'm sorry, sir, I didn't know. Here, take them back." He tossed the sugar cane back to the old man, and they landed at his feet. The old man bent over and picked them up, never taking his eyes off of Stan.

"How do I know that you aren't just one of King Kev's spies?" asked the old man, stashing the cane in his inventory. "I've kept to my agreement, I've stayed out of the city, and I have had absolutely nothing to do with any potion-related activities going on in Element City."

"Wait, you're a fugitive from the King?" asked Stan.

"What, you don't know who I am?" asked the old man incredulously. "Anyone who's been on this server for more than the past few weeks or so knows who I am!"

"Sir, I'm only level nine," said Stan as he realized at the same time that he had, to his horror, been stripped of his armor and weapon. Good thing Charlie had the clock and compass, he thought. "I've only been playing Minecraft for a little over a week now."

"What? Really? But you're so good with that axe, I'd have thought that you'd seen a good few fights, son," replied the old man, who seemed genuinely impressed.

"Wait, are you saying that *you* don't know who *I* am?" asked Stan; he'd have thought that the King would have his face on wanted posters all over the kingdom by now.

"Should I?" the old man asked.

"I'm the one who tried to assassinate the King!" fell out of Stan's mouth again, but an instant later he regretted it. What if the old man was actually in cahoots with the King? He may have just earned himself a slow death by arrows! But instead of pressing the button, the old man's eyes widened in awe.

"*You?* You're the one who tried to kill the king? At level nine? Good lord, son, you're either very brave, very stupid, or a liar.

Okay, you can come out of there for now, but don't expect your axe back until I'm one hundred percent sure that you're not one of King Kev's cronies."

Stan stepped apprehensively out of the range of the machines, and, at his gesture, followed the old man out of the cobblestone room. He noticed his axe hanging at the old man's side, right next to an iron sword and a bow. He gulped, not sure what he was going to find in the next room.

What he did find was unlike anything he had ever seen before. There were rows of wooden plank tables, all of which covered by stands that held bottles, which themselves held bubbling liquids of various colors. Chests lined the wall, and a quick look out the glass pane windows revealed that it was late afternoon, and that they were still in the jungle. In one corner of the room was a black table, covered in a red velvet tablecloth embedded with diamonds, a book levitating over it. Around this table were shelves that held books of all sizes and colors. In another corner was a bed, next to which sat a furnace, a crafting table, and two chairs. The old man sat in one of these, and he gestured Stan into the other.

"I'm sorry that I had to knock you out earlier. You see, ever since King Kev banished me from Element City a year ago, I've had to be very wary about who enters and who leaves this jungle. He's sent his men in on me multiple times, whether they be hired griefers to give me a hard time, or spies to try and figure out what I am up to. But I am sure that none of them would even joke about trying to assassinate their master.

"So I will introduce myself. My name is Apothecary1," and he extended his hand, which Stan shook.

"My name is Stan2012, but you can call me Stan. I have a quick question though; Are King Kev and the King of Elementia the same player?"

The Apothecary laughed. "Ho ho, I had forgotten how little you know! Yes they are the same, the same ruthless, tyrannical fiend. You do agree with me don't you?" he asked quickly.

"Are you kidding?" said Stan angrily. "He killed three friends of mine for no good reason and I've tried to kill him! I don't think he and I are going to be friends any time soon."

"Ah, yes, you claimed to have made an attempt on the King's life. I'm not positive that I believe that story, but I do *want* to believe it. He's killed a good number of my friends, too, and banished a few more."

It was at that point that Stan suddenly remembered. "My friends! They'll be expecting me back!"

"What?" the Apothecary asked.

"My friends, Charlie and Kat. It's almost nighttime, they'll be expecting me back soon. We're making a base back by that lake you found me at."

Instantly the Apothecary became suspicious. "What do you mean? You brought others with you? How many?"

"Just the two," replied Stan. "I have to go back to them."

"And how do I know that you're not part of the king's army since there are more of you, Stan? If that's even your real name? How do I know they aren't watching this house right now?" The Apothecary was on his feet, his hand going to the iron sword at his side.

Stan decided to take a huge gamble. If it failed, he would be killed. If it succeeded, he would convince the old man that they were on the same side. "Because we're planning on overthrowing King Kev."

The old man stared at him. Stan knew that, based on what the old man had said, even speaking about overthrowing the king was highly treacherous. The Apothecary had a different look growing in his eyes. It was respect.

"Are you serious, my young friend?" asked the Apothecary.

"One hundred percent," replied Stan. "If you'd like, I'll explain to you everything that's happened to me so far in this game, and how we plan to go about overthrowing him. My only condition is that I go and find my friends."

The Apothecary agreed, and he gave Stan his axe back. He also gave Stan a compass to find his way back to the lake. When he got there, he found a hole in the ground with light coming out of it and some pumpkins scattered around it. Upon examining the hole, Stan found that there was a ladder going down the side of it. Stan climbed down the ladder and at the bottom he found an underground room.

There was a dirt roof, a stone floor, and walls made of a combination of the two. In the corner sat a furnace, a chest, and a crafting table. Two beds sat against the wall, while Charlie was standing at the crafting table making a third one. On the nearest bed sat Kat, who had a stone shovel in her hand and looked exhausted. Lemon and Rex sat on the bed beside her. They all looked up when Stan entered.

"Hey man, please tell me you brought in a lot of wood, because we need tools real bad," said Charlie.

"Guys, the most amazing thing happened!" and he told them about his exchange with the Apothecary. Kat and Charlie listened to his story with steadily widening eyes. When he was finished, there was a moment of silence before Charlie spoke.

"So, you didn't bring back any wood?"

"And more importantly," said Kat her voice rising quickly, "you told our plans to a total stranger?"

"Weren't you listening?" said Stan, exasperated. "He *wasn't* a total stranger, he's an experienced player that's been on this server a long time, and he hates the King! He's got knowledge of the server. If we're going to overthrow the King, we've got to start somewhere, why not with the Apothecary?"

"Is that his name, the Apothecary?" asked Charlie, standing up. "Doesn't that mean, like, a pharmacist, or a healer?"

"That's right," said Stan. "Maybe he knows about healing. Does anybody else know any potential medics that we could have for a potential battle with the King? I mean, if he does know medicine than maybe he could train other medics!"

"Maybe you're right!" said Charlie, nodding fervently.

"Are you even listening to yourselves?" yelled Kat. "Stan, you gave this man classified information after he shot you and gassed you! And now you..."

"Hey, that knockout gas worked instantly! Do you know how to make knockout gas, Kat?"

That stopped her. She closed her eyes for a second. Then, slowly, a smile spread across her face as she imagined the potential effect that a cloud of knockout gas could have on a group of enemies. She opened her eyes again.

"Okay, let's go meet him. But let's make some new weapons, so if he betrays us and steals our stuff, we'll have backups back here." Stan rolled his eyes as Charlie nodded in agreement.

Charlie hadn't brought up any iron ore from his mining expedition, just quite a bit of coal and almost two stacks of cobblestone. His pickaxe was worn out and broken, and he had had to craft a new one from the little wood he was able to gather by fist. Kat had also crafted a stone shovel and pickaxe to expedite the process of creating the house. The remainder of the wood had been used to make torches with the coal.

Stan quickly used his axe to gather a fair amount of wood, which he then converted through crafting into planks. They then made sticks, which, with the cobblestone, became a stone sword, a stone axe, and a stone pickaxe. For good measure, Kat used leather from some cows she had killed to craft a cap and tunic, leaving her iron ones in the chest. She also crafted a new cap for Stan. They put their good weapons and all of their excess materials in the chest, and Stan used the compass to find his way back to the Apothecary's house.

It turned out the Kat's worry for her tools' safety was for naught; the Apothecary didn't even ask for their weapons upon their entering his house. Stan saw that he had set up two new chairs to accommodate the extra guests. Stan was excited; the Apothecary seemed to be anticipating their arrival. They were all introduced, and they all sat down.

"So, now that we're all here, tell me: Why do you hate the King so much, and why do you want him overthrown?" asked the Apothecary.

Stan told the Apothecary, with the help of Kat and Charlie, everything that had happened to them since they had joined Elementia. They omitted no details, and there were certain details that Kat obviously would have preferred they had left unspoken, such as the part where she almost killed Stan and Charlie. But as Stan recounted every injustice, every instance of prejudice, every senseless murder, it only increased his feeling of hatred for King Kev, and the overwhelming desire to transfer this hatred into the old man sitting across from him.

The Apothecary said nothing until Stan finished the story at Charlie acquiring Lemon (who was sitting outside with Rex, guarding them from monsters and the King's men). Then he spoke.

"Well, I can certainly understand why you so dearly want to see my old friend King Kev dead," said the Apothecary gravely.

"What do you mean, your old friend?" said Kat quickly, and Stan noticed her hand moving towards the stone sword at her waist.

"Oh, don't worry, he certainly isn't my friend anymore," said the Apothecary, and Kat's grip relaxed, though her hand didn't move from the sword. "Trust me, that evil dictator is the reason I have to live out here as an old hermit. If I had my way, I would reopen my chain of Apothecaries in the city..."

"Wait, you mean *you* owned all of those abandoned Apothecaries that we saw in Element City?" asked Kat. Stan remembered; there was at least a store on every block, all closed up and abandoned, but all of them saying *Apothecary* on signs above each empty window display.

"That I did. You told me your story, would you like to hear mine?" Stan and Charlie nodded enthusiastically, and even Kat said, "Yes please, sir."

The old man chuckled. "All right then, please try not to get bored and fall asleep... let's see, where to begin...

"I joined this server in its very earliest days. Elementia was one of the first extremely successful Minecraft servers, and I joined Elementia within a week of its founding. King Kev, the operator of this server, used his operating powers to found Element City on that meadow. He and I were good friends, as we were with a number of others. However, I always felt unfulfilled, like I was meant to do something else in Minecraft besides build.

"Then, we learned of the alternate dimensions. Soon thereafter, the King opened Elementia's first portal to the Nether."

"Excuse me, sir," interrupted Charlie, "but could you please explain to me exactly what the Nether is? I've heard people talking about it, but I don't really get what it is."

"Of course," the Apothecary said. "The Nether is a dimension reached by constructing a portal. It is a hell-dimension of lava and fire, populated by mobs far more terrible then those of the overworld we are in now. When the portal was first opened, most of the players stayed away from it, fearing the dangers. But I kept finding myself drawn towards it. I explored every aspect of it, yet I couldn't find what it was that I was looking for.

"One day, on an update, Nether Fortresses were added. These were even more treacherous than the rest of the Nether, but they held two valuable pieces of loot: Nether Warts and Blaze Rods. The rods were used to craft brewing stands, and the warts were the base for potions.

"I had found my calling. The brewing of potions is what I was good at. I loved it so much that I opened up a chain of Apothecaries around the city, and even changed by name to Apothecary1. Those were the good days.

"But then, with the server being as successful as it was, there was an influx of new players to the server that continues to this day. All of them wanted a piece of the upper class. Naturally, the King tried to spread the wealth, but there were just too many players. I had gained a seat on the King's Council of Operators by this time, and there was a player on the council who was the King's best friend, named Avery007. Avery was an advocate for the new players, and wished to eliminate the class barrier. He was gaining a huge following; he was a very gifted public speaker.

"It was at this point that the King became incredibly paranoid, afraid that he would lose his absolute power. He had granted Avery operating powers a while before this, and he was afraid that Avery was going to overthrow him. This led him to implement the Law of One Death, changing the mode of this server to Hardcore PVP, where you cannot return to Elementia after death. He and Avery then battled to the death, using their operating powers to fly high over the city. I tell you, it was a spectacle; two operators battling is the most amazing thing you will ever see. In the end, though, Avery was overpowered. He was killed and banished from the server. By the next day, the King had killed three other people with strong followings on the server. With Avery gone, the King was the only operator remaining.

"That is very interesting, sir," said Stan, which he sincerely meant, "but where do you come into this?"

"Oh. Well, you see, I was still very much in the King's favor, although I was very upset with him for killing and banishing those players, all of whom were my good friends. But paranoia had twisted King Kev's mind by that point. There were rumors of a rebellion going around so any of the alleged leaders of the hypothetical rebellion were killed; that's why no sane player who was in league with the King today would even joke about overthrowing him.

"My problems started when a rumor came up that the Apothecaries in Element City were providing potions to a rebellion movement. I was lucky; four of my friends and I were accused by King Kev of treason on the same day. There was me, there was the chief of Redstone Experiments, Mecha11, and there were the three Chiefs of Exploration, Bill33, Bob33, and Ben33. There was a high amount of unrest in the kingdom over the number of people that the King had killed, so he pledged to never kill anyone again unless they were proven guilty. Instead of killing us, King Kev banished us from the city, warning us to never again run into a government official, or risk dire consequences. I opened my own Nether Portal here in the jungle and began stockpiling potions. I have no idea what happened to the Mechanist, or to Bill, Bob, and Ben.

"So you see," said the old man, and Stan sensed that he was about to say something important, "If you truly want to overthrow the King, I would be happy to use my knowledge of Elementia's inner workings, as well as the potions I have stockpiled, to help you in any way that I can."

"Thank you!" Charlie threw himself at the Apothecary, and began wringing his hand. "Thank you, thank you, thank you!"

150

"Yes, we really appreciate your help, sir," said Kat, and Stan could tell that she finally trusted him.

"So I have a question, sir," said Stan, voicing something that had been on his mind since that morning, "How many people do you think that we'll need to launch an assault on the King's Castle in Element City? If we can take the castle, then we'll have control over the city."

The old man thought for a moment, and then said, "Well, I imagine that the King probably has around two hundred men at his disposal. You weren't in the city long enough to know this, but the King has a jury-duty style system of selecting the military. He has two hundred citizens from the city at any given time selected to perform the city's public services. This makes one public serviceman for every four citizens. He can order these people to do absolutely anything that he wants. So assuming that the lower-level citizens of the army were to abandon the army if you attacked the castle, you would still have, say, another hundred thirty or so men to face."

Stan was shocked. He looked at Charlie and Kat. "Where can we possibly get that many people to invade the city?"

Kat was about to answer, but the Apothecary cut her off by saying, "How about the Adorian Village?"

There was a moment of silence. Then Kat said, "Um, sir, weren't you listening? The King's riot control destroyed the Adorian Village. Everybody who lived there is dead now."

"Oh, I wouldn't be so sure about that," said the Apothecary with a smile. "New players join Elementia every day. Most of them will still be inclined to follow the path to the Adorian Village. And also, don't be so sure that all of the people that were in that village are dead."

151

"How could any of them have survived?" asked Charlie incredulously. "They blew up all the stone houses and burned down the wooden ones!"

"Well," the Apothecary replied, "One thing that I didn't mention in my story is that the King has largely ignored the Adorian Village, as have the majority of the Council of Operators. Avery and I were the only ones on the council who aided young Adoria, the new player on the scene who wanted to create a village for the new players of Minecraft. We helped her design the village, and the houses within.

"Every few days, the Adorian Village has a drill (you must have missed it; you were there for such little time) in which they prepare for a large-scale griefer attack, which was essentially what you described to me. Each of those houses has an underground survival cellar, which can sustain four people for a month. The entrance is very inconspicuous, only the most observant soldier would recognize it. They also have that mine to hide in; I'd be surprised if more than a third of the inhabitants of the Adorian Village were actually killed in that attack."

Stan's heart lifted at the thought that there were far less casualties of the attack on the Adorian Village than he had originally thought.

"And I'll bet that those survivors are furious with the King right now," added Charlie. "And I'll bet that Jayden and Sally and the others are still training those players, and they have no clue where to go now."

"Well, that's settled, then," said Kat. "The survivors of the Adorian Village will be our main attackers when we attack the King's castle. One of us should go back to the village and tell the

152

others of our plan to attack the castle. The other three should try and find some supplies, like diamonds, and steaks, and golden apples. We need enough materials for an army of, say, a hundred." She looked at the Apothecary. "Any idea where we might find that? Because Charlie and I have been discussing it all afternoon, and we've got nothing."

The Apothecary replied, "I actually might."

Stan was caught off guard; he had expected the old man to say something along the lines of 'Are you high?' but certainly not having a response like that. "Wait, seriously? Where?"

"Oh, hold your horses, I don't know for sure where it is. But what I do know is that in the days of my seat on the Council of Operators, I heard rumors going around that the King had created a secret stash of armor, weapons, food, everything he would need to recreate his army if he was ever ousted from power. There were several rumors about where it was, but the one I heard most said that it's underground, at the center of Ender Desert. I'm not positive that that's where the stash is, but there definitely is a stash, and there was too much talk about that location for there not to be at least something there."

Stan jumped up. "Charlie!" he yelled. Everyone looked at him, and Charlie replied, "Yes?" with a concerned look on his face.

"Charlie, you have the best mining instincts of anyone, G said so himself! If there's anyone who could find an underground stash of supplies, it's you."

The Apothecary stood up and slammed his fist on the table. "It's settled then! I myself shall go back to the Adorian Village, and work with Adoria's pupils to train their new players for battle with the King's forces. The three of you must go into the Ender Desert and find the secret stash. I swear to you, if the stash isn't there, something will be, and maybe it will be something that you can use to your advantage."

The old man walked over to a chest, and put his leather armor into it. Stan realized with a start for the first time that the Apothecary was skinned just like Crazy Steve, save the white beard and the Potion Sashes. The Apothecary reached into the chest and pulled out a diamond chestplate. He stared at it for a moment.

"This place has given me so much, and then taken it away," said the old man to his reflection. "It's time for me to make this server a place where future generations can call home."

He pulled the chestplate on over his head, and Stan watched in awe as the old man pulled out a full set of diamond armor, including boots and leggings, and slipped them on. He then drew out his weapons of choice: Two diamond pickaxes, glinting in the torchlight. He turned back to the players.

"Charlie, come here please," said the old man. Charlie obliged, wondering what would happen next.

"Charlie, I want you to have this," said the old man, as he reached out towards Charlie, diamond pickaxe in his hand.

"What!? Wait," said Charlie, eyes widening in disbelief. "Are you serious right now?"

"Completely," said the old man, as Charlie took the pickaxe. "A good pickaxe is the best weapon and tool that you can have underground. This old pickaxe has served me well. I've brought it with me on several deep mining expeditions, as well as every time I've gone to the Nether. Besides, I have two, so I want you to have that one."

Charlie spun the pickaxe in his hand a few times, and tapped the diamond pick of the tool. "Thank you," Charlie said in silent awe, still staring at the weapon.

"Okay, I have a few things for the rest of you. But first, let me ask this: are any of you over level, say, ten?"

Stan was about to say no, but Kat jumped up and said, "I am! I killed a bunch of animals this morning, and I leveled up to fifteen!"

The Apothecary smiled. "Good, good. Now, would you like to exchange your levels for enhancements to your gear?"

"Would I!" exclaimed Kat. "How can I do that?"

"With that," said the Apothecary, and he gestured to the black table with the diamonds and red velvet on top, with the book levitating over it. They all walked over to it.

"This is an Enchanting Table," said the Apothecary. "If you have enough experience, this little gadget will let you exchange that experience for enchantments for your gear. Do you have any weapons or armor that you'd like to enchant, Kat?"

"Yeah, I have an iron sword, helmet, and chestplate back at the base," she said. "I also have this bow," and she lifted it up. "So are you saying that I could use this thing to give my sword special powers?" she asked excitedly.

"Yes," the Apothecary smiled. "After I finish giving out the rest of the things you will need to pull off this revolution, you can go back and get it," he said. He then proceeded to walk back over to his chest and pulled out a smaller chest. This one was black, and it appeared to be locked with a green orb.

"This is an Ender Chest," the old man explained, handing it to Stan. "If you put any items in this chest, they will be accessible from all other Ender Chests everywhere, even in other dimensions like the Nether. The King doesn't use Ender Chests, he doesn't trust them. When I get to the Adorian Village, I am going to put down a second Ender Chest that I have, which is, as far as I know, the only other Ender Chest on the server.

"Now, quick note about Ender Chests: They're incredibly hard to make, and once you put them down, if you pick them up again, they won't work. So only put down the chest once you've located the secret stash. When you put items in the chest, the green lock on my chest will emit purple particles, and I will take the materials out and give them to the Adorian fighters. This is the only practical way that we'll be able to transport the giant amount of materials from the secret stash to the Adorian Village.

"You got all that, Stan?" the old man asked, and Stan nodded; this was a brilliant way to discreetly transport materials across the server in an instant without arousing suspicion.

The Apothecary walked over to the brewing stands on his table. He plucked off twelve potions: nine red ones and three orange ones.

"These are potions that will help you on your way to finding the stash. I have four for each of you; I could give you more but they'll just take up space in your inventory. Just swigging one of the red potions of healing will give you a good health boost in the middle of a fight, and if you accidentally fall or tunnel into lava that orange fire resistance potion will keep you safe." He handed out three healing potions and one fire resistance potion to each player. They firmly attached them to their belts, ready to swig at a moment's notice.

"Now, Kat, are you ready to enchant that sword of yours?" asked the Apothecary.

Kat, who had been squirming in anticipation like a child about to pee, yelled out, "Are you kidding? Let's go!" and she whipped out her stone sword and sprinted towards the door, threw it open, and stopped.

"What's the hold up, Kat," asked Charlie as he pulled out his new diamond pickaxe, and Stan pulled out his stone axe.

Kat was looking out the door. In the bright light from outside Stan could see the look of terror on her face. This was odd because it was the middle of the night...

CHAPTER 12: THE DESERT

The forest was on fire. The fire was about a kilometer away, sure, but the light was still burning bright. Stan could tell that within minutes, the entire area around their house would be burned down.

"The King's men must have followed us out here somehow," said Stan. "Do you think that they've found our stuff?"

"Yes," replied the Apothecary, who was already pulling some cooked pork chops from his inventory. "They most likely have found your items, deduced that you are still somewhere around here, and are now burning down the jungle to attempt to flush you out. The fire will burn out before it gets here, but the King's men will still find the house here. You three need to get out of here, now."

"But won't they find you out here?" asked Charlie anxiously.

"I'll hide underground," the Apothecary replied. "And before they get here, I'll lay down some trip wires that will activate the arrow dispensers. They'll find the house, and they'll think it's been abandoned and try to loot it, but when the traps go off they'll decide it's not worth it. I'll be fine. But I'm experienced at hiding, whereas if they find you, they'll execute all three of you on the spot."

"But what about my sword?" Kat asked, as the Apothecary handed some bread to Stan.

"I'm sorry Kat, but you'll have to enchant something else. What about your stone sword?"

"Nah, that'll wear down really fast... I know!" and she pulled out her bow. "So what do I do?"

The Apothecary replied, "Just sit down, put your weapon down on the table, and stare at the book. The right enchantment should instantly take to your bow."

Kat walked over to the table, and kneeled in front of the table. She put her bow down on the table, and the book opened. She stared into it, and her blocky eyes started to glow, as did the book, and the bow. Seconds later, there was a flash of light, and Kat fell to the ground.

"Are you alright?" asked Stan, helping Kat up.

"Yeah, I'm okay," she replied. She stood up, and picked up her bow, which was now glowing purple with power. "Whoa," she said in an awed voice. "Infinity enchantment."

"Excellent," said the Apothecary, as he belted several potions. "Now any arrow fired from your bow will reappear in your quiver; you'll never run out of arrows again. The table must have known that you're going on a long journey."

"To that note, we'd better get going! The fire's getting closer," yelled Charlie.

"Right," said Stan. "Sir, thank you for everything you've done for us. We'll meet back up with you at the Adorian Village after we find the stash."

"Right, good luck," said the Apothecary as he laid a tripwire across the floor, and the three players, dog, and cat rushed out the back door.

They sprinted through the forest, weapons drawn. They had to fight off some monsters but had no time to pick up their drops. They kept on running, and didn't stop until they had reached the desert and had run a good distance into it.

They looked back at the jungle behind them; Stan could see that it was raining again. He sighed with relief; that should put the fire out. He guessed that it didn't rain in the desert.

He looked up and realized that he was looking directly into the sun. They had ran through the night. He also realized that he was famished; he hadn't eaten since the previous day. He ate two of the loaves of bread that the Apothecary had given him, and he distributed the remaining two to each Charlie and Kat. As he ate, Stan looked out into the desert to see what lie ahead, and his heart skipped a beat.

It was the tall, spindly figure that he had seen the previous morning in the jungle trees. In broad daylight, it looked menacing; Stan found its unnaturally long, thin arms and legs, and it's purple slits of eyes, to be incredible unnerving.

"Charlie, Kat, look!" they both looked up and saw it, too.

"What is that?" asked Charlie. "And why is it shaking?"

For the figure was indeed trembling, as if shivering with cold. Its jaw hung open, revealing terrifying black fangs, and it was staring at Charlie. Then, all of a sudden, it vanished in a puff of purple smoke. All three players looked at each other, scared to find what would happen next.

All of a sudden, there was an earsplitting clang. Stan spun around and saw that the black figure had appeared behind Charlie. It had grabbed him by slamming its hands into the sides of his rib cage. Stan watched in horror as the thing lifted Charlie, whose face showed unspeakable pain, into the air, and proceeded to then slam him, full force, into the ground headfirst. Charlie fell onto his front, and was still.

The monster then let out a shriek; it was bleeding purple blood from the cut on its side that had been inflicted by Kat's sword. Kat drew the sword back and thrust it towards the fiend, but right as the point was about to pierce its back, the monster disappeared in a puff of purple smoke. His instincts tingling, Stan whirled around and saw that the monster had indeed teleported about ten blocks behind him and was sprinting towards him fast. Stan raised his axe, and threw it as hard as he could at the monster. The axe impaled itself in the monster's chest, and it teleported away again after another shriek.

The monster reappeared between Kat and Stan, axe still in its chest. However, before it did anything, the monster looked up at the rising sun and, with a hateful glance at Stan, it teleported away. Stan stood at the ready, waiting for the monster to reappear, but it didn't. He sighed. Then he remembered.

"Charlie!" he rushed over to his friend. Kat had rolled him over to his back, and his face was red; he wasn't breathing. Refusing to consider the worst, he surveyed his friend and saw that the marks of the monster's arms had dented the sides of the chestplate, and were now pressing into Charlie's side making it impossible for him to breath.

"Kat, give me your sword, quick!" Kat didn't hesitate, and with two swift strokes of the weapon Stan cut the sides of the

161

damaged iron armor, and pulled it off. Charlie took a deep breath. Stan noticed that the iron helmet was dented beyond repair too; he pulled it off and threw the useless thing aside. Charlie gave a sigh of relief.

Kat yanked one of the red potions off of Charlie's belt, popped the cork, and poured the potion into Charlie's mouth. He swallowed, and he sat up.

"Charlie!" Kat hugged him as Stan exclaimed, "Thank God you're okay man! Geez, you seem to get beat up a lot don't you?"

Charlie gave a weak smile as Kat let him go. "Hey," he said in a weak voice, "It isn't the first time I've been beaten up, and I think we all know that it won't be the last." They all chuckled. "And I remembered reading about that thing in the book. It was called an Enderman. It has really powerful physical attacks, the ability to teleport, and it gets provoked when you look at it."

"Well, it certainly was powerful," said Kat. "It made you lose your armor and one of your healing potions. And you, you lost your axe, Stan."

In the excitement of Charlie's recovery, Stan had momentarily forgotten about his axe. He sighed in disappointment.

"Man, why do you have such a hard time holding on to your weapons?" commented Kat. "What is this, the third one you've lost now?"

Stan counted on his hand. "There was the Zombie Pigman, the one back at the house, this one... yep, this is the third. Where am I supposed to get a new weapon in the middle of the desert?"

As if on cue, there was a pained grunting sound behind them. They all turned around to see a lone zombie burning to death in the sunlight. When this zombie fell, there was the common rotten flesh, but Stan saw a glint as well. We walked over to the corpse and saw that the zombie had dropped an unused iron shovel, which he must have had in his inventory when he died. Stan fed the flesh to Rex and picked up the shovel.

"Well, it's no axe, but it'll have to do," said Stan as he gripped the shovel like a baseball bat.

"Well, the center of the desert should be to the Southeast, if I remember correctly," said Charlie as he pulled out his compass. "Let's go," and he lead the trio out into the desert.

It was a long, boring walk; the desert was incredibly flat, and they passed a few cactuses, the occasional pond here and there. There were a few Creepers roaming around that tried to chase them, but they backed off when Lemon hissed at them. It turned out that the explosive creatures really were scared of cats. When the three players arrived at what Charlie judged to be the approximate center of the desert, they found a small cave opening in the side of a sandstone hill. Charlie pulled out his diamond pickaxe, and with one last glance at the sun, Stan and Kat followed Charlie down and into the unknown mines.

* * * * *

Geno looked down in satisfaction as the sound of explosions reverberated out of the ground. Geno was his full tag, not just his nickname. He wore torn camo pants and a biker's jacket with tattoos, and an eye patch over his left eye. On his jacket was a badge, with the name of his team, RAT1, written on it in black letters. He was smiling down into the small hole. If there was any life down there, it was gone now.

The explosions stopped, and a few moments later a head of black hair and olive skin, topped by an iron helmet, popped out of the ground.

"Find anything, Becca?" asked his brutal voice.

"Nah, there's nothing down there," replied Becca as she pulled herself out of the hole; it was now plain to see that she was wearing a full set of iron armor. "I didn't see any items scattered. They must've known we were coming."

"Gee, it couldn't have been that *fire* that you set on the trees, could it, you idiot?" spat Geno.

"Don't you call me an idiot, you moron," growled Becca.

"Oh, well then let's go right now!" yelled Geno, vein in his temple popping, as he drew his diamond sword.

"Bring it!" yelled Becca, drawing the iron sword from her side. The two charged towards each other, and were about to start fighting when two arrows glanced off their armor and stopped them in their tracks.

"Hey! We don't need no fightin', kids, aight, we've got a job to do here," yelled the archer, a black player with a samurai armor skin covered by a leather tunic. "And for the record, Geno, it was me that started that fire last night, kay, it was an accident. I used my fire bow instead of my powerful one by mistake, kay? So shut up, or you both get an arrow through the head."

Geno and Becca lowered their weapons. As well as they could fight with swords, they knew that Leonidas could kill them in a second if he wanted to; they had never seen him miss with a bow.

"Whatever, Leo," said Geno, sheathing his sword. "But tell Little Miss Bomb-Happy here to not immediately destroy every non block she sees," spat Geno.

"Oh, come on though, it's so fun," squealed Becca; it was true; she was RAT1's resident demolitions expert, a job she took very seriously.

"Hey!" yelled Leonidas, so loud that the other two shut up instantly. "If ya'll remember, this is exactly how the last mission started out, with y'all foolin' like noobs! We fail one more time, the King is gonna hang our heads on his wall. So come on! If there's nothing in their old house, let's go out into the jungle, and look for 'em there."

And with that, he pulled an arrow into position and shot something he sensed moving up in the tree. He walked over the corpse that had fallen to earth and saw that it was nothing, just an ocelot, no items to collect. He walked into the jungle, and Geno and Becca followed, swords still in hands.

As they scanned the trees for clues, Becca growled under her breath, "Stan2012, where are you?"

CHAPTER 13: THE ABANDONED MINE SHAFT

I miss my axe, thought Stan as he plowed through the dirt with his shovel. He had had to fight off several monsters so far in the darkness, and he felt awkward and clumsy beating a spider to death with a shovel. He would have much preferred the smooth decapitation that the axe would have given him.

He punched through another block of dirt and stopped; a sheer cliff face was in front of him. He had dug through to the side of an underground ravine. Kat took the lead; she had found an abandoned underground house a while back with nothing inside except a chest containing a stack of torches. She placed the torches on the wall, illuminating the path ahead, keeping her bow held tight in her other hand. A few times a zombie lumbered along the cliff face towards her, and once a few arrows sunk into her tunic from a skeleton across the ravine. All these attacks saw the monster silenced by her infinite supply of arrows.

At the end of the chasm, Kat put up the last of the torches, and Charlie pulled out the compass.

"We should be near the center of the desert," he said excitedly. "If there is a secret stash, it should be around here."

And with that Charlie pulled out his diamond pickaxe and began tunneling into the wall. He went three blocks in… and his pickaxe struck wood.

"What the..." he exclaimed as he dislodged the diamond pick from the wood and saw that it was a wooden plank. "What's a manmade block doing this far underground?"

"Maybe it's the entrance to the stash room!" Stan exclaimed excitedly.

"Maybe..." said Kat, "but you'd think that the King, guarding his most precious supplies, would guard the stash with something you can't punch through..."

"Well, in any case, it's something," replied Charlie, and he began to punch through the wood with his fist. This would go a lot faster with my axe, thought Stan glumly as Charlie broke through.

Light flooded through the hole. As Charlie punched more wood planks around the first one, Stan could see that they had entered a network of tunnels, which appeared to be supported with fence posts. Train tracks ran across the ground, but they weren't complete. Torches were on the wall, and there were chests against the wall to their right.

Charlie jumped up through the hole and examined the fence post supports. Stan followed and looked down at the tracks. He wondered if he could make a train to run on them. Then he heard Kat yell.

"Hey guys, check this out!"

They walked over to her, and she started pulling things out of the chest.

"Excellent!" she exclaimed, pulling two iron ingots out of the chest. "I can make a new sword out of these! Oh man, there's tons of stuff!" said Kat. She pulled out a handful of white seeds. "These look like pumpkin seeds. They could come in handy at some point. But what's this?" She pulled out a handful of chalky blue stones.

"I think that's Lapis Lazuli," said Charlie. "It's used to make blue dyes."

"Not particularly helpful," said Kat, but she pocketed it anyways. She continued pulling things out of the chest. "There are also three pieces of bread in here ... and a bucket... what kind of seed is this?" She pulled out the bread and a handful of black seeds.

"Melon seeds," said Charlie.

"How do you know all this stuff?" asked Kat, impressed.

"I read that book at night before it got burned up back in the forest. I know about lots of stuff. For example, we are currently in an Abandoned Mine Shaft. Nobody dug this; it was here before any players knew about it. Anyways, anything else good in this chest?"

"Just this," and she pulled out a handful of red dust. "Redstone dust, right?"

"Yeah... hey, let me see those gold ingots." She handed them to him. He punched four wooden planks off the wall and quickly constructed them into a crafting table. He laid the gold ingots and redstone out on the table, and moments later he had made a new clock. The face showed that it was about noon above ground.

"Alright, so I guess we should look around this mine shaft," said Charlie, pocketing the clock.

"Good idea," said Kat, drawing her sword. "Maybe there'll be some more chests down here."

"Or maybe," said Charlie, "the King decided to put his secret stash somewhere in here. From what I understand, these things are pretty hard to navigate."

"Uh, guys?"

Kat and Charlie turned. In their excitement of finding the chest, they had forgotten about Stan. He had followed the train tracks down the corridor, and now seemed to be looking down another corridor that branched off at a right angle.

"You guys might want to check this out," he said slowly.

Kat walked over to him, followed by Charlie and the animals. The hallway in front of Stan was completely blocked off by thick spider webs, stretching from floor to ceiling. The webbing continued down the hallway as far as the eye could see.

"What do you make of this, Charlie?" asked Stan, looking uncertainly at Charlie for an answer. Charlie was shaking his head, apparently at a loss; Kat, on the other hand, stepped forward and slashed at the cobwebs with her sword.

"Kat!" cried Stan, pulling her back.

"What? There's gotta be something that way, right?" she snapped, yanking herself out of Stan's grip and continuing slashing.

"But what if there's a trap? There could be anything down that hallway, we can barely see three blocks in front of us," said Charlie, and it was true that with the cobwebs and lack of torches down the hall, visibility was very limited.

"Do I look like I care?" said Kat, still hacking through the cobwebs, followed by Rex, to the point where she was out of sight of the boys, and they could only hear her voice. "I'm sick of all of this sneaking around the King, I want to find this stash. And if I get in a fight, then so be it, I'd personally prefer a straight fight to all this... HOLY MOTHER OF.... AAAAAUGH!"

Kat's anguished scream reverberated around the walls of the mine shaft, making it seem three times louder than it actually was. Stan sprinted into the darkness towards his friend, weaving through the path Kat had hacked through the spider webs. Stan heard a pained whimper as he approached where he judged Kat to be. He pulled back his shovel and swung it, baseball style, as it connected to the spider that was digging it's teeth into the chest of Kat, lying unconscious on the stone floor, with Rex lying lifeless beside her.

As the spider fell down onto the floor besides him, Stan noticed in the low light that it was small, only about two thirds the size of a normal spider. It had the same red eyes, but it appeared to be bluer in coloration. He only noticed it for a moment though, before another one came barreling out of the darkness, straight towards him. Out of the corner of his eye, he saw Charlie kneeling down, tending to Kat, so he batted the spider back with his shovel as he did the first one. This one landed on its feet, and he had to hit it a few more times before it finally succumbed to death.

More spiders kept coming, and their numbers were increasing. Stan wondered what was happening. Hostile mobs did not attack like this, there were a variety of them, and they didn't spawn this frequently, even in such low light.

Then, slowly, as he batted down more and more spiders, with Charlie now fighting at his side, he noticed a faint glow in the distance. He dodged a spider and stepped close. What he saw was a black cage, one block in size. Every now and then, a small glow of fire would burst from the cage, and Stan could see a miniature

170

spider, blue like the ones he was fighting, spinning inside. Immediately afterwards, another spider would appear, which Stan would hastily beat down.

Stan realized that this ... thing, was spawning swarms of spiders, and if he didn't destroy it soon, they would have a serious problem on their hands. Then he saw Kat's stone sword lying on the ground, and he knew what had to be done. Without thinking, he snatched up the sword, cut aside two of the spiders, and, with all his strength, thrust the sword into the heart of the cage, impaling the miniature arachnid inside.

There was a burst of light and resonance. Fire flew from the cage, and there was a loud shrieking noise, like thousands of spiders being murdered at the same time. Then, the cage was silent; the fire within it had died, and no more monsters were being spawned from it. Stan picked up his shovel, cast aside the remains of the ruined sword, and turned back to Charlie, who was just puncturing the body of the last spider with his diamond pick.

"Good thinking, man," heaved Charlie, wiping the sweat from his brow.

"Thanks," replied Stan, and he looked down at Kat, who now appeared to be shivering in a puddle of her own vomit. "Is she going to be alright?"

"Yeah, but it'll take a while," said Charlie gravely. "Those things were cave spiders. They didn't do much damage to her, thanks to you, but they poisoned her. The poison will make her throw up anything in her system. I was stupid and tried to feed her one of her potions, but she just threw it back up. Her system will rid itself of the poison eventually; we just need to give it time. When she wakes up, she'll be very weak and very hungry."

"Man, I'm so glad you read that book," chuckled Stan. Then he had a thought. "Oh God, you didn't get poisoned, did you?"

"I doubt it," he replied. "None of those spiders even touched me. You?"

"I don't think so," said Stan in relief. "That's good. Even with the bread we got from that chest, we only have six loaves left, and I think that at least two of those are going to Kat when she wakes up."

Indeed, after guarding the unconscious Kat for a while, she woke up, and the first words of her mouth were incoherent grumbling, asking for food. Charlie gave her two loaves of bread and one of her two remaining healing potions. Even after this, Kat was very weak, and had to walk slowly. She was also on edge.

"What do you mean, my sword's gone?" barked Kat at Stan when he explained what had happened after she was knocked out.

"I told you," he said, "I used it to destroy the spider spawner."

"And you couldn't save it or something?" spat Kat in disgust. "You're useless, you know that? Absolutely useless."

"Shut up! If you hadn't been all like, 'to hell with caution,' we wouldn't have been ambushed by those spiders. It's no fault of anyone but yourself that your sword's gone, stop blaming me."

"To that note," added Charlie, who had just finished healing Rex with some rotten flesh, "I still have that stone pickaxe; you can use that until you can craft a new sword, Kat." He pulled it out and gave it to her. She looked at it in disgust.

"I need to get a new weapon," she said, spinning the pickaxe over in her hand.

"Welcome to the club," sighed Stan, his shovel still gripped in his hand. "You, at least, have your bow."

They wandered the mine shaft, and kept taking side tunnels they had never seen before, trying to find some way out or, even better, an entrance to a secret stash room. In due time, they became hopelessly lost in the labyrinth of tunnels. Stan was just about to say that they should tunnel back up to the surface when something caught his eye.

At the end of the corridor to their right was a door. It was made out of metal, and there were torches to either side of it, as well as a button. He could see a ton of light streaming from the window of the door. But what most caught his attention was the sign above the door.

It read "Underground Base of Avery007".

CHAPTER 14: AVERY'S STORY

"Avery007?" said Charlie when Stan pointed the sign out to him and Kat. "You mean that guy from the Apothecary's story? Does that mean that he lives down here?"

"Not anymore," said Kat, staring at the sign. "Remember what the Apothecary said? The King killed him; he's banished from the server forever. This must've been where he lived at one point."

"Didn't he have operating powers?" remembered Stan.

"Yeah …" said Charlie, an idea striking him. "And if he had operating powers, that means he probably had some pretty good stuff!"

"Okay, let's go in then," said Stan, shovel at the ready. "But be careful this time. We don't know what could be in there."

Charlie nodded, and he raised his diamond pick, ready to defend; Kat also drew her pickaxe and held it at the ready. Stan pressed the button on the wall, and the iron door slowly swung open.

He stepped inside, and immediately his foot caught on some string lying across the ground. An arrow flew out of nowhere and snagged his leather cap off his head. Another arrow immediately afterwards glanced off his iron chestplate.

"Hit the dirt!" he screamed, and fell to the ground as arrows continued to whiz over his head; behind him he heard Charlie and

Kat doing the same. He looked up and saw that the arrows were being fired from a machine, the same kind that the Apothecary had trapped him with when they first met. He realized that he had stepped on a tripwire which had activated the machine. He hastily brought the blade of his shovel down on the trip wire, destroying it. The arrows stopped immediately.

Stan got up and looked around. They were in a well-lit room, made mainly of stone; here and there, sections of the wall had been replaced with brick. There were various crafting tables and furnaces around the room, as well as chests. A bed sat in a corner.

"Well, this is disappointing," said Kat, examining a painting of a sunset on the wall.

"Yeah, it is," agreed Charlie, pulling a pair of iron leggings out of the chest. "This is the lair of Avery007?"

"It does seem a little basic..." said Stan, but then he noticed something. Lying atop one of the crafting tables was a book, similar to the one that he and Charlie had found on their first day in Minecraft. The title on the book they had found on Spawnpoint Hill read *Welcome to Minecraft*, with the author signed as *Bookbinder55*. But this book's title was *My Story*, and the author was signed as *Adam711*. He picked it up.

"What's that?" asked Charlie, walking over, Kat right behind him.

"It's a book, written by somebody named Adam711," replied Stan, examining the book. "What do you suppose it's doing down here?"

"I don't know..." said Kat. "Why would Avery007 care about whatever this Adam711 had had to say?"

"Let's find out," said Stan, and he opened to page one and began to read aloud.

MY STORY: THE TRAGEDY OF THE RISE AND FALL OF AVERY007

0 AWA

This first entry of my diary is written on the day that they added writing in books to Minecraft, hence the entry number, 0 After Writing Added. I am leaving this record of my life to whoever may find it, with the hope that the wisdom within should help another to carry out my cause should my enterprise fail. I shall start by explaining that though my name is presently Adam711, I first entered Minecraft under the name of Avery007. This name, to me at least, is, and always will be, who I am: the great and powerful Avery007, who tried to change the world in his valiant quest for the equality of his subjects, but was destroyed in the process.

Let me start by telling of my history. I joined this server Elementia when it was new; King_Kev, the creator of this server, was my best friend. He granted me operating powers and worked with me to establish the great Element City, which most likely will still exist whether this account is read three days from my writing this, or three hundred years. I was on the governing body, the Council of Operators, in that city, and I tried to help pass laws that would benefit the lower-level citizens that were the future of Minecraft.

As the server grew, so did my friend King_Kev's fear that the young generation would overpower the golden age players, as he called those who had played in Elementia since the beginning. I believed him to be quite wrong in this account, and I voiced this opinion on multiple occasions, destroying notions of laws that would unfairly give unlimited power to the upper class.

My actions prompted the King to pass the Law of One Death, which eternally banishes a player from Elementia upon dying once. I was horrified at this law for the sake of the lower-level players who were so inexperienced and prone to dying; never did I dream that the law was intended to rid Elementia of myself.

I tried to repel the King, but I failed. I myself was forever banished from the server; Avery007 was no more. However, I am still determined to lead the lower-level citizens of Elementia to victory over their King as my new identity, Adam711. As I write this, I have already played the game from the beginning, and have gathered enough resources for myself to lead a rebellion against the King. From my days on the council of operators, I learned of the King's secret stash of enough supplies for an entire army, hidden in a secret catacomb beneath the Ender Desert. I am on a voyage there now, determined to find these resources and use them to build an army to destroy the King.

Stan paused for a minute to look up. "So Adam711 is Avery007 in a past life?"

"I guess," said Charlie, "but the important thing is that there is a secret stash down here! I KNEW IT!"

"Hold on," said Kat, "but Avery was looking for it too. What if he found it and the stash is gone now?"

"I guess there's only one way to find out," replied Stan, and he continued reading.

2 AWA

I have arrived at the secret catacombs but I have discovered no treasure. Through examination of the premise, however, I found a log of the King that says that he had moved the secret stash to a mysterious alternate dimension known as The End, where it will be much safer and better protected. I also learned that he has given up his operating powers. That is good, it will make him much easier to kill when I do build up an army.

5 AWA

I have met with a group of low-level players, living together in a group in the Southern Tundra Biome. I am still looking for the entrance to the End, but the Eyes of Ender suggest that it is somewhere around here. Hopefully I will manage to convince these players to help me overthrow the King.

Stan flipped to the next page. It was blank.

"It stops there," he said, tossing the book back on the crafting table.

"So the secret stash is somewhere called the End," said Kat, looking confused. "Do you know what that is, Charlie?"

"Beats me," he said, looking down. "The only alternate dimension I was aware of in this game was the Nether."

"Forget the secret stash for a second," said Stan slowly. Something didn't add up... why did the book just stop like that? He asked the other two what they thought.

"I dunno," shrugged Kat. "Maybe he just got bored of writing in his little diary."

"Or maybe he was killed," suggested Charlie.

Stan was about to voice his opinion, but he was cut off by an evil laughter emanating from behind him.

Stan whipped around, as did Kat and Charlie. There, dressed in full diamond battle armor with a diamond sword in his hand, stood Mr. A, his black sunglasses dangerously glinting in the torchlight, a sly smile creeping onto his face.

Stan braced himself for a fight with his shovel, wishing enormously that he had an axe. Charlie drew his pickaxe and Kat her bow, both of whom also braced to battle. All three of them sat ill at ease; they knew that with their limited armor and less than ideal weaponry, they would be auspicious to make it out alive.

Mr. A laughed. "Don't worry, I'm not going to kill you... yet," he said, putting his sword away and smiling. "I think that it is a shame that you should come all this way, to not at least here the conclusion of the story of Avery007, don't you think?"

Stan was caught off guard. He lowered his shovel for a moment. "What are you talking about? How do you know the story of Avery007?"

"Because I knew Avery007," replied Mr. A quietly. "He was like a brother to me."

There was a stunned silence. Charlie stared at Mr. A, convinced that he was insane. Stan's face took on a mask of one trying to process this implausible information. Kat, on the other hand, merely laughed and said, "Hah! Nice try, buddy. Even if I believed for a second that that was remotely possible, from what I understand Avery was a friend of lower-level players. You, on the other hand, if you recall, tried to attack us. Somehow, I don't think you two would have gotten along very well."

179

Mr. A's face contorted with rage, and he drew his sword again. "Fine! Don't believe me! Then let me tell you what happened! It just so happens that after he met those worms that you read about in that book, Adam tried to raise an army out of them to help him overthrow the King. When he told them his idea, they figured that he was a dangerous madman and beat him to death with their stone tools! Just like that, Adam711 was gone from this server, just like Avery007!

"And so now, I have made it my sole duty to dispose of all the worthless lower-level scum on this server. The citizens, whom my friend tried to help, the citizens, that turned on him in his hour of need. The citizens, who truly are the bane of Minecraft!"

Mr. A was screaming now, the vein in his head popping. He gave an almighty scream, "AND NOW YOU DIE!!!" and rushed in with his sword, straight towards Charlie.

All four warriors attacked at the same time; Mr. A thrust his sword at Charlie's unprotected heart; Charlie threw his pickaxe at Mr. A's head; Stan swung his shovel's blade towards the front of Mr. A's stomach; Kat fired an arrow aimed at a chink in Mr. A's chestplate. The arrow missed and knocked the sword to the side, causing it to strike Stan's iron chestplate which shattered. The pickaxe missed its mark and embedded itself in the wall, and the shovel flew up and knocked off Mr. A's helmet.

Stan and Charlie scrambled to recover their weapons. Stan could see that Mr. A was dizzied by the blow to the head, while he himself felt like he was about to throw up from the blow to his stomach. Still he snatched up his shovel and ran back into engage Mr. A, but he stopped short when he saw that Mr. A was already taking heavy fire from Kat. Her never ending supply of arrows flew out of her bow almost rapid fire, glancing off the diamond of Mr. A's armor and knocking him backwards and into the wall.

"Hey guys! I think we may have a problem here!" Stan heard Charlie yell. He turned towards Charlie and saw that his diamond pickaxe had hit a button on the wall next to a bookshelf. Simultaneously, he heard a rumbling coming from above him. Seconds later, the roof above them exploded, and sand blocks fell down into the room, burying the entire underground bunker in a vortex of darkness and coarse, grainy earth.

Stan found himself buried; he couldn't judge which way was up or down, and he couldn't breathe inside the coarse blocks. He slowly realized that he still had his shovel in his hand. He came to his senses and punched around with it, quickly realizing which way was up. He dug up quickly, and right as he thought he couldn't hold his breath any longer, he punched his way into the fresh air.

CHAPTER 15: THE PORTAL

It was afternoon; Stan never thought that he would miss the sight of the blocky clouds in the blue sky as much as he did at that moment. He took deep breaths of the fresh air, amazed that after all that had happened in the past day underground, he was still alive.

Then he remembered his friends; they were nowhere to be found. Stan was about to panic when he heard a barking behind him. He turned and saw Rex trotting around in the sand next to him. Stan was puzzled. How did the dog get out? Then he remembered that the dog was able to teleport to wherever Kat was. So if the dog teleported aboveground, that could only mean that...

Sure enough, at that moment he heard a fist punching through sand, and Kat surfaced, breathing heavily from the effort. She looked at Stan.

"Don't ever let me hear you complaining about that shovel again!" she panted, down on her hands and knees trying to catch her breath. "It let you tunnel up way faster than this useless thing!" She held up the stone pickaxe still grasped in her hands.

Stan was about to reply when Lemon appeared in front of him, followed seconds later by Charlie's diamond pickaxe punching its way out of the ground. Unlike Kat, though, Charlie wasn't breathing heavily at all.

"Nice going Charlie," spat Kat.

"Yeah, honestly man, of all the places on that wall that you could have hit, why the button that destroyed the place?"

"Nice to see you too," sighed Charlie, wiping the excess sand off his clothes. "And you should be thanking me. For one, I probably trapped Mr. A down there too. I don't think he'll manage to get out of this one alive; he was already pretty weak from Stan's shovel attack. And for two, I managed to grab this!"

He pulled out a book from his inventory. The title read *The Nether and The End: How to Get There.*

Kat's jaw dropped, and Stan asked in amazement, "Charlie! Where'd you get that!"

"Oh, I saw it on the bookshelf next to that button and thought that it might come in handy," he said smugly. He stood up. "Now we can figure out our next move."

They agreed to find some shade from the hot desert sun while they planned this next move. They looked around and saw that they were in the middle of a sinkhole that must have been created when the sand fell down and buried Avery's base. They walked over and sat against the edge of this sinkhole that provided shade from the sun. Charlie opened the book to the chapter entitled "Entering the End" and read aloud.

"To enter The End, one will, before all else, require twelve Eyes of Ender." He looked up at his friends. "Does anybody know what those are?"

Neither of them did; Charlie found a glossary of Nether and End items in the back of the book and looked up the Eye of Ender.

The picture showed an orb, green-grey in color, which resembled the eye of a cat. The crafting recipe for it included one Ender Peal and one Blaze Powder. None of them knew what either of those were either, so Charlie opened the book first to the Ender Pearl .

"An Ender Pearl is most readily obtained by the killing of an Enderman," Charlie read.

"Wait, an Enderman?" said Kat. "Isn't that the thing that almost killed you this morning?"

Charlie sighed. "Yeah, it is. And it looks like we're gonna have to kill twelve of them if we want to get to the End."

Stan gulped. He remembered the Enderman's overwhelming power well, and he wasn't eager to face one again. "What about Blaze Powder?" he asked quickly. "How do we get that?"

Charlie turned the page and found what he was looking for. "Blaze Powder is a substance that is crafted from a Blaze Rod. The Blaze Rod can only be obtained by killing a Blaze, a creature indigenous to … the Nether," said Charlie, his stomach lurching; after all he had heard about the Nether, he was not eager to go there.

"So, if we want to get to the End," said Stan, piecing it together, "Then we have to kill a bunch of Endermen, and we also have to go to the Nether and find these Blaze things?"

"Oh yeah!" cried Kat, pumping her fist in the air. "Road trip to the Nether!"

"Wait," said Charlie quickly, "Not so fast. Who says that we have to go the Nether first?"

"Well, do you want to fight the Enderman again?" asked Kat. "Whatever's in the Nether, it can't be worse than something that can teleport and tries to kill you when you freaking *look* at it."

"Not to mention," added Stan, "that the King's forces are definitely still looking for us, and they're going to comb the entire overworld looking for us before they start looking in other dimensions."

Charlie tried to think of another argument of why they should not go to the Nether, but he couldn't; he did agree with the reasoning of both of his cohorts. "Okay," said Charlie, resigning himself. "I guess our next move is to go to the Nether."

As Charlie flipped through the book to figure out the way to enter the hell dimension, Kat kept on doing fist pumps and jumping around like a hyperactive puppy; she was obviously very excited to explore the place. Stan felt nervous, but he too had a growing sense of exhilaration. He was very much anticipating with potent curiosity the exploration of the new dimension, whatever it may hold.

"Okay, apparently to enter the Nether we're going to have to build a portal," said Charlie, referring to the book. "It has to be five blocks high, four blocks wide, hollow in the center, and made out of obsidian. From what I understand, obsidian is created when running water hits stagnant lava, it's almost indestructible, and it can only be mined with a diamond pickaxe."

"We passed an entire lake of lava on the way here, remember?" said Stan.

"Oh, yeah, I remember that!" agreed Kat.

"Okay, so we have stagnant lava," said Charlie, "but how are we going to get a flow of running water across it?"

"Are you stupid, Charlie?" said Kat with a laugh. "I found a bucket down in the mine shaft!"

"Oh yeah," said Charlie, feeling, indeed, a little stupid.

"Okay, then!" said Stan, clapping his hands together. "Let's make camp in this sinkhole overnight, and tomorrow we'll hike out to the lava lake and make a portal to the Nether!"

And they did just that; Kat walked over to a pond in a grassy oasis near them and filled her bucket with water, while Charlie and Stan used all the sand and dirt in their three combined inventories to make an inconspicuous sand house against the corner of the sinkhole. They quickly threw together a crafting table, a furnace, and three beds, with the wool made from the string of the cave spiders.

They also made preparations for their impending quest. Charlie made torches out of the coal and wood he had found while mining and he used the remaining coal to smelt the iron ore he found in the furnace. He used the resulting iron ingots to create two new iron chestplates for himself and Stan; Kat still had her leather tunic and cap.

After crafting the chestplates, there were three iron ingots left. Stan wanted a new axe, but Charlie said he needed one of the remaining ingots to combine with flint he had found underground; he read in the book that the way to activate the Nether portal was to light the inside on fire, and to do that he would need to craft Flint and Steel. After he created this, the two remaining ingots went to a new iron sword for Kat.

They had some leftover string and wood. These Charlie crafted into a chest and a new bow, which he gave to Stan, along with twenty arrows that he had collected from Skeletons underground. The chest was filled with the group's items that they would not be taking to the Nether: Some dirt, a lot of cobblestone, the book, the contents of the chest from the mine shaft save the bucket, and the Ender Chest. With all their necessities on them, and all extras safely stored in the chest, the three players, the cat, and the dog were all happy to go the bed.

As the wool mattress of the bed beneath him conformed to his body, Stan thought, for the first time, about the griefer whom he had probably just killed beneath the desert. It was incredibly conflicting. Although Stan was quite happy that they now had a dangerous enemy off their tails, and it was inevitable that not all of them would leave that fight intact, Stan found his insides squirm in guilt when he remembered the hell of being crushed by the sand himself. Suffocating in that buried room must have been a dreadful way to die. Even if Stan *had* dismissed Mr. A's story about Avery007 as being completely untrue, Stan still felt as though Mr. A did have an underlying reason for his hatred of lower-level players. And now he was dead, and they would never find out what that was...

Regardless of his guilt, Stan was too tired from the events of the day to dwell on it for long. It was only a matter of time before he succumbed to sleep.

* * * * *

It seemed like forever to Stan since they had had a really good night's sleep, but it was a peaceful night, and Stan woke up to the crowing of a chicken feeling refreshed and ready to tackle whatever the Nether had to offer.

They wasted no time leaving. They clipped their remaining potions to their belts, along with their weapons and arrows. Stan

187

and Kat slung their bows over their shoulders. Kat and Charlie commanded their pets to sit and hide, as Charlie had read that Rex and Lemon would be unable to enter the Nether.

Before the clock even showed that the night was over, the trio was retracing their steps back towards the lava lake. They passed some burning mobs on the way there, but they were too preoccupied to pick up the materials. They reached the lava before the sun was high in the sky.

Stan was amazed; at a passing glance the body of molten lava had seemed like a lake, but now he could see that it expanded for kilometers, forming what could more appropriately be called a lava sea. Kat was equally amazed. Charlie, on the other hand, wasted no time placing the water from the bucket on the shore of the lava. Initially Stan was confused as to why the water from the bucket seemed to stay confined to one block on the shoreline; wasn't water supposed to flow? However, water immediately began to flow from this single source block, eventually spreading out into the lava and cooling a fair amount of the lava instantly into the black-as-night obsidian blocks. Charlie ignored the coal ore and stone rimming the lake, and he picked up the source block of water with the bucket; with the source gone, the water flowing from it quickly drained away. Wasting no time, he took his diamond pickaxe to the obsidian.

It was hard work; the sun was soon high in the sky, and the heat from the lava didn't make it any easier for Charlie to continue hacking away at the black rock that seemed to resist breaking at all costs. After ten minutes, the obsidian block broke off and Charlie snatched it before it could fall into the lava below. Charlie, content at attaining his first obsidian block, gritted his teeth and got to work on the second one.

Meanwhile, Kat and Stan stood poised at Charlie's back, bows raised, ready to shoot down any attackers that ventured to close to them. It was boring, but Stan just kept the image of finally entering the Nether in mind, and he kept his poise, as did Kat.

It was when Charlie was just collecting his ninth obsidian block when, without warning, the ground in front of Stan exploded. A stunned Stan was knocked back by the force of the blast, and he skidded along the black obsidian that Charlie had created, stopping just before he would have fallen into the edge of the lava sea.

Kat had trained her bow on the cloud of dust, and was ready to snipe the first thing to rise from it when a figure burst out of the hole in the ground. Before Kat could react, the figure threw a series of fire charges to the ground, thickening the smoke and setting the ground on fire. Kat tried to stare through the thick smoke and see who was attacking them when an arrow flew through the smokescreen right at her.

It was too fast for her to dodge, but she ducked her head and the arrow snagged the leather of her cap, damaging the armor but leaving her unharmed. She sent arrows into the general direction of the attacker, and she was drawing another one when another figure ran out of the smoke. This was the first one whose features could clearly be seen. His blond hair was cut to his head, and he wore camo army pants and a black tank top, with an eye patch covering one of his eyes. He held a diamond sword, and he was rushing straight towards Kat.

His attack was cut off by Stan, who had gotten up by now and swung his shovel at the man's feet. As he tripped, Stan yelled back to Charlie, who was about to come help them, "We can handle this, Charlie! Finish the portal so we can get out of here!" At the same time, he sensed something to his right, and he turned and caught Kat's eye.

"Stan, here! You need this more than I do!" she yelled, and she dodged an arrow while simultaneously throwing her sword in his direction. He responded by yelling "Thanks!" and grabbing the sword just as the eye patch guy got back on his feet. Stan drew back and shot a couple of arrows at the man, which were effortlessly deflected, and when arrows became a futile effort he engaged the man with the sword.

Kat, meanwhile, could now see the man she was having a ranged arrow-battle with; he had dark skin and black hair, and he was wearing a leather tunic over Japanese samurai armor. The bow he was using was glowing just like hers; it had been enchanted. She had a feeling that the enchantment on a bow owned by someone who had attacked them without provocation would be considerably more sadistic than the Infinity enchantment on hers.

Charlie was vaguely aware of Stan's sword flying out of his hand in his battle with Mr. Tank Top, and of more and more arrows catching on Kat's tunic in her arrow fight with Mr. Samurai. He knew he had to finish the portal quickly. Charlie hastily placed the last three obsidian blocks into place atop the black obelisk, and he jumped to the ground, pulling out the flint and the steel ring. He was about to light the portal when a figure burst out of the ground right behind him. He whipped around, pickaxe in hand, ready for a fight.

This player was wearing full glowing iron armor; it was enchanted. The blocky black ponytail extending to her waste distinguished her as female. She didn't attack Charlie; rather, she didn't even notice him. She pulled something out of her inventory; a handful of redstone dust, and a torch that was glowing electric

190

red. Charlie stared, baffled, as she laid the dust along the ground and out of the hole, and she touched the red end of the torch to the dust. Instantly, the dust illuminated and sent off faint red sparks.

"Contact in five!" she bellowed, and she whipped out her iron sword and sunk into a defensive stance. Kat stopped, having bent over to pick up her iron sword, as she wondered what this meant, and Stan looked equally as confused, but the effect on the other three was immediate. They eye patch guy and the samurai whipped out shovels and dug a hole into the ground, and Charlie realized in horror what was about to happen; he ducked behind one of the obsidian pillars of the portal, screaming, "Get down! She's about to...!"

He was cut off when the world exploded.

Stan was knocked twenty blocks back as the sand beneath him exploded in a whirlwind of earth and rock. He was sent flying through the air, and he felt dizzy, becoming aware that he was spinning.

He landed on the ground, and, dazed, looked into the dust cloud that was where the battlefield used to be. He was confused, too paralyzed by fear and injury to think to do anything but instinctively grab and swig one of his healing potions. Instantly, the effect of the potion kicked in; he felt alert, and completely healed, and his thoughts immediately turned to the safety of his friends.

Then he saw her. Flying through the air, smoke flying from her burning leather armor, iron sword miraculously still clasped in her hand, the body of his brave friend, propelled by the amazing force of the explosion, sailed through the air like a graceful kite, disappearing upon plunging into the fiery depths of the lava sea.

Stan's vision went white. He couldn't hear. He couldn't feel the bow in his hand. All of his senses seemed to shut down as he processed the impossible information. His body seemed to be refusing to accept what he knew to be facts; he was thrust into two states of logic. For Kat could not possibly be dead, there was no way that it would be allowed to happen...

Stan's thoughts were refusing to connect, so his instincts took over; he grabbed his iron shovel from the ground next to him, ran towards the samurai archer that was now aiming an arrow at Charlie's head. Charlie's face was white, his eyes wide and his jaw dropped, as he stared at the spot where Kat had made contact with the molten liquid, oblivious to his own impending doom. Stan drew back his shovel and slammed it against the archer's head before he could fire.

The archer was knocked down to the ground, his head twisting at an odd angle. Stan could not tell if he was dead, but if not he was definitely unconscious. Becoming aware that he was screaming in fury, Stan whipped around to face the other two. He saw the guy with the buzz cut dashing towards him, diamond sword in attack position, with the girl close behind. Both were seething with rage, the veins popping, ready to avenge their fallen friend. But the rage at the death of Kat had elevated Stan's fighting abilities, even with a shovel. Stan's anger rose up in him like a pot boiling over, and he was sure that he could easily take these two armored gorillas armed with swords. He was about to shoot a preemptive arrow with his bow when something behind them caught his eye.

There was a disturbance in the surface of the lava sea; a ripple, or rather, a bubbling, was appearing right next to the shore. What happened next was so unbelievable that had Stan not been there he wouldn't have believed that it had really happened, no matter how many eyewitness accounts he heard.

Out of the lava burst a player, surrounded by a glowing red aura, her iron sword red with the heat it had absorbed from the lava. Kat flew out onto the sand, and without hesitation proceeded to thrust her sword into the back of the girl in full iron armor. The sword seemed to melt a hole through the back of the chestplate and out the front.

The look on the girl's face changed from outrage to shock as the sword entered her body. Kat, on the other hand, looked like the embodiment of some hellish entity as she used all of her superhuman strength to fling the girl over her head, off of her sword. The glowing iron body flew through the air and it entered the lava right at the edge of the stone shore.

Stan didn't allow himself time to think about how his friend wasn't burned to death, nor did he allow himself time to be happy. All he knew was that the one remaining fighter with the buzz cut would be upon him soon, and he would be livid that his two companions were down. He ran towards the obsidian frame, where Charlie stood in shock.

"Light the portal!" he bellowed, and he became aware that Kat was running right behind him, deflecting arrows from the buzz cut man with her sword as she did.

Charlie pulled out the flint and the steel ring, and struck them together. Sparks flew out upon collision, and they fell into the obsidian base. The sparks flew into the air, beginning to glow purple. When they reached the center of the portal, they grew until the entire inside of the portal was glowing purple. The portal to the Nether was open.

Charlie jumped into the purple glow and disappeared, purple sparks flying through the portal. Stan threw all hesitancies he had about entering the hell dimension away, and he dove through the purple barrier. He suddenly felt like he was buried in the sand over Avery's base once again, being squeezed from all sides. The very unpleasant sensation lasted for about three seconds, and then Stan tumbled out onto a surface that felt like dirt that was crusted over, and refilled his squeezed-empty lungs with warm, dry air.

On the other side of the portal, Geno was dragging the body of Becca out of the lava. He pulled out two illegally brewed potions from his inventory, and poured them into her mouth. The flames that were burning her armor and skin immediately subsided, and she gave a weak cough. Relieved, he quickly whipped around and poured a third potion into the open mouth of Leonidas. There was a faint click, and his head spun around and back into place.

Geno looked up and through the portal. On the other side, he could see that all three players were punching the bottom block of the obsidian portal. Realizing what they were about to do, Geno desperately sprinted towards the portal, trying to dive through before it closed. Just as he was about to fly through the portal, there was a crack, and the bottom obsidian block of the black frame ceased to exist. There was a flash of purple light, and the entrance to the Nether disappeared.

Geno skidded to a stop right before his momentum could carry him through the empty obsidian frame and into the lava sea. He cursed in anger, and he looked back at his companions. Leonidas was sitting up and caressing his neck; Geno knew that he would be alright. Becca, on the other hand, was still lying on the ground, her breathing shallow. Geno worried about her, but he was sure that there would be at least one medic in the legion of the King's army awaiting RAT1's command in the jungle.

It was all for the best, decided Geno, as Leonidas slowly got back to his feet. Geno was confident that under his command, RAT1's battalion of troops would ensure that Stan and his friends, now stranded in the Nether, would not make it back to the overworld alive.

CHAPTER 16: THE NETHER

Stan's knuckle was bleeding from helping Charlie punch through raw obsidian. Presently though, he wasn't worried. His entire brain was processing two simultaneous emotions. He was breathing hard, amazed and relieved that they had managed to escape those thugs back in the overworld.

He was also amazed and in shock as he stared at Kat, who was still glowing red from the molten lava. But now, as Stan took a closer look, the glow wasn't coming from the residual heat of the lava; Kat seemed to have a red aura surrounding her body. She was sitting on the ground, panting, next to Charlie, but other than being winded, she looked completely unharmed.

"So tell me Kat," panted Stan, talking for the first time since entering the Nether. "How exactly did you manage to survive swimming in lava?"

Kat looked up at him. She lifted up an empty bottle. "Fire Resistance potion," she huffed, tossing the bottle to the side, "and healing potion to get rid of the damage from the burns." She tossed a second bottle to the side. It shattered next to the first one on the red and black speckled rocks. The sight of these odd blocks prompted Stan to look around the area.

Around the eleven remaining black obsidian blocks of the broken portal, Stan could see that they had spawned inside a cave. The entire cave was made of the black and red speckled rocks. Stan guessed that this was a fairly widespread block in the hell-dimension. The cave was wide open, and he could see that one end was illuminated. The air was arid, and very warm; Stan imagined that water was nonexistent here.

Charlie glanced at the broken portal. The obsidian block that they had to punch out had cracked into three pieces; there was no way to repair the portal with the remaining chunks of the black rock. "We're gonna have to find some new obsidian if we're ever going to fix the portal," he sighed, chucking the useless obsidian chunks to the side.

"Well let's not even try to fix it just yet. Whoever that was who just attacked us, I bet that they're with the King," said Stan. "And I'll bet that it's just a matter of time before they make their way into this dimension and hunt us down. We've got to find these Blaze rods as quick as we can, and once we figure out how to fix the portal, we shouldn't do it until the last possible minute so they can't follow us."

Kat and Charlie nodded, and Stan suggested that they make their way out of the cave. They picked up their items and left the broken portal behind them. They walked to the mouth of the cave, and three jaws simultaneously dropped at what they saw.

The entire world seemed to be a colossal cave, made almost entirely of the red and black speckled rock. Flooding the bottom of the cave was a sea of lava that made the one they had just left in the overworld seem miniscule by comparison. A few small, dark-red islands dotted the face of the lava. Hanging from the ceiling, which ranged greatly in height, were stalactites that were made of a glowing type of crystal, as well as several giant lava falls that flowed viscously from holes in the ceiling and into the molten basin. It was beautiful in a fiery way, but it was also terrifying; all three players

197

were simultaneously imagining the unknown perils of exploring the scorching land.

The players' first view of the Nether was soon obscured, however. After about ten seconds of surveying the landscape, a giant white form rose in front of them. Stan stepped back in awe, and had to look up as the giant creature floated up in front of them. It appeared to be a giant, white, levitating jellyfish; its body was a cube, and there was a mess of tentacles hanging from underneath it. Its eyes were shut, as was its mouth. Stan was amazed; it was by far the largest mob he had ever seen in Minecraft.

Suddenly, the monster's eyes and mouth opened, and it gave out a scream. It was a high-pitched baby-like screech, even shriller than that of the Enderman, which seemed oddly in contrast to the blazing fireball that came shooting from its mouth.

"Get down!" Kat screamed, dropping to the ground.

Not needing to be told twice, Charlie and Stan followed in suit. Stan's eyes followed the path of the fireball until it hit the back wall of the cave, at which point it exploded. This explosion was different than a TNT or Creeper explosion. The blast of a Creeper was stronger than this blast, which emitted a shockwave of heat that scorched Stan's eyebrows from a distance. The remaining blocks that weren't destroyed were set alight, and began to burn brightly.

Another fireball came flying, and the players rolled to the side just in time to avoid impact, while the section of the ground they were just standing on was blown apart. Stan looked at the hole that had been blasted in the ground and saw that they had been standing on a ledge; one wrong step, and they would fall down into the lava sea below.

Stan whipped out his bow and arrows and tried to snipe the next fireball out of the air. He missed; the arrow instead hit the flying monster in the forehead. Its eyes flew open, and the monster gave an animal bellow of pain. The mob levitated upwards and spit three more fireballs that hit the roof of the cave. The entire top of the cave exploded, leaving the three players exposed to an absolute rain of fireballs from the evil mob.

"We've got to split up!" cried Charlie as he tumbled sideways to dodge another fireball. "It can't shoot at all of us at once!"

"But there's nowhere to split up to!" yelled Kat desperately, and she was right. They had backed up to a cliff, and the ledge had been completely blown apart by fireballs except for the part where the three players were standing. The giant jellyfish opened its mouth, and the fireball that was sure to drop them all into the burning sea below flew out, right on a collision course with the players. Stan held his shovel in front of his face and prepared himself for an explosive death.

Right before the fireball could make contact, a form burst out of the wall behind Stan and flew in front of him. It was a player, dressed in a scarlet jumpsuit with olive skin and black hair. He held a diamond sword in his hand, which he hastily swung in front of him in midair, hitting the fireball, and then landing on the cliff below him. The projectile changed trajectory and headed on a return course to the monster that had shot it. The fireball exploded in the mob's face, and it tumbled backwards a few feet, screaming.

"Get behind me!" yelled the player, as the monster recovered and blasted another fireball their way. Stan, Kat and Charlie obliged and watched, amazed, as the player deflected another fireball, this time missing the monster and sending the fireball deep into the cave. Another player burst through the hole in the wall.

This player was dressed the same as the player with the sword, but he had red hair and pale skin, and he held a fishing rod in his hand. Stan watched in astonishment as the player threw the rod back, and cast it, with the bobber flying towards the flying jellyfish. The hook entered the monster's head, and it cried out in pain again. It tried to fly away again, but the redheaded player expertly maneuvered the line, dragging the mob back down. All the while, the monster was still shooting fireballs, and the swordsman kept deflecting them.

"Nice cast, Bill!" yelled the swordsman as he parried another fireball to the side.

"Thanks, Ben!" the redhead cried in response, as he kept changing the power of the cast to keep the monster from flying out of range. "The Ghast is in optimal position! We're ready, Bob!"

At this, yet another jumpsuit-clad player burst out of the wall, this one pale and blonde. He held a glowing bow in his hand, and he fired an arrow at the monster in midair. He landed on the ground and looked back at Stan, Kat and Charlie.

"If any of you three are archers, now's the time! Aim for the eyes!" said the blonde archer, Bob, with a manic grin on his face. Stan was a little unnerved by the grin at first glance, but he then noticed the same expression on the face of the fishing rod player, Bill, and the swordsman, Ben. They weren't just fighting off this mob, which he had heard one of them call a Ghast; they were *loving it*!

Stan and Kat pulled out there bows, and they began shooting at the Ghast. The monster's eyes were punctured by the dozen arrows protruding from them, and its fireballs seemed to be going in a more confused pattern. One of the fireballs flew towards Kat, and she whipped out her sword and deflected it, just as Ben had been doing.

"Okay you three, let up!" cried Bill, pulling back hard on the fishing pole.

Bob lowered his bow and got back against the wall, but Kat and Stan looked at Bill, confused.

"But it's still alive!" yelled Stan.

"Yeah, why should we let up?" asked Kat.

"Because Ben loves this part!" bellowed Bill, laughing like a maniac, as he threw his full weight back against the fishing rod. The damaged Ghast lurched back down towards the ledge; it was very close to them now. Stan flinched as he felt the heat of the desperate Ghast spamming out yet another fireball.

Ben, a manic glint in his eyes, deflected the fireball off into the distance and ran towards the Ghast, which was now almost level with the ledge. He took a flying leap at the Ghast, his sword in his right hand, and he drove his weapon into the forehead of the giant monster. It screamed in anguish as he grabbed the Ghast's face with his left hand while repeatedly thrusting his sword into the Ghast's head. The giant mob stopped launching fireballs, and started to fall apart from the repeated sword slices.

Ben pushed off the monster's face with a white item in his hand; his sword spiraled down and landed on the ledge. He himself landed next to the weapon and pocketed the white item. Ben then looked up, and his companions stood next to him, looking on with satisfaction as the hacked up corpse of the Ghast fell into the lava sea below. Bob turned around.

"And that, gentlemen and lady, is how we amazing people kill Ghasts."

And with that, the three fighters bumped their fists together in midair and yelled in unison, "HELL YEAH!"

"Okay, that was officially really impressive," remarked Kat, still sweating from the battle with the Ghast.

"Well, we've had practice," said Bob, slinging his bow over his back. "You kids have got to be more careful. Ghast fighting can be one hell of a pain; it's really easy to get blasted sky-high in this place."

"You guys seem like you have a lot of experience here," said Charlie. "How many times have you three been to the Nether?"

"Are you kidding? We live here, man!" Bill laughed. "And that's not an exaggeration either, we've lived here ever since that backstabbing jerk King Kev banished us here."

"And by the way," said Ben as Stan opened his mouth in surprise, "we don't care what you think about the King, if you have a problem with our opinion we'd be more than happy to fight you." Bill and Bob nodded in agreement.

"Oh trust me," smirked Kat, "I'd use a considerably more vile word to describe the King."

"Yeah," said Charlie. "I agree to that, and I'm sure Stan does too. After all, he was the one that tried to kill that terrible king."

"Wait, what?" Bob did a double take. "You tried to kill the king? Man, you got guts, noob!"

"How the hell are you possibly still alive?" asked Bill, amazed.

"Did you come to the Nether to hide from the King's forces? Cause there's no way that you would still be alive if you were in the overworld," commented Ben.

Stan looked up. "No. As a matter of fact, we're trying to overthrow..." but he was cut off when Kat punched him in the arm.

"Shut up, you idiot!" hissed Kat. "Don't give away too much..."

"You're overthrowing the King?" interrupted Bob in a hushed, awed voice.

There was a moment of silence. The look on Kat's and Charlie's faces confirmed that Stan's outburst was indeed true. Kat slapped her head, sure that these three players were about to reveal that they were really secret agents of the King. But then...

"Man, that is freaking awesome!" cried Bill. "It's about time someone stood up to that pile of pig crap."

"If we weren't banished to this dimension with no way to get out," said Ben, "we would have done it sooner or later."

"Wait a minute... do you guys have a portal out of here?" asked Bob. This got the others ears perked up.

"Yeah! It'd be great to finally get out of this awful hell-dimension. We've been here for so long..."

"Yeah... maybe the Apothecary is still around..."

"Wait, you know the Apothecary?" said Stan. "We met him back in the jungle! He's helping us organize a rebellion with the people in the Adorian Village. How do you know him?"

"We used to work with him on the Council of Operators back in Element City," said Ben. "We were the Chiefs of Exploration before the King associated us with some fake rebellion and kicked us all here to this hellhole."

"Oh yeah! He mentioned you guys!" said Charlie, remembering their lengthy conversation with the old man. "You guys must be Bill33, Bob33, and Ben33."

"Testify," said Bill, raising his fishing rod and then lowering it. "Although nowadays, we go by the title of the Nether Boys."

"Anyways, do you guys really have a portal out of here?" asked Bob. "We've been marooned in this blistering wasteland forever, I'd kill just to see a sheep or a cow or a tree again!"

"Well, we do have a portal," said Kat, "but it's broken right now; we need one obsidian block to fix it. We have the means to fix it, I have a water bucket and Charlie has his diamond pickaxe," Charlie raised it in confirmation, "but we can't leave here until we get some Blaze rods. If we're gonna pull this rebellion off, we're going to need access to the King's secret stash of supplies in the End, and we can't get there without the rods."

"Also," added Charlie, "we can't fix the portal until we're ready to leave, or else the King's forces will be able to get in to follow us and we'll all be screwed."

"Well, it ain't gonna matter one way or another," said Bill. "You're in the Nether now, kids; water will evaporate the instant it leaves the bucket, so there's no way to make obsidian here."

Stan's heart sunk; how were they going to get out now?

"Still, I think that we may be able to help you out. It just so happens that we have one block of obsidian back at our house," said Ben. "We'll make a deal with you. We'll give you the obsidian block so you can fix the portal. You let us use your portal to get out of the Nether, and in exchange, we'll help you get your Blaze rods."

"Sounds good," said Stan, and he looked at Charlie and Kat for confirmation. Both nodded and smiled, and Kat said, "You've got yourself a deal."

"So where exactly are we supposed to find these... Blazes?" said Charlie, remembering that Blaze rods were dropped by this type of enemy.

"We'll talk about getting your Blaze rods when we get back to our house," said Ben.

He jumped into the hole he and the other two had made in the wall, and the six players followed the tunnel. It went down for a good while, and when they came out they were at the level of the lava sea. They began walking across the open plain of red and black speckled stone, which Bob told Stan was called Netherack. At the edge of the plain was a small rise, and before they crossed over it, Bill raised a hand.

"Hold up, we should check to see if there are any monsters on the edge of this rise. Bob, Stan, you two go and check. Shoot down any hostile mobs that you see, and then we'll go on. The house is just over this plain."

Stan pulled out his bow and walked with Bob over to the rise. Bob poked his head over and looked at the plain, and his eyes widened.

"Whoo, whee! This oughta be fun, right Stan?" said the blonde archer. Stan poked his head over the wall to see what Bob was talking about. What he saw made his stomach fall out.

He had seen these mobs before. On a stormy day, en route to Element City, he had fought a great battle against this creature. Could this possibly be the same mobs that he had fought with his friends in that terrible battle? But there was no mistaking the pink rotting skin, the brown loincloths, the golden swords...

It had managed to take down Charlie, Kat and Rex, and it was only because of the lightning-charged Creeper that Stan had managed to defeat it... and that was just one...

But now, Stan was staring into a plain, an entire wide-open stretch of flat land with lava on both sides. And roaming around this wide open space was an entire herd of about fifty sword-wielding Zombie Pigmen.

CHAPTER 17: THE FORTRESS AND THE BLAZE

Stan drew back the arrow without thinking. All he knew was that he wanted to get this massive fight over with as soon as possible, and with as little sword fighting as possible. He let the arrow fly, right as Bob cried out, "Stan, no!"

The arrow went right through the hollow eye socket of the nearest Pigman, and it fell to the ground. The others around it looked down at their fallen comrade, and in a unison motion all of their eyes locked on Stan. In a swarm, the entire herd of Pigmen surged forward, towards Stan and Bob.

"Man, those things are neutral!" cried Bob as he downed another one of the Pigmen with an arrow. "If you don't attack them, they won't attack you!"

"What do you mean?" asked Stan as he pulled out his shovel and knocked one of them that had almost reached the top of the rise back down the plain. "In the overworld one attacked me!"

"Well I don't know why that was, but right now we've got a serious problem on our hands!" He clubbed a Pigman with his bow and it flew backwards and landed in the middle of the herd that was now climbing the rise in a swarm. "Get back, get back!" Bob continued to yell as he walked backwards and fired arrows into the throng.

Stan and Bob ran back down towards the others, and Bob yelled, "Zombie Pigmen, incoming!" When the other two Nether

Boys looked at Bob in confusion, he said "Stan shot one of 'em." When Kat and Charlie looked at Stan in horror, remembering the one from the overworld, he said, "There's, like, fifty of them coming now! Prepare yourselves, this is gonna be one hell of a fight!"

The Zombie Pigmen started to stream over the rise. Stan, Kat, Charlie and Ben raced in to battle the herd. Bill and Bob stayed back and started attacking with their respective weapons.

The fighting was intense; Ben was an expert at disarming the rotting pig-warriors, and then cutting them out of existence. Kat, on the other hand, required a lot more effort to defeat the Pigmen than he did, being unfamiliar with the sows' fighting techniques. Charlie had adopted a unique strategy; he had used his pickaxe to swiftly hack a ditch in the brittle Netherack ground, and when the Zombie Pigmen stumbled into the ditch in pursuit of him, Charlie drove his pickaxe into the monsters. Stan meanwhile adopted the timeless zombie-fighting strategy of beating them into submission with a shovel.

By far, the ones doing the most damage were Bill and Bob. Bob's arrows downed pig after pig after pig, and Bill had adopted an unusual strategy of catching the Pigmen on his fishing hook from afar and casting them deep into the lava sea. They wouldn't burn, but instead they just swam around aimlessly in the molten lava, not interested in the fighting anymore.

It took a while, but the seemingly endless supply of Zombie Pigmen finally trickled down and eventually stopped when Kat decapitated the last one. Bob went alone to check whether or not the coast was clear; it was, and the six players walked across the plain and soon came to the house of the Nether boys at the base of a steep Netherack hill. The house was entirely covered in Netherack, so it blended into the environment in such a way that you would have to know the house was there to see it. The inside was made entirely of cobblestone, which, for Stan at least, was a sight for sore eyes. It was the first of the familiar block that he had seen since entering the nightmarish Nether.

They saw a crafting table, a furnace and some chests; other than that the house was completely empty. Stan asked why they had so few possessions after living here so long.

"We were banished here, don't you remember kid," said Bill, slinging his fishing rod over his back. "And besides, if you try to sleep in a bed in the Nether, the bed will explode."

"Okay." Stan didn't even bother questioning it; he was so past wondering about the many breaches in the laws of physics in this wonderful, dangerous game called Minecraft.

"So to get your Blaze rods," said Bob, sitting on the cobblestone floor and leaning against the wall, "we're going to have to get to the Blaze spawner in the Nether Fortress."

"Yeah, the Apothecary mentioned something about the Nether Fortress," said Kat, chiseling her initials into the cobblestone wall with her sword's point. "What exactly is the Nether Fortress?"

"It's a maze made out of dark red brick that's incredibly dangerous to navigate," replied Ben. "Luckily, we happened to live right near the closest Nether Fortress, and even luckier is that we've done a little exploring of it and it shouldn't take too long to get to the Blaze spawner. We'd better be prepared though; once we enter that room we're going to be up against a never-ending swarm of Blazes, and those things are hell to kill."

"What makes them so hard to kill?" asked Charlie.

"Well, for one, they can fly," said Bill, "and for two they have the annoying tendency to spam fireballs at you. When the three of us first made it into the Blaze spawner room, we barely made it out alive. Great fun, really, but we didn't even try to fight them."

"Mind you," interjected Bill, "we've had a lot more experience fighting Ghasts since then, and we could probably figure out a winning strategy for killing them, but we should still be careful."

"The Nether Fortress is very near to this location," said Ben. "We actually chose to build our house here in case we ever wanted to explore it some more. We actually have a few times, it's awesome to explore that giant labyrinth. Anyways, it's right up this hill outside," he said as he exited the house, and he started up the hill, followed by the other five.

It was quite a sheer hill; more like a cliff face, really. At one point, another Ghast tried to blast them off the Cliffside, but Ben managed to kill it with deflected fireballs, and they kept climbing.

"Damn, why is it so hot in the Nether?" said Kat, gritting her teeth as she wiped the sweat from her brow. She was closely followed by Charlie, and then Kat.

"Well...I'm guessing... the fireballs and...the lava sea may... have something to do... with it," panted Stan as he dragged his shovel behind him climbing the hill. "And who are you... to complain? You're... wearing shorts... and a T-shirt!"

"And also you're... not wearing... one of these freaking heavy... iron chestplates!" gasped Charlie. Kat glanced down quickly at her neon pink shorts, and then again at the light tunic over her orange T-Shirt. She blushed in embarrassment and did not speak again for the rest of the climb.

210

At the top of the Netherack cliff, there was a monster standing by that tried to attack them. It was a large cube of magma of various shade of dark red, and glowing yellow eyes, that opened up like a spring as it leaped forward to attack Ben. He calmly identified it as a Magma Cube and sliced it in two with his sword. Stan was totally caught off guard when the two halves of the monster morphed into two smaller Magma Cubes. One of them caught him unawares as it tackled into him, and he would have been knocked back down the cliff had Bill not caught the strap of his chestplate with his fishing rod. Ben kept killing the Magma Cubes, and the pieces of the dead ones kept reanimating. They were easy kills, though, and soon all of them were dead for good, leaving a pasty orange substance on the ground that Bob pocketed for later use.

"Magma cream," he pointed out. "You use it to make Fire Resistance potions."

Now that the Magma Cube was good and dead, the players turned their attention to the structure in front of them. It was composed entirely of dark crimson bricks, and there were stairs that lead up to a tunnel made out of the bricks that had torches lining the walls. The tunnel went straight into the side of another Netherack cliff. There were no distinct architectural features of the building; as a matter of fact; Stan was surprised to see that the exterior looked very plain.

"Those torches weren't put there naturally," said Ben. "We put those up the last time we visited this place. If we follow them, it should lead us straight to the Blaze spawner room."

They walked into the corridor. Stan was pleased to realize that it was slightly cooler within these brick halls. He followed the Nether Boys as they took turn after turn, following the torches.

Slowly, Stan began to realize just how big the complex was. There were windows in the sides of the corridors, and more often than not there was nothing to see out them except for Netherack. However, now and then he could see that they were suspended over the lava sea, and a few times he saw magnificent lava falls flowing from the ceiling of the Nether and into the lava sea. Stan realized that he may well die during the fight with these monsters, so he took the time walking down the corridors to appreciate just how beautiful the landscape of Minecraft was.

After going down endless corridors, with a few rooms that had staircases and small farms of some type of seed in them which Stan guessed was the Nether Wart the Apothecary had told him about, they finally arrived at a corridor that was not lit with torches. At the end of this corridor, Stan could see a block with a yellow figure revolving within a black cage, very similar to the block that spawned Cave Spiders in the abandoned mine shaft. He knew that they had reached the Blaze spawner.

"So what's our strategy?" asked Charlie eagerly.

"Personally, I say we should just go in there and beat the things to death before they get a chance to attack us," said Kat, pulling her sword from her waist.

"Not so fast, sister," said Bill. "Those spawners can set up to three of those things on you at a time. As much fun as it would be to charge in there and beat the living crap out of those things, I think we have to think this one through a little more. Anyone have any ideas?"

There was silence for a moment. Then Charlie spoke up, much to Stan's surprise, and said, "How about I drink my Fire

Resistance potion and draw their fire, while Bob, Kat and Stan shoot them down?"

"Nice thinking, bro," said Bob. "Be careful though. Even if you don't catch on fire, the Blazes can still do mêlée attacks and the fireballs still damage you, even if you're not set on fire."

Charlie agreed to be careful, and they got ready for their plan. Charlie gave all of his things to Kat to hold, and Ben and Bill hid behind Bob, Kat and Stan, all of whom had their arrows notched, ready to fire.

"Wait, I'm almost out of arrows," Stan said. "Do you have any extras, Bob?"

"Sure," he said, and he handed half of his arrows to Stan. With everything ready, Charlie swigged his Fire Resistance potion, and he charged into the Blaze spawner room.

Charlie could see that the room was jutting out of the side of a Netherack mountain, and that the walls were completely composed of fences. In the center of the room, the black cage gave off some fire particles, and the yellow figure within started spinning rapidly. Before Charlie could study the little figure any closer, a full-sized Blaze appeared right above the spawner. Charlie couldn't help but stare; it was the most bizarre thing he had ever seen.

The head of the Blaze was a yellow cube flecked with orange, and it had beady eyes that were locked on to him. The head was on top of a column of smoke, which had a lot of yellow rods orbiting around it. The entire thing was engulfed in flames. Charlie was just getting over how zany the entire composition looked when the Blaze opened its mouth and three fireballs shot out.

Charlie rolled to the side; the three fireballs hit the walls in three puffs of fire. The Blaze's head rotated and fixated on Charlie again, and it rose into the air and shot out three more fireballs. Charlie dodged again, and before the Blaze could take another shot, three arrows flew out of the corridor and impaled the Blaze's head. The pyro fell to the ground, extinguished, with only an orange stick remaining, which Charlie snatched up. He barely had time to examine the Blaze Rod when two more Blazes appeared, and six more fireballs flew towards him. One of the Blazes fell from three more arrows, but it didn't drop a rod. The other one fell seconds later, and the rod fell to the ground. Charlie was too preoccupied with the four more Blazes in the room to pick up the rod at the moment.

Back in the corridor, the archers were shooting arrows as fast as they could, but the spawners were creating new enemies faster than they could shoot them down. Bill sat solemnly against the wall; he knew there was nothing that a fishing rod could do in such a closed off space. Ben, on the other hand, stood rigid behind the archers, sword gripped in his hand. Like the other Nether Boys, he was a pretty easy-going guy, but if there was one thing he hated, it was to be left out of a fight.

"He must've collected enough rods by now! Let's go in there and destroy the spawner!"

He made to go down the corridor, but Bill pulled him back.

"No, Ben, not yet," he said calmly. "You can go in there when it's time, but right now nobody has a chance of surviving in there besides Charlie."

"Do you see a better time on the horizon?" Ben asked in exasperation.

Indeed, back in the spawner room, Charlie did not see the fight ending well at all. There were now eight Blazes circling around the room, with the spawner creating them at a rate of two spawned for every one shot down. He had more than enough Blaze rods to craft twelve Blaze powder units required. He sincerely wished that they would hurry up and direct their fire towards the spawner before the potion wore off; he had already been hit by numerous fireballs.

Charlie was momentarily distracted by a shout that he heard from down the corridor. He turned to see what it was, and in that second he was knocked to the ground by a fireball to the back of his head. Dazed, he was wondering whether or not the potion was still working when the crimson-clad figure of Ben burst into the room, turned his sword to the side, and thrust it through the bars of the cage. There was a hissing noise, and the little Blaze inside the cage ceased to exist. Ben dodged the fireballs of the remaining Blazes, and Charlie watched in awe as he took out three of the flying pyros with one well-timed sword slash, not getting hit once. The archers shot down the rest of the Blazes a moment later, and, as if on cue, the red aura around Charlie's body that distinguished him as fire-resistant evaporated, leaving him vulnerable once more.

"Well, that was fun," he said, grinning. Ben pumped his fist in the air and yelled at the top of his lungs "HEEEEELLLLL YEEEE-AAAHHH!!!"

The six players met back in the corridor, and congratulated each other on their spectacular performances against the Blaze spawner. Stan was much more excited on the way back than he was on the way there, seeing as they were finally going to get out of the fiery hell-dimension. They reached the final turn that would lead back to the Nether Boys' house, and were about to turn the corner when they heard voices from ahead.

Ben, who was in the lead, held up is rectangular hand to stop them, and he peered around the corner. An instant later, he pulled his head back around, and he fell to the floor, eyes wide, breathing quickly.

"What is it?" Kat asked.

"What's out there?" Charlie breathed.

Stan remained silent; he was just imagining. He had seen all kinds of terrible things throughout the two worlds of Minecraft, but only one thing could install such instant terror onto the faces of a fugitive.

Ben closed his eyes and grimaced, and Stan knew what he was about to say even before the words left his mouth.

"It's the King's forces," said Ben gravely. "They've found us."

CHAPTER 18: A DARING ESCAPE

Geno looked down at his partner sprawled out across two wool blocks on the Netherack ground. Geno knew from experience that sleeping in a bed in the Nether was a bad idea, and so he had decided that the wool blocks would have to do. Obviously, it would have been better for Becca if she could have lain down in a bed. However, as King Kev had made it clear to RAT1 that they must catch the assassins at all costs, Geno had decided that the unconscious Becca would have to get her rest in the hell dimension. As he thought this, Becca started to stir.

"Oh god..." she moaned, slowly sitting up as she held her stomach. "It hurts so bad..." She noticed Geno sitting there. She looked around and noticed the fires burning everywhere, and she really snapped into focus when she saw the armored men patrolling everywhere with bows in hand. "Geno, what the... what is going on? Where are we?"

"We're in the Nether," he said, "hold on, I'll explain everything." He sat down on a lone Netherack block next to Becca.

"Well, what's the last thing you remember?" Geno asked.

"Ah..." Becca mumbled. "Crap... well, Stan had just hit Leo with a shovel.... And we were going after him... and then... damn... that's it, after that it hurt like hell for an instant, and the next thing I know I'm waking up here... how long have I been out?"

217

"Almost a day," Geno said. "Seriously, though, how do you remember their names? I looked at those pictures of them just as many times as you did, and I know what they look like fine, but I still don't know them by names."

"I still don't know how you haven't gotten that yet, Leo and I both did," she said, condescension dripping from her voice. "But anyways, what happened?"

"Well, it turns out that the girl that flew into the lava…"

"Kat," interrupted Becca automatically.

"Whatever," continued Geno. "Well it turns out that she had a fire resistance potion on her, and so she went back through the lava and jumped out behind you. The little turd stabbed you in the back and flung you into the lava. I dragged you out of the lava and healed you and Leonidas, and while I was doing that they escaped through the portal and broke it.

"After that, I set you up on the bed in your inventory, and Leo stayed to guard you while you rested up. I ran back to the jungle and I lead the legion of troops back here. The medics got to work on fixing up you and Leo, and we fixed the portal. I sent a couple of scouts into the Nether to see where they were. When they came back, they told us that they had just entered into the Nether Fortress.

"So here we are. As far as we know, they're still in the fortress. Thirty men are circling the fortress, ready to take them out if they try to escape. We know better than to try and find them inside that maze, so we're trying a… different tactic." A sly smile broke on his face at these last words.

"And…" said Becca, a wide smile spreading across her face as well; she liked where his conversation was going .

"We're gonna blow the entire fortress off the side of the mountain," Geno said, sounding like a child anticipating Christmas. "Right now Leo and a team of ten guys are laying TNT around the entire structure. When they're done, they're going to detonate the entire fortress, and if they're still in there, they're going to die, and if they try to escape, the snipers will get them."

"Excellent!" Becca chortled; she loved watching stuff blow up, and if her stomach didn't hurt so bad she would insist that she march up there and help them lay down the explosives. "When are they getting back?"

As if in response to her question, Leonidas jumped down from atop the fortress, redstone torch in hand.

"Well, that's it," he grunted. "Dynamite's lied down all over this fort. Soon's they lay the redstone down here, we're ready to blow dis thing up."

"What took you so long?" sneered Geno; it had taken twice as long as he had anticipated for Leonidas and his team to set up the explosives. "Hurry it, up or they'll get away!"

"Hey, at least you don't see me waitin' around here like a useless sheep for your girlfriend to wake up!" snapped Leonidas.

"He's got a point, Geno," said Becca, "It was nice of you to stay here in all, but next time you should go and help lay down the explosives."

Geno grunted and turned away from his friends. Honestly, he thought, sometimes I wonder why I don't just kill both of those two...

The figure in iron armor laid down the final redstone wiring along the ground, and he looked up to Leonidas.

"The wiring is ready sir, and the premise has been evacuated. You may commence detonation when ready."

Leonidas nodded, and the man backed away from the redstone wire, closely followed by Geno, who looked irate as he carried Becca on one shoulder, the latter of whom was still prattling on about how Geno needed to think things through more. Leonidas was about to touch the redstone torch to the wiring when he hesitated for a moment.

Did he really want these players dead? No, he did not. As a matter of fact, though he would be killed for admitting it, he secretly admired the fact that they had enough defiance and courage to try and overthrow the tyrannical king. The server was so much better before the King had become so paranoid...

Leonidas remembered an earlier time, a time of peace, a time of prosperity, when the King was fair and kind to those of all levels. Then came the darker influences to the King, mainly his advisors, Caesar and Charlemagne. They had stolen Leonidas's peaceful life in the desert. At the threat of the death of his family, the King's men forced Leonidas to commit heinous acts for RAT1 until he was completely desensitized to murder.

And now he was about to kill three players that were trying to prevent the duplication of his fate to other young players of Elementia.

All of this ran through his head in less than a half a second. Leonidas wished he could refuse, but he knew the consequences, and he knew that there was nothing he could do to prevent it from happening. There was no hope for him anymore.

Leonidas touched the redstone torch to the wire, and the secret pain that he had kept bottled up was projected in the tear that trickled down the side of his blocky cheek as the entire Nether Fortress exploded in a shockwave of fire.

* * * * *

Stan was a half a mile underground, but he was still seriously shaken when the sound of the mega-explosion above him went off. He had to give credit to Charlie; it was his quick thinking and mining instincts that had gotten them deep enough to be safe from the explosion that was created by RAT1. He knew now that they were being hunted by the assassin team known as Royal Assassin Team 1, or RAT1, which was composed of sword master Geno, demolitions expert Becca, and archery prodigy Leonidas. Apparently, according to the Nether Boys, they were a highly esteemed search-and-destroy group that the King sent out to destroy particularly evasive or dangerous targets.

Well, thought Stan as Charlie began to tunnel upwards, he was honored that the king believed that he and his friends were a threat worthy of addressing by the most highly-acclaimed assassins in Elementia, but this also came with a problem. Namely, the king believed that he and his friends were a threat worthy of addressing by the most highly-acclaimed assassins in Elementia. If these guys were willing to follow them all over two worlds, Stan guessed that he and his friends would have a pretty hard time finding their way to the End with these assassins in pursuit of them.

For the time being, however, Stan thought as Charlie hollowed out a little Netherack room for them to plan their next move in; they had to focus on getting out of the Nether. Stan voiced this opinion to the others as soon as Charlie had finished the room and set up the torches.

"We have all the Blaze Rods we need, so the next thing we need to do is get out of here, and break the portal. That way," he reasoned, "we'll be able to start hunting the Endermen, and they'll be stuck in the Nether, at least until they figure a way out. We can use that time to get as far away from the portal as possible."

"Good thinking Stan," agreed Kat. "Now that we've got people after us, we've got to get to the End as quickly as possible."

"Yes, I concur," said Charlie, nodding. "We'll stop back by our old house to get our stuff and pick up Rex and Lemon, and then we'll go off into the desert. We'll keep moving around so they won't find us and we'll hunt Endermen at the same time."

Kat nodded, and Stan said, "Okay then." He turned to the Nether Boys, who had been huddled together and whispering aside from the others. "So what about you guys?" he asked. "What are you guys going to do when you get out of the Nether?"

"Well, firstly, we're going to kiss the sand beneath our feet..." said Bill.

"Then, we're going to breathe in air that's under 80 degrees Fahrenheit..." said Bob.

"And then, perhaps, build a shrine to the clouds and swear that we're never going to take them for granted again..." said Ben.

"Okay," said Kat, rolling her eyes, "we get it; you're going to be very happy to be back in the Overworld. But what are you going to do? Long term, I mean."

"Oh," said Bill. "Why didn't you just say that?" Charlie sighed.

"Well, we were just saying that we want to go back to the Adorian Village to help you guys organize the rebellion."

"Really?" asked Stan, his heart lifting.

"Absolutely," said Ben. "You keep your end of the deal and get us out of this hell, and we've got nothing to lose by helping you guys out."

"Alright, well, thanks guys," said Charlie. "Now, it's only a matter of time before they realize that we weren't killed in that explosion, and after they do realize that, they're going to look everywhere, including underground. Now, if my calculations are correct, we should be located right under the cave that has the portal in it. If they got in here, that means that they've fixed the portal themselves, so that shouldn't be a problem anymore.

"So here's what I want everyone to do," and they all leaned in to listen; Charlie had clearly thought this through. "I want Kat and Bob to jump out of the hole that I'm going to make above us, and be prepared to shoot down anybody in the vicinity. Stan, Ben and I will run towards the portal, and we'll attack anybody that gets in the way of us. However, we shouldn't have that many people to deal with, because I want Bill to use his fishing rod to fling any people between us and the portal out of the way so that Bob and Kat can shoot them. Any questions?" Nobody had any.

"Okay then, get ready," said Charlie. Kat and Bob drew their bows and arrows out, Stan drew his shovel, Bill drew his fishing rod and Ben drew his sword. Charlie took his pickaxe and, trying to conceal his heart pounding within his chest, he gave three swift blows to the Netherack block above him. It shattered, and Kat and Bob burst out of the hole, quickly followed by Stan and the others.

Stan had to do a double take at the scenery to truly believe their good luck. He had thought that this was a daring escape, certain to be met with some opposition, but there were no guards around the portal, which was indeed glowing purple and complete once again. Stan looked back as he dashed towards the portal. He could see five men guarding the mouth of the cave, but the six players were silent as they dashed towards the portal, and the guards could not hear them.

Stan was still giddy at their good luck as Charlie dove through the active portal. He was closely followed by Ben, and he himself was about to dive through when a figure stepped around the edge of the portal and into his path.

Stan didn't even think or look at the figure as he beat it senseless over the head with the shovel. The figure fell, and it gave a squeal of pain. Stan was stepping into the portal when he realized that something odd had happened. Why would it squeal?

Stan looked down at the unconscious body and realized in horror that he had not just knocked out a guard; this was a Zombie Pigman, whose skull he had just crushed. He looked around in terror for the hoard of angry undead warriors charging at him, lusting for his blood; there were none, as this Pigman had apparently been alone. However, he did see an even scarier sight.

The sound of the Pigman's death had alerted the guards to his presence. The five of them were now charging towards the portal, shooting arrows as they did. Stan became aware of Kat, Bill and Bob diving through the portal, and he did too. He experienced the horrible squeezing sensation for the few seconds, and then tumbled out onto the sand in the dawn's early light.

"They're coming though!" Stan yelled to his five friends, who lay panting on the sand. Stan raised his shovel and began beating the bottom right block of the obsidian portal, and Charlie joined him, as did everybody else. Through the purple particles, they saw the five guards rushing towards the portal, coming to attack them. At the head of the pack was a man that had the skin of a cow, but with iron boots, leggings and helmet, and an iron axe in his hand. Stan punched faster and faster to break the black block that was so frustratingly solid, and the block broke into several useless chunks at the same moment that the cow-man burst through the portal and set his axe on the nearest target, Kat.

The other five players stepped out of the war zone as Kat and the barbaric warrior battled, their iron weapons moving as fast as silver spirits in the dim pink light. It was obvious that Kat was the superior fighter; she remained calm, while the axe-fighter's wild attacks became increasingly desperate. One false axe swipe later and the axe flew out of the man's hand and skidded across the ground, coming to a stop at the base of the broken Nether portal.

Kat kicked the man to the ground and raised her sword. She held the sword above her head and looked down into the man's face. He was lying sprawled on the ground, breathing heavily from the kick that Kat had inflicted upon his chest. Kat raised the sword.

"Kat," said Stan suddenly, putting his hand on her shoulder, "don't. He's unarmed, what good will it do?"

225

"It'll stop him from ratting us out to the King!" said Ben.

"If we let him go, it'll just come back to bite us!" cried Bill incredulously.

Kat's sword was shaking. The look on her face showed pained confusion.

"Kat," said Charlie. "Just don't..."

But his response was cut off when Kat's sword found its home in the cow-man's chest.

CHAPTER 19: THE TOWN OF BLACKSTONE

The player's items burst out around him in a circle, indicating the death that Stan already knew to be true. Kat pulled the sword out of the man, and she looked down at the body in disdain. She then looked over at Stan and Charlie, both of whose faces showed disbelief and horror at the murder of an unarmed player by their friend.

"I'm sorry," said Kat, and Stan couldn't tell who she was talking to, him and Charlie, or the dead player. "I am so, so... *sorry*," and at the last word her voice cracked and she sunk to her knees and erupted into tears.

Bill walked up to the weeping form of Kat and knelt down besides her. "I'm sorry, Kat, but these are the tough things about war. It's eat or be eaten; if you had let him go, than he would have followed us, and relayed our position back to the King's forces, and we'd be captured within the next half a week."

Kat had stopped crying, and she looked up to face Ben. "I know that," she sniffled, wiping her eyes on her T-shirt sleeve. "But it doesn't make it any easier."

"I know that," said Ben. "You know, when I first joined Elementia, I had to kill my old sword fighting mentor to save Bill's life. I realize that killing people, even if it is in self-defense, is hard. But if we are truly going to overthrow the King, then there are certain things that are going to have to be done. We are going to have to kill people to get to where we need to get; that is a fact. But we'll be saving hundreds more, and making life better tenfold for thousands. You understand, don't you, Kat?"

Kat stood up, breathing deeply. "I understand. You're right Ben, thank you."

The two players hugged. Three of the other players looked on solemnly, but Stan looked away. He was filled with an overpowering feeling of disgust, and right then and there, he swore that he would never kill a player unless he himself was in mortal peril, no exceptions.

After the moment of peace was over, the Nether Boys stood back as Stan, Kat and Charlie looked through the stuff that the player had been carrying. Stan picked up the iron axe, relieved to finally have his choice of weapon back, while Kat pulled on the iron helmet, leggings and boots. Charlie picked up everything else: apples, fire charges, TNT blocks, redstone dust, a redstone torch, and a compass.

"So, do you guys know what you're going to do now?" asked Bob.

"Yep," replied Stan. "Thank you for all your help. We'll rendezvous with you guys and the others back at the Adorian Village after we've made our way to the End."

"Alright, see you guys then," said Ben, and the three boys turned and ran back towards the looming jungle trees in the far distance. As they were running off, Ben turned around again one last time. "And be careful in the End! I've never been there, but I hear it's way more dangerous than the Nether!"

"We will! Thanks!" cried Charlie, and the Nether Boys ran off into the distance. As they did so, Stan, Kat and Charlie ran in the opposite direction, back towards their old campsite. Even without the compass, Charlie knew the way back, and they had reached the sand abode before the sun was at its highest point in the sky. Needless to say, the animals were very happy to see their owners again.

"Hey, boy! How've you been!" laughed Kat as Rex pounced on her and started licking her face, and she fed him some rotten flesh she'd picked up from a passing zombie. Charlie stroked Lemon behind the ears, and he purred affectionately, rubbing up against Charlie's hand. Stan went over to the chest and took some select things out of it, readying themselves for departure. They had decided as they walked over that they would leave some non-essential things in the chest to give the illusion that the base was still in use. Stan put the book on entering the Nether and End, and the Ender Chest into his inventory; the rest of the items they decided to keep in place. They also decided to leave their beds. As they would be traveling a lot, they would have no need for them.

The three players resolved to spend the time until dark, when the Endermen came out, to go hunting for food. All three players went separate directions, but stayed fairly close to the sinkhole. Stan went to the far side of the hole, and he saw a herd of cows wandering around the oasis where they had gotten the water for the obsidian, eating the grass and drinking the water. He walked up to them and started downing them with his axe, one after another. He was chasing the one cow with an axe, ready to kill it, when he noticed something that he hadn't before. About twenty blocks in front of him was a straight line of railroad tracks, stretching in both directions as far as the eye could see, with one end headed towards the jungle and the other headed out into the desert.

Intrigued, Stan walked closer to examine the railroad tracks, but he stopped when he heard a rumbling sound coming from the jungle end of the railroad, and he noticed something in the distance coming down the tracks. Fearing it to be the enemy, Stan dove into a shallow trench near the edge of the tracks that was deep enough to conceal him yet still allowing him to see.

The train passed Stan at high speed; it consisted of seven mine carts, four of which containing chests, two of which containing what appeared to be furnaces. In the remaining mine cart, which was situated in front of the two furnace cars and behind the chest cars, sat a man with pale skin in an army uniform. The train thundered past and into the distance; Stan was incredibly curious as to where this man was going. Resolving to be back before Kat and Charlie noticed he was gone, he ran down the railroad tracks after the train.

The train was much faster than he was, and before long it had disappeared from view, but Stan kept running, following the tracks. He was wondering how he was ever going to catch up to this man when he heard another rumbling behind him; a lone mine car with a furnace was chugging down the line, spewing black smoke as the two before it had. Stan supposed that this cart must have fallen off another train; he had noticed that on the train he had seen before, the carts weren't fastened to each other very well. Willing to accept the gift, Stan let the mine cart catch up to him and he jumped on, riding it at full speed towards the end of the line.

The sun was showing it was about noon by the time Stan saw the buildings in the distance. They were simple wooden huts, and they were the lone structures in the middle of the endless miles of desert. Wondering why in God's name anybody would want to build their house in such a barren land, Stan jumped off of the cart just before it entered what appeared to be a railroad station.

He snuck over behind two chests, and he noticed the train that he had seen before. The man that had been riding it stepped out, and he appeared to be talking with a man that was dressed like Abraham Lincoln who had a distressed and desperate look on his face. Eager to hear what was happening, Stan crawled underneath the station platform so that he was right underneath the two men and could hear every word they were saying.

"...is no excuse for you not producing your quota," said the soldier in an angry tone.

"But, sir, please, as I've been trying to explain, our miners have run into problems," responded another voice, which sounded stressed out. "We were mining out the areas that you had requested, and we hit a rather large lava spring, we are going to have to slow production until we can fix it, otherwise the environment would not be safe..."

"Do you think the King gives a damn about safety!?" barked the soldier. "He needs all the resources he can get his hands on, especially in these troubled times, for as I'm sure you're aware, there is an assassin on the loose..."

Stan gulped; he sincerely regretted coming this close to the soldier now.

"...and the King needs all available resources to put him out of commission! And it is my responsibility to make sure that the town of Blackstone, as Elementia's primary coal producer, generates more than its share, not less! If there isn't enough coal, the King gets angry with me, and ergo, I get angry with you! This is

231

your last warning, Mayor. If you fail to produce your quota one more time... well, you can imagine..."

There was a clinking sound and the mayor cried out in terror. Stan jumped up to come to his aid, while forgetting that he was under the wooden platform; he hit his head on the underside of the plank above him and he saw stars. When his eyes came back into focus, he saw the soldier leaving on his train, and he became aware in horror that the block of wood above him had been burned away; the clinking had been a steel ring against flint! And it was a wooden station...

The mayor was doing all he could to punch out the flames, but they were spreading too fast. Throwing caution to the wind, Stan stood up through the hole and helped the mayor punch out the flames. The mayor's eyes widened in surprise, but he did not question Stan's sudden appearance, and was simply grateful of the help he had miraculously received; within a minute all of the flames were extinguished.

"Thank you, kind stranger," said the mayor, bowing his head in respect. "Without your bravery, we may have lost one of the few respectable buildings we have left in this city."

"No problem," said Stan, "I'm glad to be of help. So what is this place, exactly?"

"This, my friend, is the humble town of Blackstone, population twenty three, and Elementia's chief producer of coal," replied the mayor. "And may I ask where you come from, my good sir?"

So he doesn't recognize me, thought Stan. That's good; generally attention doesn't work too well in my favor. "I've lived in a lot of places," Stan said. "Let's just say I get around."

"Well, if you are in need of a place to stay for a while, we would be happy to have you here," said the mayor. "It is rare that anyone shows such kindness to the people of this town, and on the rare occasion that it does, they deserve to be rewarded."

"That is very kind of you sir," said Stan, "but I have to return to my friends by nighttime. Do you by any chance have anything to eat?" asked Stan; he had had only an apple since breakfast, and he was very hungry.

The man smiled; there were wrinkles in his blocky cheeks. "Of course, sir. Right this way. He walked out of the station, followed by Stan, and they exited the station and began walking down the main street of the town.

Stan had never seen such a pathetic-looking excuse for an important town in his life. The unpaved main street was the only street, and on either side it were ten or so small houses, so patched together with sand, dirt, cobblestone and sandstone that it was impossible to tell what the original material was. Stan noticed that on the sides of a few of these houses were small wheat gardens which were surrounded with fences. Against the front of these houses leaned players.

There was no way to describe the look of these players except broken. Their heads hung, looking towards the ground, with the sun glinting off the metal helmets on their heads. Most of them had iron pickaxes dangling down from their hands. They all wore leather armor everywhere except their heads, which were obscured by the helmets, so it was impossible to tell them apart at a glance. When they sensed Stan walking into the town, a few of them glanced up. Stan could see much pain reflected in their faces, which were scarred in a variety of states, and the players projected a defensive caution at this new player, young and whole, who had the audacity to waltz into their village unannounced.

"Just ignore them," mumbled the mayor, sensing Stan's unease. "They're just tired and upset from all the extra work the soldiers have been forcing them to do lately. They're looking for a fight; they need to take their anger out on someone. So don't look anyone directly in the eye."

Stan took the mayor's advice and looked straight forward towards the end of the street, keeping his hand cautiously but subtly close to the wooden handle of the iron axe dangling at his side by his belt. Keen to avoid eye contact with the temperamental miners, Stan forced himself to focus on the building at the end of the street. It was the largest, and by far the most well-kept building. It was made of brick, and it was a large, rectangular complex with no windows and two side by side metal doors on the front. Unlike the patchy houses that held the miners, this building seemed to be in a state of good repair. Stan inquired the mayor as to its purpose.

"That is the government's storehouse. They come by rail to this village every other day to collect the coal quota, but all other materials, including cobblestone, iron, and even buckets of lava from the sources of springs that we encounter, go in there, along with any other ambiguous blocks we find.'

"Did you mean to say that the army controls the flow of materials leaving this village through that storehouse?" asked Stan; he was gaining a pretty good idea of what was happening in this crippled town.

"Yes. Though nobody dares admit it out of either fear or a stoppage of caring, the government leeches all the resources out of this town, and never gives anything back in return. If some blocks of

234

our house are stolen, we have to smuggle cobblestone blocks up from the mines to repair them, an offense punishable by death. Our miners have actually gotten into fights and killed each other over accusations of stealing parts of each others' houses."

Stan sighed in realization that he was correct in his suspicions that the government's oppression of the people extended this far into the desert. His brain was beginning to formulate a plan of how to liberate these people from the bonds of the King when they arrived at the house directly adjacent to the warehouse that read Mayor on a sign next to the front door. This house was a little bit larger than the other houses, though in an equal state of disrepair. The mayor pushed open the wooden door and they walked inside.

The inside of the house had a wooden floor, walls made of the same materials as the outside, suggesting the walls being one block thick, and windows, some of which still had glass panes. The entire house consisted of one room, which had a crafting table, a furnace, two double chests, two chairs and two beds. The entire room had a defeated air to it, and at each step the floorboards creaked in seeming sounds of despair.

"Nice place you've got here," Stan lied through his teeth, as the mayor grabbed two steaks from his chest and handed one to Stan. "I notice there are two beds here, and two chairs. Does somebody else live here with you?"

In apparent response to his question, a coughing issued from a hole in one corner of the room that Stan had not noticed before. From it emerged the most disheveled player that Stan had seen thus far. He was dressed in a white lab coat with grey pants, and his grey hair stuck up in all directions. He would have look akin to Albert Einstein if he didn't look so beaten. His face was sallow and sunken-in, he had an unearthly stench that Stan could smell from across the room, and he was completely covered in coal dust that was mixed with what appeared to be shiny, red material that Stan identified as redstone dust. He held two bottles in his hands, one of which was empty, one of which held a liquid of sickly blue-grey color. The man gave an almighty belch before addressing the mayor.

"Hey, Turkey, we're running low on SloPo, when do you think the nomads'll be back?" his voice was slurred and giddy, reminding Stan of a man who was deep into the stages of delirium. "Are the nomads gonna be back tomorrow? They'll be back tomorrow, and then I'll get my SloPo. I do love me muh Slopo. But, wait, I'm gonna need money! Turkey, remind me to get some money later tonight, okay, old buddy, Turkey old friend?"

At that point, the player stopped his conversation with himself and noticed that he and "Turkey" (who Stan could only assume was the mayor) were not alone in the room. The man turned his dilated pupils to Stan, and inquired the mayor. "Who's the new meat, Turkey? He another new miner to come from, from, from the Elementia prisons? Hehehe, good luck, little buddy, you ain't gonna last two days down in that ravine!" For some reason, the player seemed to find this extraordinarily funny, and he rolled around on the ground, banging his fist on the floor to the point where one of the wooden planks actually broke off.

The mayor simply walked over to the hysterical player on the floor and calmly said, "Mecha11, you are hereby sentenced to labor in the coal mines of Blackstone, in the Ender Desert, for as long as you should remain in this server."

The effect of these enigmatic words on the player on the floor was instantaneous. He immediately got up and got to his

236

knees, and he started crying, and he got out through his tears, "As you wish, my King." Then, without warning, he stood up, shook his head, and his face looked confused. Then he appeared as if something was dawning on him, and he looked at the mayor. "Damn you, mayor, why do you have to do that?"

"Well," the mayor replied agitatedly, "That's the only way that I can get you out of your trance when you're SloPoed without a golden apple, and there's somebody I want you to meet."

Stan, who was extremely confused as to the events that had just transpired, nodded politely and tried to keep the look of confusion and fear off his face as the man was introduced as Mecha11, head of Redstone Mining Pioneering. The name rang a bell in Stan's memory.

"Wait, *you're* Mecha11?" he asked, dumbfounded that this wreck of a player was once in the same tier of people as the Apothecary and the Nether Boys. "I've heard of you! My name is Stan2012, and I've met the Apothecary and the Exploration Chiefs, Bill, Ben and Bob!"

A flash of recognition crossed Mecha11's face, but it soon returned to its uninterested state as he collapsed into one o the wooden chairs. "Well, I'm glad to hear that they're still chugging. And speaking of chugging," he said, and he made to drink more of the potion in his hand, but he mayor slapped his hand to the side.

"Mechanist, please, don't be rude! This young man helped to stop the army from burning our train station to the ground, he deserves your respect."

"Yeah, great job, kid," the Mechanist sneered in a sarcastic drawl. "You made it so that we still have a gateway for the army to keep taking advantage of these people who've already wasted their lives slaving away in the Blackstone mines. So you'll forgive me if I don't thank you by offering you a free muffin."

"Shut up, Mechanist!" whispered the Mayor in urgent tones.

"What? You hate the army, the King, just the same as everybody else!"

"Yes, but there are those who you should *not voice that opinion in front of*!"

There was a moment of silence, and it lasted until Stan realized that they were referring to him.

"What, me? You think *I'm* a spy for the King?"

"He's sent them in before," said the mayor, still keeping a keen eye on Stan for any sudden movements.

"No, trust me, I am not with the King," said Stan, and then, a thought occurring to him, he decided to take a huge gamble. "As a matter of fact, I intend to overthrow him myself."

The Mechanist laughed. "That's cute," he said. "You really think that you're capable of overthrowing the King, don't you."

Stan was taken aback; it was not the first time that his plot had received skepticism, but there was something in the Mechanist's voice that made Stan want to hear what he had to say.

"Yes, as a matter of fact I do," he replied firmly. "I've already raised an army, and as soon as we gather the necessary supplies, which we have access to, we are going to march into Element City, kill the King and his officials, and reform Elementia into a better place."

The mayor's eyes had simply widened a little when Stan first mentioned his idea to overthrow the King, but at this latest description, he was actually running around the room from window to window, checking to see that there were no soldiers listening in. The Mechanist, completely unconcerned with being overheard, threw back his head and laughed again.

"You really do think that you can do it! That's cute." Stan found the condescension in his voice infuriating. "But let give you a piece of sound advice, kid: GIVE IT THE HELL UP!" He shouted this with such power and volume that Stan actually jumped, and the mayor whipped around with an iron pickaxe drawn, ready for an impending attack, and though none came, the Mechanist continued to talk in an unnecessarily loud voice.

"The King's forces are spread, far and wide, all over this server. All of them are equally as cruel and brutal as he is, and there are hundreds of them. The King is not an operator anymore, but he still has an almost limitless cache of resources from the days when he was! Also..."

"Hey, I already know all of that!" interjected Stan. "And let me just point out that I intend to tap into one of those caches in order to gain the supplies for my army!"

"My God, kid, you have no clue what you're talking about; because it's not just the King you have to worry about! You realize that about a third of the citizen population is heavily aligned with the king; he has a double standard for the upper class! My point is, even if you do manage to take down the king, which is an impossible dream itself, you'll never be able to completely destroy the king's evil ideals."

"You don't understand!" cried Stan. "I've met people, I've talked to them, you don't understand just how much people hate the King, and want him dead."

"Ha!" sneered the Mechanist, an ugly look taking to his face. "The irony that you lecture me of how people hate the King! You think I don't know that? Listen to me, kid, and I'll give you the full story of what King Kev has done to me personally! I was the head of Redstone Experimentations back in the old kingdom. It was me who designed Element City's monorail system, it was me who wired King Kev's entire castle, and it was me that designed all of the weapons systems that guards the King's castle from invaders like you. For the love of God, I invented the TNT Cannon for him!

"And how does the King repay me? He banishes me to spend life in this desert hell, just because people who hated him copied my weapons systems and used them against him! If there is anybody who wants the King dead, its people like me, like the Apothecary, like the Exploration Chiefs, who were close to the King, and who he banished from his kingdom!"

"And that doesn't make you want to want to try and take control of Elementia from him?" asked Stan, his eyes flashing with passionate rage at the King and at the old inventor across from him who was being so difficult. "For the record, the Apothecary and the Exploration Chiefs have both agreed to join my army."

"Then they're bigger fools than you!" said the Apothecary with a joyless shout of laughter. "They ought to know that nothing good comes from rebelling against the King's supreme authority. If you were wise, you'd do the same thing as me, and try and make the best you can out of the world that the King has created. Me, I love making redstone mechanisms, and so I put by skills to use here by making piston machines to make deep-earth mining easier.

240

"I hate the fact that I'm helping the King by making mining for him easier, and so I don't feel guilty when I get SloPo from gambling with the Nomads that pass through here," and he raised his bottle of blue-grey liquid, leading Stan to realize that it was the Minecraft equivalent of alcohol. "I've made myself a life out here. Thanks to the King, it's not happy or fulfilling, but I can't change it, so why not make it as nice for myself as possible?"

And with that, the Mechanist took another swig of SloPo. The effect was instantaneous, and his head fell back and rolled to the side, passed out.

Stan was filled with a new level of infuriation at both the King and the Mechanist; he could never forgive the Mechanist for just giving up on life after it got hard and not even trying to fight back. On the other hand, his new knowledge at the kinds of mistreatment that the King had extended to even his friends, who had trusted and served him, imparted in Stan a furious desire to do something drastic against the King. He looked down at the mayor, who had been sitting in his chair, trying to block out the noise with his mind throughout the whole argument.

"Mayor, I need you to gather all the miners in the village in front of the warehouse. I have an announcement to make to them," said Stan.

The mayor stood up and looked Stan in the eye. "If I do what you say, will I regret it?"

"I sure hope not," replied Stan as he walked out the door.

He had noticed that there was a wooden platform in front of the brick wall of the warehouse, which was illuminated by torchlight. It was a perfect podium for the message he was going to try and get across to the desperate coal miners. By the time the sky was pink and the sun was about to disappear under the desert skyline behind the warehouse, all of the almost twenty five coal miners had congregated around the wooden platform. When they were all settled down, Stan stood up and began to speak.

"People of Blackstone! My name is Stan2012. Many of you may have heard rumors that an assassin has tried to murder Elementia's dictator, King Kev, during his last proclamation to the public. I am here to tell you that that assassin was none other than myself."

There were a few surprised intakes of breath from the crowd, and Stan saw a few miners move their hands and firmly grab their pickaxes, unsure of what was going to happen next.

"Since that incident, I have been on the run. Many have asked me what my motivation was for trying to kill one of the most powerful men on the server." That part was a lie, but Stan thought it sounded impressive, and it was a good line to segue into the next part of his speech. "I am here to tell you that I tried to kill the King because he is an evil tyrant that needs to be brought down!"

A few miners looked around, half-prepared to see the King's forces ready to attack them for treason, but most of the miners were staring intently at Stan, nodding with respect on their faces.

"I am currently raising an army against King Kev and I am going to lead this army to victory by taking control of the King's castle in Element City! I intend to kill the King, along with any high officers that refuse to surrender. The days of the present terrorist regime are numbered, and the King's Elementia will fall, to be replaced by an Elementia where all men are given equal opportunities, and slavery, as is so commonplace in the kingdom now, including you all here, is nonexistent.

"Many of you are probably wondering how I have the audacity to talk out against the King, when the possibility is high that I may be turned over to the authorities. And the reason for that is, I do not fear the King! I accept that the King is a powerful enemy, and he has resources that will make it easier said than done to bring him to justice. However, and this is the reason that I am willing to speak so freely, I believe that we have resources too. I say we because I am positive that there are more of you in this village that hate the king then are sympathetic with him. If we all band together, we have a realistic chance to take the King down!"

"I am going to walk over to the train station now, and all those who would like to join my army and take down the King with me should follow me. Anybody who remains, I will fight and kill in order to prevent them from telling information of my plan to the King. However, I also expect anybody willing to join me to help me fight against those who are unwilling. This is your test, people of Blackstone. You may join me and fight those who did not join me, or you may not join me and fight those who did. Those who wish to join me have sixty seconds to walk over to the station, starting now."

And with that, Stan jumped off the platform and ran through the crowd of people (who stepped to the side to let him through; he was vaguely reminded of the crowd on the day he shot the King). He stood at the threshold of the train station and turned around.

Five seconds ticked by, and nobody moved. Stan wasn't surprised; he hadn't expected anybody to make up their mind right away. Then ten seconds ticked away, and then fifteen, then twenty. When thirty seconds went by and nobody had joined Stan, he drew his axe. He had promised to fight anybody who didn't join him, and it looked like he was going to be in for one hell of a fight. At forty seconds Stan was starting to panic when there was a shuffling in the crowd.

One single miner, who looked similar to Stan although blackened with coal dust, who was wearing an iron helmet and holding a stone pickaxe, walked across the empty expanse towards Stan. Another followed, and then the entire mass of miners seemed to come over and join Stan's side.

By the time the sixty seconds were up, there was not a soul left on the side of the warehouse. Every single miner had abandoned the building that contained the materials that the government had claimed for their own. They now stood at the train station, ready to partake in Stan's quest to overthrow the King.

The mayor walked up through the crowd to talk to Stan. "Thank you, Stan," said the mayor, tears in his eyes. "You've inspired these people to fight back, and you've inspired me to lead my people to join in your army. Tell me what to do; I am at your service." And the Mayor bowed his head in respect to Stan.

The two talked for a few minutes, and they worked out what the plan was. The mayor was going to lead the miners of Blackstone down the railroad tracks and they would follow these until they reached the Adorian Village. There, they would tell Jayden and Sally and company that they met up with Stan2012 in the Ender Desert and were there for the militia. The mayor was convinced that the miners could put their skills to use in the Adorian Village's mine, gathering blocks for use in the war effort. Also, the miners were apparently very good pickaxe fighters. Stan, meanwhile, was given a powered mine cart and some coal that would get him back to his friends, where he could continue his quest to enter the End.

Stan and the mayor shook hands, and Stan was about to leave when he thought of something. He walked down the main street, where the miners were preparing for departure by emptying their houses of their meager possessions. He passed the warehouse which was now being looted for supplies by several of the miners. At last he came to the shared house of the mayor and the Mechanist. He opened the door, and the Mechanist was sitting in the chair, no bottles in hand, apparently waiting for Stan.

"Well, congratulations, kid," said the Mechanist. He was not smiling. "You just convinced twenty-two more people to go on a suicide mission. Well done."

Stan controlled his anger, and he looked at the Mechanist with a face of determined calm. "You know," he said, "we could sure use an expert of redstone mechanics in the war effort. And if we win, you could reclaim your position as Elementia's chief redstone inventor. What do you say, Mechanist? Are you coming?"

The Mechanist looked down at the ground for a few moments, his eyebrows scrunched up, clearly trying to decide. Then he looked up at Stan, looked him in the eye, and gave him a solid shake of the head.

Stan, resigning himself to the fact that this player would not join him, turned to walk out the door. He was just stepping down the steps when something hit him in the back of the head, knocking him down to the street. He spun around, axe in hand, ready to confront the Mechanist who had attacked him, but instead noticed a book that had landed next to him. He picked it up, and in the dim light from the setting sun he read the title.

It said, *Full Schematics of Element Castle's Redstone Defenses*, by Mecha11.

Stan, amazed, looked up at the Mechanist, who was standing in the door way, looking down at Stan with a sad expression on his face. "It's your funeral, kid," he grunted, and he slowly walked back into the house, pulling the wooden door shut behind him.

Stan looked in awe at the book; the book which would allow them to safely predict the locations of all of the King's hidden automated traps in his courtyard whilst attacking. He only allowed himself a minute to admire the Mechanist's gift, however, for the sun had just disappeared behind the desert skyline, and he could already see zombies and skeletons roaming around in the vast sandy expanse.

Stan ran back to the train station, where the miners were gathered in a huddle, preparing for their journey down the rail line. Stan shouted a hasty goodbye to the mayor, who waved back in reply, and he hopped into the mine cart and inserted some coal into the furnace of the engine behind him. The effect was instantaneous; the furnace ignited, and the train took off at terrific pace.

Stan watched as the dim lights of the town of Blackstone disappeared in the distance behind him. He was rushing down the rails at high speed, and he was just finishing eating a pork chop that one of the miners had given him when an arrow hit glanced off his iron chestplate, nearly knocking him off the mine cart. He looked ahead and saw a skeleton, standing in the middle of the track, drawing another arrow back. He deflected this arrow with his sword and, having an idea, stuffed his second and third pieces of coal into the engine. The engine gave a puff of black smoke, and the train picked up speed. Before the skeleton was able to fire its third arrow, the train slammed into it and the monster exploded into thousands of white fragments.

Stan sighed in relief, but he would have repealed that sigh if it were possible after seeing that the track in front of him was packed with the biggest swarm of zombies he had ever seen. There must have been at least twenty of them. And what's more, he could see the sinkhole about twenty blocks behind them; he could only run over a few zombies before he would have to jump out of the vehicle and face the rest on foot.

CHAPTER 20: THE MONSTER SLAYER

As the train sped towards the zombies, they turned their attention towards it and started mindlessly lumbering towards Stan. Stan stood up in the train car, his axe raised, ready to fight off any zombies that tried to immediately attack him. The train hit the zombie hoard, and it plowed through the center, automatically disintegrating about five of the twenty fiends. Stan jumped out of the car and ran back towards the sinkhole.

He slid down the sandy cliff with the zombies in hot pursuit, and as he did, he saw Charlie, Kat and Rex, outside engaged in a battle with two spiders and a skeleton. The spiders were engaged and dying fast, but the skeleton was far out of Stan's friends' range. He raised his axe and threw it at the skeleton, clobbering it with one blow. At the same time, Kat stabbed the spider's eyes out and Charlie cut open the arachnid's stomach with his pickaxe, tossing the corpse aside. Stan snatched up his axe from the dead skeleton and joined his friends.

"Hey, he lives! Good to see you, Stan!" exclaimed Charlie, smiling.

Rex jumped up to lick him, Lemon rubbed up against his leg and purred, and Kat asked him where he'd been.

"Boy, guys, do I have a ton to tell you, but we've got other problems at the moment!" Stan yelled. The wave of zombies had started to pour into the sinkhole. Stan and Kat stared at the rotten green wave with dropped jaws of horror.

"What did you do!?" screamed Kat.

"I don't know, they just spawned! We've gonna have to fight them!" Stan yelled over the moaning.

"We can't possibly take down a zombie hoard that size, and we can't go back inside either, the monsters already broke the door down!" exclaimed Charlie, panicking.

"We'll have to try," yelled Stan, and he killed the first undead mob with three swift axe blows to the chest. Kat, Charlie and Rex all rushed in to fight as well.

It was mayhem; every zombie they killed was replaced by what appeared to be two more flooding in from above the sink hole. Stan gritted his teeth, and as he hacked and slashed his way through the hoard, all he could think was, where are they all coming from?

In time, despite the rapid hacking, slashing, stabbing, and biting of the three players and dog, the unending swarm of undead pushed them back against the wall of the sinkhole. Stan was starting to think about giving up from exhaustion and the sheer overwhelming number of zombies when he heard a scream from above.

"YAAAAAAH-HOOOOOO!" the man yelled as he landed in front of the players. There was a metallic clang from his boots as he yelled, which was odd because they were made of leather and glowing. Stan guessed that they had been enchanted to absorb fall damage. The player whipped out a diamond sword that was also glowing. As the zombies closed in on him, he swung his sword back behind his head with his right hand, and he swung it around him, cutting every zombie in the front row of the onslaught.

Stan felt a powerful wave of energy emit from the glowing blade, and he could tell that it was no ordinary sword. Indeed, all of the zombies in the front row were knocked back by the invisible shockwave emitted by the sword, falling into the ones behind them and reducing the entire zombie attack to a squirming pile of disorientation.

The player turned to face Stan and the others. He was dressed exactly the same as Stan, the standard look for Minecraft, but he had dark shades that covered his eyes. "Hey, guys!" he exclaimed; he had a heavy New York accent. "I thought you guys could use some help, so I'm gonna help you fight these freaking mobs off. Just FYI, there was on old dungeon caved in next to the train tracks with a Zombie Spawner inside. Don't worry though, I destroyed it, the zombies'll stop coming. All that we have to do is to fight off the rest of these zombies down here, and we're home free. Don't say anything, just fight, and then we'll talk."

The player turned around, sheathed his diamond sword, and drew another one from the other side of his belt, this one made of iron, but with a distinct red glow to it. Stan was too amazed by this savior that had descended from nowhere to question him, or, at least, until he and his friends were out of immediate danger. The zombie hoard was back on its feet by now, and Stan rushed in to greet the zombies, exhilarated by the fact that there would be no more of them coming.

Though he was busy bringing down zombie after zombie with his axe, Stan couldn't help but be amazed with the capacity for fighting that this mysterious player displayed. It was soon apparent what the glowing red enchantment on the iron sword was. The first time the player slashed a zombie across the chest, the zombie burst into flames, as if the night were over and the sun had come back up. This sword with the Fire enchantment cut through zombie after zombie with a level of sword fighting expertise that Stan had never seen before, with the unfortunate victims becoming lifeless, flaming corpses on the ground.

By the time they were down to the last five zombies, Stan, Kat, Charlie and even Rex had stopped fighting and simply stood out of the player's way. They watched in awe as the player stabbed through one zombie, threw it into two more and then rolled over to the three Zombies and killed them all with one downward thrust. He spun around and parried another zombie's attacking arm to the side, cutting it in two at the waste as he ducked under the monster's armpit. Finally, he swung his arm backwards and decapitated the last zombie, which was right behind him, without even looking to see where it was. With that, the player sheathed his iron sword, and gave a sigh of relief and closure.

The most impressive thing, however, was that though Stan and Charlie had dents in their iron chestplates, and Kat had dents all over her full iron body armor, from being repeatedly hit by the zombies, as the sun rose Stan could not see one scratch on the mysterious player with shades. He did not wear any armor; he had pulled off the leather boots after landing in the sinkhole. This player had fought the entire battle completely unprotected, and he had not taken a single bit of damage.

Whoever this player is, thought Stan, I'm glad he's on our side.

"That was amazing!" said Charlie, coming over and shaking the player's hand. "My name is Charlie, and these are my friends,

Kat and Stan." They both nodded, distinguishing themselves. "What's your name?"

"They call me DieZombie97," said the player, wiping some sweat off his brow. "Former head of the Brotherhood of Elite Hunters, three-time champion of the Grand Elementia Spleef League world tourney, and self-proclaimed King of the Desert. However, you may call me DZ," he added with a smile. "May I ask what you three are doing out here? Very few people choose to camp alone out here with all of the monsters and nomads that roam this freaking sandy wasteland."

"Well, we're kind of on a mission right now, and there are certain people we'd like to avoid," said Stan, presently wary about giving away to much information to this stranger, albeit a stranger who had saved their lives, but still. "What about you? I assume you live out here, Mr. King of the Desert, and you don't even have armor!"

"Excellent point, my young friend," said DZ, leaning against the sandstone at the bottom of the sinkhole wall. "Well, the reason I live out here by myself is that I have found it to be a very pleasing life, detaching myself from the insanity of the modern world. I used to be very successful back in my day, you'll forgive me for bragging, but I have found that it is quite pleasant and peaceful to live alone out here, beating the living crap out of the night folks, and occasionally getting to ward off the nomads. As for the no armor, eh, it's an old habit from my days playing Spleef."

"What exactly is Spleef?" asked Stan; he had wondered about this a few times before, but he hadn't had a chance to ask yet.

"Sheesh!" cried DZ, taking them all by surprise. "You people've never heard of Spleef? What levels are ya'?"

"Why does it matter?" asked Stan defensively; he would not tolerate any more of this bias against lower-levels, even if DZ had just saved their lives.

"Oh, I'm not prejudiced, don't worry!" laughed DZ. "No, no, prejudice against the lower-levels was the reason I *left* Element City. I was just wondering because if you'd been on here for long, you'd have heard of Spleef."

"Oh, well in that case, we're all in the thirties," replied Stan, which was true; what with all the monsters and animals they'd killed around the Nether and the Overworld. Kat, Charlie and Stan were now levels thirty four, thirty three, and thirty one, respectively. Indeed, it occurred to Stan as he said this that the three of them wouldn't even be considered lower-level players anymore. Then he realized that DZ had also said something else. "Wait, why'd you leave Element City again?"

"Because I hate the King," replied DZ offhandedly. "Anyways, Spleef is a game where any number of people... well in the league rules the official numbers are..."

"Hold up," interjected Kat. "Why do you hate the King so much?"

"Because he backstabbed a bunch of his friends because he's a paranoid jerkface. Anyways, in league Spleef two teams of three players each go into an..."

"And so you hate the king? You'd like to see him overthrown?"

"Well, yeah, if anyone had the guts to organize a rebellion, I'd join. So you've got these two teams in the arena, and they destroy the floor, which is made of snow, and try to knock the guys on the other team through the gaps..."

"We're doing that! We're organizing a rebellion against the King right now!" Charlie exclaimed.

"...and the last team with a player standing is... wait, what?" DZ started to pay attention to them for the first time. He lowered his shades and looked down at them. "Hold up... from what I know, nobody allied with the King would even joke about overthrowing him... you're freaking serious?"

Stan looked at Kat, and she looked at Charlie, and he looked back at Stan, and he knew they were all thinking the same thing. "Yes, we're serious!" Stan said. "If you want, you can join us. We're raising an army right now to try and overthrow the King. As soon as we get supplies, which we're on a journey to find right now, we're going to hook up with some players back in the Adorian Village and we're going to storm Element Castle!"

"So... hold up..." DZ sat down, trying to take in the enormity of what Stan was saying. "So you already have an army... and supplies? But how are you going to infiltrate the castle? Even assuming your army could stand a chance against the King's, isn't Element Castle rigged with those freaking... automatic... uh... redstone booby trap, er, thingies, that are meant to stop invading armies?"

Kat's and Charlie's faces fell, realizing that they had overlooked that particular stage in the plan, but Stan reached into his inventory and pulled out the book that the Mechanist had given him. "I got this book from the guy that designed all those redstone traps for the King, and it tells what and where they are. We can use this to anticipate and avoid these traps."

Stan's friends, as well as DZ, looked at him inquiringly, and he briefly explained about his detour to Blackstone and his meeting with the mayor and the Mechanist. Kat and Charlie were elated to here that twenty two new fighters were now heading towards the Adorian Village to help the war effort. DZ, meanwhile, took to their plan with enthusiasm.

"Well, if you guys have an army and are going to overthrow the King, then I want in! The sooner that jerkface comes down, the better. What can I do to help?" His face was split into a smile of determination; this was the most earnestly positive reception of their plan Stan had seen yet.

"Well, you can make your way back to the Ado…" started Stan, but he was cut off by Kat pulling him backwards. "What are you doing?" he asked as he was pulled into a huddle with Charlie.

"Okay, guys, look. We have to kill, like, twelve Endermen if we're going to get into the End, and who knows what kind of ridiculous crap is in that dimension? They must have called it the End for a reason," articulated Kat.

"Where are you going with this?" Stan asked.

"Well, how about instead of telling DZ to go back to the village with the others, we ask him to come with us? He seems to know what he's doing," Kat said.

"That's a great idea, Kat!" exclaimed Charlie. "He seems to have a way with those swords."

"Hold up, wait a second," said Stan. "Are you sure we want to ask this guy we just met to come with us?" Stan, truthfully, had seen a little off-put by DZ's reaction; it had seemed a tad too sincere for him.

"Well, why not? It's worked so far, you know, with the Apothecary, the Nether Boys, and these people in this Blackstone you told us about," Kat replied.

"Yeah, and with the Apothecary you were yelling at me for pushing our luck, and now you want to push it some more? Can we say hypocritical?"

"Oh, come on, Stan!" sighed Kat in exasperation. "I have a good feeling about this guy; just trust me on this one."

"Are you sure that it's not just because you think he's cute?" sneered Stan, and he regretted it an instant later.

Kat let out a hiss of rage and she flew at Stan and punched him squarely in the stomach. Both of them flew backwards; Stan had the wind knocked out of him by the power of Kat's fist, and Kat had in her anger forgotten that Stan was still wearing his iron chestplate. They were both on their feet again in seconds and were about to have a second go at each other when something stopped them; Charlie's hand shoved Kat back down, while his foot did the same to Stan.

"Enough, both of you!" yelled Charlie. "You're acting like Geno and Becca, like you're crazy and willing to kill each other over the stupidest things! Those are the people we're trying to get rid of, remember?" He turned to Kat. "Kat, there is nothing wrong with being cautious, so don't just completely blow him off." He whipped around to face Stan. "Stan, that was just uncalled for, and besides, if he wanted us dead he could've just let us been mauled to death by

256

those zombies, okay?" He stepped back so he could talk to both of them at once. "I say that we invite DZ to come along with us, but we keep an eye on him until we're one hundred percent sure that he's trustworthy, okay?"

Stan and Kat were silent for a moment. Then, they both nodded. They did not, however, look each other in the eye.

Charlie walked over to DZ, who had remained oblivious to the fighting and was now absentmindedly chiseling "Burn in Hell King Kev" in the sandstone wall with his diamond sword. "DZ?" The warrior turned towards Charlie, sheathed his sword, and looked Charlie in the eye.

"Hey, Charlie. Have you decided what you want me to do yet?"

"Yes we have," Charlie replied firmly, with Kat and Stan lurking embarrassed behind him. "We would be very happy if you would come with us. We have to collect twelve Ender Pearls, and use them to craft twelve Eyes of Ender with our blaze rods so that we can find a fortress and enter the End. Would you like to come with us?"

DZ nodded. "I'm in. I've been living out here for so long, and it's been fun, but I'm about ready to do something to give back to this server; it's given me some fun times."

Stan remembered what the Apothecary had said, right after agreeing to help them raise their army. *This place has given me so much, and then taken it away. It's time for me to make this server a place where future generations can call home.* In all of his travels around Elementia so far, he had began to forget the amazing things one could accomplish in this game, given the time and opportunity. People had had great times on this server, and they could really get attached to it. Time and opportunity, however, would not be available to Stan until after King Kev was slain; this he knew for a fact.

"And also, the End sounds freaking awesome, I want to find out whatever it is we're supposed to do there, and beat the living crap out of it!"

This statement snapped Stan out of his train of thought, but one piece of it caught in his mind. "DZ, what do you mean, 'whatever it is we're supposed to do there'? We have to find the King's treasure, that's it."

"Oh no, Stan buddy, you don't get it," laughed DZ. "I've never been to the End... I don't think anyone has, actually, barring the King... but I do know that it's not a normal dimension like the Overworld and the Nether. From what I hear, there's a specific task you have to do there, and until you do it, you won't be able to leave."

"And... what kind of task is that?" asked Stan apprehensively, not sure if he really wanted to know the answer.

"No idea," replied DZ, shrugging. "Maybe a puzzle, a boss battle, a friendly game of Parcheesi... when we go there, we just have to go prepared, that's all. You three seem like you know what you're doing, I'm sure the four of us could tackle whatever ridiculous stuff is in the End."

"Yeah, you're right," agreed Kat. "Anyways, we'll cross that bridge when we come to it. What we have to do next is to get twelve Ender Pearls."

"Like these?" asked DZ, holding up a handful of several blue-green orbs.

"Yes! Oh my God!" cried out Charlie in amazement. "DZ … where did you get those?!"

"Where do you think? I've been wandering this desert for longer than you there've been in Elementia put together, you know how many Endermen you run into during that time? I tell you, it's freaking annoying when you're scanning the horizon for danger, and you accidentally look at one of those emo freaks…"

"Yeah, we know, we've fought one before," replied Stan as Charlie took the Ender Pearls from DZ and counted them out. "They're powerful, they teleport, and they aggroed when you just look at them."

"Probably the three worst qualities a monster could have," added Kat solemnly.

"Testify," replied DZ, as Charlie put the pearls into his inventory.

"Okay, we have six Ender Pearls," he said, "thanks to *DZ*," and he shot an annoyed glance at Stan, who looked away in concealed embarrassment. "So now we need to find and kill six more Endermen. Easy enough," he said.

"Eh, not exactly, bud," said DZ. "Endermen don't always drop Ender Pearls, we're gonna need to kill a lot more than six."

"Wonderful," said Charlie, hanging his head. "But where are we going to go now? We can't stay at our current base, there's no door and no wood around, and we can't stay in one place too long anyways or the King's forces will find us."

"I know what we can do," said DZ. "Sometimes, if I'm low on health and I need a place to stay, I look around for an NPC

Village. The guys that live there are nice, they know how to make food, and they're always willing to provide you with shelter."

"Oh, I don't know if an NPC Village is such a good idea," replied Kat quickly.

Stan and Charlie looked at her in surprise. "Why not, Kat?" asked Stan. "What do you have against NPC Villages?"

"Yeah, Kat, remember when we first met?" asked Charlie. "You said that you were looking for an NPC Village because they'll give you really good stuff."

"Um, well, yeah, uh, about that," stammered Kat as she fidgeted around, "sometimes they, uh, don't like people, I mean not *all* people, DZ obviously got along fine, I mean... uh..." Stan had never seen Kat look so uncomfortable before.

"Ah, come on Kat, the three of you seem nice enough," said DZ, laughing. "I'm sure they'll like you just fine. Besides, the King's forces have a tendency of imposing wheat quotas on the villages, so they all hate him. I'm sure they'll take to us if we tell them we're going to overthrow the king."

"Well... then, uh... I sure can't think of... uh... any reason not to go," sighed Kat with an extremely forced smile. It was becoming exceedingly obvious that, for reasons unbeknownst to Stan, Kat wanted nothing less than to go to an NPC Village.

"Okay then!" exclaimed DZ with a smile, apparently oblivious to Kat's discomfort. "I'm pretty sure that there's one just a day's journey southeast of here. If we start now we should be able to make it there by nightfall, and we can start our Enderman hunt."

DZ started walking a little towards the left of the rising sun, and Stan and Charlie walked enthusiastically behind him. Kat, on the other hand, had her head down and was plotting out the way she would handle being marooned in the terrible NPC Village.

CHAPTER 21: OOB'S HELPING HAND

It was not long before Stan was beginning to seriously regret allowing DZ to come with them.

His exceptional sword fighting skills, and the fact that he had already acquired half the Ender Pearls necessary for their voyage into the End, did not make up for the fact that by nightfall of that day, the NPC Village was nowhere in sight. They had already exhausted their meager supply of food that Kat and Charlie had gained through hunting the previous day. DZ was only able to contribute one raw chicken, which they could not eat for fear of food poisoning. DZ apologetically explained that his philosophy was generally to eat something directly after killing it, so he rarely had food on him. This revelation did not elevate Stan's opinion of him as they continuously trudged through the endless sea of sand.

As the sun glowed bright over the pastel pink of the western horizon, Stan let out a shout of frustration. Charlie and Kat looked at him in concern.

"DO YOU HAVE ANY IDEA WHERE YOU'RE GOING?!" yelled Stan, the vein in his head pulsing, and spit flying out of his mouth as he unleashed his biding anger at DZ.

DZ looked around unconcernedly, apparently unaware that Stan was on the verge of sociopathic rage. He scratched his head innocently. "Well, now that I think about it, if the sun rises in the east and sets in the west... that means it moves... so if I keep going to the left of it... Ooooh! Then I WON'T be going southeast! I'll be going in CIRCLES!" He laughed. "Wow! That was pretty stupid of me, wasn't it?"

Only then did DZ come to the realization that all of his comrades were staring at him with incredulous looks on their faces. Charlie was staring at him as if he had just stated that he was going to attempt a staring contest with an Enderman, and Kat's mouth hung open, her eyes now wide enough to take up her entire face. Even Rex and Lemon were looking up at DZ, as if they too were aware that he had just done something remarkably dense.

Stan was the only one who was not looking shocked, but about ready as a lightning-charged Creeper to explode with rage. His eyes were closed, his teeth were gritted, and the vein in his head was bulging.

"Do you mean to tell me," said Stan in a quiet yet dangerous voice, "that we have been following you all day long, and you have been leading us in circles?"

"Apparently," said DZ, shrugging, "Ah, quit worrying, it don't matter much, we'll set ourselves straight tomorrow."

"And you are really still somehow oblivious to the fact that we have no food, no shelter, and standing between us and daytime is NIGHTIME!!!??" Stan yelled the last word so loud that Charlie actually fell backwards in shock. DZ just stood there with his mouth slightly agape and his eyes unblinking as Stan lashed out at him.

"YOU HAVE BEEN WITH US FOR LESS THAN ONE FULL DAY, AND YOU HAVE ALREADY CAUSED US MORE TROUBLE THAN YOU'RE WORTH!" bellowed Stan. "WE ARE NOW STUCK IN THE MIDDLE OF GOD KNOWS WHERE, AND IF TONIGHT IS ANYTHING LIKE LAST NIGHT, WE WON'T SURVIVE! WE HAVE GOT IT TOUGH,

YOU GOT THAT DZ? WE ARE TRYING TO DO SOMETHING IMPOSSIBLE! WE'RE FIGHTING THE KING, WE'RE FIGHTING NATURE, HELL, SOMETIMES IT FEELS LIKE WE'RE FIGHTING MINECRAFT ITSELF AS WE TRY AND DO THIS THING! IF YOU ARE NOT GOING TO BUCK UP AND TAKE IT SERIOUSLY, THEN IT'S JUST AS WELL THAT YOU GET THE HELL AWAY FROM US WHERE YOU CAN'T DO ANY MORE DAMAGE!"

Stan was breathing heavily like an ox now, nostrils flaring, veins popping. Kat and Charlie were in awe; they had always known that Stan had had a streak of recklessness and anger in him, but this display was far more violent than any they had seen from him before.

DZ looked at Stan with a new look on his face. It was a combination of shock, fear, and sorrow. DZ looked the apoplectic Stan in the eye and sighed, "Hey, I'm sorry, alright? I'm doing the best I can, I'm used to being a nomad out here, I'm not use to finding places. I promise that I'll try to take our job a little more seriously. But don't forget to have fun, alright?" he gave a weak smile. "It is still a game, right?"

Stan gave a snort of derision. "This is more than a game, DZ. It gives people another life; you of all people should know that. And the King is making these people's lives miserable, and it's up to us to fix that. We can have fun after our work is down."

DZ looked sadly at Stan. "I hear you buddy. But just remember what they say: At the end of your life you regret the stuff you didn't do more than the stuff you did do. So remember to have fun with what we're doing, because out here, there's no telling when our lives are going to end."

264

The enormity, power and sincerity behind this statement hit Stan like a shockwave, and he realized it was true; he could very well be dead by tomorrow in the middle of this desert, in the midst of this quest for justice.

They continued to trudge through the desert, nobody saying anything, and Stan looking downcast and humbled. The sun sank behind the desert hills, and the moon rose high into the star-speckled night sky. The optimistic view of the situation was that traveling was easier because of the lack of heat from the sun.

The pessimist's view, and the view of all four travelers, was that they were out of food, they had no source of light, and monsters were materializing on all sides of them. The attacks of Zombies came in hoards, the Skeleton shot arrows from afar, and the Spiders climbed up the cactuses that were everywhere and jumped down onto the players. Even the Creepers posed a threat. Lemon scared most of them away, but there was one point at which DZ was driven away from the main group by two spiders and a skeleton, and just as he managed to kill the second spider, he heard the telltale hiss and was blasted into the air a second later.

DZ landed on a cactus and found himself unable to move due to a shooting pain in his right leg. He looked down and saw that the cactus had tore into his flesh; he knew that he couldn't fight anymore with no food in his stomach to heal him. Instead he drew his glowing diamond sword and his swung it into the hoard of oncoming zombies now upon him. The blade barely ripped the monsters' blue shirts, but the shock emitted from the sword was enough to throw the zombies back into a heap, averting that danger for the time being.

DZ gritted his teeth; he knew that he had to do something quickly. His thoughts drifted to the cactus besides him. He drew an iron shovel out of his inventory and quickly hacked away the sand around the cactus, pulling himself into the hole, and resealing it with dirt he had on hand. The zombies, now on their feet again, mindlessly wandered towards him, but they found themselves walking straight into the cactus; with no brains to tell them otherwise, they kept trying to walk straight through the cactus until they were eventually felled by the spines.

When the last of the zombie noises had diminished from above him, DZ destroyed one of the dirt blocks and popped his head out, confirming that all the zombies were dead. He then looked over to Stan, Kat, Charlie, and the animals, all of whom were all quickly being overrun by the mobs.

"Over here!" DZ yelled, gesturing for them to come into the hole. They didn't need telling twice; all three players sprinted over to DZ and hopped into the hole. To say they made it in the nick of time was an understatement. Lemon's tail had just vanished into the dirt hole when a spider leapt towards DZ. He punched it back and placed the dirt block into place, securing the four players and two pets into the dark hole. Too tired to do anything else, DZ barely heard Kat tiredly mentioning something about dropping her sword outside before he keeled over asleep.

* * * * *

"Hello? Hellooooo!"

"Go away..." muttered Stan sleepily; his exhaustion from fighting off the mobs last night did not increase his desire to sleep as much as his present dream regarding him and Sally rejoicing after the fall of the King. Whatever mundane, secular task the others wanted him for, he was certain it could wait.

266

"Helloooo! Anybody home? You dropped your sword! Helloooo?"

"Wha... what?" came Kat's groggy voice from the other end of the hole. "Someone found my sword?" she asked in a stupid-sounding voice.

"You were dreaming Kat," yawned Charlie, "now *go back to sleep.*"

"Hellooooooooooooooooooooooo?"

Stan winced as the hole flooded with light; Kat had punched through the dirt roof to find the source of the caller. "Hello?" Though Stan was now pressing his hands to his ears to block out the noise, he could still clearly hear her. "Did someone say they fou..."

Kat's voice faltered for a moment. When it returned, it was with a shaky. "Oh. He-hello, there."

There was something in Kat's voice that registered wrongly with Stan. Suddenly quite awake, he grabbed his axe and jumped out of the hole after her. He turned his head and asked, "What's going..." But his voice faltered.

Kat was standing, looking extremely uncomfortable, next to the strangest-looking player that Stan had seen; at least, Stan thought it was a player. It definitely looked human, but it, or rather, he, looked more like a Neanderthal than a modern person. He was wearing a brown robe over darker brown pants and shoes, and he was the same size as the players. His face looked absolutely ridiculous; his head was taller than Stan's, he had green eyes with a brown unibrow, and his nose was gigantic; it actually fell down lower than his mouth. His hands were clasped together in front of him, Kat's sword grasped awkwardly between them.

267

Stan's immediate response was to blurt out the question of what that thing was, but as long as it, or, he, was still holding the sword, Stan felt that he'd better try to be at least a little sensitive. Charlie, on the other hand, who had just come out of the hole, went wide-eyed and blurted out, "Whoa! Kat, what the hell *is* that thing?"

Stan glared furiously at Charlie and his hand instinctively went to his axe, but the thing did not looked angered; in fact, he was looking around the desert, and looking, truthfully, rather stupid. The thing looked at Charlie.

"My name is Oob," he replied. "I found this sword on the sand early in this morning. I have looked for its owner and now I have found you." Oob spoke slowly, as if he had to think about every word that he said.

"Hey, an NPC!" exclaimed DZ, as he climbed out of the hole after Charlie. "What's your name, man? I've never seen you before, and I've been to most of the villages out here in the desert."

"I am Oob," the NPC Villager said simply, and he began wandering around aimlessly. Charlie and Stan looked at Oob, wondering whether he was being inconsiderate of them or just extremely stupid. DZ just laughed, and gestured to Stan and Charlie and muttered so Oob couldn't hear, "Don't worry, these NPC guys are pretty dumb, after they get to know you a little they'll take to you." DZ approached the villager and tried to talk to him again. Charlie seemed very interested in Oob, but Stan had just noticed Kat.

She looked more ill at ease than Stan had ever seen her, including the time he told the Apothecary that she had tried to kill him and Charlie when they first met. It was obvious the source of her discomfort; she kept on acting all jittery every time the villager made the smallest move. She actually sneaked up behind him and snatched her sword back from him instead of asking him for it. He didn't seem to notice.

"...because seven ate nine!" exclaimed DZ, finishing his joke and causing Oob to laugh hysterically. He had clearly spent a fair amount of time around NPCs and knew how to get them on his good side.

"I like you players! You are very kind to me and I become very happy when people are kind to me. Would you like to come and visit my village? We would be happy to have you with us," said Oob to DZ.

"That'd be awesome, man!" replied Charlie before DZ could respond. "We've been out here for a while and we could really use some food. You seem like a nice guy, Oob," said Charlie, and he gave Oob a friendly punch in the shoulder.

"Follow me then, my friends," said Oob, and he walked out into the desert. Charlie walked right next to Oob, chatting with him and, judging by the occasional outburst of laughter, telling more stupid jokes. DZ was walking behind them, next to Stan, and he was smiling, but Stan was anxiously keeping an eye on Kat over his shoulder. She was walking behind them all, and the look on her face clearly said that she was dreading going to the NPC Village, but Stan still had no idea why. He decided to find out.

He fell back next to Kat and she immediately made a noticeable effort to not meet his eye.

"Kat, I don't think it's any secret that you don't want to go to the NPC Village," Stan said.

Kat remained silent.

"When we first met, you told me that you found stuff in the chest of an abandoned NPC Village. Judging by the way you're acting, I'm beginning to think that that might not be completely true."

Kat was still silent.

"Kat, what happened at that village?"

"I killed him."

Kat had stopped walking. She had this look of incredible pain on her face. Stan was confused and disturbed by her face. She looked like someone repenting for some awful crime. When she next spoke, her voice was detached and distant.

"I went to an NPC Village, and all these villagers were being so nice to me. And I took their stuff. I took the sword, and I killed their blacksmith. And they all just stared at me. Then he told me to leave. Their priest stepped out of his church, stared at me, and told me to leave the village, and to never come back. And then... there was this stomping... and it got louder... and louder... and so I ran... I didn't look back... I didn't even have the decency to look that priest in the eye..."

Kat was staring down at the ground. She took a deep breath and then sighed. She looked at Stan. "I was a different person back then, Stan. I always had been. I used force to get what I wanted, and I didn't care what the consequences were, because I knew I could cancel out those consequences with more force." Kat paused. "Just like King Kev," Kat added in a mutter, echoing Stan's thoughts.

"We've got to beat him, Stan," said Kat. Her voice suddenly became serious, and she looked him straight in the eye. "After I met you guys, everything changed. I'm not the same person I was. You and Charlie are just so great; you get so legitimately upset over injustice, all injustice, even stuff most people just brush off. You've changed me. And I know that we're doing the right thing. We have got to take this lunatic down and bring justice to this place. And you've got to lead it Stan. You're something special, and you're the right one to do it." Kat was now radiating that same power she had when she burst from the lava and attacked Becca at the lava sea. Every word that she said went straight to Stan's heart. He felt empowered.

Stan had not said one word throughout Kat's entire monologue, but he knew that she was right. Kat was certainly a very different person than the girl who had ambushed them from the woods with a stone sword, and he knew that it was he and Charlie who had influenced Kat for the better. Furthermore, though he wasn't sure how he felt about it yet, he knew that he was somehow special. He had been sure that some otherworldly power had possessed him to win his two-on-one fight at the sword fighting dojo, to effortlessly destroy that Snow Golem with the axe, and to shoot that arrow at the King. He had felt it again the previous night as he yelled at DZ. Those actions did not feel like they had come from him, but from some higher level of thinking, as if the universe itself was calling him to act.

Stan remembered how, a million years ago, a million miles away, in an Adorian Village not destroyed by hatred, Sally had asked him if he believed himself to be special, and Crazy Steve had given him a calculating look. They knew; they had sensed something about him, some aura. In retrospect, they showed it, too. Sally had had him fight Kat and Charlie two-on-one, and had Crazy Steve not been killed in the midst of their talk, Stan was sure that he would have mentioned something about this sixth sense to him.

Stan had all these thoughts playing around at the back of his mind, but as the silhouettes of buildings appeared on the desert horizon against the rising square that was the sun, the prospect of food convinced Stan to store these thoughts in the back of his mind for later contemplation.

* * * * *

"Oh muhn, I nuvr tawdied misdah tashtah bredsamush," mumbled Kat through a mouthful of bread. Stan agreed. The bread that the villagers had given to them was indeed a vast improvement over the hungry darkness they had endured for the past day. The sun showed that it was almost noon, and while Lemon and Rex sat outside, Stan, Charlie, Kat, DZ and Oob were all sitting in Oob's house in the NPC Village.

The village itself, Stan found, bore a fond similarity to the Adorian village. The majority of houses were made out of wooden planks and cobblestone, with glass pane windows and wooden doors. The entire village was centered around a cobblestone well with gravel paths branching out around it. Behind most of the houses were miniature farms that consisted of rings of wood with rows of wheat crops and water within.

Two buildings stood out from the houses. A tall cobblestone building with multiple stories was the tallest thing in the village. Oob had pointed it out to Stan as the church, where their priest, also their leader, lived. Next to the village was a wide building, with the entire left side exposed, revealing two furnaces and a pool of lava. This building was called the forge, Oob said, home of the blacksmith who kept the villagers' tools in good repair.

272

"We are very happy to have you here. It has been so long since we have had players behave kindly towards us," said Mella, Oob's mother who lived in the house her husband, Blerge, and Oob.

"What do you mean, Mella? Have other players done stuff to you guys?" asked Kat.

"Oh, yes," she replied, a grim look taking to her face. "Long ago, before Oob was born, the forces of the one named King Kev forced those in our village to pay a tribute of wheat from our farms. There were often shortages, and many of us starved." Mella started to wander around the house again. Stan had realized that this was a quality of all NPC Villagers, that they all had a tendency to wander aimlessly regardless of what they were doing.

"What happened? Why did the King stop bothering you?" asked Kat encouragingly.

"What? Oh, yes," replied Mella, as though she had momentarily forgotten that they were there (Stan suspected that she actually had). "Not long after Oob was born, a player made a deal with the King that in exchange for that player's services, the King would no longer collect tribute from our village. We have seen no players since they took that brave player away." And with that Mella, again, began to wander.

Seeing that she was obviously out of it, Stan chose to ask Oob, rather than Mella, the name of the player. Oob's face took on a kind of elation in response.

"Oh, we have vowed to never speak the name of the Sacred One again! We have received a sign from the almighty Notch that in repayment for his sacrifice, we are never to speak the name of the Sacred One again!"

273

"The almighty Notch? Who is Notch?" asked Charlie, just as the back door opened and Blerge, Oob's father, walked in from tending the farm.

"He's the guy that created Minecraft," hissed DZ under his breath to Charlie, out of the hearing of Blerge, whose face showed utter disbelief.

"You do not know of Notch, the Creator? Without the almighty Notch, life as we know it could not exist! At the beginning of time, Notch created this village, which protects our people from the evil mobs! Notch makes the sun rise and set, and he is the master of all the creatures of this world! Without him, we would all be at the unchecked mercy of Herobrine, master of evil and destruction."

As Blerge kept on talking about the almighty Notch, Stan found himself intrigued. Did these villagers really worship the guy that created Minecraft? Well, it makes sense, he thought, their entire world is this game. Personally, though he obviously couldn't see himself worshiping the guy, Stan thought Notch was pretty awesome for creating such an excellent game.

"That sounds really interesting, Blerge," said Charlie, and Stan thought that he did seem legitimately interested in the behavior of these NPC Villagers, "So now I have a question. We're trying to overthrow the King, you know, the guy that used to force you guys to pay him stuff?"

"Oh yes," said Blerge, an his unibrow knitting over his eyes. "That man caused my people much suffering. I should be most happy if four kind players such as you were to take his place. You treat us very kindly, while the one called King Kev believed us to be inferior to them."

Stan opened his mouth to interject, but he quickly caught himself. It was very hard to say that he was equal in any way to this race of NPCs, especially considering that since he had joined the village, he had seen two villagers wander straight into cactuses and almost kill themselves. But Stan still had respect for the village people and that, he thought, was the difference between King Kev and himself.

"So," asked Charlie to Blerge, "would you be willing to let us use your village as a base? We still have to collect six Ender Pearls in order to get to the End, and we could use a place to stay until we've killed enough Endermen."

Blerge had began to wander again before Charlie had finished his request, so it was Mella who answered Charlie, "I am sure that it would be fine for you to stay with us for as long as you need, my friends. However, before we may tell you certainly, we must consult Moganga, the priest and leader of our village. She will tell you whether or not you may stay. Come, I shall take you to her." And with that, Mella started to the door, and Oob followed her (Blerge was still wandering around the house).

"Wait," asked Kat, speaking for the first time in quite a while. "This is your house. Why does this Moganga lady get to decide if we stay or not?"

"Because the almighty Notch commands it," she said, and she exited the house, as if this were a satisfying response. Oob left behind her, followed by Charlie and DZ, then Stan and, after a moment, Kat.

CHAPTER 22: THE SIEGE

As the group walked down the gravel street towards the tall stone church, Stan was vaguely aware of Charlie, DZ and Oob chatting in front of him, while he himself kept a careful eye on Kat out of the corner of his eye.

Ever since Kat had confessed to Stan what had happened to her in the last NPC Village she went to, Kat had been very calm and pensive, quite in contrast to her usual self. She had also seemed much more at ease around the villagers now that she had gotten her crime against their race off her chest. Now, however, Stan did sense a diminished version of her previous tension as she approached church. Still, she entered and, after Stan explained to yet another villager, named Libroru, that walking into a cactus would hurt, Stan followed Kat inside.

The church was made entirely of cobblestone, with a ladder on the side leading to the upper stories. There were torches on the walls, and a cobblestone altar sat in front. A villager in purple robes stood and faced the altar. When the players, lead by Mella and Blerge, entered, the priest turned towards them.

"Hello, players," said Moganga, gesturing to Stan, Kat, Charlie and DZ. "Oob has told me of your arrival. Welcome." She turned towards Mella and Blerge. "With what may I help you, my brother and sister?"

"These four players have requested the use of our family's house as an outpost for their hunting of the Endermen," replied Blerge in a powerful voice. "I appeal to you to ask the almighty Notch as to his judgment on the matter."

"I see. I will attempt to connect with the almighty Notch, my brother," replied Moganga. Her eyes closed, and her single eyebrow began twitching. She remained this way for about two minutes, and by the time her eyes reopened, Blerge and Mella had began to wander around the church. Oob stepped forward.

"What is the word of the almighty Notch, Mother Moganga?" asked Oob with a serious face.

"The Almighty Notch has spoken to me," replied Moganga, and Oob's face lifted. "The Almighty Notch has blessed the endeavors of these players and calls us to offer them refuge, provided that we are able to cope with the evil that will befall us beneath the full moon tonight."

"Oh, God," muttered DZ. "Are you saying that the full moon is tonight?"

Moganga nodded, and Oob and DZ looked crestfallen. Charlie asked, "Wait, what's the big deal about the full moon?"

A grim look took to DZ's face as he replied, "A siege is the big deal. Every full moon, if there are players staying in an NPC Village, then a giant hoard of mobs will attack the village. And I mean, giant. Makes the ones we killed off back at that sinkhole look like nothin'. And even though they're mostly Zombies, you get plenty of the other kinds, too."

"Years ago," said Mella, who had stopped wandering, "when the Sacred One was still with us, the sieges used to befall us every full moon. We were able to survive as a species because, in those days, Zombies could not break through our doors. However, during every siege, a horrible monster would terrorize our village alongside the Zombies, a skeleton riding upon a spider."

"A Spider Jockey," muttered Charlie. His eyebrows knitted, and his eyes widened in anxiety. "I've read about those things. All the range of a skeleton combined with the agility and rapidity of a spider. That does not sound like a fun combo to me."

"Oh, you are right on that, bro," agreed DZ, looking sober. "Whenever I see a freaking Spider Jockey out in the desert, I avoid it. If it sees me, I run like he... I mean, like anything," he said, checking his language for his presence in the church. He looked at Moganga. "So every time there's a siege, a Spider Jockey comes and attacks the villagers?"

"That is correct," replied Moganga. "It would often kill one of us before the Sacred One drove it away, and the Sacred One was never able to kill it, despite his status as an elite archer. As a result, the Spider Jockey will return tonight. If you consider this, and the fact that the Zombies have recently learned how to break through doors, then you will realize that you players staying here will make the village a very dangerous place for our people."

Stan wanted to add that that wasn't saying much, seeing as he had seen three villagers almost commit suicide by walking into cactuses, but he kept the thought to himself.

"Therefore, I make this offer to you. You may stay with us in the village while you hunt the mobs called Endermen, and in return you will defend us from the siege and kill the Spider Jockey. Do we have an agreement?"

"Yes, ma'am," replied Stan, and his friends nodded in assent. Indeed, Kat and DZ both seemed thrilled about the prospect of fighting a hoard of evil mobs. Charlie, on the other hand, still had a hint of the old nerves he had shown so often when they had first met. Stan had thought that this nervous tendency would be gone from him by now, after all they had been through, and he certainly couldn't have a nervous Charlie in the End. As insurance, and a sort of final test, of the power of Charlie's nerves, Stan spoke up.

"Okay, here's how we should do this. DZ and Kat, you stay back in the village, and kill all the zombies that try and break into the village houses. Charlie and I will go out into the desert around the village, and we'll kill all the mobs that spawn out there. We'll also hunt the Spider Jockey."

Charlie's eyes widened. He opened his mouth in what Stan was sure would be a protest, but Kat had already said, "That works," and DZ nodded in agreement. "Okay," she continued, "let's suit up. The sun is setting, and this is gonna be a long, long night."

Looking slightly put out, it was with a slightly pained expression on his face that Charlie followed Stan, Kat and DZ back to Oob's house, where they had stored their armor and weapons in a chest.

DZ's arsenal was by far the lightest; with no armor, he held nothing but an iron sword glowing red with the Fire Aspect enchantment in his hand, and two diamond swords at his side. One of these swords was glowing with the Knockback enchantment, while the other one remained inflorescent.

Kat, on the other hand, was the most bogged down with gear, being the only one with a full set of armor. She had on an iron helmet, leather tunic, iron leggings and iron boots, and she held an

279

enchanted Infinity bow in her hand. Her arrows and iron sword hung at her hips.

Stan also had quite a bit of paraphernalia on him. He wore only his iron chestplate, and he had his axe in his hand and a bow slung over his back, with arrows hanging at his side. Oob had provided him with a sash to strap across his chest, to which he attached the two Potions of Healing and the one Potion of Fire Resistance that he still had from the Apothecary.

Charlie was adorned in an iron chestplate, his diamond pickaxe grasped in his sweaty hand. He had the same sash and potions as Stan, but no bows and arrows. Instead, he took the Fire Charges that he had taken from the dead soldier at the Nether Portal, and he attached them to his belt and sash.

As the sun sunk deeper and deeper, towards the desert hills, the sky's color shifted from light blue, to azure, to pink, to violet, and finally, to black. Kat, Rex and DZ took their places patrolling the gravel pathways of the village, while Stan, Charlie and Lemon walked down the main street towards the desert. It was like a ghost town; the NPC villagers were all holed up in their houses, preparing for the impending siege. The eerie wind blowing in off the desert hills all contributed to the ominous sense of foreboding that now lay around the darkened village as Stan, Charlie and Lemon ventured out into the dune sea.

When they had reached a moderate distance from the village, Charlie looked at Stan. "Okay, Stan, clearly you volunteered me to do this for a reason. Spill."

"I wanted to make sure you were tough enough," replied Stan, not looking at Charlie as he scanned the hills for any signs of a horde of zombies. "The End is going to be terrifying, whether you like it or not, Charlie, so better to buck up now than when we're faced with that world."

Charlie's mouth opened in outrage, but it soon closed because he realized that Stan was right. Charlie felt that he had become much braver since meeting Stan, but whatever was in the End was sure to be much more dangerous and trying than anything in the overworld or the Nether. To insure that he was up to it, Charlie agreed that he ought to not run from precarious situations when they arose, for the sake of training himself.

The sun eventually fully dipped below the distant sandy knolls, and the full moon was soon at its zenith in the sky above, the stars gleaming like diamonds in the black infinity of the sky. Neither Stan nor Charlie were able to appreciate the natural beauty around them, however; both were now preoccupied with the very real likelihood of hundreds of Zombies pouring over the hills.

Sure enough, it wasn't long after the sunset that Stan's ear became vaguely aware of a rumbling, like the sound of hundreds of feet swarming forward in unison. The sounds of bones rattling, spiders clicking, Enderman crying and, most prominently, Zombies giving their empty moans of despair became louder and louder until, finally, the first wave of zombies appeared.

Stan and Charlie rushed into action; there were hundreds of targets to choose from, so it was not long before the pickaxe and axe, in the hands of the two experienced fighters, had torn, smashed, and beat down dozens of the beasts. However, many more were now thronging towards the village. Stan rushed to engage them. Charlie was about to follow in suit when he saw sight that made his stomach dissolve.

Another wave of monsters had appeared over the horizon, this one composed not just of zombies, but of skeletons, spiders, Creepers, and Endermen. And leading the charge, ordering the attack on the village by gesturing with its hand, was a skeleton, which was sitting, bow in hand, on the back of a spider. The Spider Jockey…

Charlie knew that this was his fight. He had to be the one to obliterate that Spider Jockey. However, he knew that he could not do that with all the other hostile mobs streaming onward… formulating a plan, he pulled out a TNT block and a redstone torch that he had gotten from the dead soldier, placed it on the ground and yelled at the top of his lungs, "HEY! OVER HERE, YOU UNDEAD FREAKS!"

His plan worked; the mobs' attention turned from the NPC Village, and instead the dozens of mobs swarmed towards Charlie. With seconds to spare, he touched the tip of the redstone torch to the TNT block, scooped up Lemon in his hands, and jumped into a ditch a few blocks back. An instant later, just as Charlie saw an Enderman above him, raising its arm to strike, the TNT block exploded with the same force as a Creeper. Charlie was knocked back by the explosion, landing on his rear a few blocks away, but that was nothing compared to what happened to the rest of the mobs.

The explosion occurred right as the greater part of the mobs were over it, and as Charlie looked down into the crater in the sand and saw that none of the demons had survived; the crater was littered with bones, arrows, rotten flesh, and (to Charlie's delight) two Ender Pearls. He picked up the latter and looked back to the horizon to see what remained of Spider Jockey's henchmen.

Besides the Spider Jockey itself, the only mobs left in the desert were three Creepers, staring at Charlie from behind their leader. One of them began to shake in anger at the death of his comrades, and it began to lumber towards Charlie, but the Spider Jockey raised its hand to signal a halt. Charlie's eyes locked on the empty eye sockets of the skeleton. They both knew the same thing to be true: this fight was to be one on one.

If this was to be the case, Charlie was sincerely wishing that he had brought a bow with him and, as if a miracle, he noticed that one of the skeletons had dropped one, and it was sitting in the crater. He scooped up this, along with all the arrows lying alongside it. Though he had never been much of a shot at archery, Charlie was on such an adrenaline high from the massacre of the undead that he was sure that he could shoot just as well as Kat or Stan under the circumstances. Climbing out of the crater, he gave one last defiant look at the Spider Jockey, and he charged.

The Spider Jockey charged at the same time. The skeleton fired off two quick shots with his bow, which Charlie dodged and knocked aside with his pickaxe. As he came up from his dodge, Charlie threw his pickaxe boomerang style towards the Skeleton's head. It seemed to be on a collision course, but at the last second the spider pounced to the side, saving its rider for the time being.

Charlie was unphased. He drew his bow and, while still running forward, fired off three shots as the skeleton did the same. Charlie dodged two of the shots, while a third deflected off his armor. The Spider Jockey was not so lucky; though the Spider was able to hop out of the way of the first two arrows, the third one sunk straight into one of its eight red eyes; the spider spat in pain and began thrashing around, causing the skeleton to hastily jerk the arrow out of the Spider's face, restrung it in its own bow, and fire it back Charlie's way.

Charlie ducked the arrow and he was upon the monster; the spider bared its teeth and launched itself at Charlie, but Charlie delivered a quick jab to its face and it keeled over sideways, not dead but certainly disoriented. Charlie took the opportunity to grab the pickaxe lying nearby on the ground. By the time the Spider Jockey had regained its footing, it was too late. The skeleton notched an arrow in its bow just as Charlie drove his pickaxe into the Spider's side. The spider fell to the ground, twitching reflexively as it bled from the hole in its side. The skeleton was thrown to the ground, its arrow fired haphazardly into the air, and as it looked up at the impending warrior that was Charlie, it waved its white bone of an arm forward.

Charlie barely had time to ponder what this meant when he noticed the three Creepers converging on him. He closed his eyes and braced himself for the powerful explosions. Instead, however, he heard a hissing sound distinctively different than that of a Creeper. Charlie opened his eyes to see Lemon chasing the Creepers away, and Charlie pursued them until he reached a ditch in the sand.

Lemon stood at the top of the ditch, still hissing at the three Creepers, all of which were cowering in fear in the corner of the wall of sand. The Creepers were too scared of the cat to even look up as Charlie ended their lives with three quick strokes of the pickaxe. Relieved, Charlie turned, ready to scratch Lemon behind the ears in thanks.

Instead, Charlie looked up just in time to see an arrow pierce his cat through the stomach.

Time ran by in slow motion as Lemon descended in a graceful, almost angelic arc off of the sandy ledge and into the ditch, finally coming to rest in Charlie's waiting arms. Charlie's stomach filled with the sensation of a knot being tied in his gut as his cat gave one last feeble meow, and Lemon faded out of existence.

Charlie's mind was white with shock. He stood staring into his empty arms, where his dying pet had just breathed its last breath, unable to comprehend what had happened. He had only had Lemon for a short time, but during that time he had become as fond of the cat as he had of Kat and Stan, knowing that whenever he awakened from this nightmare created by the King, he would have Lemon by his side.

Then, in an instant, the shock and horror within Charlie spontaneously morphed into rage, and an insane, animal desire to utterly destroy the one responsible for Lemon's death. He looked up to the ledge above the ditch, and he saw the skeleton that had been riding upon the spider aiming another arrow straight at his head. Charlie's reflexes, already heightened by battle, increased to the point of becoming superhuman as he caught the flying arrow in midair, inches from his own face, re-notch it in his own bow, and send it back to its owner, the flint tip shattering the bone-dry skull into dust.

Charlie pulled himself out of the hole, still seething and bloodthirsty for the destruction of more of the undead; the desert was, however, completely vacant. Charlie had managed to kill all of the Spider Jockey's forces single-handedly. Though Charlie was still enraged beyond rage that they had gotten Lemon, he did allow himself something that he had never given himself before: credit.

From the time the first mobs appeared to the present, there was one emotion that he had had none of at all. He had not been afraid.

Emotions of pride, sadness and fury swirling within Charlie, he raced back towards the light of the NPC Village to combat the mobs he now saw roaming the streets.

* * * * *

Stan could have filled a chest with the rotten flesh of all of the Zombies felled by himself and his comrades while defending the village. Stan's axe brought zombie after zombie to its second death. Kat was even more effective, her sword able to parry the zombie's attack aside, letting her fight them at close range alongside her dog. However, by far the most devastating blows to the undead came from DZ, his red-tinted iron sword needing only to cut a Zombie once, while the element of fire did the rest.

Though the moon was still high in the night sky, Stan was just thinking that the siege was dying down when he suddenly felt himself lifted into the air. Though upside down and very disoriented, he managed to glimpse an Enderman lifting him high in the air, and making to smash him into the gravel street. Stan braced himself for impact when he felt a lurch, and he fell quite gently to the ground, his fall cushioned by the dead corpse of the Enderman. Eager to see who had killed the monster, Stan looked up just in time to see Charlie pulling his diamond pickaxe out of the back of the black, hominoid head, his expression dark and distant.

"Thanks, Charlie," said Stan as Charlie helped him to his feet. "How did it go?"

"They're all dead. The Spider Jockey too," said Charlie in a monotonous voice that seemed awfully out of character. Something had obviously gone wrong. Stan was just making the connection of what was out of place when Charlie muttered, "Lemon's dead."

It was like a dull blow to the stomach; Stan was filled with sympathy for his best friend. He knew how much joy Lemon had brought to Charlie, and he knew that Charlie would be a much different person now.

"How've you guys been holding up here?" Charlie asked, his voice lifting almost imperceptibly, as if he were involuntarily trying to make himself happier.

"I think we're done," exclaimed DZ, joining them after sticking one last Zombie. He had a small scratch on his left forearm, and he looked exhausted, but besides that he was fine. "I got the last one over here, and I'm pretty sure that Kat finished those over there."

At that very moment, Kat's face peeked out from around the corner of Oob's house, but she did not look triumphant; quite the contrary, her face was pale and looked horrified.

"I think you guys need to see this," she whispered, her lips barely moving.

The three players ran to see what she meant. As he was running, Stan heard Oob's voice coming from within his house.

"Players? Yoo hoo! I have something to show you!"

"Not now, Oob," muttered Stan in response as he rounded the corner of the house and saw what Kat was staring at. His gut contracted painfully at the sight.

Stan had seen many large groups of evil mobs together throughout his time in Minecraft, but never before had he seen one as large as the one now lumbering down the gravel path towards the NPC Village. There must have been at least two hundred evil mobs in all. This group was not just zombies; there were skeletons, spiders, Creepers, and Endermen, too.

"Players?"

"Not now Oob!" barked Stan as he raised his axe; he was far too tired to fight anymore, and his body was screaming at him to ignore these mobs and just go to sleep.

"But it's very very very very very important!" came Oob's exasperated, rushed response.

"Oob, buddy, we're kind of busy defending your butt right now, so talk to us later, alright," said DZ, and he did something that Stan had only seen anyone do once before; DZ drew out two swords, with his red-iron sword in one hand, and his unenhanced diamond sword in the other. Stan supposed that this was an advanced form of sword fighting.

"Oh, come on!" came Oob's voice, and his face appeared in the window. "Don't you want to see my new little brother?"

Stan suddenly snapped to attention. "Wait, what did you just say?" he asked.

"Oob, did you just say you have a new brother?" asked Charlie.

Oob's face disappeared for a few seconds, and when he came back up he was holding up a miniature version of himself. It seemed that he did, indeed, have a new brother. "Mother and Father decided that if we are to remain in the village, we must have new members. Then they stared at each other for a few moments, a heart icon appeared above their heads, and my new brother Stull appeared!" Oob's smile was so big that it was visible even beneath his colossal nose.

"Wait..." said Charlie, and Stan could tell that he had just realized something. "Oob... how many buildings are there in your village?"

"Including the houses belonging to those killed by evil mobs, there are thirty-one," replied Oob.

"And, counting your new brother... Stull... how many people live in the village now?"

"I am the tenth resident of this NPC Village," answered Stull in a surprisingly deep voice for an infant.

"But that means that... if there's really ten..." said Charlie, completely ignoring the fact that his question had been answered by a newborn baby, "and thirty one... then that means that... soon..."

Charlie's thinking-out-loud was cut off by a metallic rumbling sound.

Stan, Charlie, Kat and DZ all whipped around as the figure charged down the road. This beast was enormous; it was metallic, a little taller than the players and about twice their width, and it had long, gangly arms. Vines grew all over its body, and save its gleaming red eyes its face bore a direct resemblance to a sort of grey NPC villager.

As the beast charged forward, Stan was afraid for an instant that it was going to attack them, but it flew right past them and into the hoard of mobs that had now entered the village. The thing raised its great long arms, and swung them side to side in rapid and crazy attack patterns, with each new swing knocking mobs apart as if they were life-sized sculptures of gelatin. The victims of this thing truly did end up liquefied under its pure physical strength.

"What is that thing?" asked Stan in awe, his mouth agape at the awesome battle taking place before him as the beast eliminated wave after wave of hostile mobs.

"It's an Iron Golem," replied DZ, looking at the beast with admiration. "They spawn in large villages and help defend the village people against these sieges."

"And Stull's birth gave this village ten people, officially making the game classify it as a large one," added Charlie as he watched the carnage.

The evil mobs were simply no match for the Iron Golem. The second they came within the range of the iron arm, they had no chance to initiate any attacks before they were crushed.

Stan suddenly remembered something, and he looked at Kat. Her face was solemn, as he had expected it to be. He remembered that she had described a metallic clanging noise that followed her after she pillaged the last NPC Village she went too. That village had undoubtedly had an Iron Golem too, placed there to defend the village from having its citizens taken advantage of. He expected her to look scared or at least a little uncomfortable; but indeed, Kat now seemed fully at ease and it appeared that she, finally, had forgiven herself.

For an hour, the four players watched in stunned silence as the Iron Golem laid waste to all evil mobs to enter the NPC Village. The last mob to die was a skeleton. Right before it could shoot, the

Iron Golem delivered a roundhouse punch to its head, knocking it dead to the ground.

The Iron Golem then stood still, glancing into the horizon, ready to defend the village at all costs. It looked very impressive, silhouetted against the white square of the rising sun, a sure indication that the siege, at last, was over.

CHAPTER 23: THE TWELVE EYES OF ENDER

As the sun rose over the NPC Village, Stan surveyed the village to see the effects the siege had had. He was relieved to find that no villagers had been injured during the siege, but he was surprised to see that the villagers seemed truly devastated when they heard of the loss of Lemon. From what Stan had understood, they had never seen a cat before Lemon, and they had had great joy in petting him.

"He was so gentle and kind," said Oob with a frown on his face and a tear trickling down his cheek. "I am so sad that he is no longer with us." DZ was about to comfort him when the villager started wandering again, making his consoling moot.

The villagers also seemed very fond of the Iron Golem, who seemed to showcase a gentler side around them, and especially around the children. As the newborn Stull played a game of tag with another villager child, a girl named Sequi, the Iron Golem joined in, tagging the children with a light, harmless tap on the head, as opposed to the wild, fanatical arm swings he had used to destroy the evil mobs the previous night.

Stan, Kat and DZ were all quite contented that the village was safe, and Kat in particular was now noticeably pumped up with anticipation for the Enderman hunt that was now next on their to-do list. Charlie, on the other hand, was taking the loss of his cat very hard. He spent the first day after Lemon's death sitting on the wood blocks that made up the border of Blerge's wheat farm, staring out into the desert sky, a pensive look on his face and an occasional tear rolling down his cheek.

As the afternoon rolled around, and DZ entertained the villager with more bad jokes, Stan and Kat caught each other's eyes for a moment and knew that they had to go talk to Charlie. They went around to the back of the house, and they sat down on either side of Charlie. He raised his eyes slightly to both sides in acknowledgement of their presence, and he proceeded to look down at the sand below him.

"You doing all right, man?" asked Stan.

Charlie didn't answer.

"What's the matter, Charlie?" said Kat.

Charlie still didn't answer.

"Charlie, I'm really sorry about Lemon," said Stan, "but we've got to keep going. We've got a King to take down, remember?"

"What's the point?" asked Charlie in a dejected voice. Stan was alarmed at how depressed he sounded. "All that's going to happen is more people dying." He looked up at Stan. "My cat just got killed, and I feel miserable. What's going to happen if you get killed? Or you, Kat?" he asked turning his head the other way to face Kat.

"Charlie, there's no other way," said Kat, a grim expression on her face. "Believe me, if I thought there was any other way to change the way things run on this server, then I wouldn't be with you guys right now. But sometimes war is the only option. It's a horrible option, but it's the only one we've got."

"If we don't take down the King, then things are going to just get worse from here, you know that, Charlie," said Stan. "The King's been abusing the people living here for too long, and he's not letting up. And now, we have people, a lot of powerful people, ready to risk their lives to take him down, and we're closer than ever to getting the supplies to do it. Are you saying you just want to give up?"

Charlie sighed before answering. "No, you're right, and I know you're right. It's just…" He paused as a tear rolled down his cheek and he wiped it away. "…it's not any easier…"

Kat leaned over to Charlie and gave him a hug. Over her shoulder, Charlie glanced at Stan, their eyes locked. Stan knew from the look in Charlie's eyes that, as much as neither of them liked it, Charlie knew that they must carry on.

Stan became vaguely aware of another presence joining them. He looked up and saw Oob looking down at them, the Iron Golem standing just behind him.

"You are doing the right thing, Charlie," said Oob, his face more serious than Stan had ever seen him. "And I thank you for making life better for us."

Stan smiled. This was the reason they were doing this, he thought. The lower-level players, the NPC Villagers… wasn't this the reason that they were ready to fight? These people weren't able to defend themselves, and while the King capitalized on this weakness by extorting them, there would always be those willing to defend them. The Apothecary, the Nether Boys, DZ… even the Iron Golem, Stan realized, were ready to defend themselves and others if the need arose, but that didn't mean that they were vicious monsters.

Hadn't Stan seen the Iron Golem, just this morning, playing tag with the villager children?

As if in response to his thoughts, Stan heard a metallic creaking and looked up. The Iron Golem had stepped forward and walked right to Charlie. Charlie looked into the Golem's red eyes, and the Golem extended its metal hand. Clasped in it was a red flower, a rose. The Golem's gift to the heavy-hearted Charlie.

Charlie smiled, and took the rose. "Thank you," he said to the Golem, and the iron obelisk nodded its head with a metallic creak in response. Charlie stood up and looked at his friends. "Come on, guys. We've got some Endermen to kill."

Glad to see that his friend was out of his stupor, Stan followed Charlie and Kat back to Oob's house, where they found DZ already waiting and ready for hunting.

"Hey guys! You ready to kick some teleporting butt?" he asked, eliciting the first smirk anyone had seen on Charlie since the siege. DZ took notice. "Hey Charlie, you doing better man?"

"Yeah, I'm all right. I've gotta say, though, I do have an odd desire to kill some Endermen right now," replied Charlie.

"Now that's what I'm talking about, man! ENDERMAN HUUUUUNNNNNT!" DZ sung, pumping his fist in the air and doing a little dance of excitement.

"Come on, guys. Let's suit up and get out there," said Kat, pulling her armor out of Oob's chest.

After they had put on all their armor, and equipped themselves with all their weapons, the four players and dog set out into the desert, with Oob, Mella, Blerge and Stull waving to them from within their house.

"Okay guys, so here's the plan," said Kat. "We'll all just look around the desert; the terrain is pretty flat out here, so we shouldn't have much trouble finding any Endermen. When someone sees one, they call out, and everyone jump to that player's back to defend them. How many Ender Pearls do we have again?"

"Well," replied DZ, scratching his head, "I had six before, what about you guys?"

"I got two last night," said Charlie.

"And I got one," added Stan.

"Excellent!" said Kat, grinning. "We only need three more! Alright, everyone, start looking!"

Stan was excited; he had not realized just how few Ender Pearls they still needed to collect. He started scanning the darkening horizon, and the sun had just ducked out of sight behind the distant hills when Stan spotted his first Enderman. It was holding a sand block, and upon recognizing his view, its jaw dropped, and it stared back and shook as if it were racked with spasms.

"I've got one!" yelled Stan, and the other three players rushed to defend his back. Sure enough, when the Enderman appeared behind Stan, it immediately found itself cut by two swords, an axe, and a pickaxe before it teleported away. It reappeared an instant later behind Kat, who spun backwards and decapitated it. She looked down at the tall, black corpse, and sure enough...

"Yes!" she exclaimed, as she scooped up one of the turquoise pearls from Enderman's body. "Ten down, two to go!"

And sure enough, the Enderman hunting was quick from there on out; with the desert plains providing minimum obstructions to their vision, they were easily able to locate two more Endermen very quickly, adopting the same strategy. Of the two, however, only one yielded an Ender Pearl.

"Yeah, that happens sometimes," said DZ, seeing the look of outrage on Kat's face as she found that the second Enderman had no Pearls. "It's no big deal; we'll just kill another one."

No sooner did DZ say this than Stan sensed a presence behind him. He spun around, ready to combat an incoming mob, but what he saw instead caught him totally off guard; had he not been wearing an iron chestplate, Leonidas's arrow would have impaled his heart. He gave a short shout of pain that alerted the others to the presence of his assailant.

They wasted no time in reacting. Kat and DZ hastily drew their bows and fired two arrows in Leonidas's direction. He ducked one, and the other caught in the wood of his bow. Charlie and Kat rushed in to engage Leonidas at close range, where they had their advantage. DZ, however, was otherwise occupied, as Geno had just burst out of the ground, diamond sword glinting in the moonlight. Stan pulled himself to his feet, watching as DZ and Geno, probably the two most powerful swordsmen he had ever seen, locked blades in ferocious combat.

Stan became aware of a sizzling behind him. He spun around and brought his axe down into the line of redstone dust on the ground, cutting off the electric charge that would have activated the TNT block that had somehow appeared directly behind him. He

297

destroyed the TNT block in one punch, and he drew his axe to combat Becca, who was now rushing in to engage him.

Becca may have been the demolitions expert of RAT1, but she certainly knew her way with a sword. Stan had had quite a bit of experience, and his prodigy with the axe had doubled since he first learned the skill from Jayden in the Adorian village; yet, Becca was able to fight him on an equivalent level. It was only by a lucky uppercut that his axe managed to knock Becca's iron sword out of her hand and into the air.

Becca was not deterred; she immediately drew two Fire Charges and with a quick flick of the wrist she was gone in a billow of black smoke. The force of the small burst fire knocked Stan backwards, and as he looked up he saw that there were also plumes of smoke where Leonidas and Geno had just stood. No sooner had he opened his mouth to ask where they had gone when an arrow came flying out of the smoke and embedded itself into Stan's right forearm, which was unprotected by his armor.

Through there was pain shooting up and down his arm, Stan did not allow himself to look at the wound. Instead, he drew his bow and fired arrows into the smoke, dodging the ones that flew back out towards him, until he heard a grunt of pain that told him that he had hit his mark. Only then did Stan allow himself to yank the arrow out of his arm.

Stan ignored the throbbing pain, gritted his teeth and looked around. Becca was now engaging DZ in combat by sending fire at him with Flint and Steel, and Geno was fighting Kat. Stan did not see Charlie at all. The smoke in front of Stan had subsided enough for him to see the figure of Leonidas drawing another arrow.

Stan spun his axe around in midair to deflect the arrow, and he charged Leonidas with his axe. Leonidas fired two more arrows, but Stan simply knocked them aside with his weapon. Just as Stan was about to cut Leonidas's bow in two with his axe, he caught the glint of something in Leonidas's hand. Stan tried to change his course, but Leonidas had already thrown the potion bottle at Stan, and it burst on his forehead, dazing him and knocking him to the ground.

Stan felt dizzy, and the world rotated around him as if he were in some hallucinogenic nightmare. He was vaguely aware of wisps of grey smoke rising off of his body, and found himself with not even enough energy to lift himself up off of the ground. Though he was aware that his axe was still clasped in his hand, this sensation was indistinct, and Stan knew that whatever that potion was, it had dulled his nerves and reflexes. As he became aware of this, he became aware as well of the fact that Leonidas was pinning him to the ground with his foot, and that he was yelling to Geno and Becca.

There was screaming, Stan was sure of it, and it was a girl; out of the corner of his eye, he could see Becca still fighting with DZ, and he knew that it must have been Kat who had fallen fighting Geno. His suspicions were confirmed when he saw Geno being pushed back by frantic attacks by both Rex and Charlie, who were clearly enraged at the state of Kat, whom Stan could not see. He knew, though, what he must do.

Leonidas was shooting arrows in the direction of Charlie, still standing on Stan. He therefore didn't notice as Stan, with a great deal of focus to overcome the groggy effects of the potion, released his axe and fumbled around with his hand until his fingers clasped on his bow. Stan's head was throbbing with the effort of moving, but he the bull-man named Minotaurus who had destroyed the Adorian village knew that this was the only way to save Kat. Feeling like his head was about to split open, Stan's shaky hands notched an arrow in the bowstring, pulled back, and fired.

The arrow shot straight upwards and into Leonidas's tunic, through the leather into his chest. The wound was not deep, and Stan doubted that it would be fatal, but Leonidas still cried out in pain and surprise as he tumbled backwards off of Stan's chest.

The relief in weight helped Stan's focus immensely; immediately, the effects of the potion were only but half as bad. Stan was now able to sit up; he saw Kat lying unconscious on the ground, and he noticed Geno turn for a moment and recognize his injured teammate; in the second of lost focus, Rex's body slammed Geno in the stomach, knocking him backwards. He skidded across the ground, finally stopping when his head slammed into a nearby cactus; the thorns entered his head, and a trickle of blood began to flow from the wound.

Stan heard a clang. He whipped his head around (though he regretted it as soon as he did, his head still aching from Leonidas's potion) in time to see Becca's sword flying into the air. Wasting no time, she kicked DZ in the stomach, knocking the wind out of him, and she ran. "Come on, Leo!" she cried as she sprinted off into the night.

Stan became aware that Leonidas was no longer next to him; he had gotten up and was now slinging Geno's unconscious form over his back. He made to follow Becca, but then he stopped for a minute. He turned back to look at the players. DZ was still doubled over, and Rex was still growling in Leonidas's direction, but Stan looked at Leonidas. There was something in his eyes, Stan suddenly realized, something that Stan couldn't place. Was it pity?

Sadness? Jealousy? Whatever it was, Stan knew it was out of place in the ruthless assassin that Leonidas was.

"Leo, RUN!" came Becca's cries; she now sounded a distance away. DZ had gotten back to his feet now and, his face contorted in rage, he had strung an arrow pointed at Leonidas. Then, with one last look, at the three of them, Leonidas was gone in a burst of Fire Charges; DZ's arrow flew into the fire and hit nothing but air.

But in a moment, Stan realized that this was not true. A figure appeared from nowhere, engulfed in tongues of fire; an Enderman, DZ's arrow sticking from its chest. Stan didn't bother drawing a weapon; the monster was on fire, and it would die before it could reach him. Sure enough, the tall spindly figure succumbed to death at Stan's feet, leaving the twelfth Ender Pearl on the sand as the body evaporated.

Suddenly, Stan remembered what had happened to Kat; he ran over to her and saw that Geno's sword had cut across her chest, just below her neck. Stan wasted no time in pulling out one of his two remaining Healing Potions and administering it to the wound; the cut instantly sealed, and Kat, though remaining asleep, gave a deep breath that Stan took to mean that she would be all right.

* * * * *

Stan was in deep thought as he sat on the front steps of Oob's house. Mella and Blerge were inside the house, caring for the still injured Kat who was now lying incapacitated in a bed. Charlie was in the village library, using the crafting table within to turn their Ender Pearls and Blaze Rods into the twelve Eyes of Ender that they would need to locate and enter the End. DZ, Oob, Ohsow the village butcher, Stull, Sequi and the Iron Golem were congregated around the well, talking and playing together.

Stan was aware that the next day they were to fight a great battle, and as he sat here with nothing to do but wait for the others to finish their tasks, he found it the perfect time to contemplate various thoughts that had become present in his mind over the course of their journey.

After the last night, Leonidas was at the front of his mind. Stan wasn't sure what, but there was definitely something off about the way that he had looked at them. He had fought Leonidas twice so far, and both times he had initiated violence against him and his friends for no good reason, and Stan had thusly marked him as equal in savagery to Geno, Becca, King Kev and the lot of them. Still, something about that look from the previous night made Stan feel slightly guilty about classifying him as such...

Then there was Mr. A. They had thankfully not seen Mr. A since their encounter in the Abandoned Mine Shaft, but the griefer's self-professed motives for his hatred of Stan and his friends seemed awfully misguided... assuming, that is, if anything he said was true at all, which seemed more unlikely the more Stan thought about it. What Stan had heard about Avery007 from the Apothecary was that he was a kind player, someone who stood up for the rights of those not able to do so for themselves. Stan could not imagine any scenario in which Avery might befriend a dark-hearted griefer like Mr. A.

He was definitely lying, decided Stan, and he told himself so firmly. Still, Stan believed that Mr. A had fabricated the story based on a real experience; he had seemed too passionate while telling the story for it to not have some basis in fact. That being said, it was all the same that Mr. A's hatred was injudicious, and Stan intended to tell him so should they ever meet again. Which was unlikely, seeing as he probably died in the sand trap...

Stan dismissed the unpleasant thought from his mind and his thoughts settled on himself. For some reason, everybody seemed to see something special in him. Crazy Steve had seen it, Sally had seen it, and Kat had seen it too. Though he couldn't pinpoint what it was, Stan believed that there was something, some force, some otherworldly entity that influenced him in difficult situations. Despite the fact that he knew nothing of what that power was, how he was able to use it, or whether or not it even existed, he knew that this power of questionable reality would be put to the ultimate test in the End.

There was one more thing that Stan would definitely have liked to think about, to dwell on, and to consider the possibilities of. However, he refused to let himself think too heavily on it, for it might distract him in the End; no, not until he had conquered the End would he allow himself to think about Sally.

It was just as well, thought Stan as he became aware of Charlie leaving the house; his thinking time was officially over. He stood up and walked over to Charlie, meeting in the middle of the gravel path.

"You've got them?" asked Stan in a whisper, though he was not sure why he spoke in this manner.

"Yeah," replied Charlie, and he held up one of the Eyes of Ender. It was the same size and shape of the Ender Pearl from which it was crafted, but it looked like a green cat's eye with a constricted pupil. Even as Charlie held it inactive in his hand, Stan felt a sense of electricity in the air, as if the Eye itself was emitting energy into the air. Upon closer inspection, Stan noticed tiny wisps of purple smoke rising from the eye.

Charlie pulled the other eleven Eyes of Ender from his inventory, and he grinned. "Awesome, aren't they? We are officially all set to go into the End."

Stan was glad to see Charlie in such a good mood; what with Lemon's death, and Kat's injury, their time in the NPC Village had seen Charlie grimmer than Stan would have believed possible of him. Besides being worried about the state of his friend, Stan knew that Charlie would need to be confident and in high spirit for their epic foray into the End.

Stan and Charlie were still admiring the Eyes of Ender when DZ walked over to them, Oob and Ohsow in tow.

"So a horse walks into a bar, and the bartender says, 'why the long face?'" said DZ, and the two villagers burst into hysterical fits of laughter. DZ walked over to talk to Stan and Charlie as Oob and Ohsow inquired as to what horses and bartenders were.

"So, we've got the Eyes, then? Excellent!" he exclaimed as his question was answered by the grins on both of their faces, and the green orbs in DZ's hands. "So we're going to leave tomorrow?"

"I guess so," replied Stan, "providing that Kat is feeling up to it."

At that exact moment, the door to Oob's house flew open, and out of the doorway burst Kat. She wasn't wearing any armor, and there was a leather band across her chest where Geno had cut her, but besides that, she seemed back to her normal self. She literally ran out of the house and took a flying leap, landing right next to the boys.

"Hey, Kat! You're awfully energetic for someone who just almost got herself cut open," said Charlie with a smirk.

"Are you kidding? I feel awesome!" she said, bouncing on the balls of her feet. "Blerge and Mella made a bunch of bread, and Moganga added some stuff called glowstone dust to it, and that stuff made me feel so much better!" She turned to Stan. "I owe you a huge thanks though, Stan. Without that potion, Moganga said that I would have died."

"Ah, it's no big deal," said Stan, shrugging but giving a humble grin all the same. "You would have done the same for me."

"Very true," replied Kat.

"So Kat, I take it by the fact that you're more energetic than we are that you're gonna be able to go into the End tomorrow?" Charlie asked.

"Are you kidding? If you guys weren't tired right now, I'd be willing to go right now!"

"Well, I just finished a nap earlier, I'm not tired at all," said Charlie.

"Yeah, same here," said DZ.

"Me too," said Stan, his face lighting with excitement. "So… are you guys ready? You want to go into the End right now?"

There was no hesitation; Kat, Charlie and DZ all nodded at the same time.

"Okay," said Stan, his eyes blazing with inner fire. "Let's get ready."

* * * * *

The NPC Villagers were all quite disappointed to hear that the players were leaving the village; according to DZ, they had all become very fond of the players, and to DZ and Charlie in particular. Nonetheless, the villagers all rose magnificently to the challenge of supplying the players with the supplies that they would need to conquer the End. While the villagers were usually unwilling to give anything up unless in exchange for Emeralds, which they saw as a form of currency, the villagers gave the players everything that they could.

The farmers, including Oob and his family, supplied the villagers with a generous amount of bread, so that they would be well fed on their expedition. The players also received a copious restocking of arrows from the farmers, and Charlie was given Flint and Steel from a villager named Vella. Leol, the village blacksmith who lived in the forge, was probably the most helpful of all; he willingly replaced Stan's and Kat's weapons with a diamond axe and a diamond sword, respectively. He also gave each player a diamond helmet and chestplate. Moganga helped in her own way, by taking the players' diamond gear and, after fifteen minutes emerged from the church with the gear glowing with enchantments of Protection for the armor and Sharpness for the swords.

In return for all of these commodities, the villagers only asked for them to do anything possible to take down King Kev.

The sun was high in the sky when the four players, suited up and with weapons equipped, they lined up, facing the villagers. Stan looked out onto the faces of the villagers, and particularly of those of Stull and Sequi, who were seated on the shoulders of the Iron Golem, and of Blerge and Mella, who were holding hands as tears rolled down their cheeks. Though it would have been characteristic, none of the villagers were wandering.

Oob stepped forward from the ten villagers and Iron Golem, and it was implied that he was speaking for the entirety of the village's population of ten.

"Brave players, we would like to thank you for the services that you have done us personally, in killing the Spider Jockey that had plagued our village. We would also like to thank you for the work you are doing to make life on this server the best possible for not just the people of our village, but of the citizens of this server as a whole. You will be welcome back to our village at any time that you would like, and you will be welcomed with open arms. Goodbye, and good luck."

The entire village simultaneously nodded in unison. Stan was more touched by this simple gesture from these simple people than he had been from anything he had seen in Minecraft so far. Even if it hadn't been for the Adorian Village, or the deaths of Blackraven and Crazy Steve and the like, he would have been very keen to defeating the King for the sole purpose of making life better for these NPCs.

Stan didn't hear what Charlie said in response to this; he was too busy reaffirming the image of King Kev in his mind as public enemy number one for abusing these people, and all other people in Elementia. As the four players gave an about face and headed away from the village, Stan was more sure than ever that there was nothing in the End that was unsurpassable if they kept in mind the image of an Elementia free of King Kev.

CHAPTER 24: WITHIN THE STRONGHOLD

The trek through the desert was long and drawn-out, as Stan had expected. He knew that the Ender Desert was large, but he hadn't realized just how expansive the biome really was. Stan had been to forests, plains, and jungles since he had been on Minecraft, but this desert biome was by far the largest biome that he had encountered, and it all looked the same. There were small knolls of sand blocks scattered here and there, and cactus dotted the landscape, punctuated by an occasional pool of lava or water.

Stan didn't understand how Charlie, who was navigating, didn't get lost in the endless dune sea. He walked up to ask him about it at one point, but he didn't need to, because he saw. Charlie had an Eye of Ender in his hand, and every so often he would toss it into the air, and in a burst of purple particles, the eye would float forward a few blocks in a certain direction, then fall back down into Charlie's outstretched hand. Charlie seemed focused, so he didn't ask, but Stan believed that the Eyes were most likely floating towards the entrance to the End.

Stan fell back next to Kat. "So do you have any ideas, at all, about the End? Like where it is or what's in there?" he asked her.

Kat glanced at him and smirked. "Honestly, man, I have no idea where the End is. And frankly, whenever I think about what we're actually gonna find there, I end up almost crapping my pants. Whatever it is, though, it is *not* gonna be easy to get to. I'm willing to put money on the fact that the King was only able to make a stash there because he was able to use his operating powers."

"What *are* operating powers?" asked Stan. At Kat's look of disbelief, he said, "Well, I've heard a couple of people *mention* them before, but I've never actually found out what they are."

"Well, basically," said Kat, "operating powers are special powers that you get when you start a server, or you can be given them from somebody else with operating powers. Basically, if you have operating powers, you get to be a total badass. You can create and destroy any blocks you want instantly, you can shoot arrows and fireballs from your fingers, you can create explosions anywhere you want, and you can fly." Now it was Stan's turn to make a face of disbelief. "Yeah, that's right, fly. Really fast, too. Basically, operating powers make you a Minecraft superhero. Also, you can let people back on the server after they've been banned."

"Wait, what?" exclaimed Stan. His eyes were glowing now, and a grin was spreading over his face. "With operating powers, you can return people to the server after they've been killed?" Kat nodded. "Is there any way that you can get them? Can you learn them somehow?"

Kat gave a short laugh, and a dark look crossed her face. "Stan, if there were any way to learn them, there would be ridiculous structures popping up all over the place, and people would be returning from the dead all the time! The point of operating powers on servers like this one is to regulate activities on the server, and to prevent griefing; you can't just *learn* them."

Stan felt a little let down at the idea that he couldn't become an operator through training or any type of work or practice. It would have made him practically impossible to stop when he tried to destroy the King. But this thought raised a new, alarming one in his head.

"The King doesn't have operating powers, does he?" asked Stan quickly as he tried not to imagine what fighting someone with operating powers would be like.

Kat rolled her eyes. "Stan, haven't you been paying attention to anything that anyone's told us about the history of this place?"

Stan didn't answer; truthfully, history was his worst subject in school, and he could never remember anything about history in real life, let alone in Minecraft. Kat sighed, and answered his question in a tone of exasperation.

"The King gave up his operating powers a while ago, Stan. Trust me, if he still had operating powers, we wouldn't have gotten out of the gate of the King's castle. The King thought that if he gave them up, then he'd be equal to everybody else, and it would make people stop wanting to revolt against him."

"Well, that plan kind of blew up in his face," replied Stan with a smirk. "Look at what we're doing!"

"You say that," said Kat grimly, "but he the King's plan did work for a decent amount of time, seeing as we're the first who have even tried to overthrow him since he gave his powers up, unless you count what Avery did."

"Yeah, but that's just because most people are too scared of his forces," retorted Stan. "I can't have been the only one to notice that back at the castle, over half of the people there helped us escape."

Kat opened her mouth as if to say something, but a pensive look crossed her face and she closed it again. Instead, she reached down and scratched Rex between the ears, and continued trekking onward. Stan did notice, however, that her sword was now in the tight grasp of her right hand. Stan, sensing that their conversation was over, now amused himself by watching DZ, who was practicing advanced sword fighting techniques on a wandering sheep that was running for its life.

* * * * *

The sun was on a sinking path when Stan finally spotted tall formations on the distant skyline. As the four players and Rex approached them, Stan saw the welcome sight of mountains towering up over the desert plains. The setting sun splashed a brilliant array of colors on the sky, and there was an element of natural beauty of the masses of land rising from the ground, silhouetted against the sunset. The group actually stopped walking for a moment because Charlie had dropped the Eyes in his hand, transfixed at the beauty of the landscape. Kat had to literally pull Charlie away from staring into the sunset in order for the journey to continue.

Charlie had found love at first sight; the mountains absolutely took his breath away. He found himself continuously drawn to the majesty of the mountains, from the herds of wild sheep roaming the steep slopes, to the black veins of coal ore speckling the rocky cliff faces, to the springs of water and lava that occasionally ran out of the sides of the mountains. Eventually, Kat took over the navigation, as Stan had to keep Charlie from getting distracted and Kat, after the episode in the desert, flat-out refused to let DZ navigate.

Kat could tell from the Eyes of Ender that they were nearing their goal; the trajectory of the Eyes thrown in the air lead the group to a cave situated in the cliffside. As they headed down the cave, Stan putting up torches as they went, Charlie suddenly spoke out.

"Hey guys!"

"We get it, Charlie," said Kat through gritted teeth as she fumbled with another Eye, "the mountainside grass *is* more beautiful than the grass in the forest, we get it."

"No, not that, *that*! Look at those blocks there!"

Stan put a torch up at the point that Charlie had gestured too, and in the light a row of blocks stood out from the natural stone around it. These blocks appeared to be bricks, but they were grey instead of crimson.

"I don't recognize these blocks, do you guys?" asked Charlie.

Kat shook her head, and DZ said, "Negatory, sir," but Stan, though initially in the same mind as Kat, suddenly saw the blocks with remembrance. "Weren't those the same blocks that the King's castle was made out of?" he asked.

The other three players looked confused for a second, but then it dawned on them that Stan was indeed correct; the King's castle had indeed been made out of these same stone bricks. Kat tossed one of the Eyes of Ender into the air; it started to float towards the stone bricks. Kat snatched the Eye out of the air and grinned.

"The way into the End is through here!" she said excitedly. "Charlie, mine through this wall!"

Charlie pocketed the book he had been holding in his hand and drew his diamond pickaxe. "I just checked in the book, and it said that the Eyes of Ender would lead us to what's called a Stronghold, and that the portal to the End will be inside. This must be the outside of the Stronghold... hey, what the..." said Charlie as he struggled with his pickaxe. As he had spoken, he had mined one of the stone brick blocks, but the second one that he had tried to mine into now had his pickaxe wedged in it.

"It's... not... coming... out..." grunted Charlie as he tried to pull the pickaxe out of the block. Stan noticed that it was not wedged in the block as much as it was stuck to it. The block appeared to be made out of some sort of slimy, gelatinous goo that was now latched to Charlie's pickaxe like glue.

"Oh, let me see that, you little wimp," snapped Kat as she grabbed the handle of Charlie's pickaxe from him. She was stronger than he was, and in an almighty tug she wrenched the pickaxe from the gooey block and started bearing down into it full force with the diamond tool.

"Why is this block so difficult to mine?" Kat asked to no one in particular as she again and again wrenched the pickaxe from the stone block.

Stan watched bewildered, but he was relieved to see that the mysterious block was about to break. Right as the block was about to break, out of the corner of his eye, Stan noticed a horrified look flicker across DZ's face. DZ cried out, "No, Kat, stop! I think that block might be..."

But it was too late. As Kat gave the stone block one last strike, it burst apart like a water balloon exploding, dousing everyone in grey slime. But the worst part was that out of the goo burst had sprung something small, fast, and grey that now latched itself onto Kat's face. Kat screamed, and wildly tried to swat the thing off of her, but it was no use; the tiny monster crawled all over her body, moving too fast for Stan's eyes to track. Nobody tried to get it off for fear that an attack on the monster would hit Kat instead. Every so often Kat would elicit a sound of anguish, indicating that the creature had bit her, stung her, or something of that nature.

As he tried to track the monster to get a clean shot at it with his axe, Stan noticed that Kat's hands were now swatting at various places at her back, suggesting that the monster had crawled down inside her armor. Kat's fist pounded the back of her chestplate to no avail, as her flailing fists did nothing to penetrate the diamond of her chestplate. However, she gave Stan an idea.

He spun his axe around and, with the butt end, tapped the back of Kat's chestplate with moderate force. The diamond armor compressed into Kat's back, knocking her forwards. Stan heard a hissing and a crunching coupled with Kat's grunt of pain, and something small and scaly fell out of the back of her armor. It was a small grey insect that looked like some sort of odd armadillo-porcupine-worm cross breed. The monster made spiderlike clicking noises for a few seconds while it twitched, and then it was still.

"That was Block 97!" shouted DZ, drawing his sword. "I've heard stories about it; it spawns those things, Silverfish! Get ready, there's gonna be more!"

Stan looked around, bewildered, unsure what DZ was talking about, but sure enough, all around the inside of the room they had just mined into, stone bricks ruptured into sprays of goo, and a swarm of Silverfish was on the move towards the players.

The monsters were not particularly strong in comparison to the bite of a spider or the arrow of the Skeleton, but they were much smaller and faster, like miniature spiders. Stan managed to kill each of them with one powerful blow of the axe, but each time one of the monsters fell, it seemed to awaken more and more Silverfish spawned from the stone brick walls.

Stan was tiring of fighting them quickly, not from their strength, but just from their overwhelming numbers. Stan was about to suggest to the three players fighting besides him that a retreat back out of the mine was in order when the monsters started appearing in less and less numbers, and a few moments later they had stopped appearing altogether. The players were breathing heavily; the four of them plus Rex must have killed two hundred and fifty Silverfish in the space of about two minutes.

Stan wiped the sweat off his brow, and he pulled the tail end of a Silverfish off of his axe blade and looked at DZ. "What just happened, DZ?"

DZ was breathing heavily; he appeared to have killed the most Silverfish of everybody, judging by the pile of grey scales a block high at his feet, and he caught his breath before responding. "Those were mobs called Silverfish. They spawn when you break a block called Block 97, which is disguised as a stone-based block found in a type of structure, which I guess is a Stronghold. The annoying part is when you attack them, they'll spawn other Silverfish from nearby Block 97."

DZ sighed, an amazed look coming to his face. "I didn't know that Silverfish or Block 97 really existed, I thought they were just rumors or upcoming features or something."

"So," said Stan, putting two and two together, "we can't mine any blocks in this Stronghold? The way to the End is in this fortress, and we can't mine anything in here?"

"Correct-o," said DZ, nodding. "We can't mine anywhere around here or we run the risk of spawning another swarm of Silverfish, and frankly, I can't be the only one that doesn't want to fight those freaking parasites again."

"So," said Kat, her voice heavy as she realized what that meant, "we have to navigate this entire thing by foot?"

DZ nodded, and Stan threw back his head and groaned, and Kat hung her head in despair. Charlie on the other hand, looked at them with amusement.

"Oh, come on, guys, don't be like that! For all we know, the entrance to the End could be just around the corner! Don't be such a bunch of downers, let's at least give it a shot, what's the worst that can happen?

Well, Charlie was right about one thing: while they were navigating the Stronghold, the silverfish continued to remain the worst thing that they had encountered. It was a fairly peaceful walk, save a few zombies that spawned in dark corners and storage rooms. That being said, navigating the fortress without mining directly through any of the walls was possibly the most frustrating task that Stan had endured. The Eyes of Ender still pointed them towards something, apparently located deep in the heart of the Stronghold, but there were so many stairways, corridors, turns and sides rooms that it was near impossible to navigate the maze. After they passed the same book-and-cobweb-filled library for the third time, Stan turned to the others, and, struggling to keep his voice level, inquired as to whether or not they had really passed the library before.

"No," said DZ, pointing down a hallway they had just passed, "you're thinking of the library down that way, it had the jail cell next to it, remember?"

"You're thinking of the storage room," said Kat, "the one that had all that cobblestone in it, the jail cell is the one with the iron bars."

"But there were also iron bars in that hall back there next to the side corridor, are you sure you're not thinking of those?" asked Charlie.

"No, I'm sure that it was a full wall of iron bars," said Kat.

"Why don't you let me see the freaking Eyes of Ender, I'll show you..." started DZ, but he was cut off by Stan.

"DZ, after all that crap back when we first met you, don't think that you're getting your hands on *any* kind of navigational tools," snapped Stan in retort.

"There is a room with lava and a portal made of a strange white stone, are you looking for that?" came a fifth voice.

The four players turned around to face the voice, and Stan couldn't believe his eyes. Standing in the middle of the stone brick hallway, a primitive stone hoe grasped in his hands, was Oob. As the players stared at him, the NPC villager smiled and waved at them until Charlie broke the silence.

"Oob!? What... what the... what are you *doing* here? Why aren't you back in the village?"

"I would like to help you conquer the End dimension. I feel that I should do my part to help you defeat the one called King Kev. I have been following you, and now I am ready to help!"

"Oob!" shouted Stan, infuriated that their plans would now have to be changed to compensate for returning Oob to his village. "You can't come with us to the End, are you crazy? You'll get slaughtered!"

"But I would like to help you! Come, I have found the way to enter the End!" And with that, the villager hobbled back down the hallway.

Sensing impending danger, Stan urgently sprinted down the hallway after him. Oob entered the room at the end of the hall, which was significantly brighter than the rest of the Stronghold. Stan was only halfway down the hall, and he watched on in horror as Oob was knocked back into the hallway, his head slamming into the wall, an arrow protruding from his shoulder became visible. Stan's mind went blank except for the thought of the villager now slumped up against the wall. Stan knelt down next to Oob, his mind going into medical overdrive as he pulled out his last Potion of

317

Healing, vaguely aware of Charlie, Kat and DZ rushing in to engage Oob's assailant.

The arrow had sunken deep into Oob's shoulder, and the blow to his head had left him unconscious. Stan, adrenaline heightening his intuitions, made the on-the-spot decision to use his last Potion of Healing to cure Oob. As Stan applied the blood red potion, the arrow popped out, the wound instantly resealed itself, and Oob's chest gave a peaceful rise and fall. Confident that the villager would be okay, Stan burst into the brightly lit room to deal with his attacker. What he saw made his jaw drop.

He was standing in a stone brick room with pools of lava in all four corners, and windows fitted with iron bars lining the walls. In the center of the room was a stone brick staircase. A black cage block set at the top of the stairs, but no figure revolved within it; this spawner had been disabled. Behind this black cage sat a frame of blocks unlike anything Stan had seen before. The base of these blocks appeared to be made of lunar rock, and the top had an ornate turquoise pattern. These strange blocks were arranged in a five by five ring with no corners that formed a frame, and Stan could see that through the center of the frame was a drop into a pit of lava.

However, the feature drawn most immediately to Stan's attention were the bodies of Charlie, Kat, and DZ all lying lifeless on the ground. Kat had a considerably sized lump on her head, DZ had a slash across his chest, and Charlie had an arrow protruding from his heel. Rex lay sprawled out, feebly whimpering, on the ground besides them. Above the four bodies stood Mr. A, wearing the same diamond helmet and chestplate as Stan himself was wearing.

Stan stared in shock; he had accepted it as fact that the griefer had perished in the sand trap. Stan noticed movement out of the corner of his eye and saw that Mr. A had pulled something from his inventory: an Ender Pearl, un-crafted into an Eye of Ender. Stan supposed that Mr. A believed that Ender Pearls would activate the portal. In the intense wave of hatred that had erupted in his stomach since he had spotted Mr. A, Stan was about to make a scathing remark to that effect when Mr. A threw the Ender Pearl towards Stan. Not knowing exactly what would happen, Stan hopped backwards and the Pearl landed at his feet.

To Stan's horror, in a burst of purple smoke the Ender Pearl was gone, and Stan was staring at a pair of legs adorned in black pants. Stan dared himself to look up, and he saw Mr. A standing right in front of him, his arm bringing the sword down across Stan's body.

The impact of the sword, though slightly lessened by the axe that Stan managed to reflexively raise to block the attack, sent Stan tumbling backwards. He came to a stop beneath one of the iron bar walls, and Stan barely had time to raise his axe in defense when Mr. A brought the sword down onto Stan again, putting his full body weight down through the sword onto the axe handle that was now pinching Stan's neck to the ground.

Stan began to see white and red flashes as the axe handle drove further and further into his neck. Determined to die in defiance, Stan focused all of his remaining energy into thrusting the axe off of him, and Stan took a frenzied swing with his axe, still blinded by the lack of air, hoping against hope that he would hit something.

Miraculously, Stan heard the clang of diamond hitting diamond, and he knew that his axe blade had struck Mr. A by the grunt of pain. Stan used this lucky blow to buy time to regain his vision, and when it finally returned, he saw Mr. A notching an arrow and pulling back the string. Stan ducked the arrow and, rage fueling his bloodlust, he used his axe to engage Mr. A's sword in a mêlée battle.

The hacking and slashing was intense and heated to a remarkable degree. Stan's scowl was mirrored on his adversary's face as the two battled around the ornate portal in a dance of death. Stan was aware that he was greatly outmatched, so he was absolutely astounded when, by a lucky shot, his double uppercut combination hit Mr. A's hand, sending the sword spiraling into the air. Before Stan could follow through, the griefer let loose a barrage of Fire Charges that exploded at Stan's feet in a short series of starbursts. Stan stepped back, away from the smoke, ready for the inevitable retaliation. Moments later Mr. A's form flew through the smoke, sword back in hand, and Stan had to jump backwards onto the stairs leading to the portal in order to avoid being cleaved in half by the sword slash that cracked the stone stairs when it hit.

Mr. A pressed the attack, driving Stan up the stairs, to the very edge of the portal. Stan leaned backwards to avoid the whistling blade of the griefer's sword, and he found that there was no ground below him, just a pit of lava. Stan kicked off the base of the portal and landed on the other side. The battle commenced, this time with a pit of lava separating Stan and Mr. A. The griefer let loose a flurry of wild stabbing attacks with his sword. Stan was able to dodge the first few, but then one of the sword jabs caught Stan in the hand, and his axe flew backwards.

Stan knew that it was useless, there was no way he could turn his back on Mr. A to retrieve his weapon. Energy coursing through his veins, Stan raised his arms, ready to defend his exposed face from the barrage of arrows that would find a weakness within a few shots. The first arrow glanced off his helmet, and he felt the helmet rattle his brain, making it ache incredibly. Stan prepared himself for the next arrow that could very well kill him, when he heard a savage cry of pain, and he dared to look up.

What he saw was Oob, standing on the edge of the portal, his stone hoe moving through the air as if he had just swung it; and Mr. A, in midair, falling headfirst into the pit, and landing with a terrible, scathing splash into the pool of lava beneath the portal, spraying Stan with a wave of fire particles that bit like wasp stings.

Stan stared at Oob, and then at the pit of molten fire with the griefer struggling to survive. Slowly, Stan made the connection that the NPC had just saved his life. At the moment, however, Stan

320

did not sing Oob's thanks but, rather, looked sadly into the pit of lava containing the enemy that had plagued him from his second day in Minecraft. The turbulence in the molten liquid had stopped, there was no more struggling; Mr. A was no more.

"It didn't have to be like this, Mr. A," said Stan, depression deeply intertwined with his words. "We could have been friends, you know. There was nothing that could have stopped us from being on the same side, the side of right. There was just the King. The players didn't betray your friend Avery, it was the King that did that. I only wish that I could have helped you see it sooner, before it was too late." Stan cast one last long, sad look into the lava that was now stained with the blood of his enemy, and he turned to the NPC Villager.

"Oob, thank you. I would be dead without you, and I was wrong. Wherever we go, whatever we do, you are welcome to come with us and help."

"Amen to that," came a voice from behind them as the villager beamed.

Stan turned around. DZ was standing up, smiling at Stan and Oob. Charlie was standing behind him, looking proud, and Kat was feeding Rex with some rotten flesh she had on hand. Charlie held two empty glass bottles in his hand; it seemed that he had used his last two Potions of Healing to jointly heal himself, Kat and DZ. Relief breaking across both their faces, Stan and Oob rushed down the stone steps and met the three players and dog in a group hug. When they broke apart, Kat looked at Stan.

"I saw what happened," she said, looking from him, to Oob, and back. "You two were fantastic."

"You really were," said Charlie, and DZ enthusiastically nodded his consent.

"I just wish that it didn't have to end like this…" said Stan, and he glanced back towards the portal and the pit of fire beneath it, but Kat took him by the cheek and turned him away.

"It's okay, Stan. You did what you had to do," she said, her eyes deep and meaningful, which calmed Stan.

"Yeah. It really sucked that you had to do it, but you did the right thing," added Charlie.

"You're right," said Stan, and he looked at the ground for a moment, letting the memory of the player called Mr. A leave his mind, like letting a balloon soar up to the heavens; and with this his mind was clear again. When he looked up at the three players looking back at him, it was clear what had to be done.

"It's time, isn't it," he said. It was not a question. They all knew that the time had come.

"Let's end this," said Kat, nodding in Charlie's direction.

Charlie walked up the white frame of blocks, took a deep breath, and pulled out the twelve Eyes of Ender. Each ornate portal frame block had a hemispherical indent in the middle, the perfect fit for one Eye of Ender. Charlie walked around the outside ring of the portal, carefully fitting one Eye of Ender into each of the twelve blocks that made up the portal frame. When the last Eye was fitted into place, the twelve eyes glowed purple simultaneously, and for a few second, they did nothing but give off an eerie sound and emit copious amounts of purple particles. Then, all at once, the space within the portal showed not a drop down into a pit of lava, but a dark, spectral space that seemed to go on forever, speckled with luminous dots of all colors, giving Stan the impression that he was staring into some deep, untouched realm of the cosmos.

Stan, Charlie, Kat, DZ and Oob gathered around the portal, looking into the ominous black depths. Stan looked around at his friends.

"Are we ready?" he asked.

A scan of everyone's face showed four brave, well-equipped warriors, ready to tackle whatever the ominous End dimension had in store.

With an almighty yell of "BOO-YAH!" DZ jumped off of the portal frame and into the black portal, which swallowed him instantly. Charlie was about to jump into the portal next, but he was interrupted when Oob fell into the portal by way of his aimless wandering. Charlie followed behind him. Kat scratched Rex behind the ears (They knew from Charlie's book that dogs could not enter the End, but they were confident that Rex would manage to find them on his own should they re-enter the overworld alive) and, with closed eyes and a deep breath, she too disappeared into the depths of the End portal.

Stan looked around at the room; he realized that this underground chamber of stone and lava may very well have been his last view of the overworld in Minecraft. Taking a deep breath, and with the image of a dead King Kev and a free Elementia in his head, Stan jumped off of the portal frame and fell into the black void in a freefall.

CHAPTER 25: THE END

Whereas the travel through the Nether Portal had felt as though he were being squeezed through a tube, Stan found that immediately after entering the End portal, he landed feet-first onto a platform of black rock that he recognized as obsidian. Also, although the Nether had been hot and dry, Stan felt no significant change in the atmosphere of the End other than an apparent dormant static that hung in the air.

Stan looked around and saw his friends, like himself, were looking at the room that they had spawned in, which appeared to be made of a type of lunar rock similar to the base of the frame of the End portal. They were completely surrounded by it, and Stan felt his stomach drop. Were they underground? Was the task of the End to mine around until they located their goal? He voiced this question to the others, and immediately, the air of the group turned to panic.

"Hey, guys, don't worry, alright?" said Charlie, taking his pickaxe to one of the stone blocks. "I'll mine around a little bit, I seriously doubt that the final challenge of Minecraft would be a gigantic mining world." Charlie angled his aim diagonally and started to tunnel upwards. The others followed him.

The further upwards they tunneled, the more Stan's unease grew. As Charlie's pickaxe broke the surface and struck air, Stan couldn't shake the feeling that there was something...

"...watching us!" cried Stan as he was charged by a pair of Endermen. He cut the first one on the side with his axe, and it teleported away, while the other one was killed instantly by a lucky shot that took off its head.

"They're freaking everywhere!" yelled DZ as the wounded mob reappeared behind Stan, and DZ ended its life with a stab of the sword. "Look down!"

Without thinking, three players obeyed DZ's command and stared at the moon-white ground. Stan heard DZ's voice calm voice (which was amazing, seeing as Stan was terrified at what the End turned out to be so far) give a command.

"Oob, I need you to look around and tell us how many Endermen are out there."

"What?" came Oob's disgruntled voice. "Won't the large, scary black things kill me?"

"Don't worry, you're an NPC, they won't notice you."

"But..."

"Just do it Oob, I swear you'll be alright," came DZ's voice, a slight edge to it now.

A few moments later came Oob's response.

"They are everywhere. I see their eyes going even far off into the distance. How are we to defeat all of them?"

"Don't worry, guys, I got this," said DZ, as if sensing the air of panic in the group increase tenfold. "I know how we can kill them. Take these, I found them as we were going through the mountains." Stan heard DZ fumbling, and a few moments later Stan saw a block land at his feet. It was orange, and it appeared to be some kind of plant, but it was only when Stan picked it up and saw the eerie face carved into it that he realized that it was a pumpkin.

"And what in the name of God do you expect me to do with this?" came Kat's irate voice from just to the left of Stan.

"Take off your helmet and put it on your head."

Stan was struck by a sudden notion that his battle with Mr. A may have knocked something loose inside DZ's head. Charlie said in tones of dripping sarcasm, "Yeah, you first, DZ."

"Gladly," said DZ calmly, and Stan sensed that he had stood up; using his peripheral vision, he barely viewed DZ standing upright and looking quite ridiculous with his head stuck into the bottom of the pumpkin. The carved pumpkin face was where DZ's own face should have been.

"DZ, you look like an idiot, where are you going with this?" hissed Kat, as if she were afraid talking too loudly would provoke the crowds of Endermen roaming ominously amongst them.

In response, Stan's strained oblong vision picked up DZ walking right up to an Enderman and staring directly into its eyes. Amazingly, the Enderman didn't begin to shake, teleport behind him, or, for that matter, acknowledge his presence at all. DZ used this to his advantage, and one stab through the chest later, the Enderman was nothing more than an Ender Pearl sitting idly on the ground.

Before any of them could voice their stunned amazement, DZ explained. "You can see out the eye holes of the pumpkin, and even though you can't see that great, the obstruction prevents the Endermen from being able to detect you. Seriously, they have no idea that you're even there, you can just walk up to them and kill them."

Stan didn't need any more encouraging; with great gusto, he ripped his diamond helmet off of this head, haphazardly shoved it into his inventory; he proceeded to snatch up the pumpkin and jam it awkwardly onto his head. DZ was definitely right about one thing: the pumpkin *did* considerably obstruct Stan's vision, and it was only through squinting that he could tell the forms of Kat and Charlie, both adorning the pumpkins.

"Alrighty boys... and Kat," said DZ, and Stan was sure from his tone that a manic grin had spread on his face beneath the pumpkin, "Let the Great Enderman Massacre begin!"

Massacre truly was the appropriate word for it, for without being able to detect the players' lines of sight, the Endermen were powerless to stop the players from ambling right up to them and felling them one after another. Even with Oob not helping (his stone hoe was not strong enough to destroy an Enderman in one hit, and the villager certainly was not capable of beating one), all of the Endermen that they could see were dead within the space of three minutes.

"Dude, that was AWESOME!" called out Charlie to Stan, as Stan pulled the axe out of the monster he had just beheaded after throwing the weapon during a back flip.

"Thanks. Frankly, this was so easy, what are you to do but make up trick shots to keep things interesting?" smirked Stan, and he pulled the pumpkin from his head and wiped the sweat off his brow (though he had exerted almost no effort, it was very hot inside the pumpkin head). The others followed in suite.

Now that they had their pumpkins off and no Endermen to deal with, the four players plus Oob took their first real look at the End. The entirety of the ground seemed to be made of the moon-rock-like material, and the sky was a dark static pattern that didn't seem to move and was almost completely black. It was hard to make out the tall, black, looming pillars that were set against the black sky on first sight. These pillars were a wide square at the base, and extended various distances into the sky. There was a light source illuminating the top of each of the pillars, but Stan was not close enough to see what it was.

The most interesting part was that, as far as Stan could see, the End was not an infinite dimension like the overworld or the Nether; they were on a moon-rock island, floating in space, with around ten of the tall obsidian pillars protruding from the ground into the static heavens.

Immediately, something about this setup sat wrong with Stan. He looked at the others and saw from her face that Kat had realized it too, although DZ and Charlie hadn't. They were still pondering their surroundings, while Oob was (incredibly) wandering off yet again.

"Guys, the End isn't infinite. It's like an island," said Kat slowly as Stan dragged their villager friend back by the back off his brown collar, Oob's eyes still unfocused and clueless.

"Yeah, we've noticed," said Charlie, shrugging. "So what? Easier work for us, less places to look."

"That's just it," said Stan, dropping Oob and letting him fall to the ground like a sack of potatoes. "Less places to look. So why would the King move his stash here, when there are literally unlimited places to hide it in the overworld or the Nether?"

"I don't know, maybe because there are Endermen freaking *everywhere*?" stated DZ with the air of someone explaining that Earth revolves around the sun.

"DZ, you four players easily defeated all of the Endermen by doing nothing more than putting pumpkins upon your heads. Clearly, there is something more dangerous here that will prevent us from searching for the King's possessions," said Oob.

"He's right, DZ," said Charlie, realizing that Stan, Kat and Oob were right. "There's definitely something else going on here that's going to stop us from looking for the treasure."

"And what do you suppose that will be?" asked DZ indignantly, having been rustled by Oob making a more intelligent comment than himself.

Then they heard it. A long, piercing roar cut through the otherwise quiet End environment. It sounded like the scream of an

Enderman magnified by a thousand, with elements of tyrannosaurus and elephant noises mixed in to form one ultimate, blood-curdling roar.

"What... was... that?" whispered Charlie feebly.

"Oh... my... God," whispered Stan, as he spotted something in the sky that made his stomach implode with terror.

A pair of purple slits were present in the sky at first glance, but they grew larger, and larger, and larger, and before very long, the eyes of all four players plus Oob were locked in terror as the shape of a massive, black and silver winged beast with glowing purple eyes rocketed through the sky and straight towards them.

Not thinking much about it, just acting through a hidden instinct unlocked by fear, Kat, Stan and DZ simultaneously drew their bows and launched their arrows into the giant monster's face. Stan's and DZ's bounced off of the monster's silver scaly forehead, but Kat's arrow sunk straight into the monster's left eye. Right as the monster was about to barrel into them; it gave a roar and thrashed its head in agony, and changed courses to fly back up into the black sky.

It was then that Stan got his first full look at the monster. What he saw was absolutely horrifying; they had just shot arrows into a gigantic black dragon. Its mighty wings were flapping through the air creating rushes of wind like a jet plane, and a silver armor exoskeleton ran the length of its body, creating a web of protection extending over its almost-equally-tough-looking black hide.

Stan watched in wonder and foreboding as the wounded dragon circled the black obsidian pillars, and he watched in amazement as glowing orbs of white energy flew from atop the pillar and onto the dragon's face. The dragon roared again and flew on, and a moment later, Kat's arrow fell to the ground besides the players, having popped out of the dragon's eye.

"Guys, I think whatever's up there is healing him!" exclaimed DZ, his sword drawn and his eyes intensely focused on the dragon.

"Then we've got to destroy it," said Stan, already formulating a plan in his mind to do so.

"Okay, here's what we do," said Kat, her brow knitted in determination. "Stan, DZ, you go destroy whatever's on top of that pillar. Charlie, Oob, you two distract the dragon, and don't let it notice Stan and DZ. I don't think the dragon will like us destroying whatever it is up there."

"What about you?" Stan asked.

"I have a feeling that we're gonna be seeing some more Endermen soon," said Kat firmly, already pulling the pumpkin back into place on her head. "I'll take care of them. Now GO!" she screeched, for she had just noticed the dragon speeding towards them for another attack. Charlie drew his pickaxe, and Oob his hoe, and the two weapons plus Kat's sword simultaneously cut into the dragon's snout, sending it away for the time being.

"DZ! Start grabbing Ender Pearls!" cried Stan, picking up the orbs from the sea of Enderman corpses they had left in their wake.

"What? Why would we do that?" asked DZ incredulously.

"When I was fighting Mr. A, he threw one of these things at me and appeared right next to me with purple smoke all around him," said Stan, snatching a group of three from the ground. "I think that you can use these things to teleport! Watch this!"

Before DZ could interject, Stan had hummed the Ender Pearl with all his might into the sky, aiming for the top of the black obsidian pillar nearest him. His aim was spot on, and the pearl flew towards the top of the pillar. Stan closed his eyes, and moments later he felt the surge of pain to his knees that caused him to stumble, a sure indicator that something had happened. Once he had regained his footing, Stan opened his eyes.

His plan had worked; Stan was now standing atop one of the looming obsidian pillars. In the center stood a cubic crystal, rotating slowly within a fire erupting from a block of bedrock. The crystal flashed shades of light blue and pink, and on each side, strange red symbols flashed.

"Stan! Where are you?" came DZ's anxious cry from dozens of blocks below him. Stan looked down and saw DZ looking desperately around. He could also see the dragon flying away from Charlie and Oob, indicating that they had scored a hit, and Kat sneaking up behind an Enderman.

"I'm up here!" called Stan. He saw DZ look towards his voice and their eyes locked. "The plan worked! There's some sort of psychic crystal thingy up here, I'm pretty sure that 's what's healing the dragon!"

"That's great, Stan! Quick, figure out how to destroy the freaking thing!" came DZ's seemingly quiet yell across the landscape and up to Stan.

Stan decided to go for the most obvious method of destroying it first; he backed up to the very edge of the pillar, wanting to be as far away from the crystal as possible when he tried his method. He notched an arrow, and sent it directly into the center of the crystal. There was a superheated flash that made Stan's vision go white for a minute, but when it cleared he saw that the only thing left of the crystal was a block of bedrock that was set on fire.

"Just shoot the crystals, DZ!" Stan called down to his friend. "That makes them blow up!"

"I'll tell you what Stan!" came DZ's voice from down below. "You destroy all the crystals by teleporting around up there, and I'll shoot them down from down here!"

"Sounds like a plan!" Stan yelled back. He looked around and saw that, indeed, each of the pillars did seem to have a crystal rotating on top of them. He knew that they would not be able to properly fight the dragon until all of those crystals were destroyed. As scared as he was, he had to give credit to the King; this truly was the quintessential hiding place for anything valuable.

Stan saw DZ taking aim at the obelisk immediately to the left of him, so Stan turned to the right and drew another Ender Pearl from his inventory. He threw it with all his might, and once again he squeezed his eyes shut. Within a few seconds, there was the considerable pain in his leg region again. When he opened his eyes, he was standing on a different pillar, with yet another crystal ominously revolving before him. And again, with one arrow, the crystal exploded in a psychic burst fire.

Relieved, Stan gave a quick glance to his left just in time to see DZ's crystal explode, having been struck in the center by a land-to-air arrow. However, out of the corner of his eye, Stan saw something that made his stomach drop out. A flash of purple light, the rush of beating wings... Stan only barely had enough time to whip around and pull out his axe to drive it between the dragon's eyes. The axe only left a slight dent in the dragon's hide, which was quickly repaired by the nearest remaining crystal; nonetheless, it had the desired effect, and the dragon changed its trajectory and fled.

"Sorry, Stan!" came Charlie's yell from back down on the ground. "It flew away from us and came at you. I tried to shoot it but I missed."

"Well, aim better next time!" snapped Stan irritably. They were in the middle of an extremely dangerous fight, and there was no way that he could afford to fight a dragon on these pillars; one head butt and the dragon would knock him down to a terminal height.

Stan busied himself again with destroying the crystals. He saw DZ blow up another of the crystals, so he teleported to the next pillar over, destroying the crystal with another arrow. With DZ shooting from the ground, and Stan using his teleport-and-shoot strategy to great effect, it wasn't long before Stan sunk one last arrow into the solitary remaining crystal. The accompanying explosion marked the end of the dragon's healing capabilities.

When DZ saw the last burst of fire come from the last obsidian obelisk, he let out a yell of wild excitement, for now, the dragon would be possible to fight. Moments later, Stan appeared next to DZ in a burst of purple smoke.

"That's the last of 'em," said Stan with a sigh.

"Awesome," replied DZ. "How'd those Ender Pearls work out for you?"

"Great," answered Stan. "My knees hurt like all hell, but other than that I'm great. Wanna go kill a dragon now?"

"Let's do this!" cried DZ, and, sense of excitement building, they ran to join Oob and Charlie.

"Hey guys!" exclaimed Charlie as he drew back his pickaxe after striking the now-fleeing dragon. "Are the crystals all gone?"

"Yep, Stan just destroyed the last one," said DZ. "Have you guys figured out anything about how the dragon attacks?"

"Well, from what I've seen, the only thing that the dragon does is just keep flying towards us and trying to head butt us, but if we just keep on hitting it in the face when it gets close enough we should manage to kill it pretty quickly."

"Really?" asked Stan, raising an eyebrow. "That's all you guys have been doing? Just hitting it when it gets near you? And that's been hurting it?"

"Yes," replied Oob. "There has been a surprising lack of difficulty in fighting the dragon. The dragon has not come close to hurting either of us using its current attack pattern."

"Well," said Stan, looking around, "I guess the difficulty of this place isn't supposed to be fighting the dragon itself, but destroying the crystals, fighting the dragon and avoiding the Endermen all at the same time."

"Yeah," said DZ, nodding, "That sounds right. I guess we were right to come here as a team. The King seems to have picked this place as a good defense against just one or two people, not five."

"And I gotta say," added Charlie as he looked around, "Kats been doing a really good job fighting off the Endermen, I haven't seen any since we first... OH MY GOD!!!"

Stan looked at what had made Charlie scream, and his jaw dropped in dread. For he had been looking at Kat as she pulled her sword out of the back of an Enderman she had just killed, completely oblivious to the dragon that had set its sights on her and was now swooping down upon her. It never got there though, for just as Kat sensed the impending force about to slam into her, she spun around in time to see the form of Charlie hurl himself between the dragon and herself.

Charlie's pickaxe came down a little too late; Kat didn't see where it hit, but the dragon thrashed around in agony, it's front left claw thrashing out wildly and cutting a dent through the center of Charlie's chestplate. As the dragon flew up into the black sky, Charlie tumbled across the white ground for a few blocks. Kat's confusion and fear of the dragon condensed into an immediate desire to help her friend now lying lifeless near the base of the nearby obsidian pillar.

Kat's heart pounded out of her chest as she ran over and knelt down to examine Charlie. She rolled him over and found that, to her immense relief, he was not dead, though his face was screwed up in intense pain.

"Charlie! Thank God, are you okay?" asked Kat as she pulled off his chestplate to examine his wound.

"Don't worry, I'm fine," grunted Charlie, wincing as the chestplate coming off revealed a slash through his shirt and across his chest and stomach. "It's not deep," he added, seeing the skeptical look on Kat's face. "I'll be fine. Have you seen my pickaxe, though?"

* * * * *

"Hey, DZ, what's that on the dragon's face?" asked Stan, as he noticed something glinting on the dragon's snout. He was determined not to let the dragon find its way over to Kat and Charlie, nor Oob who was off wandering (though whether he was running from the dragon or aimlessly wandering was not evident). Stan stood with his axe at the ready as the dragon swooped in for another attack.

It didn't matter that DZ had not responded; the dragon came into close range, and Stan had to bite his lip to keep from laughing. Charlie's pickaxe was still attached to the dragon's face, lodged deeply into its right nostril. It looked absolutely ridiculous, but Stan still waited before he brought his axe down into the dragon's nose before he let the laugh out.

"Oh, God, that's great, that is *priceless*, don't you think, DZ?" Stan got out between laughs, but when he looked to DZ for a response, what he saw made him immediately forget about how the dragon looked. DZ's arm traveled through the air in an arc, a clear testament to the Ender Pearl he had just thrown in the air, directly at the dragon.

"What the hell are you doing!?" shouted Stan at his insane friend. DZ turned around and looked Stan in the eye.

"Ending this," DZ replied simply before disappearing in a burst of purple smoke.

Stan looked around, bemused; finally realizing that DZ must have landed on the actual dragon by the way the dragon was now thrashing around in midair. Now sure beyond reasonable doubt that something had been knocked loose in DZ's head, it was all Stan could do to watch the scene in horrific anticipation. He didn't risk sending an arrow up at the dragon for fear that he might hit DZ. Stan looked over at the others and saw that Kat and Charlie were now apprehensively transfixed on the dragon. Even Oob had stopped wandering to watch the spectacle now unfolding in the air.

Stan thought he could see the unclear form of a figure moving up and down in a rhythmic pattern, and the dragon's head was thrashing side to side, spitting in agony. Stan realized in amazement that DZ was straddling the dragon's neck, driving his sword again and again into the long black neck. Stan then watched in sheer disbelief as the figure atop the dragon ran along its neck and leapt off its head and into the air, spun around, and fired an arrow directly into the dragon's face. The dragon froze in midair, and Stan noticed an Ender Pearl fall down to the ground next to him, followed in a burst of purple smoke by DZ.

Stan's mouth opened to say one of ten thousand things on his mind to DZ, but DZ simply put his hand to Stan's mouth, gestured to the sky and said, "Just watch."

And there was something to watch indeed. Rays of white light seemed to be breaking through the black hide of the dragon's skin like sunrays through morning mist. The dragon seemed to be in suspended animation as it rose higher and higher in the sky, more and more rays of light breaking through the skin until, finally, the dragon exploded in a rapid series of explosive bursts not unlike those of a Creeper explosion. When the smoke cleared, the sky was a peaceful black once more, and the dragon had ceased to exist.

Kat, Charlie and Oob had all walked over to DZ by now. Their eyes simultaneously shifted from the place the dragon had been to DZ; all four of them were now staring at DZ as if he was some king of the gods, descended from above with the sole purpose of ridding the world of the dragon.

"That," Kat got out after nearly a full minute of stunned silence, "was literally, by far, the single most impressive thing I have ever seen in my life."

"Very good job, DZ," Oob added kindly.

"Yeah, no words to describe how awesome that was," agreed Charlie, while Stan still stood there stunned.

"Thanks guys," said DZ, brushing himself off and projecting an air of humility suggesting that what he had just done was about as common and unimpressive as killing a single zombie. "By the way, I grabbed this for you, Charlie," and DZ pulled an item from his inventory and handed it to him.

"My pickaxe!" exclaimed Charlie as he took his weapon back from DZ. Then he took a closer look, and he shoved the pickaxe out to a distance from his body. "Oh God! What the is that purple... slimy.... crap... type-stuff on the end?"

"Oh, that," replied DZ. He looked a little sheepish as Charlie examined the noxious purple slime now coating the diamond ends of the pickaxe. "I... uh... kinda mighta snatched it out of... you know... the dragon's nose..."

There was a moment of silence as they all examined the slime-covered pickaxe. Then, they all burst out into gales of laughter; perhaps the relief of finally defeating the dragon had gone to their heads and made them see the slimy weapon as more amusing than it really was. Perhaps it was that they had all just simultaneously realized that the inevitable next step on their journey was to confront the king. For whatever reason, though, the players laughed for minutes on end, only stopping when DZ sensed

337

a presence behind him and was forced to spin around and kill the Enderman behind him by decapitation.

The mob seemed to snapped the players back to their sense. Charlie looked at the others.

"Okay, so now we've got to find the King's treasure," she said, wiping his pickaxe on his pants leg, cleaning it of snot. "Everybody spread out and look for anything that seems indicative of a hiding spot. If you find anything, call me over, and I'll mine it out."

The group spread out in a web, scanning every block of the moon-rock surface of the island that was the End. They took care to not raise their eyes from the ground, the better to not provoke any Endermen. It was quite hard to look around this way, and so it was not altogether surprising that Oob was the first one to call out.

"Charlie! I think that I may have discovered something!" cried Oob. Within minutes, all four of the players had gathered around a small indent in the ground around the base of one of the obsidian pillars. Charlie took this inconsistency in the otherwise very flat ground to be a clue, and he started mining the area out. As he did, Stan noticed that he seemed to be swinging the diamond tool with a decided effort, and more than once Stan noticed Charlie's hand rush to his stomach for an instant. Charlie seemed to have dismissed the injury the dragon had given him as trivial, but Stan knew that they would be better off hurrying to get Charlie out of the End.

It was about ten blocks underground that Charlie's pickaxe finally broke through a block behind which light shown through. He enlarged the hole enough so that the players could climb through, and they all looked around in awe. The room was of medium size, lit with torches, and there were chests around all corners. Each player ran to a different chest and threw them open; Stan was seized with elation when he saw that his was full of golden apples and various potions. He looked around and saw that Charlie was pulling various sets of enchanted diamond armor out of the chest he had open, whereas Kat was pulling out fire charges and dozens of blocks of inactive TNT. DZ's arms were spilling over with hundreds of uncrafted diamonds.

The more chests they opened, the more valuable materials appeared. Stan was besides himself. The King's secret stash had surpassed even his wildest expectations. He was sure beyond any measure of doubt that, provided that the Apothecary had indeed secured the manpower in the Adorian Village, they would have more than enough materials to launch a full-scale invasion of the King's castle.

As he thought this, Stan remembered what the Apothecary had told him to do when he found the secret stash. For the first time in the weeks since he had received it from the Apothecary, Stan pulled the Ender Chest out of his inventory and, for the first time, he set it on the ground. Immediately, the Eye of Ender that acted as a lock on the chest glowed purple, and particles of smoke began to rise off of the chest. With trembling hands, Stan grasped the black lid of the chest and, on tenterhooks, swung it open. What he saw made him gasp.

Inside the chest was a purple mist, swirling about in the chest's center like a vapor in suspended animation. Through the mist, Stan saw the smiling face of the Apothecary looking back at him. Stan was seized with an immense joy to see that his friend was still alive and well.

"Stan!" cried the Apothecary. "It's so good to see you!"

"Likewise," replied Stan, who didn't think that he could stop grinning if he tried. "You would not *believe* what we've been through in the past few weeks."

"I'm sure that I wouldn't," replied the Apothecary with a wise smile. "I'm assuming that, because you've activated the chest, you've found the King's secret stash?"

"Yes we have!" replied Stan, picking up a glowing diamond sword that Charlie had thrown on the ground whilst looting the chest. "Although," Stan added, thrilled to see that the Apothecary had given a hearty laugh of joy, "the King's secret stash actually wasn't under the Ender Desert. Believe it or not, we're in the End right now!"

The old man's eyes widened; he looked shocked. "*The End? The End dimension?* What is it doing there?"

Stan gave the Apothecary the brief summary of what they had found in Avery's underground base, not omitting all of the encounters that they had had with Mr. A over the past weeks. The Apothecary seemed quite upset that the griefer was now dead.

"Well, I'm very sorry to hear that," replied the Apothecary, looking downcast. "I always find it a shame when one player has to kill another. Mind you, I believe that you did what you had to do, he would have killed you had you not done the same to him, but he seemed like a very confused individual whose death was needless."

"I agree," replied Stan, who honestly completely concurred with everything his old friend had just said. "But, at least it's over now."

"Yeah. Honestly, though, I still can't believe that you guys wound up in the *End*," said the Apothecary, putting his hand to his forehead and shaking his head. "I was wondering what was taking you so long to respond, I was hoping that you hadn't been captured or killed."

"Well, we're alright here, don't worry. The only one who needs medical attention is Charlie, he got scratched by the dragon, but it's not bad, and..."

"Whoa, whoa, did you say dragon? The *Ender Dragon*? I thought that that was just a myth!"

"Tell that to the slash across my chest," replied Charlie, who had just come over next to Stan and was holding his wound with a weak grin.

"Here, take this," said the Apothecary, and he proceeded to pluck a blood red potion off of his sash, and, to Stan's amazement, he reached into the mist, and placed the potion into it where it just floated there as if a message in a bottle lost at sea.

"Go on, take it!" exclaimed the Apothecary. Tentatively, Stan reached into the swirling purple mist and found to his surprise that the potion was quite tangible. Stan grabbed the potion out of the chest and held it up to the torchlight, as if to check that truly was real. When he realized that it was, he wasted no time applying the potion to the wound on Charlie's chest, which instantly resealed itself.

"If you put something in an Ender Chest, you can then access it from any other Ender Chest on the server," explained the Apothecary. "That's why I gave one to you. Now that you've found the stash, I want you to put all of the loot into the chest, and I'll take it out and store it here in the village, where we can use it for the war effort."

"Sounds good," replied Kat, for she, DZ and Oob were all listening by that point. The four players (Oob was an NPC villager, and therefore could not properly pick up most items) wasted no time in unloading all of the valuable materials contained in all the chests into the single, black Ender Chest. Just as quickly, the Apothecary took the items out of the swirling mists and handed them off to places that Stan couldn't see; he assumed that they were people who put the items in safe chests in the village.

"Okay, that's the last of it," said Stan as he placed the last item, a stray Potion of Swiftness, into the chest, and the Apothecary took it out.

"Okay, so, Apothecary, here's my next question: Do you have any idea how to get *out* of the End?" asked Charlie.

341

"You mean you don't know?" hissed Stan in disbelief as the Apothecary responded. "I don't know. Are you telling me that you went in there without any knowledge of how to get out?" he asked.

"It would appear so," said Stan, barely containing rage, and he was about to lash out at Charlie when Kat interrupted him.

"The book guys, remember?" she said with an exasperated sigh.

"Oh yeah," replied Charlie, blushing as he pulled out the book about the Nether and the End. "Apparently... ah, yes, here it is, apparently since we've defeated the Ender Dragon, a portal back to the overworld will have appeared, and when we go through it we'll go through a process called 'Enlightenment,' whatever that means, and then we'll reappear back at Spawnpoint Hill."

"What's Enlightenment?" asked Kat. "I am *so* done with tasks right now... I just want to get back to the Village and plan for some serious King-Kev-ass-whooping, I'm sick of tasks!"

"Don't worry, it says here that we don't have to do anything but just listen while we sit there and are teleported back to the Spawnpoint," read Charlie.

"Okay then, I'll see you at the village," replied the Apothecary, and with one last wave, he closed his Ender Chest so that the purple mist now hung in endless black space.

The players climbed out of the King's stash room and saw that, indeed, a portal back to the overworld had appeared in front of them. It appeared to be a fountain, made out of Bedrock, with four torches illuminating some sort of black egg atop a bedrock pillar at the center. Wanting desperately to be back in the overworld, however, the four players rushed up to the portal and one by one, DZ, Oob, Kat, Charlie and Stan all jumped without hesitation into the black portal that would take them first through the Enlightenment, but then, thankfully, back home.

ENLIGHTENMENT [1]

I see the player you mean.

Stan2012?

Yes. Take care. It has reached a higher level now. It can read our thoughts.

That doesn't matter. It thinks we are part of the game.

I like this player. It played well. It did not give up...

....

This player dreamed of sunlight and trees, of fire and water. It dreamed it created. And it dreamed it destroyed. It dreamed it hunted, and was hunted. It dreamed of shelter.

Hah, the original interface. A million years old, and it still works. But what true structure did this player create, in the reality behind the screen?

It worked, with a million others, to sculpt a true world in a fold of the ⍰⍰⍰⍰⍰⍰⍰⍰⍰⍰, and created a ⍰⍰⍰⍰⍰⍰⍰⍰⍰⍰⍰ for ⍰⍰⍰⍰⍰⍰⍰⍰⍰⍰, in the ⍰⍰⍰⍰⍰⍰⍰⍰⍰⍰.

It cannot read that thought.

No. It has not yet achieved the highest level. That, it must achieve in the long dream of life, not the short dream of a game.

....

Take a breath, now. Take another. Feel air in your lungs. Let your limbs return. Yes, move your fingers. Have a body again, under gravity, in air. Respawn in the long dream. There you are. Your body touching the universe again at every point, as though you were separate things. As though we were separate things.

Who are we? Once we were called the spirit of the mountain. Father sun, mother moon. Ancestral spirits, animal spirits. Jinn. Ghosts. The green man. Then gods, demons. Angels. Poltergeists. Aliens, extraterrestrials. Leptons, quarks. The words change. We do not change...

....

Sometimes the player thought itself human, on the thin crust of a spinning globe of molten rock. The ball of molten rock circled a ball of blazing gas that was three hundred and thirty thousand times more massive than it. They were so far apart that light took eight minutes to cross the gap. The light was information from a star, and it could burn your skin from a hundred and fifty million kilometers away.

Sometimes the player dreamed it was a miner, on the surface of a world that was flat, and infinite. The sun was a square of white. The days were short; there was much to do; and death was a temporary inconvenience...

....

And sometimes the player believed the universe had spoken to it through the sunlight that came through the shuffling leaves of the summer trees...

and the universe said I love you

and the universe said you have played the game well

and the universe said everything you need is within you

and the universe said you are stronger than you know

and the universe said you are the daylight

and the universe said you are the night

and the universe said the darkness you fight is within you

and the universe said the light you seek is within you

and the universe said you are not alone

and the universe said you are not separate from every other thing

and the universe said you are the universe tasting itself, talking to itself, reading its own code

and the universe said I love you because you are love.

And the game was over and the player woke up from the dream. And the player began a new dream. And the player dreamed again, dreamed better. And the player was the universe. And the player was love.

You are the player.

Wake up.

PART III: THE BATTLE FOR ELEMENTIA

CHAPTER 26: THE SPEECH

And Stan did wake up. He found himself standing on the warm, familiar ground of Spawnpoint Hill as gently as his entry into the End had been. He was in a stupor, filled with awe at what the Enlightenment had turned out to be; perhaps this was what had made him oblivious to the blunt spikes that were attempting to penetrate his diamond armor.

"GET DOWN!" screamed Kat, snapping Stan out of his pensive state, and Stan realized with horror that they were under heavy fire from arrows. He fell to the ground, and he looked up wildly and saw four dispensers surrounding him, firing arrows from all four sides. Stan's eyes went from the dispensers to the trails of glowing red dust leading to them, and he realized with a start that he and his four friends were lying atop a stone pressure plate.

Quick as a whip, Charlie drove his pickaxe into the smooth stone plate, which shattered into chunks. Instantly, the bursts of arrows from the machine subsided. The players and Oob awkwardly stood up in the limited space between the arrow dispensers. As they worked their way out of the center of the small maze of machines, Stan realized the intentions behind the arrow machines and was revolted. The machine had been put there by the King to instantly kill anything that appeared there! Had the players not been wearing diamond armor, they would have been murdered on the spot!

After Charlie had taken his pickaxe and torn down the arrow machine, the five of them quickly congregated. Stan wasn't really focused on the others, though; he took the opportunity to look around Spawnpoint Hill, which he was standing on for the first time since he had joined the game.

Stan shook his head in incredulity; the serene hill was not changed in the least from the scene that had been Stan's first impression of Minecraft. Actually, that wasn't right, Stan thought as his eyes drifted over to the section of bare dirt blocks where the dispensers had stood minutes before, which had not yet been re-covered with grass. These dispensers demonstrated the change that had taken place within Elementia much more than any large structure ever could. Stan's first moments in Minecraft had been met with the warm, comforting light of torches to ward off the mobs and a chest of food, a tool of defense, and a guide of how to play. Any players that had entered Elementia since then had had nothing to see except four arrows to the cranium.

Now that they were but a stone's throw from launching their endgame on the King, Stan took a moment to think about it. He realized that what had once seemed like a crazy, whimsical desire had manifested itself within Stan's very being, and had evolved into a crazy, consuming obsession. Stan wanted the King dead, and, for the first time, a new realization crashed over him as he stared at that simple uncovered dirt: He wanted to do it.

Stan wanted to be the one to personally smite the King with a sword, bury an axe into the King, send an arrow flying between the King's eyes. By whatever manner the King was destined to die, Stan wanted the blood to stain his hands. Stan's time in Elementia so far had been pockmarked by so much death, destruction, and multifaceted misery that Stan wanted nothing more than to be the one to end the responsible life, no matter what the cost.

The odd thing was, even though Stan desired his axe felling the King with every fiber of his being, he somehow knew that even if he had not sought the confrontation, it would have inevitably happened anyways. Stan couldn't tell how he knew this... maybe it was the higher power of dubious existence contacting him again... but Stan knew that, like it or not, he and King Kev were going to lock sword and axe on that battlefield, and only one of them was leaving that confrontation alive.

Stan was so deep in his thoughts that he hadn't even realized that they had started walking back down the road, still shaded by trees in the same manner as on that first day. He smiled as he recalled in fond retrospect how he and Charlie had panicked and barely managed to keep a lumbering Zombie at bay that first day. And now look at us, thought Stan, and his smile widened as he looked at the diamond-clad and heavily armed Charlie, and he glanced again down at himself and the similarly-adorned players traveling alongside him.

Stan found that first Zombie that they had encountered, and the way they had handled it, much more amusing than he thought that he ought to. Perhaps it was just how far they had come and gone in such a short time, perhaps it was nerves that were showing themselves in short bursts. In any case, when Stan noticed a Zombie out in the woods give him a sideways glance, he walked over to it and, as it neared him in the slow manner that the Zombies do, he made a point of killing the Zombie with a succession of swift punches to the rotten face, his axe sitting idly in his inventory.

At the fifteenth punch, the Zombie's head snapped to the side, and as Stan picked up the rotten flesh, he became aware that everybody was staring at him (except for Oob, who had managed to wander into a nearby small lake and was looking about as if wondering how he had gotten there). Unabashed, Stan just smiled up at them and tossed the rotten flesh into the air, where it was snagged by Rex before it hit the ground (Stan hadn't noticed exactly when the dog had reappeared, but he was so far past questioning it).

"Ah, nostalgia," he said with a chuckle as Rex chewed hungrily on the rotten flesh, and the dog shot Stan a fond look. "Remember that first day, Charlie? The Zombie, the shelter, the spiders?"

A reminiscent look came to Charlie's features. "Yeah. It was a simpler time," he said longingly. "It's weird to be back, isn't it?"

Stan nodded. "It's like visiting your old elementary school twenty years later."

Charlie gave a casual "Yep" of agreement, and the four players continued walking the path, with Oob following slowly behind him. They passed an old dirt-and-wood shelter with no top that Stan realized was the one that he and Charlie had built on that first night. They inspected it and found a wooden pressure plate inside, which Stan assumed led to some sort of booby trap. Stan walked over to the hut and was about to split the wooden pressure plate with his axe, but in his haste he accidentally stepped on it, and he heard a faint click.

His brain registered what was about to happen seconds before it did. "Hit the dirt!" Stan bellowed as he jumped away from the decrepit shack, and the others barely had time to follow in suit before the TNT below the fortress ignited, creating a crater the width of the road where the shelter had just stood.

Stan pulled himself up and looked into the smoldering remains with disgust. What sort of sadistic monster would rig this basic shelter with explosives, on the chance that a new player would come back and seek refuge within its humble walls? It made Stan's insides churn to think that King Kev and his sympathizers had actually sunken to the levels of spawn killing innocent new players.

Stan looked at the ground as the group continued walking, picturing again and again, over and over in his head, the image of his arrow penetrating King Kev's forehead, or his axe burying itself in the King's chest. It was only when he noticed that the group had stopped walking, and that they had taken on a pronounced silence, that Stan looked up. He wished that he hadn't.

The Adorian village was in complete and total ruin. This village that had embraced the travel-weary Stan, Kat and Charlie just weeks earlier was now nothing more than a ghost town, with only the most basic of stone frames of houses having survived the fire. As the group walked down the main street, their faces simultaneously took on expressions of horror; even Oob, who had never been to the village before, sensed the magnitude of the complete and total razing of the village that had taken place.

The only structure in the village that was still in the least bit recognizable was the brick town hall where they had first met Adoria; even that had had significant chunks of it blown apart by TNT explosions. Next to where the front doors of the building had been, Stan felt another dull blow to his stomach; the brick next to the doorway had been tainted with a bloodstain that still had no less than five arrows stuck directly in its center. Next to this evidence of carnage, a wooden sword stuck in the gravel, blood now sitting dry on the handle.

The feeling of disgust, horror, and consuming fury that had racked Stan's body the last time he had seen this village came back in full fury, and Stan felt himself about to vomit again. Before anything could come however, an arrow whizzed past Stan's left shoulder and Stan heard a clang of flint on diamond and heard DZ's "Oof!" of pain. Stan's eyes found a pickaxe flying past his other shoulder, and when he turned back an assailant in full diamond armor was upon him. Before he could react, Stan felt the dull blow of a bow slamming him across the forehead.

Stunned by the blow to the head, Stan wildly looked around and saw two forms in full diamond battle armor, moving too fast for Stan to recognize. Through the blunt pain in his forehead, Stan saw a figure struggling with Kat over a diamond pickaxe which ended when the figure punched Kat in the face. The figure grabbed the tool back from her, then slammed her over the head with it, knocking her to the ground. Stan also saw DZ engaged in a sniper battle with what appeared to be a skeleton in full diamond battle armor.

Stan was unsure of whether or not he was hallucinating, but for some reason his brain tried to focus on the fact that for one, skeletons didn't wear armor, and for two, they weren't that fast. Stan stole a glance at the other assailant and saw a glint of yellow in between the light blue of the helmet and the chestplate, and the truth dawned on him in an instantaneous rush of comprehension.

"Archie, G, stop attacking! It's us!" he hollered.

There was a moment of silence as the two figures, both of whom had gained the upper hand in their respective fights, looked at Stan, and contemplated him. The skeleton pulled off his helmet to reveal a mop of wild red hair, while the other pulled off his to expose a golden figure identical to Stan.

"Stan?" asked Archie, not daring to believe it. "Is that... is that really you?"

"Yeah, or at least I think I am, that blow to the head shook me pretty good," Stan muttered, his head still shrouded in fog.

"Oh my God! I'm so sorry!" cried Archie as he rushed over to Stan and handed him a blood red Potion of Healing, which Stan graciously downed in a single swallow. Instantly his head cleared up, and he took Archie's outstretched hand to pull himself up.

Kat and Charlie were both on the ground; Stan hadn't realized up to that point just how skilled Archie and G were in player-to-player combat. Charlie was being treated for the arrow wedged in a chink in his armor by a figure in a scarlet jumpsuit whose blonde hair distinguished him as Bob, the archer of the Nether Boys.

G was on his knees, cradling Kat's head in his arms. He poured half of his potion on the pickaxe wound on her forehead, and the other half went into her mouth. Kat's eyes fluttered, and when they fully opened and she saw who was holding her, she gave an exclamation of joy and embraced G. They stayed in each other's arms for half a minute until they realized everybody else staring at them, which left the lot of them feeling slightly awkward.

The feeling didn't last though. As soon as everyone was back on their feet, the greetings started.

"Hey, Stan! How're ya' doin', buddy?" asked G as he offered Stan a high five, which he returned.

"Not bad, not bad. Killed a griefer, slayed a dragon, found some diamonds… good times, good times," he responded with a grin.

"Sounds like it," said Archie. "The Apothecary told us all about what you guys did. Sounds like one hell of a vacation."

"Well we did go to hell, among other places, if that's what you mean," said Charlie with a chuckle. "So, how many people do you guys have organized?"

"Well," said G, scratching his head. "The Apothecary came to us soon after you guys left… said that you were organizing a rebellion against the King, and he wanted to help… well, seeing as the King had just burned down our village, killed our leader, and slaughtered half of the people here, we didn't have to think hard about believing him."

"We headed straight back here after you helped us out of the Nether, Stan," said Bob, who had just helped Oob out of the chimney he had hidden in during the ambush. "Bill, Ben and I joined up with the militia. Then, a whole gaggle of miners, lead by this guy who they all called Mayor, showed up, like, a day and a half after we did."

"Those guys were from Blackstone," Kat pointed out.

"You mean the coal mining town out in the desert?" Archie asked.

"That's the one," Stan replied. "I ran into them pretty soon after you guys left, Bob, and they all agreed to come and join us. Well, most of them did, anyways," said Stan bitterly, his thoughts flashing over the drunken Mechanist, "but those who didn't aren't going to join either side any time soon."

"Speaking of which," said Bob, a slight edge to his voice that caught all of their attentions, "who is this fine gentleman over here?" and he jerked his head in the direction of DZ, who had been staying out of the conversation (not knowing any of them), and practicing complicated attacks with two swords on a nearby lamp post.

"Oh, this is DZ," said Kat, and DZ, hearing his name, rushed over and hastily added, "But you may know me by my full name, DieZombie97." And with that, he gave a white, toothy smile.

Archie, G, and Bob's eyes all widened. "Wait, you're DieZombie97?" asked Bob in disbelief.

"*The* DieZombie97?" asked G incredulously.

"See?" said DZ pompously, grinning at Stan, Kat and Charlie, all of whom were amazed that their friends apparently knew of DZ. "I told you I got around in the Spleef Arena a few updates back."

"Man, you're *awesome!*" exclaimed Bob, running up and wringing DZ's hand up and down.

"I thought that King Kev had killed you!" said Archie, a wild happiness on his face.

"Nah, that was just a rumor. Didn't bother staying around to contradict it though cause, you know, then it probably wouldn't have been as much of a rumor as a fact," said DZ with a laugh.

"So where've you been all this time? After that last Spleef championship you just kind of disappeared!"

"I've been living out in the desert," said DZ. "I realized that a world run by government generally ends up pretty corrupt, so I decided I was better off by myself out in the Ender Desert. That is, until I ran into these three," and he jerked his thumb at Stan, Kat and Charlie.

Archie continued to talk to DZ; G and Bob asked the other three about Oob, who was now cowering behind Charlie at these three players who, he believed, were still likely to kill them all.

"So, how did you guys come across this NPC? And, more importantly, why is he still with you?" asked Bob. The three players explained briefly about all they had seen and done after Stan had left Blackstone.

"So, what's your name, Oob?" asked Bob, speaking gently to the NPC who was now cowering behind Charlie, looking terrified. "I hear that you're pretty brave; I've never heard of an NPC taking out anything living before, and they just told me that you took out a griefer that had attacked them three times before!"

Oob looked around Charlie's shoulder and replied timidly, "Yes. He had hurt Charlie, Kat, and DZ, and he was trying to hurt Stan. They are my friends, and I do not want them to be hurt."

"That's awesome of you, my man," replied Bob with a kind smile, which Oob hesitantly returned. "We need more guys like you. In fact, a bunch of us guys that don't want to see good people hurt, like you, are gonna try and take down the King of all the players, so he won't be mean to them anymore! You want to help us with that, buddy?"

Oob raised one eyebrow. "If I did not want to help, then why would I be here?" he asked as if asking a dim child why they had tried to lick an electrical socket.

Everyone chuckled, but Archie quickly pointed out that they had been standing exposed in the open for far too long. He walked off towards the entrance to the mine, Bob and G on his tail, and the other five followed in suit.

"So, why are you guys setting up your operations underground?" Charlie inquired of G, but G didn't answer; he was too busy speaking with Kat, whom he was now walking next to with less than an inch of space between them. Rolling his eyes, Charlie redirected the question to Archie.

"Are you kidding? Do you know how many griefers we've had to put up with so far? It's ridiculous!" he said throwing his arms in the air. "The King had sent probably about fifty scouts to this village so far, we'd be sitting ducks out in the open! We have about ten of those guys in a prison in our underground base, but the rest of them have been driven away by our automated defenses."

"You mean, you set up redstone circuitry?" Charlie asked.

"Oh, sure," said Archie. "It was just basic stuff at first, you know, your arrow dispensers, your tripwires opening pits, stuff like that. But then, when the guys from Blackstone showed up, there was one guy with them, went by the name of Sirus666. Oh man, he completely vamped up our systems after that. Our camp is now automated with defense that'll pretty much instantly hurt anything that comes near it, and that'll kill them if they come to close. You should see some of the ridiculous things he's designed... long-range TNT cannons, automatic lava launchers, rigs that drop you into a pit filled with Silverfish... you name it."

By now they were deep in the mine, and they walked up to a section of wall that looked just like any other, a ridge over a smooth stone wall. G detached himself from Kat for a moment to take his pickaxe and toss it up on top of the ledge. Instantly, there was the click of a pressure plate being activated, and the wall split open to reveal a passage just wide enough for a player to walk through. They filed through in a single file line, with G staying to the back and snatching his pickaxe before entering and resealing the entrance.

After a short walk down the corridor, Stan found himself in an open room. It was composed mainly of stone blocks, with cobblestone flecking the walls here and there. There were various chests, torches, doorway, signs, and a Nether Portal in the room, but Stan only had eyes for the five players sitting in the center of the room in wooden chairs, who all turned to look at them when they entered.

The Apothecary, who had been toying with the brewing stand in front of him, gave them all a warm smile. Bill and Ben, with their respective fishing rod and sword swung over their shoulders, gave a hearty "Hey!" of greeting to the group. Jayden surveyed them all with a tired grin. However, there was only one player who jumped up and sprinted at the entering group at top speed, launching herself into Stan's arms.

"You're back!" exclaimed Sally as the others filed into the room to meet the players now walking over to greet them. "I'm so glad you're here... I was worried sick while you were out there..."

"Don't worry, Sally, I'm here," said Stan, rubbing her back and feeling more at peace than he had in a long, long time. "I really missed you, you know. I can't tell you enough how glad I am to be back here."

"Eh, it's good to see you too, noob," smirked Sally as she instantly became twice as composed and stepped backwards, out of Stan's arms but still holding his hands. "It's a crazy world out there, huh? I hear that someone's been doin' a little bit of dragon slaying lately, eh? Noob, that is freaking epic stuff!"

Stan smirked; yep, this was Sally, all right.

"What's funny?" she asked.

"Nothing, nothing," said Stan, although he had to bite his lip to keep from laughing. It seemed that Sally was trying to cover up her emotional outburst from moments earlier by being all cool and collected and frankly a little tomboyish; Stan found her need to try and do this quite endearing.

"So what've you guys been up to around here? I bet it' not more dangerous than recruiting abroad for a rebellion, killing a dragon, getting rid of a notorious griefer..."

"Oh, cry me a river, do you have any idea how annoying it is to put up with ten griefers a day? What did you have to deal with, one idiot that the *NPC* managed to beat and three sad excuses for assassins, over a couple of weeks? And besides, we've had to mine out a whole new section, and we lost two of our guys to a lava flow the other day. Also, I believe that the dragon you killed attacked you by, oh, let's see, flying directly towards you and flying away if you shot it before it got there? Does that sound about right, Stan?"

Stan was stunned. Why did he even bother to ever try and win an argument with this girl? In any case, it didn't matter. He wasn't in the mood to talk right then anyways.

"What've you guys got in the way of food around here?" he asked Sally, looking around for a chest or something.

"Actually," replied Sally, sitting down on the nearest chair and gesturing to Stan to pull up a seat next to her, "we've got a guy who just went down to the mess hall to get food right before you left, he'll be back soon."

Stan was hungry, but he occupied himself until the player with the food got there by talking to Jayden, the Apothecary and the other two Nether Boys while Sally talked with Kat, Charlie, DZ and Oob.

"Hey, Stan! *Nice axe!*" exclaimed Jayden as he caught sight of the diamond axe hanging at Stan's side. "Where did you get that?"

"The blacksmith in Oob's village gave it to me. I tell you, those NPC's were great, they gave us everything we needed to get to the End and back, and they really seemed to like us."

"I'm not surprised," said Jayden bitterly. "The King's been abusing the NPCs for as long as I've been on this server, imposing wheat quotas on them and whatnot."

The Apothecary was delighted to see that they had managed to get back from the End in one piece, and he asked Stan what Enlightenment was.

"Well... actually, I have no idea what it was," said Stan truthfully. He had seen the words of two beings in apparent conversation about him while he was going through the portal back to Spawnpoint Hill; however, he had no idea who these beings were, why they were talking about him, and exactly what they meant. He explained it the best he could to the Apothecary, but it still seemed ambiguous. He made a mental note to himself to discuss it with the others later. Stan was just starting to discuss useful axe fighting techniques he'd learned with Jayden when he heard a voice.

"Okay, people, steak and pork chops right over here!"

The shout tore Stan away from Jayden, and he spun around in disbelief. Because he knew that voice, he had heard it before. There was no way that he could possibly be alive... he had watched in helpless horror as the flames razed his house to the ground, and bricks had been thrown through the windows by the prejudiced bigots back in Element City... yet there was no mistaking as Stan saw the player, the distinguishing black body, feathery texture, and yellow beak were all there. As Stan looked in utter incredulity at him, the skepticism was reflected on Blackraven's face. They held each others' gaze for a moment, then Stan ran to Blackraven with wild joy breaking onto his face, followed an instant later by Charlie and Kat, both of whom shared looks of equal disbelief.

"You're... you're alive!" Charlie managed to get out. Charlie's features were lifted in a way that Stan had not seen in him since before the death of his cat.

"Why yes… last I checked… but what are you three doing here?" Blackraven responded.

"What do you mean, what are we… what are *you* doing here?" asked Kat through her tears of joy; she was elated that the one who had taken them under his wing, so to speak, had survived the cowardly attempt on his life in Element City.

"Simple, I crawled into the hidden cellar underneath my shop," said Blackraven, still looking back and forth between each of the players. "But what are you three doing here?"

"Wha… what are you talking about? We were the ones that started this whole thing!" Charlie exclaimed.

The expression on Blackraven's face showed unfathomable confusion, and he opened his mouth when Jayden called over. "You didn't know, Raven? These three were the assassins I told you about; that's kind of funny, did we really never get around to telling you who they were?"

"Are you serious? These were the three guys I told *you* about! You know, the players I had employed when that mob griefed my shop?"

"No kidding? You know Blackraven?" asked Jayden.

"No," said Stan, irony dripping from his voice. "We ran over to greet him because he's a complete and total stranger."

Jayden scowled.

* * * * *

Stan soon learned that in the time that he and his friends had been gathering supplies, the team in the village, headed by the Apothecary, had concocted an entire plan of action for launching an attack on King Kev. The attack would be launched a week after Stan, Kat and Charlie had returned from their journey. That time would be used to turn the supplies they brought back from the King's

360

cache into suitable gear for the hundred and fifty fighters that were based in the village and formed the Grand Adorian Militia. The time would also be used to train Stan, Kat, and Charlie in special combat skills for the upcoming offensive.

The reason for the special training was that each of the three players have been given a specific task in the upcoming battle. Kat was in charge of ensuring the death of every member of RAT1, who were sure to participate in the battle in support of the King. Charlie was to be in command of a special team of a dozen troops that was to defend the base of the tower so that Stan was not to have any opposition when he undertook his task.

The Apothecary, through his former allegiance to the King, knew that the King commanded his battlefield troops from the bridge of the castle. Stan's task was to travel to the bridge of the castle by means of Ender Pearls, and engage the King in combat. Stan was to ensure that neither of them left the tower whilst the other was still alive.

As for the others, they had designated tasks too; The Nether Boys were in charge of killing the King's main advisor, Caesar; Sally was in charge of taking down the bull-man named Minotaurus who had destroyed the Adorian village; Jayden was in charge of destroying Charlemagne; and the Apothecary was the field medic. The other high-level players, namely DZ, Archie, G, Blackraven and the Mayor of Blackstone, were to be the five commanders of the five legions of troops whose job was to capture or, only if absolutely necessary, kill, as many of the King's men as possible.

The redstone defenses of the castle provided a different obstacle; however the book that Stan had gotten from the Mechanist had mitigated this threat considerably. Stan gave the book to Sirus666, who Stan recognized as the first miner to join his side in Blackstone. Sirus would infiltrate the King's fortress undercover a day beforehand, and he would do his best to disengage the incredibly complex redstone circuitry by the time the attacks began.

Stan felt his nerves beginning to snowball as the climactic confrontation drew nearer. To keep from psyching himself out, Stan played a trick on his mind whenever he found himself thinking about how nervous he was about fighting the King, he would try and remember every single detail of everything he had learned in training since returning to the village.

And there was no shortage of information to remember. Stan spent the next five days, from the time the sun surfaced on his golden clock to the time it completely vanished, training harder than he had ever done for anything in his life alongside Jayden and DZ. Jayden was the most experienced in the workings of fighting with an axe against a sword, and DZ had the most knowledge of anybody in the village about the King's style of sword fighting. As Stan soon found out, it was not uncommon for the King to fight with two swords instead of one, an uncommon fighting style reserved for only the most skilled sword fighters.

However, nobody who saw him during those five days doubted that Stan's prowess with an axe was exceptional, as was his determination to surpass King Kev in skill. After Stan had managed to disarm DZ of both of his swords and had shattered his iron chestplate with one swing of the axe, Jayden called out, "Okay, Stan, I think you're ready! Anybody who crosses you that doesn't have some sort of, like, incinerator ray or something is absolutely dead! Besides, we can't waste any more iron, that's the sixth chestplate you've broken today!"

Kat was also accelerating under her customized training regimen. She spent the week leading to the invasion under the tutelage of Sally, who was teaching her how to fight with twin swords instead of just one. With dual-wielding blades, it was possible to combat multiple enemies at a time, or to have an upper hand in a one-on-one combat situation. Though Kat came out of Sally's program still preferring one sword to two in most situations, she felt firmly that there was no way that she was going into battle against the full force of the King's army with only one diamond sword strapped to her hip.

Charlie's pickaxe fighting improved exponentially while he studied under G and Sirus, the latter of whom was apparently a pickaxe-fighting prodigy as well as a redstone mechanics expert. While G taught Charlie new skill after new skill in hand-to-hand combat, Sirus taught Charlie a way in which it was possible to tunnel underground like a mole, and burst out in whichever direction he needed. Charlie appreciated this skill most of all; he believed that the art of ambushing suited him well. Charlie also spent a relatively short amount of time with Archie, during which he improved his skill with a bow to a respectable level.

All other players in the village who were over Level fifteen were assigned the task of overseeing the remaining hundred and twenty or so lower-level players of the Grand Adorian Militia. They trained in combat skills for the battle with the King's army half the time; the other half of the time was spent crafting the items that Stan and his friends had brought back into useful things such as swords, armor, flint and steel, and other such paraphernalia.

The Apothecary even took a small group aside that devoted themselves completely to brewing potions and splash potions, which were a throwable variety of potions that could be weaponized. They did soon run into a flaw in their factory-line assembly of potions, however; they had not found any magma cream or Potions of Fire Resistance in the End. It was quickly decided that it was too risky to enter the Nether to hunt down a Magma Cube or a Blaze to get some. This was unfortunate, especially considering that the King's castle was ringed in lava. For those fighting near the edge of the castle, such as Charlie and Stan, such a potion might have been a real asset. It was not essential, however, and when approached about it, neither Stan nor Charlie complained, and rather said that they didn't care (although secretly they both would have heartily enjoyed the extra insurance of protection).

* * * * *

At long last, the night before the assault on King Kev's castle had come. At high noon tomorrow morning, the Grand Adorian Militia would march into enemy territory. The plan was to engage the King's forces in combat, subdue the royal army, kill the King, and liberate the lower-level citizens still trapped within the walls of the city. They would march into the city under Stan's lead, and he would have command of the entire Militia throughout the offensive.

And the thought of doing this made Stan feel like he would soil his pants.

Stan was lying in the bed of one of various compartments that had been carved into the walls of solid rock. Kat, Charlie and DZ occupied the other three beds in the room. Stan could tell from the absence of snores that at least Charlie and Kat were both lying awake. Stan heard whispering and rolled over to see the source; he watched as G leaned over, embraced Kat and held her for half a minute, and then crept out of the room without another word. Stan was smiling at the sweet gesture, and he rolled back over and found himself staring right into a second pair of eyes.

"Hey, noob," they whispered.

"Sally!" Stan hissed as he scrambled to the backside of the bed and away from her. "Don't *do* that!"

"I'm sorry, but it was just too perfect," she smirked. "I had to come in here and have at least one more midnight chat with you before we go off to war tomorrow."

"Oh, come on, don't go saying 'at least one more,'" said Stan as Sally sat down on the bed beside him. "We're both going to come back tomorrow and you know it."

Sally smiled at him. Stan smiled back, but what Sally couldn't see were the gears grinding beneath his face. In truth, he had really never even considered the possibility that some of them might not... no, *would* not make it back from the battle alive. What if Kat

364

or Charlie died? Thought Stan, and in the space of about one second, about twenty horrific what-if-scenarios came crashing through his brain. He made a decided effort not to reveal the pit opening in his stomach to Sally.

"We should probably get some rest," he said as he grabbed the hand of the girl who was now his greatest enemy, the girl who could die and leave him devastated beyond repair. As if sensing his tension through the bond of their hands, Sally leaned forward and kissed Stan on the cheek. "I'll see you in the morning then, noob," she said, and she stood up and walked out the open door, closing it behind her.

Stan turned back towards the wall, and from behind him he heard an almost imperceptible sigh of disappointment. He whipped around and saw a face staring at him through the moonlit window; he recognized one of the lower-level players that he had seen around the village. Clearly, he had been expecting to see something, but had been let down, and his head ducked down and out of the window.

Stan shot the now empty window a disgusted look. "Nothing to see here, kid. This is Minecraft, not GTA," and with that Stan rolled back over and fell asleep almost instantly.

* * * * *

"But I would like to fight as well!"

In all of the excitement and tension surrounding the preparations for the Grand Adorian Militia's first offensive, the matter of Oob, who had wandered around the base for most of the week prior, had been largely ignored. As the sun rose over the skyline of the Great Woods, Charlie and DZ were now in a heated argument with the villager over the Oob's participation in the battle.

"Oob, you've gotta stay here!" cried Charlie with increasing exasperation. "You'll get slaughtered out there!"

"I helped in defeating the griefer called Mr. A, and therefore I should be allowed to fight!" protested Oob, showing more focused determination than he had ever shown before.

"Oob, you gotta understand, that was an ambush," explained DZ. "You snuck up behind him, and you killed him. Out in the battlefield, there are people everywhere! It wouldn't be hard for one of them to sneak up on *you* and kill *you*!"

"I do not care!" cried Oob, starting to cry like an oversized child. "I will gladly die if it means I assist in killing even one of those associated with that terrible King!"

In the end, it took the combined efforts of DZ, Charlie, and the Mayor of Blackstone to force Oob into a compartment room where he would be unable to follow them into battle. Stan and Sally, who were sitting in the chairs and fitting themselves into enchanted diamond chestplates and helmets, watched on in amusement.

"You know, it breaks my heart to keep the little guy from fighting, he wants it *so* bad," sighed Stan.

"Well, if you have to choose to either keep your heart or his neck intact, I think the latter is probably for the best," said Sally, to which Stan nodded. Sally looked at him. "Can you believe this is actually happening?"

"I truly can't," answered Stan, which was completely true as he looked around the main room of the underground bunker at the hundred and fifty players now wearing armor of leather, iron and diamond. Swords, axes, bows and the like hung by their sides, and Stan couldn't believe that it was an arrow, drawn back by him, shot by him at the King, that had put it all in motion. He knew that the King had had it coming to him for a long time, but it was still too much to comprehend that this was all begun by his rash, anger-driven action.

"You know," said Sally, "we don't have a plan of escape or retreat. We only have a plan of attack. Everybody in this room is willing to die for the ideal that you personify, Stan. You should say something to them."

"What?" said Stan, taken aback; her suggestion to make a speech caught him off guard. "What should I…"

Sally reached out and grabbed him by the shoulders before he could finish. She yanked him into her until their faces were almost touching. "You know what to say. You're special, and you know it. I saw it in you the moment I first laid eyes on you." Her voice was intense, and Stan was hanging on every word that escaped her lips. "You're not average Stan, you're so far beyond average. I saw the way you fought against Kat and Charlie with that sword. I heard about the way you took down that snow golem. Those were not things that anybody could have done except for you, whether you believe it or not. I love you, Stan, because you are not just above average, you are on a higher level than that."

As Sally's pep-talk drew to its abrupt close, it was not the fact that Sally had told Stan that she loved him for the first time that resonated in Stan's mind. No, the last words that Sally had said were the ones that struck Stan: *You are on a higher level.* Stan's experience during the Enlightenment, the conversation between the two beings that he had witnessed, came rushing back to him again. But now, now they had a whole different meaning.

Stan had briefly discussed the Enlightenment with Kat and Charlie at some point (Stan didn't remember exactly when), but they had just thought of it as a cool, well-written poem that tried to sum up the universe in words, with interesting results. Now though, as Stan looked back on those words, he realized what Sally was trying to say.

The poem, spoken by the two beings on the highest level of universal knowledge, whom had spoken some words that Stan's mortal mind could not decipher, had spoke of a one, a player that had reached a higher level, who had the ultimate power of the universe within him.

"It's me, isn't it," he breathed. Sally nodded, as if she had been reading his thoughts. "I've got to kill King Kev because it's me." And again Sally nodded. Stan was not even entirely sure what he meant when he said 'it's me,' but then again, he had not yet reached the highest level, and so he could not hope to understand. For the time being though, Stan finally realized the full meaning behind the poem as he could understand it at the time.

There were players, humans, entities, or whatever you chose to call them that were at a higher level than the rest of their respective societies. Being at a higher level freed them to do fantastic things, to do things that no other beings had the ability to do. Call them geniuses, call them prodigies, call them gods, Stan now knew that he was in the league of these others, these players, these higher beings. They had not yet reached the highest level, but they had reached the highest level one could reach in the grand scheme of life, of the universe, of the game.

As he looked into Sally's eyes, Stan knew that she had recognized this higher level within him from the start. Crazy Steve had seen it too, and Stan was sure that Sally was experiencing the same indescribable mix of confusion and undoubting sureness that he was; they had no more to say to each other. Stan stood up on the chair and cleared his throat.

"People of the Grand Adorian Militia! May I have your attention please!"

It was odd how quickly the room went completely and totally silent. Stan continued, not knowing what he was going to say next but knowing that whatever it was would be right.

"In a few moments, we will be leaving this village. We are embarking on a journey that will take us far past the point of no return, and by the end of this day, all of us will be either victorious

368

or dead. There is no need for me to tell you this, as you knew what you were in for when you joined this militia."

Stan paused for a moment, and he felt a disquieted murmur circulating the room, as if unsure of where he was going with this. Stan continued.

"We are going to win this fight. We are going to win this fight because we are good. We are going to win this fight because we are on the side of justice. We are going to win this fight not just because we want it more, not just because we are better-equipped than our enemy could possibly imagine, but because in the grand scheme of the universe, justice will always prevail.

"If we look back on the history of this world of Minecraft, the world of Earth from which we originated, and any other intelligent world in this universe, you will find that there will always be evil. This is nature, and we cannot change nature. However, there is also an overwhelming power of good to balance that evil, and we do have the power to change what side we choose to ally ourselves with. I have nothing but contempt for the King, who fraternizes with evil so, and whom it is my job to kill today. I have nothing but pity for the men and women that he has swayed to his side with his dark temptations.

"However, although evil will always be able to tear us down, this is only because it is indescribably easier to destroy than create. This game, Minecraft, is not about destruction, however; it is about creation. You will find that creation far outweighs destruction in this universe. That is because, for every one evil being in existence, there are a hundred righteous beings to counteract. We are those righteous beings! We are the ones that the universe has enlisted to make this land of Elementia great once again! We are one hundred and fifty players, of one server, of one world, of one universe. And it is our job to save that one server, in the one world, in the one universe, from the darkness that runs unchecked around us!

"So let us go forth, my brothers and sisters of good! Let us go to the stronghold of power which now lies in enemy hands, and take it back for our own! Let us restore Elementia to the vision that its founders once had for it! It's time for us to make this server a place where future generations can call home! This is our quest, players! THIS IS OUR *QUEST FOR JUSTICE!*"

As Stan enunciated these last three words, the floor of the room broke out into a cacophonic symphony of cheers and shouts, which revved like a jet engine and soon polymerized into a unanimous chant of "JUS-TICE! JUS-TICE! JUS-TICE!"

Stan looked out into the crowd and saw the Apothecary and Blackraven standing side by side, smiling their ancient, wise smiles at him ... DZ and the Nether Boys were going absolutely insane, whistling and chanting and yelling things such as "YOU GO, STAN!" louder than the rest ... Jayden, G and Archie all rose their respective weapons to their foreheads, and gave Stan a three-man salute, then joined with DZ and the Nether Boys in their wild cheering.

The three faces that meant the most to Stan, however, were right beside him. Kat and Charlie stood side by side, beaming up at Stan with no words, simply staring at the champion of goodness that their best friend had become. Sally was still sitting down, and was staring at the floor, but when she sensed Stan looking at her, she glanced up at him and gave him her characteristic amused smirk, which meant more to him than any words ever could.

* * * * *

Five minutes later, the troops were assembled in five, twenty-five-man-long lines, with Kat, Charlie, Jayden, Goldman and Sally at the heads. The players in the lines, suited up in full war gear, were still riled up and excited from Stan's speech, and occasional outbursts of "JUS-TICE! JUS-TICE! JUS-TICE!" were not uncommon.

Ahead of the main body stood Stan, flanked behind by Archie and Bob, the two best shots of the Militia. The archers were there to shoot down, with their enchanted bows, any projectiles such as TNT Mortars or fireballs that should threaten the whole of the group.

Stan ordered the forward march, leading the Grand Adorian Militia through the Great Wood, across the bridge that had been constructed over the hole that the TNT Tower created during the thunderstorm, and through the main gates into Element City.

It was a ghost town; the bustling streets of Element City as Stan remembered them had been deserted. He had not known whether or not the fighting would extend into the streets, or if some kind of citizen militia would combat them, but in fact the only signs of life that he saw were fearful eyes surveying him from within the houses. Clearly, these people were under the impression that the invading Militia would pose a threat to them as well as the armed forces; however, Stan had no intentions of attacking unarmed citizens.

"The signal, Archie," was the only thing that Stan said, keeping his voice in a careful monotone. Like they had planned, Archie pulled out his bow, notched an arrow, and pulled back the string. As soon as the flint tip touched the glowing wood of the bow, the tip of the arrow burst into flames via the enchantment on the bow. Archie let the arrow fly in an arch high over the city, not aiming at anybody; this was the signal.

Thirty seconds. If Sirus had not responded to the signal within thirty seconds, it would be assumed that he had been captured or killed. About twenty seconds ticked by before Stan noticed two shimmering dots of light flying up over the city. Sirus had managed to disable some of the castle's redstone defenses, but not all of them. Unphased, for this was about what Stan was expecting, he ordered the Militia to continue the march forward.

The walk down the main road was uneventful. The Militia was psyching itself up for the offensive that was now just minutes away by chanting "JUS-TICE! JUS-TICE! JUS-TICE!" louder than ever before. By the time they had reached the outer wall of the King's castle, the Militia was in a frenzy, and Stan had to make a quick announcement reminding them that their aim in this battle was to wound if possible, not kill.

As he turned around, he noticed a pleasant surprise: Sirus was running down the length of the wall, a determined smile on his face.

"Hey, Sirus!" Stan exclaimed as the player, who looked the same as Stan but with a lighter color scheme, reached him. "Fancy seeing you here, I didn't expect to see you until we'd gotten in. You got news for us?"

"Yeah, I managed to deactivate most of the redstone traps and pitfalls, but there are a few still in place, such as arrow and fireball dispensers, although I think I managed to deactivate most of the really deadly ones, you know, your TNT cannons, your Automatic Lava Flows, your tripwires into bottomless pits, but we'd still better be careful, though, cause like I said, the arrow and fireball launchers are still online, I couldn't hack into those, they're too well guarded, so..."

"Okay, Sirus, okay, calm down," said Stan, cutting off Sirus's report, which he had delivered very quickly and in the twitchy manner of a mad scientist.

"Okay, okay, but you'd also probably better know that I rigged a TNT pit under this wall, just hit that button there on the wall and it'll blow up! Hehe," he said, his face wild with excitement.

"Nice touch, Sirus," said Stan with a grin. He had been planning to have the Blackstone miners simultaneously break through the wall, but this way would be much quicker. He turned to his troops.

"Soldiers of the Grand Adorian Militia! In a few seconds, we will punch the button on this wall, destroying it. When we do, you are at liberty to charge into that courtyard and put out of order anything or anyone that moves in the name of King Kev. Again, I remind you to avoid homicide at all costs. We are not like them, and therefore we will not kill like them. Good luck to you all, and I will see you again once King Kev has fallen."

Tumultuous applause followed this. Stan looked back at his leaders, and the same grim determination was reflected on all of their faces. Even Rex, who stood between the stone-faced Kat and Sally, was baring his teeth in anticipation of the fight he knew was to come.

Stan turned around. This is it, this is happening, he thought. I am about to blow my way into King Kev's castle and try to kill him in combat. Adrenaline coursed through his veins like a powered mine cart down a track, and as the troops looked up at the wall, a pregnant silence fell. Then Stan spoke.

"Sirus, PUNCH IT," he said in tones of steel.

Sirus's fist slammed into the stone button, there was a hissing, and a second later the force of the explosion crashed across the Militia like a wave, obliterating the wall and giving them a clear view of the castle. Leaving all pretense of hidden fear behind him, Stan gave a savage yell and charged.

CHAPTER 27: THE BATTLE FOR ELEMENTIA

King Kev surveyed the courtyard from atop the same bridge that he had stood on when he had given the announcement that fateful day. Now, however, his head was not unprotected; quite the contrary, a diamond helmet and a diamond chestplate covered his body, two diamond swords equipped with the highest of Sharpness enchantments hung by his side, and a bow with enchantments of Power and Fire was slung across his back. He stood here alone. He knew that the player called Stan2012 would seek him out with the intentions of killing him. Stan would be quite happy to find that the initial parts of his invasion would go exactly according to plan; the King respected Stan for his determination, and so he had decided to give Stan the satisfaction of tasting victory. The end results of the battle, however, would fall far short of Stan's plans.

King Kev had known that the impending attack on his castle was inevitable, but it was really owed in majority to his spy within the Grand Adorian Militia that he had come to learn the exact day, time and style of the attack. The King had found the plans incredibly simplistic. Given that the attack was being made in the majority by lower-levels with inferior combat skills, the King had expected the leaders of the militia to come up with some clever approach.

The King had decided that he would simply play along with Stan's game, and send his regular army of a hundred and fifty men in against their Militia of a hundred and fifty strong on the castle courtyard. Then, they would see the power and skill behind his men, the power, skill and loyalty that would be the reason that he himself would never be ousted from power in Elementia.

Sure enough, the sun was at its apex in the sky when the wall in front of his castle burst open. This unnerved the King a bit, because his spy had informed him that they would be tunneling through the wall. No matter, it was of no concern; the means of their entry was of no importance. The important thing was the backup redstone traps that had been hidden away from their saboteur that would now weaken them to the point of being sitting ducks for the King's army.

But... wait, what was happening? The players were charging forward, and they were surging towards the castle walls in a widespread wave... but no traps were going off! What was the meaning of this? He had been aware of every move that their little redstone saboteur had made, and they had only allowed him to find a set of decoy traps... so how was it that they were pushing forward still with no resistance!?

Shock and horror overtook the King's features as he snatched up the microphone and bellowed with a reddened face, "Traps are down, I repeat, traps are down! Minotaurus, charge! Caesar, follow! Charlemagne, follow! RAT1, you know what to do! You are now the only defense against them, so CHARGE!"

As the King looked with an apprehensive face at his men now charging, very belated, into the swarm of oncoming Adorians, a thought struck the King. He looked down at his pale, blocky hand. It would only be just the once, and the possibility of somebody discovering that he was the one responsible were slim... but no, he thought better of it. There was no way that he could use his most powerful, most dangerous weapon of all.

For although the weapon would no doubt obliterate the Adorian fighters in one fell swoop, it was more dangerous to the King himself than it was to them. No, even when Stan2012 himself was up on the tower, battling him, the King would not resort to using his ultimate, most secret, weapon.

* * * * *

Stan stood still in the middle of the ongoing charge, waving them forward, and it was only when their men had gotten halfway across the courtyard that the King's forces charged out of the castle. Stan wondered why they had waited so long to come out from the castle. Besides this, the Militia had found a complete and total lack of opposition from the automatic redstone traps he had been sure they would encounter. All of this left Stan thoroughly nonplussed.

He was about to disregard the uneasy feeling and begin teleporting towards his fight with the King when he noticed that the dirt block in front of him was breaking. Stan drew his axe, prepared for an Elementia trooper to burst from the ground, blade drawn and ready for combat. Stan was instead treated to the sight of a stone shovel penetrating the ground, followed by a head that came up in no big hurry.

Stan was shocked. He had seen the head before, he knew this player.

"Howdy 'do, Stan," said the Mechanist with a sly grin as he brushed some dirt particles from his bushy eyebrows.

"*You*? But what... how... what are you *doing* here?" Stan asked in bewilderment, wondering what bizarre chain of causality had lead this old inventor from his secluded, drunken solitude in Blackstone to beneath the battlefield of the biggest revolt against the King since the time of Avery007.

"Well, it got kinda boring back in Blackstone with nothin' to do, so I figured that, you know, after I ran out of potion, I might as well come here and help you guys. And lemme tell ya', that potion ran out pretty damn fast..." Stan noticed that, now that he wasn't drunk, the Mechanist spoke in a Texas accent.

"So wait... you're here to *help* us?" asked Stan, his heart lifting.

"Already did," replied the Mechanist with a grin, holding up a redstone torch in his hand. "Ain't you wondering why you haven't run into any opposition from the redstone contraptions? I'll give you a hint... I designed them, and I'm here."

Stan's eyes widened as he realized what the Mechanist was saying. "Are you saying that you disabled the redstone traps manually?" he asked disbelievingly.

"Better than that," replied the Mechanist. "See that guy over there?" he asked, referring to a player with an executioner's hood and an iron axe that locked against the pickaxe of Sirus. "Well watch this!" the Mechanist said, and he went back underground. Stan watched in amazement as, just as Sirus was disarmed, a pit opened up beneath the executioner, dropping him into the depths below the ground and resealing itself before the Mechanist reappeared.

"I built an entire redstone computer underground here a while back, and I remember how to work it!" said the Mechanist proudly. "Even King Kev never knew about it, and it controls all the redstone circuitry in the city! Hell, the thing's my baby, it lets me override any signals given from the castle with the flip of a switch.'"

Stan felt as though an enormous weight had been lifted off of his chest; the redstone defenses had been a huge variable in their attack plan, and now they were eliminated completely. Stan opened his mouth to give an earnest thanks, but the Mechanist waved him off.

"You can thank me later, Stan, don't you have a King to kill?"

"Oh yeah!" exclaimed Stan and, feeling more confident than ever, he pulled his first Ender Pearl off of his sash.

* * * * *

"Oof," came the dull thud as the player with devil horns was knocked to the ground. Charlie drew back his pickaxe, his eyes peeled for more attackers. He and his team had had an intense fight through the thickest of the combat, and were now struggling to maintain their position at the base of the King's drawbridge. The drawbridge was underneath the lava moat, now, preventing any troops from entering or exiting the castle. Charlie knew that his team was just a thin membrane that separated Stan and the King from a slew of backup support from the King's forces, should King Kev call on them.

Indeed, the King's men did seem very discontented that the Adorian forces had established a foothold so close to the base of the castle; and many of them were now swarming back towards them in retaliation. Charlie was just about to panic at the fresh wave of the King's men thronging towards him when he remembered his special weapon. He hastily pulled four blocks of iron out of his inventory and placed them in a T formation on the ground. The men at the head of the King's charge realized what he was about to do a second before he did it, and they began to double back, but it was too late.

Charlie threw a pumpkin onto the formation of iron blocks, and in a flash, the stack of blocks had morphed into an Iron Golem. The giant metal beast surged forward into the oncoming legion of soldiers, and even the skilled strikes of the diamond weapons of those foolish enough to challenge the Golem were unable to do much more than aggravate. The Iron Golem actually smashed one of the men's skulls between his flailing iron limbs, and by that point it was exceedingly obvious that the only sane course of action for the other soldiers was flight.

Charlie cheered the Iron Golem's praises just like the other fighters in his task force, but secretly, Charlie was just happy that the monster he was created was doing the fighting instead of him. While the majority of the other Adorian fighters had to be constantly reminded by Charlie (in an increasingly sharper voice) that they were not to kill unless absolutely necessary with the exception of the designated leaders, Charlie found this rule to be quite liberating; he had seen so much carnage and mindless slaughter in his few short weeks in Elementia that he found himself despising the day that he would kill somebody. Doing this would lower him to a level that he could never break free of again, he would just be another part of the butchery. In short, the longer that Charlie went without murder, the happier he would be.

"Plat! You are here, Plat?"

Charlie's brief second of deliverance was shattered when he realized that that voice was horribly, horribly familiar. It was a voice that was out of place, that he had done everything in his power to keep from being here. Dread already knotting his stomach, Charlie whipped around to face the villager who was chasing after the Iron Golem.

"Plat! Plat, it is me, Oob! Do you not recognize me?"

Charlie was about to shout out at Oob in anger, first pointing out that the Iron Golem was not the same one from the village (whom he had apparently nicknamed Plat), and then wring Oob within an inch of his life for coming to the danger of the battle. Charlie suddenly found no need to say such things, however, when Oob's face took on a look of confusion, and the bloodied blade of a diamond sword stuck point-first out of his stomach.

Charlie acted without thinking; Oob's body fell to the ground face-down right as Geno pulled the sword out of his back with a short grunt. Charlie's eyes immediately sought out a preexisting crack in the center of Geno's diamond chestplate, into which Charlie thrust forward with his pickaxe. The point struck the exact center of the circular fracture, and the chestplate fell apart, the pickaxe entering deep into Geno. The wound from Charlie pulling his pickaxe out of Geno's chest probably would have been enough to kill him, even if Charlie hadn't then proceeded to swing the pickaxe across Geno's neck, breaking it with a sickly snap and causing Geno's body to fall to the ground, his items bursting out in a ring about him.

Charlie didn't give a second thought to Geno; he was acting entirely on a desperate surge of adrenaline as he poured the first of his three Potions of Healing into the gaping hole in Oob's back. Charlie saw the vital organs that had been severed by Geno's sword reconnect themselves, but it was still a dire wound. Charlie robotically poured the second potion into the wound, and the wound healed further, although it was still far more serious than any wound that Charlie had seen. Charlie rolled Oob onto his back, and the last healing potion came pouring into the hole in Oob's stomach. At last, the wound resealed itself, although it was still heavily red.

Now that Charlie had done all in his power to help Oob, the panic slammed into him like a powered mine cart going downhill. His breath raced, and his eyes were wide, bloodshot, and he was now racked with desperate sobs as he silently begged Oob to stay with him. Then, incredibly, the villager gave a small, strained cough, and Charlie was filled with a jovial elation as one of the men in his legion, seeing the pain on Oob's face, tossed over one of his own Potions of Healing. Nodding his thanks, Charlie generously applied it to the wound. Oob's eyes fluttered for a moment before closing again, but it was the deep, heavy, peaceful rising and falling of the villager's chest that shown like a beacon to Charlie, and he knew that Oob would survive.

Before he moved Oob's gaunt body, however, Charlie caught one last look at Geno before his body faded away. His items were still on the ground, and the sword stuck out of the dirt, Oob's blood still wet on the cerulean blade, the last remnant of the leader of RAT1. Charlie had now committed murder for the first time. Geno would never again be able to return to Elementia. He was gone forever, and this was solely due to the actions of Charlie.

But the worst part was, even though Charlie knew he should be horror-struck that he had just ended another life, he felt nothing. This was war, and they were all marked men; Charlie only now realized that it truly was a dog-eat-dog world, and if it hadn't been Geno then it would have been him.

A massive explosion somewhere in the background returned Charlie to the real world. And so, picking up the sword and strapping it to his belt as a token to remember his deed, Charlie returned to the battle, sickened, but not really, at the knowledge that he was capable of murder.

* * * * * *

"Kat, DUCK!" shouted DZ in alarm. Kat acted impulsively, ducking the arrow and following with her eyes the arrow that DZ sunk into the kneecap of the girl with twin swords and no armor. The girl fell to the ground and yanked the projectile out, and she was making to get up when Kat pinned her to the ground with her foot. Kat grabbed the blade of her sword in her hand and rammed the handle into the girl's head, not killing her but assuredly knocking her out.

"Thanks, DZ," said Kat as she spun her sword back around and redrew the diamond one at her side, double-wielding the two swords.

"Don't mention it," he muttered back as he locked combat with a dwarf-skinned player with a glowing iron axe. Kat was about to help him when she noticed something from the corner of her eyes that set off alarm bells.

Not far from where they were, Bill had Caesar, one of the King's seconds in command, tangled in a line from his fishing rod, while Bob tried to shoot at him with arrows. What Bob couldn't see, and Bill was too focused on controlling Caesar to see, was that Caesar had slid his sword up his side in such a way that he could break out of the tangle of line whenever he wanted. In fact, instead of trying to go away from the arrows, Caesar seemed to be ducking them to get closer to Bob, and Bill was rapidly failing at his attempt to restrain him.

Kat saw what Caesar was trying to do, and with a kind of blind, intense panic taking over her body, she made a desperate attempt to stop Caesar's impending attack. Her diamond sword spiraled through the air towards Caesar just as Caesar drove his diamond sword from his side and severed the fishing line, freeing himself. Kat's plan half worked; just as Caesar was about to thrust his sword through the stomach of the utterly unprepared Bob, Kat's sword struck Caesar in the back of the head and his eyes slipped out of focus, his sword jutting out at an odd downwards angle. He had already made the forward thrust, however, and the sword still traveled forward with enough speed to shatter Bob's kneecap and sever his entire lower left leg from his body.

All of this happened within the space of about a second, a second that lasted an eternity. A dreadful sense of helplessness, combined with a surge of adrenaline, caused time to run slowly for Kat within the space of that one second. Caesar's grunt of disorientation, followed by Bob's awful howl of pain, registered enough with Kat to snap her back to the real world and see that Caesar had whipped around to attack Bill, who was armed with nothing but a stick for self defense. Kat ran directly into the thick of the fray, hatred doubling her swiftness, ready to defend Bill from the attack, but she was beaten too it by Ben, who appeared in an instant out of nowhere to force his sword towards Caesar's face.

Caesar sidestepped the attack, the sword doing nothing more than opening a light cut on the side of his neck. With too little room to inflict a sword attack, Caesar punched Ben in the face, then spun to the side, pitched an Ender Pearl far into the distance, and re-drew his diamond sword in a defensive stance. Ben hopped back to his feet and, his features contorted in rage, he swung his sword overhand onto where Caesar's helmet was, which disappeared in a cloud of purple smoke so that the sword only struck air.

Kat didn't let herself worry about Bob, she knew that his brothers would take care of him. Sure enough, as she ran over to join DZ, Bill and Ben rushed over to heal their brother on the ground. After all, Kat still had a task at hand as long as Geno, Becca and Leonidas were still alive.

"What just happened?" exclaimed DZ as he looked over and saw Bob lying on the ground.

Kat sensed the emergence of danger before she saw it, and it was somehow just intuition by which it became her turn to yell at DZ to duck. He did, and not a moment too soon; the diamond blade flew forward into the spot where his head had just been, and Kat took the opportunity to thrust her own sword firmly into the attacker's own face. She didn't bother to retrieve her sword from the flesh of the man called Charlemagne whom she had just killed; instead, she snatched the glowing diamond sword that he had been holding in his hand. This one, she knew, was enchanted with Fire, far better than the sword with Sharpness that she had.

DZ stood up and glanced around wildly back and forth between Bill and Ben desperately treating their brother and Charlemagne's body which had just vanished, sending Kat's sword clattering to the ground.

"Did you... how did he... what the hell?" DZ asked, his eyes deeply infused with perplexity.

"Caesar stabbed Bob in the knee and then Ender Pearled away, and then Charlemagne tried to kill you from behind so I stabbed him in the face," Kat said hurriedly, her instincts on overdrive as they stood in the midst of the battles. To Kat's surprise, DZ's face fell at the news; she had expected him to be at least a little happy that one of their most dangerous adversaries had just taken a sword to the forehead.

"Figures," he spat out with a dark look and a grim chuckle, turning around and drawing his bow.

"What's that supposed to mean?" asked Kat in annoyance; she felt so vulnerable standing still, and was itching to get back to the battle.

"That's just the way it goes, isn't it? You killed Charlemagne, so do you think Caesar is ever going to forgive you? And Caesar

383

probably just took away Bob's ability to walk, and do you think Bill and Ben are going to sleep well while Caesar's still alive? Of course not! It's a feaking vicious cycle is what it is!" DZ looked legitimately pissed now, thought Kat, and it couldn't be at a worst time.

"DZ, honestly," yelled Kat over the chaos of the fighting, "If you want to have some sort of moral epiphany thing, can't it wait until after we've done what we're supposed to do? I still have an entire team of assassins to kill!"

"You know, stuff like this is the reason I went out to live in the desert in the first place, why do you have to kill them? Because they want to kill you? You realize that if you just freaking put aside your differences, you're really not..."

"Oh, for God's sake, I don't have time for this now!" bellowed Kat as she sprinted off, leaving her morally confused friend in the dust. She had just spotted one of her prime targets, and she was not going to let her leave alive.

"HEY BECCA!" shouted Kat and it almost seemed planned as a clearing opened in the group of people and Becca spun around to face Kat. She had seen better days, Kat noted; under one of Becca's baggy and bloodshot eyes was a cut that indicated a sword wound, although the blood splattering her glowing iron chestplate indicated that she had won that fight. When the two girls' eyes locked over the clearing, Kat was stunned to see Becca's eyes full of a terrifying quality she had never seen before; it was a sort of mix of desperate desire, incessant hatred, and ill-suppressed fear. This insane look made it exceedingly obvious that the demolitions expert of RAT1 wanted nothing more than to impale the diamond sword in her hand into Kat's flesh.

Kat heard a growling at her side, and she looked down and was instantly filled with joy; Rex had rejoined her. Immediately after the start of the battle, Rex had gotten into a tussle with a tamed wolf of the Elementian side, and Kat had left him to his own devices, trusting that he would be alright and that he would find her if she needed him. Indeed, the dog's sudden appearance at Kat's side had convinced her that both of her assumptions were correct.

Becca made the first move. Her face broken into the unhinged grin of a killer maniac, she threw and Ender Pearl and teleported to Kat's feet, into the deadlock of her waiting sword. The two warriors pushed into each other and ended up being thrown back, and then they pounced into heavy combat. Kat soon realized to her dismay that she had seriously underestimated Becca's skills with the sword; although her directive was that of the demolitions expert, the girl was nothing short of a sword master. Kat ground away on the offensive, but Becca blocked each attack effortlessly, laughing and not even breaking a sweat. Kat knew that it was only a matter of time before Becca took the offensive, at which point she would be in deep trouble.

Kat, remembering her training with Sally, went out of her comfort zone and drew her second sword, fighting Becca with the dual blades. However risky this move may have been, it worked. Becca was totally unprepared to take on somebody of even Kat's modest skill with twin swords. Before long, Kat's left sword had sent Becca's single sword spiraling in the air, and Charlemagne's sword in Kat's right hand cut Becca across the chestplate, melting through the armor and creating a trail of burn marks as it went.

Becca's eyes bulged as she gave a very sudden, and very powerful scream. Kat was knocked off guard, which gave Becca enough time to rip off her chestplate and rush in to engage Kat at close combat. In a flash, Becca knocked Kat's swords out of her hands by hitting two pressure points on both wrists.

Kat was utterly unprepared; she had never been trained in hand-to-hand combat before, as Becca so clearly had. Try as she might to resist, Becca had Kat pinned to the ground and was undoubtedly about to do something horribly sadistic to her when an arrow punctured the ground, inches from Kat's head.

Both girls looked up and saw Leonidas standing in the clearing, his bow raised, ready to take Kat out at a moment's notice. Or… was he? As Kat focused on his brown face, screwed up in concentration, there was a tangible amount of tension in his eyes. His eyes kept almost imperceptibly changing focus between Kat and Becca as if… and Kat's eyes widened as the thought occurred to her… he was trying to decide which of them to shoot.

But why? Why was it that Leonidas, whom Kat knew to be a prodigious shot, was not immediately now putting an arrow through her skull? Was it really because he was contemplating shooting Becca? What the hell was going on? Why was it that she, Kat, was still alive?

Kat felt a jerk around her naval; she had been so intensely focused on Leonidas's hesitancy to shoot that she had not noticed Becca putting her into a full nelson, and she was now being held up in prime position for shooting. I should have known, thought Kat bitterly, he was just stalling for Becca to get me into the right position. Or was that it? Even as she sat here now, captured, more immobile than Leonidas could ever dream of finding her, beads of sweat were still tumbling down Leonidas's forehead like miniscule waterfalls, representing what Kat wondered could be suppressed conflict.

She never got a chance to learn whether or not Leonidas would have shot her. Kat felt herself fall forward and slam to the ground, and as she looked up, her jilted vision caught sight of Rex flying over her. The dog had knocked Becca off of Kat, and was now charging down Leonidas. Kat saw Rex tackle the archer to the ground, his arrow leaving his bow in a random trajectory.

Recognizing that her time for escape had come, Kat elbowed Becca in the face, kicked her way out from beneath her and snatched up her glowing red sword from the ground nearby, proceeding to slash the recovering Becca across the chest. Becca's entire body burst into flames, and she couldn't even scream in pain from the blood now gushing from her mouth, a token of Kat's elbow. Kat squinted her eyes in repulsion as Becca flailed around, trying desperately to escape the inferno now engulfing her body, finally succumbing to the inevitable and collapsing face down on the stone courtyard. But not before she pushed a small stone button on the ground that Kat had not noticed before.

Kat knew what happened after Becca pressed a button. She glanced over at Leonidas, who seemed to be in a state of shock that his partner had just essentially betrayed him. Even Rex's ears perked up, his animal instincts picking up something horribly, horribly wrong.

The entire world seemed to become a three-part combination of light, sound and heat as the TNT trap hidden beneath the Earth went off. Kat covered her head with her arms, and she felt her armor completely blown off by the sheer force of the explosion. A sensation of flying upwards overpowered all of Kat's senses, and she willed herself to open her eyes to view the scene around her.

The blackened corpse of Becca spun through the air, spewing items like blood. Leonidas was absent from the world which had become composed of white pillars of energy

Then, altogether, the white pillars disappeared and Kat found herself hundreds of feet above the ground, burns covering her arms. She looked down and saw the giant hole of blackness the blast had opened in the center of the battlefield.

As the falling began, two final thoughts rolled through her mind: *Becca is dead... And Leonidas...*

Then Kat's head hit the dirt and her mind stopped.

CHAPTER 28: THE ULTIMATE SACRAFICE

Stan was two thirds of the way to the base of the castle when a massive explosion shook the center of the battlefield. He was cursing himself for taking too long to confront the King. It wasn't entirely his fault; when Jayden had been ambushed by the griefer with the ski mask who had killed Crazy Steve, along with two of his goons, was Stan really going to stand there and let Jayden fight three-on-one? Now that one of the griefer's friends was dead by Jayden's hand, the other incapacitated by wound from Stan's blade, and the griefer himself left to the mercy of Jayden, Stan was feeling that the whole ordeal had taken entirely too much time.

As Stan finally reached the lava moat at the base of the castle, he was momentarily deterred by the sight of Archie and G engaging in raging combat with the giant beast-man, Minotaurus. Stan wasn't worried about them, he was sure that they could take him on; what did unnerve him a bit was the looks of supreme rage upon both of their faces; indeed, the only time Stan had seen them look that angry was back in the Adorian Village, right after Minotaurus had killed Adoria.

Praying that nobody else had died, and remembering that completing his own task was the only way to ensure that nobody else did, Stan pulled out his last Ender Pearl and with an almighty toss, the green orb flew up to the castle bridge. Stan closed his eyes, and allowed himself to be consumed by the rushing flow of teleportation, opening his eyes only when he felt solid brick beneath his feet.

Stan opened his eyes and found, to his relief, that his aim had been true; he now found himself standing on the bridge of the King's castle. The green below him was punctuated by small multicolored dots that were his battling friends and foes. Knowing, then, what he would find, Stan took a deep breath, assured himself one last time that he was ready, and turned to face his adversary for the first and most definitely the last time.

He stood there, on the other end of the bridge, staring Stan down like a hawk eying a particularly juicy mouse. Slowly, he reached across his body to the sword hanging at his left side, and, grasping the hilt, slowly pulled it out and pointed it at Stan. Stan could see a second sword dangling at his right side, and a bow slung across his back. As the sun glinted off of the diamond covering his chest and head, and the sword now fixated with unwavering confidence towards Stan, there was no smile on King Kev's face as he gave Stan a look that clearly offered him the first move.

Stan had planned for this, and in response, he reached for one of the two iron axes strapped onto his back. King Kev's eyebrows twitched in surprise for a moment, and then fixated back into a scowl. Stan was not surprised; had the King pulled out any but the highest tier of weapon, he would have been surprised, too.

Keeping his game plan in mind, Stan held the King's gaze for a few moments, those remorseless blue eyes erasing all doubts he had about the battle he was about to undertake. Then, the fates of Adoria, Crazy Steve, and so many others forced their way out of his throat, manifesting themselves in a war cry as Stan charged the King.

King Kev's expressionless face morphed into a slight hint of a smile, citing Stan's apparent foolishness for charging in head on, but Stan had a plan. A few blocks before he would have come into the range of the King's sword, Stan threw the iron axe with all his strength at the King. The King had clearly not been expecting this, and he dive rolled to the side. His diamond sword rose just in time

389

to counter the diamond blade of the axe Stan had pulled from his inventory.

The King thrust upwards with his sword, regaining his footing, but still giving Stan the offensive, which he pressed with pleasure. It was becoming very obvious, very quickly, however, that the caliber of King Kev's sword fighting far surpassed any which Stan had seen, any which DZ possibly could have demonstrated to him. Being in the midst of the battle for his life, Stan was at the top of his game, but it still seemed that the King was only toying with him, his blade fluidly moving through the air as if he could predict the motions of Stan's axe.

Sensing that his current approach would get him nowhere, Stan tried a new approach and cut to the side, slamming the wooden handle of his axe across King Kev's chest, hoping to knock him off of the bridge and into his inevitable demise below. The contact of wood on diamond reverberated in the form of a shock wave through the King. The unpredicted offense momentarily stunned him, but it was not to last; as Stan was about to drive him over the edge King Kev placed his hand onto one of the battlements and, in a showcase of incredible upper body strength, he pushed off his hand and sailed into the air.

It was with implausible agility that King Kev positioned his bow and fired five arrows in rapid succession at Stan. The King was clearly a prodigious archer as well, for despite the fact that he was in midair, the arrows still found Stan, bouncing off of his armor. When the King hit the ground, his features were twisted with a fresh wave of fury. He wasted no time making it clear that he had the offensive now.

There was nothing Stan could do. The King was now fighting with a technique of the sword that Stan had never seen before, and despite his best efforts, it was less than ten seconds before Stan's axe lay far from his reach, having clattered across the stone and stopping less than a block short of falling from the edge of the bridge.

Stan could barely breathe; his chest moved, but only slightly, as it was pinned under King Kev's foot. Stan could not think clearly. His mind was thrashing between two trains of thought, one panicking for his impending doom, the other scrabbling to formulate a plan to escape his cruel fate.

"I don't like people who try to kill me, Stan," said the King, his voice shaking with rage, and it occurred to Stan that it was the first time he had ever heard the King speak in person. His voice was considerably lower (and more menacing) than it had sounded projected over the courtyard. "I tend to find them, rather unpleasant, you know? The kind of people that cause problems. The kind of people..." and his voice went steely, his face ugly with hatred, "... that I don't want in my kingdom."

The King jammed his knee downward, into Stan's chest. The pressure seemed to increase tenfold; he half hoped now that the King would kill him soon, before his vital organs collapsed. It seemed he would get his wish; the King now drew his bow, and notched an arrow. Desperate to go down fighting, Stan aimed one last defiant jab upwards at the King's face. Feeble as it might have been, the King still had to weave his head to the side to avoid it. With a look that said more than any insult ever could, King Kev pulled back the string. Stan closed his eyes.

When the weight lifted from his chest, Stan knew that it was over. The arrow had entered his temple, and he had gone the same way as Crazy Steve. It was odd though, he realized, he hadn't felt a thing...

Stan opened his eyes and saw with a start that he was not, in fact, dead; he could see the body of King Kev flying backwards and away from him, his diamond helmet spinning about in a lopsided pattern beside him. But by what force? Stan looked up, and his immediate reaction was that the pressure on his innards must have impaired his cognitive function, because he could not be seeing correctly.

The figure standing over him, holding Stan's axe in attack stance, was dead, Stan had watched him die. And if he had been alive, there was no way that he would be here, would have saved Stan's life from the King...

But as Stan's vision came back into complete focus, he saw that this truth against all truths was true, and that the armored form of Mr. A was indeed reaching down, offering Stan a hand up.

"Are you alright, Stan?" asked the griefer, and Stan heard unmistakable, genuine concern in his voice.

Sure that some aspect was wrong, it was only tentatively that Stan answered "Yeah..." and grasped Mr. A's hand, letting himself he pulled back to his feet.

"Here's your axe," Mr. A said, and he held it out to Stan, who accepted it gratefully but cautiously. A small sound of "Wha..." escaped Stan's lips before Mr. A cut him off.

"Stan, I'm sure you have a million questions, and I would call you an idiot if you completely trusted me right now, but I want you to know two things. One: I am not going to hurt you. Two: I'm going to help you kill the King. I'll explain everything else in a second."

Indeed, questions were exploding inside Stan's head like TNT, but he focused himself on the form of King Kev, who had wasted no time regaining his footing and retrieving his helmet, and who was now looking at Mr. A with surprised fury. Stan decided to let things play out, trusting that he would understand everything within the next couple of minutes.

"Who are you? What are you doing here!?" barked the King in wild rage.

Mr. A smirked. "You don't recognize me, do you, Kev old boy," he responded.

The King's eyes widened, his mouth dropped open, and the grip on his sword tightened; obviously something about this phrase sat ill with the King.

"That... that voice..." said the King, growing white, as if he had seen a ghost (which, Stan reminded himself, was still very possible). "Is that... are you... is that really you, Avery?"

"What, not happy to see me, Kev?" Mr. A asked. "That's okay... I wouldn't be, either."

Stan's mind was in double time, trying to process what he had just heard. Had the King just called Mr. A, Avery? But then... that couldn't mean... *what*?

"How are you here, Avery?" asked the King, a tangible element of fear in his voice. "You're dead. I killed you. There's no possible way that you're alive."

"I'm... kind of thinking the same thing, Mr. A," replied Stan, his voice shaky. "What... I mean, how are you alive? And why..." Stan's head hurt even saying it... "...does he keep calling you Avery?"

"I'm sure you both have quite a few questions. Before I kill you, Kev," to which he gave a chuckle and King Kev shook in rage (or perhaps fear; it was unclear), "I will give a brief summary of my life, which I think shall put to rest any question that either of you may have."

"After you killed me, Kev, I found myself unable to ever return to Elementia again. I was miserable; I had done so much in this place, and it was gone. I decided that it was my duty to return, and to do everything possible to make sure that what happened to me didn't happen to anyone else here ever again. That was when I created a new account, and I rejoined Elementia again under the name of Adam711, a name not too dissimilar to who I feel I always will truly be, Avery007.

393

"I played the game of Minecraft from the beginning, gathering all my necessary resources and eventually building myself up into the warrior that I was when you killed me Kev. It wasn't enough, though... I wanted so desperately to take you down. I quickly learned of a settlement composed of players that you had banished, Kev, and who were living in the Southern Tundra Biome. I knew that if there was anywhere that I could start to raise an army to destroy you, it would be there, seeing as the Adorian Village was still in its infancy at that time.

"I arrived at that settlement, and it was miserable; the snowy wasteland of the tundra had no trees, barely any animals, and those poor players were struggling to survive. That settlement is probably dead by now... not that you'd give a damn, Kev... but I was sure that, at the time, they would join me in my plan. They did not, however; they must have become extremely paranoid from living in poverty for so long, for the moment I tried to enlist them to my rebellion, they beat me down with their stone tools, calling me a dangerous monster that they couldn't afford to deal with. And just like that, Adam711 had died, went the same way as Avery007.

"I became twisted, dark... the same way you are now, Kev, as a matter of fact... I started in a cycle of dark thoughts, and I eventually tricked myself into believing that the lower-level players of this game, who didn't join me in my plan that frankly must have sounded deranged to them, were the reason that the server was in the state of decline that continues to this day. I now know that it is because of you, Kev... but at the time I was in a bad place in my thoughts. Determined to extract my revenge, I rejoined the game a second time, this time in my current body and name, Mr. A."

"It was not long after I rejoined that I ran into you for the first time, Stan. I had already killed a number of new players, and that golden sword was the best weapon that I had found. I now deeply regret all of those actions, and I realize there is nothing worse in this world than attacking the innocent... but regardless, you three escaped me. As the first ones to ever do so, I found myself unable to want anything except for you, Kat and Charlie dead. As you know, I hunted you down, gaining better materials for myself as you did the same, and it culminated when you knocked me into that lava pit over the End Portal.

"I believed, and I know now, that you supposed that I had died in that burning pit. I *would* have, too, had it not been for the Potion of Fire Resistance that I had in my inventory. As I lay there, under the lava, I heard what you said Stan. I thank you for what you said, because I came back to my senses after that. I realized, for the first time since my reincarnation as Mr. A, how very corrupted I had become. I hated myself for what felt like forever, and I resented myself for all I had become as I floated there in that burning pit. I realized, then, that the only way I could redeem myself for my actions was to help you. You had told me that you were plotting to overthrow Kev, and I swore right then and there that I would do whatever it takes to help you overthrow Kev. He's the corrupt one. He's the reason I died. He's the reasons *everyone*'s been dying.

"And so now, I'm here to kill you, Kev," finished Mr. A, or, Avery, with an almost amused smile on his face. Stan was incredulous, but, as he thought about it, it made sense as he fit together all of the pieces of the story in his head. Mr. A had not been friends with Avery007; he *was* Avery007.

King Kev had not moved throughout Avery's speech, but his face now showed obvious fear at the fact that his best friend-turned-enemy had returned from the grave not once, but twice. Then, slowly, King Kev's face broke into a bemused sort of grin.

"Very well, if you'd like to duel, Avery, I'd be more than happy to oblige you," he said slowly, danger dripping from his voice. "But let me just remind you... I've beaten you once, and you can be sure that I'll do it again."

"I think the lack of operating powers will make a difference this time, don't you think, Stan?" came Avery's response, and he looked over at Stan, who responded with a confident grin. Avery was genuinely remorseful for his efforts against lower-levels, and as he had just saved Stan's life, Stan felt very confident in trusting him. He looked over at the King and saw what could only be described as eagerness crossing his face as Avery drew his diamond sword. King Kev, in response, drew a second diamond sword in his left hand.

Avery rushed in to engage the King on one side, quickly followed by Stan on the other. The four blades clashed one another, but clearly King Kev's prowess with the sword extended to dual wielding. Stan fought as hard as ever, but the King seemed to be able to fight just as well with his left hand as with his right, despite the fact that King Kev's right hand was then being used in the fight against Avery. Before long, the King feinted backwards and thrust his sword into Stan's chest. The point glanced off of the armor, but the impact threw Stan backwards, and he skidded away from the King, who sheathed his sword and went into a single-sword combat with Avery.

Stan didn't even try to re-enter the fight, because this was a caliber of sword fighting as he had never known was possible. Throughout his time in Elementia, he had kept on thinking that he had seen the best swordfighters in the land, but as he watched King Kev and Avery lock blades in the dangerous dance, he knew that the King was holding nothing back, nor was Avery, and that he could never fight even close to the level of these two players.

"What's... the matter," grunted Avery as the swords continued to clash. His voice had a taunt to it. "You getting... tired... Kev, old boy?" he added with a weak smirk.

Indeed, after fighting all-out for a minute, the two fighters did both seem to be tiring. The King's face was red and screwed up with effort, and Avery was sweating buckets. Still, though, Avery found the breath to continue to torment the King.

"Not... so easy... with no... operating powers... is it... KEV!?" shouted Avery, and on the last word the tip of Avery's sword locked into the handle of the King's and the sword went flying into the air and over the edge of the bridge. Desperation ripe on his face, the

King reached for the sword at his side, but it had already been cut from the side by a quick blow from Avery's blade, and the King was now completely defenseless, staring down the elongated, sharp point of Avery's diamond sword.

"Any last words, Kev?" panted Avery, a triumphant smile breaking on his face.

The King moved quick as a whip; rather than responding to Avery's sarcastic inquiry, the King leaped backwards, drew a hidden sword from his inventory, and attacked. Avery smirked, and Stan didn't understand why King Kev would attempt such a risky maneuver; Avery had the upper hand, what was he playing at? But as the sword swung forward, Stan realized with a jolt that the luster on the diamond sword, made ambiguous by the gleaming sun, meant that the King had the element of surprise on his side.

"Avery, look out! The sword is..."

But it was too late; the Knockback enchantment on the glowing weapon released a shockwave as King Kev swung it, a shockwave which hit Avery across the chest with blunt force. As Avery stumbled backwards, he suddenly found himself tumbling very quickly towards the edge of the bridge as the King released another rapid succession of attacks. At the very edge of the bridge, an uppercut sent Avery flying wildly into the air, and it was less than a second before the King had sheathed his sword, loaded his bow, and sent an arrow flying into Avery's head.

Stan sprinted to the edge of the bridge and stood, transfixed in horror, as his friend fell from the bridge, his items falling about him. Stan couldn't pull his eyes away until the end, and the end was finally reached when the body of Mr. A, Adam711, and Avery007 disappeared before it could fall into the lava moat below.

Stan felt as though a sizable chunk of him had been ripped out, and he couldn't stop staring at the spot where the form of Avery, his most dangerous menace turned valiant supporter, had just faded from his existence of Elementia for a third time. Then,

Stan's eyes were ripped from the spot as an unseen force sent him flying into the center of the bridge. Stan looked up and saw King Kev, charging him sword in hand, looking as feral as Rex had that first day he had burst from the forest, intent on feasting on Stan's throat.

The King's sword spun in his hand twice more, and two more deadening bolts of energy struck Stan, making him roll in the most painful of fashions across the bridge. In his agony, Stan barely was able to look up and see the pulsating purple face of the King standing above him, staring him down.

"Don't expect as merciful an end as I gave to Avery," whispered the King a voice that spoke death, and Stan found himself flying into the air via another uppercut. An instant later, the wind left his body as if by a punch, and Stan felt an excruciating flare scorch his back; the King had thrown a Fire Charge at him in midair. Stan fell back down the earth and felt his legs break. This was a new level of pain, higher than Stan had ever known was possible, and the process repeated itself twice more, made humiliating by the King's cruel, sadistic laughter.

Stan could not open his eyes, he could not see, he could not feel. He was aware of a scuffle going on far off in the distance, but all he was aware of was how much he wanted to die. Surely, there was nothing in the universe that could be worse than this, this terrible pain, the burn of his failure, and the sheer helplessness of being at the complete and total mercy of the evil King...

Then, all at once, the pain vanished. Sure now for the second time in five minutes that he had died, Stan attempted to open his eyes, and found out, to his utmost surprise that he was still alive, and he was laying face-down on the stone blocks. There was a distinct smell in the air, which Stan recognized as a Potion of Healing. Stan heard a voice that he did not recognize, shouting with incredible power, "OH NO YOU DON'T!"

Stan pulled himself to his elbows and saw to his amazement that he did know the speaker of the voice, although he had never known this player to speak above a normal decibel before. Stan was watching in awe as the King stumbled blindly backwards, clutching his eyes, as the Apothecary pulled more and more potions off of his sash, sending them directly into the King. Surrounded in a cloud of noxious gas and colored in potions of all hues, the King was unable to see the Apothecary as he whipped the diamond pickaxe from his belt and made to drive it into King Kev's stomach. Clearly, though, the King was not completely incapacitated by the gas and potions, as he had the sense to raise up his sword in a feeble block. The blow sent the King stumbling backwards, blindly sending out wild shockwaves with frantic sword slashes so to fend off any attackers as he regained his eyesight.

To wise to walk into the King's frenzied attacks, the Apothecary instead ran back over to Stan and helped him to his feet. "Are you alright?" he asked.

"Yeah, I'm fine," replied Stan. "Thanks for saving me... but what are you doing up here?"

"Well," the old man replied, "I wasn't needed very much on the field... you'll be happy to know that we've started to drive the King's forces back... and I looked up at the bridge and saw a body fly off! So I figured I'd come up here to see what had happened... but you're both still alive! Who was that, who was just killed?"

"That was Avery007," replied Stan quickly, sensing the King regaining his footing and readying his sword, "but...:

"*What?*" exclaimed the Apothecary, looking flabbergasted. "Avery? But he's dead! *He* killed him!" And he jerked his thumb at the King, who was now looking furiously at Stan and the Apothecary.

"Look, it's a long story, I'll explain later, oka... OH GEEZ!" cried Stan as he raised his axe to counter the sword that the King was about to bring down onto his skull. Stan felt the shockwave pass over his head, rustling his hair, and the Apothecary sent a blue potion flying into King Kev's face. He stumbled backwards, spitting in pain, and Stan knocked him back with the butt of his axe.

Stan and the Apothecary looked at each other, and they seemed to make a mutual agreement to continue talking after they had jointly finished the King. It was lucky, thought Stan, that Avery had weakened the King in the fight, or else he would be putting up a much greater resistance; but indeed, the King seemed to have given up all hopes of being able to combat the two players driving him backwards across the bridge. Potion after potion, axe blow after axe blow, glanced the King against the diamond chestplate (it was beginning to crack), and at one point the King dropped his sword, which Stan gratefully snatched up. With the Knockback enchantment on the sword, it was only a matter of moments before the shockwaves and splash potions had knocked the King inside of the hollow tower at the right end of the bridge.

As the limp but still alive body of the King smashed into the wall, his hand caught on one of two levers on the stone brick wall next to him, and the switch flipped downwards. Immediately, light flooded the tower as battlements opened systematically around the tower, perfect sniping posts for archers. The King took no notice however, his face was screwed up, apparently in anticipation for what he knew was about to come. King Kev had no weapon, no energy left, and he had his back to the wall against two players, one with potions and one with his own sword. There was only one track for his future now.

"Do it, Stan," said the Apothecary grimly, and as Stan looked down into the terrified, close-eyed face of the man who had the blood of so many innocents on his hands, Stan wanted to do it. Oh, he wanted to do it *so* badly. It would take one simple motion to thrust the King's own sword through his chestplate and through his body, thus ending his reign of terror on the server forever. Stan raised the sword.

Then Stan was gone. He was not in the tower with King Kev and the Apothecary anymore; he was standing in the Ender Desert, alongside Charlie, Bill, Bob, Rex, Lemon, the crying figure of Kat, the comforting shoulder of Ben, and the body of the King's soldier with the cow-skin that lie dead besides them. The pain that Stan felt at seeing his friend murder an unarmed player crashed over him like a tidal wave, and he remembered his vow to never murder an unarmed player again.

And here he stood, his sword raised, over the body of King Kev, as defenseless as a newborn baby, his face screwed up in anticipation of the deathblow that was to follow.

"You must, Stan," came the Apothecary's voice from behind him, sad and sympathetic, but urgent as well. Stan raised the sword higher still. Of course, he must... it was his duty, and the King deserved it... this may well be his last chance... but still...

Without warning, the King's eyes flew open, bulging out of their sockets. Then, several things happened that were so fast, and so senseless, that Stan barely had time to comprehend the events around him.

The King drew an arrow back in the unobserved bow and let it fire, but not towards either Stan or the Apothecary, between them. Although it was not intended to hit either of them, the sudden movement was enough of a shock to Stan that he dropped the sword, right into the outstretched hands of the King. The King swung the sword, emitting a shockwave that slammed into Stan and the Apothecary, knocking them off balance. The King then proceeded, with a manic frantic air, to yank down hard on the second lever on the wall, spin the diamond sword in his hands to face himself, and drive the sword through his cracked diamond armor and into his own chest.

White shock whipped Stan across the face like another shockwave as the King's body was knocked backwards by the force of his own suicide, slamming into the stone brick wall and falling limply to the ground. How could this be? thought Stan, his instincts setting off alarm bells all throughout his body, for this could not be right. Why would the King take his own life? That was not in the plan at all, they had not even considered that as a possible outcome! Yet still the King lay, a lifeless corpse, his items strewn about his body indicating that this was no trick, this was no illusion of smoke and mirrors; King Kev was dead by his own hand.

Stan glanced at the Apothecary to see how he had interpreted this zany turn of events. But instead of the now vanishing body of King Kev, Stan followed the old man's horrified gaze to the lever which the King had pulled as his last action in Elementia. Stan heard the rumbling, and an instant later he realized what that lever must have done. The word "RUN!" had barely left his lips when the tower exploded.

Stan held his glance with the Apothecary for as long as he could, but the explosions enveloping the air around him propelled him backwards with tremendous speed. The last glimpse he saw from his elderly friend was the items bursting from his body in a ring, which disintegrated alongside the body in the inferno of the explosion.

Stan was aware of the crash as he was propelled through the glass window of the tower, and he knew that he was falling down, and the explosions were coming down after him. Stan opened his eyes and saw to his amazement that he was still alive, and that he had received only trivial injuries from the explosion; on the other hand, his diamond armor had been completely blown off. It was no matter, though; Stan looked down and saw that he was falling at terminal velocity straight towards the King's lava moat.

The explosions behind Stan seemed to be destroying the entire building, which fell down in a wave like an avalanche, right above Stan's falling body. As he neared the lava, only one thought filled his mind. *King Kev is dead. My work in Elementia is done.*

Stan felt the heat a split second before he entered the lava.

CHAPTER 29: THE LAST CASUALTY

Charlie was looking around in satisfaction; everywhere you looked, the members of the King's army were fleeing the courtyard, desperate to preserve their lives, as the Adorian forces took more and more of the vital command posts. The Adorians had as good as won, with Elementian corpses littering the ground and many more now being held unarmed at sword point in a makeshift holding camp that the Adorians had established on the battlefield.

As his men cheered at the sight of the retreating enemy forces, Charlie pulled an Ender Pearl from his inventory. "You guys stay here and watch for any stragglers! I'm gonna go help Stan!" cried Charlie. He held the orb firmly in his hand, and he had just thrown it up onto the bridge when he heard an explosion.

Charlie whipped around and saw in horror that the top of the tower on the right side had exploded in a burst of stone and fire, and then another detonation went off right below it. Charlie then found himself staring at stone, as the Ender Pearl had take effect and he was now standing on the stone bridge of the castle. Charlie looked up and sprinted over to the edge of the broken bridge, looking down in shock as the explosions continued down until the castle tower ceased to exist, its base flooded by a lake of lava.

"Char... lie..."

Charlie, dreading what he would find when he turned to face the voice, looked towards the sound and saw to his horror the broken body of the Apothecary, lying stagnant amongst a pile of loose stone, his items in a ring around him. As Charlie rushed towards him, realizing to his dismay that he was out of potions to heal the old man, Charlie wondered how it was possible that the Apothecary was still alive... items bust around you was generally a sure sign of death.

"I'm here, Apothecary, I'm here..."

"Stan... King... there..." came the raspy voice, and then, in an almost imperceptible movement, the old man pointed a finger to the smoldering air where the tower had sat moments before. Then, the finger dropped to the ground, and the old man let out one final breath.

Hoping against hope that there was still a chance, Charlie placed the old man's body over his shoulder and walked over to the edge of the bridge, Ender Pearling back to ground level and leaving the medics to deal with the Apothecary. Immediately, they pronounced him to be dead, and as if on cue, the moment they gave this diagnosis, the body vanished.

Charlie didn't feel hurt; he didn't feel much of anything at that point. He had just looked over at the pillar of dust and smoke hanging in the air where the tower had stood, and he knew that Stan and King Kev were both dead. There was no way an explosion of that magnitude was survivable, already they were saying that the Apothecary should have died instantly, and most likely Stan and the King were both already wounded when the bombs went off, and by the Apothecary's gesture they were in the heart of the inferno.

Charlie began to assess the battle, logging his thoughts in a book he had on hand. They had won many great triumphs in the battle. Charlemagne, Geno, and Becca were known to be dead, King Kev and Leonidas were thought to be dead, and the whereabouts of Caesar and Minotaurus were unknown. That meant five of their seven main targets were now most likely dead, and the other two, as enemies of the state, would assuredly be captured before long.

Besides this, of the approximate hundred and fifty Elementian fighters who had come into battle, half of them were dead, fifty of them were now being held as prisoners, and the remaining twenty five or so had managed to escape. All in all, the offensive was a huge success.

Except for the losses. Charlie now looked back on all who had been killed and wounded in the battle. About half of their fighters had been killed as well, but of their leading officers, only four of them were of dire or uncertain fates besides the Apothecary.

Bob had suffered the worst of all. Although not dead, he had taken a sword through the knee from Caesar, and he would never be able to walk again. This, it seemed to Charlie, was almost a crueler fate than death.

The only Adorian commander known to be dead was Sally. It was despicable; Charlie had seen her go down by a lucky strike in Minotaurus's initial charge. It had not been pretty, and it had not been easy, to know that the sarcastic, hard-talking, but in essence kind-hearted girl who had taught Kat and so many others in the way of the sword was now gone from Elementia forever. And when Stan found out...

If Stan was still alive, that is. And the chances of that were one in a million. Charlie was sure that Stan was in that tower with the King when it exploded, and if that was the truth then Charlie couldn't have fathomed any way that Stan could have survived. Had the explosion not destroyed him as it had the Apothecary, Stan would have had nothing but hitting the ground at fatal speeds to welcome him. Even if by some remote chance he had hit the lava moat and not been instantly killed by fall damage, there had been a shortage of Potions of Fire Resistance, and Charlie knew that if Stan had indeed had none, he would have burned to death. All that being said, it could be said with confidence that Stan had died.

That left the last high-ranking Adorian. Ever since she had engaged Becca, the last place DZ had seen her, nobody had seen or heard from Kat. In the searching of the bombed out TNT trap, her items had not been found, and so there was no evidence suggesting that she had definitely died.

As Charlie finished writing the report, he saw the other Adorian commanders congregating around him: Jayden, Archie, G, DZ, Blackraven, the Mechanist, the Mayor of Blackstone, Bill and Ben, the last two of whom were carrying Bob between them. Avoiding looking into their hardened and despairingly painless faces, Charlie read off his report to the lot of them. Each of them grimaced and gave a heavy sigh upon the news of Stan's death, and Charlie could tell that, like himself, they were too numb and desensitized for the incomprehensible pain to hit them just yet. Then he read of Kat's fate.

"Wait, you mean, we still haven't found Kat yet?" G asked, alarmed.

"Not yet," replied Charlie. "We've got to..."

"Find her, that's what we've gotta do!" bellowed G. He looked very angry now. "If there's even a chance she's still alive, we've got to devote all of our resources to finding her!"

Jayden, bags under his eyes and cuts across his war-beaten face, put a hand on his friend's shoulder. "G, we've got to wrap things up here, and then, trust me, we'll put everything we have into..."

"SHUT UP!" said G in a type of loud whisper, putting his hand up. "Did you hear that?" he asked before anybody could retort. "*Did you hear that?*"

Despite the fact that many of the people in the circle, particularly Ben, wanted to yell at G to give it a rest, they humored him and listened, sympathetic to any desperation he had that might turn into the voice of his lost crush. However, in the silence, a hoarse voice did carry through the windless silence of the abandoned battlefield.

"Help... help..."

Charlie knew that voice anywhere, and he could tell where it came from. He was second only to G at arriving at Becca's TNT trap, and it dawned on him that nobody had actually checked *inside* of the crater. Charlie watched in amazement as G mined through the blocks and alongside the ledge where Kat lay on her side, her breathing shallow and raspy from being in the midst of Becca's endgame attack. G moved her head into his lap, and from his inventory produced a red potion of healing. He poured it down her throat, her eyes blinked open, and a smile of affection took to her face, which G returned with tears in his eyes.

"Maybe you should give those two some time alone," came a voice from behind Charlie and the others.

Charlie couldn't believe it... the voice he heard was the one other in Elementia that he would always recognize, regardless. Only G and Kat, who were too busy reuniting in the hole, did not turn around with the look on their face indicative of the ghost they were now seeing return from the grave. But he was not a ghost; a red aura danced around him, his armor gone and his clothes tattered and burned, and a diamond axe held clutched in his hand, the triumphant, smirking form of Stan2012 walked out of the light of the now-setting sun.

A spontaneous burst of jubilation erupted from the leaders, and they rushed forward towards Stan. Charlie was the first to reach him, embracing Stan like a brother, and only then did he truly believe that his best friend was alive. DZ, Jayden and Archie followed, tailed closely by Blackraven, the Mechanist, and the mayor of Blackstone. Even G, supporting the wounded Kat on his shoulder, managed to hobble over and join the group hug. Ben and Bill gave hoots and whoops of joy, while tears of joy streamed down the face of their crippled brother still suspended between them.

"Guys... I still need to breathe..." Stan laughed from the center of his friends, and he laughed harder upon realizing that all of the Adorian warriors on the surrounding plain were cheering their praises that the hero who had slain King Kev had survived.

"Oh my God... you're ALIVE!" were the first words that Charlie managed to stammer out; he was in a state of euphoria. "How is... is the... but... the King's dead, right?"

"Yeah, but it was the weirdest thing, I didn't kill him!" said Stan. "He stabbed himself right as the Apothecary and I... by the way, did the Apothecary...

"No," said Charlie, and Stan felt another dull blow to his stomach; he had known that the chances were second only to impossibility, but he had still hoped. He became aware that Charlie was following up on his statement.

"Did you say that the King killed himself? But why..."

"I don't know, I'm still trying to figure that out myself. I mean, he wasn't going to win anyway, he was really weak from fighting the Apothecary, and Avery, and me..."

"*Avery*?" Charlie cut him off, and there was a collective gasp and murmuring in the crowd that had now gathered around Stan. "Stan, what the hell just happened up there on that bridge?"

Stan sighed, not eager to recount the deaths of two of his friends again, but he resigned himself to the wishes of the crowd. "Well, I Ender Pearled up onto the bridge, and the King was waiting for me. He was really exceptional with the sword, and he disarmed me, and then Mr. A shows up out of nowhere..."

There was another joint intake of breath. Stan saw several mouths, Kat's and Charlie's in particular, opening to interject, but, not wanting to be interrupted, Stan continued.

"...and he tells me that apparently he's the next incarnation of Avery007, and that he had turned bitter from being killed twice... I know, Charlie, it sounds crazy, but trust me, he was telling the truth... anyways, so Avery starts to fight King Kev and knocks him to

408

the ground, but then the King draws a sword with Knockback on it and launches Avery in the air and shoots him, and the King turns back to me.

"He disarms me again and sets me on fire and throws me in the air a few times just out of spite… don't worry, Kat, I'm fine now… and then the Apothecary comes in and starts attacking the King and heals me, and together we drive the King back into that tower, and I'm about to kill him…"

Stan hesitated, a feeling of guilt worming its way up inside him. He pushed it aside and made the on-the-spot decision not to mention that he had hesitated in killing the King, for if he hadn't, he realized as his insides seemed to drop to his feet, the Apothecary might have lived…

"…when he gets this really crazed look on his face, pulls a switch on the tower wall and stabs himself in the chest. That was when the tower exploded, and I guess it must have killed the Apothecary almost immediately. I would have been killed, too, if it weren't for my armor. Then I fell down into the lava, so I didn't take fall damage…"

"And how did you survive?!" burst out DZ, his face purple from the anticipation of waiting to ask the question. "Even if the lava absorbed the fall damage, you would have burned to death anyway; you didn't have any Potions of Fire Resistance, we had a shortage!"

Stan gave a small smile. "But I *did* have a potion of Fire Resistance." He turned to look at Kat and Charlie. "Do you two remember what the Apothecary gave us the first time he met us in that jungle?"

"Yeah," replied Kat. "He let me enchant this bow," she said, gesturing to the shimmering weapon strung across her back, "He gave Charlie his diamond pickaxe, he gave you the Ender Chest, and…" she said, comprehension coming to her face as it dawned on her, "… he gave us each Potions of Healing and Fire Resistance."

409

"Exactly," replied Stan. "You used your Fire Resistance potion fighting RAT1 at the lava sea, Kat, and you used yours at the Blaze spawner, Charlie, but I never used mine; actually, I had completely forgotten about it, it was just sitting there in my inventory the whole time.

"Just before I hit the lava, it dawned on me, and I drank the potion right on impact. I only got burned a little..." he said, gesturing to his singed clothing, "...before the potion took effect. Then, I was able to just swim out of the lava and walk over here.

"That being said," replied Stan, and there was a sense of finality in his voice suggesting that the recounting of his duel with the King and his castle was finished, "did I miss anything important?"

"You missed Charlie's report," came the response from Blackraven, and Charlie immediately felt a pit open in his stomach. Of the four of the leaders of uncertain or mortal fates, two of them had been discovered to be alive and likely to make a full recovery. But the other two, and one in particular... Charlie couldn't see any way to break the news to Stan. He decided, though, that it would be best to give the general report first.

"Yes, well, the report, uh, er," said Charlie at Stan's expectant glance. "Both sides had about a hundred and fifty fighters. Of those, about half of them died on both sides. On the Elementian side, though, only about twenty or so of them managed to escape, and we have about fifty captives."

Stan nodded his head, but felt uneasy; these deaths were about what Stan had anticipated, and he was happy to hear that so few Elementians had escaped, and that they had so many prisoners... but then, why did Charlie still look so distressed? And Stan had the distinct feeling that one face was missing from the crowd... he knew that he ought to know who, but his head was so clouded from the potion...

"Of the targets we set out to destroy, the following are dead: King Kev, Charlemagne, Geno, and Becca. Leonidas is assumed to be dead, and Caesar and Minotaurus are known to have escaped."

"Of our commanding officers," continued Charlie, an unnatural pitch in his voice as the palpable tension in the crowd drastically increased, "two are of damaged or terminal fates."

Stan winced and bowed his head, determined not to let his certain tears to be conspicuous.

"Bob, of the Nether Boys, was struck through the knee by Caesar's sword. Although he is still alive, he will never be able to walk properly again. And the other one... Sally..."

The single name struck Stan like a lightning bolt, a beam of energy originating from the atmosphere of dread that had been growing in the crowd since Charlie had began to re-read his report. Stan knew now the face that was missing from the crowd ... the single face that mattered most to him in the world, that he had been too forgetful under the potion effects to see immediately...

"What happened?" Stan asked, his voice hollow and resonate. Charlie did not answer. He had collapsed on the ground, crying like a child, unable to say the name again. A feeling of dread filled Stan's insides, and he half hoped that it would stay unspoken, for to say it aloud would make it irreversible and permanent... Still, though, Jayden stepped forward and choked out the strangled whisper, turning Stan's positive fear tangible.

"Sally was hit by a lucky blow from Minotaurus's axe in his first strike. She's dead, Stan."

Stan fell to his knees, but he did not feel. He was not aware that he was unable to produce one damn tear, and he was oblivious to the fact that half a dozen hands were now reaching him and embracing him. The only thing that was true now in Stan's mind was that Sally was dead. His girlfriend, the one he had cared for most in all of his travels through Elementia, was now gone forever.

Stan took care to harden his face before standing up; he couldn't shed tears in front of these people who held him as their leader. Those closest to him were surprised to see the lack of emotion that had taken to Stan's considering that he now knew his girlfriend to be dead.

"Will you be all right now, Stan?" came the plain voice, and Stan turned his head to see Oob, a bandage on his abdomen, asking him if he, the leader of this offensive, would be okay. Again, the reason that Sally had died, that the Apothecary and Avery had died, and the reason that Adoria and Crazy Steve and so many others had died came rushing back to Stan.

King Kev was dead, and his government had fallen. Elementia now had a clean slate, and right now, everybody was looking to Stan. Stan pulled out a small pile of dirt blocks he had on him, gestured to those adjacent to him that he needed space, and placed them into a staircase formation; he slowly dragged himself up the stairs until he stood head and shoulders above the rest of the crowd. Instantly, the crowd was so silent that Stan could hear the bubbling of the lava that had nearly been his grave in the background. Swallowing his suppressed emotions, Stan cleared his throat, and, determined that this moment would change his destiny forever, began to speak.

"My brothers, my sisters, united under the name of Adoria, the martyr for whom we went forth into battle today, you have done it. King Kev is dead. All of his sympathizers are dead, fleeing, or captured. As such, we now have a country called Elementia with no leaders, no structure, and no government. It would be stupid to say that a political system this size can function properly with no government, and therefore a new one must be instated.

"This government must be established under certain principles. The circumstances in which King Kev became corrupted, and turned Elementia into the monster which we have all just fought to destroy, must never be allowed to exist again. I am very much aware of your mindset, my fellow citizens. I ask you, please, to cheer now if you wish me to succeed King Kev as the new King of Elementia."

Simultaneously, the crowd, spanning for a decent radius around Stan's podium, erupted into a cacophony of cheers and hollers. This extended not only to the low-level soldiers, who were now eyeing Stan with the sort of reverence fitting of a god, but to his friends and colleagues. Of all of the cheering, it was Charlie, Kat, DZ, Bill, Bob, and Ben that made by far the loudest of the tumultuous resonance, showing their clear love of the idea of King Stan replacing King Kev. Smiling, but knowing what must be done, Stan raised his hands, and within ten seconds the crowd had hushed themselves once more.

"I am honored and humbled by your belief in me, but there is no way that I could ever wear King Kev's crown. There shall not be a King of Elementia, as the monarchy will always cause corruption on an irreversible scale. Instead, here is what I ask of you; follow and listen to me as I lead the remains of the Kingdom of Elementia to reorganize itself into the first Grand Republic of Elementia. The voices of the many shall speak as a voice of one, and fair and equal treatment shall be the order of the day. I fully intend to run myself as president of this new Republic, and should you elect me I promise to not dictate, but to guide the people of Elementia into a brighter tomorrow. If you believe the thought of the Grand Republic of Elementia to be a greater idea than that of myself as King, I ask you to now applaud."

Someone standing beyond the walls of the courtyard might have thought that another TNT trap had detonated, so loud was the sheer blast of frenzied cheers that filled the skies above the courtyard. Three times as loud as the first applause, the noise which hurt his still potion-affected ears was Stan's one, miniscule complaint about the scene.

I promise you, Sally, thought Stan as he surveyed the panorama, a single tear trickling down his cheek, I promise you that your death will not have been in vain. Everything I do, everything I direct on this server from this point forth, I do in your name, Sally. And also in your name, Adoria, Steve, Avery, Apothecary. To all of you, and all of my friends, I thank you, for helping me. I could not have gotten here without you.

And Stan lost himself in the spontaneous, pompous festivities now breaking out across the court as the Kingdom ceased to exist, the final and greatest casualty of a war on wrong, the last casualty of Stan2012's quest for justice. A new era had dawned for Elementia.

CHAPTER 30: THE NEW ORDER

The arrow-machine now broken and long-gone, Spawnpoint Hill was exactly the same as the first moments that Stan2012 had spent in Minecraft. The sun had just dipped under the forest skyline, and Zombies lumbered in a clueless fashion in the underbrush within the forest, no light from the new moon to distinguish them from players. There was a crashing sound before long, though, and seconds later the giant, hulking form of Minotaurus burst into the clearing, his axe raised, ready to destroy any mobs in the way. To his relief, there were none.

Caesar staggered into the clearing behind him, his leg badly damaged from an ambush by a Spider Jockey in the woods. Had it not been for the sharpshooting abilities of Leonidas, who now followed the Roman-adorned player into the clearing, Caesar may have died at the mob's arrow point.

"So what now?" asked Minotaurus to the other two, after the trio had caught their breath. "Where is there left to go?"

"What about the Southern Tundra Biome, do you think they'd know us there?" grunted Leonidas.

"No, that won't do," growled Caesar irritably, "that's become a dumping ground for undesirables since you've been imprisoned... there is always Ender Desert, though..."

"Bad call, man, there's *so* many Nomads in that place it ain't even funny, man, and like hell Stan ain't gonna put a high bounty on our heads," replied Leonidas.

"So… where is there left for us to go?" asked Minotaurus again. This question made the three players finally take in the severity of their situation. The other two were about to struggle out an answer when they heard a voice.

"You are welcome with me," it said.

The voice was calm, collected, and deadly, and so it was slowly that the three players turned to see the figure now standing atop Spawnpoint Hill. The three pairs of eyes simultaneously widened in horror. This figure they were seeing… he didn't exist, did he? Minotaurus held his axe in attack position, Caesar drew his swords, and Leonidas loaded his bow, and was about to fire when the voice spoke again.

"Stop, Caesar894, and Leonidas300, and Minotaurus."

The individual, whom they never believed to have subsisted until now, took them all back by calling them by name. As they stood shell-shocked, the figure continued.

"I know of your current situation. Your leader, the great and powerful King Kev of Elementia, has fallen at the hands of the lower-level scum he was forced to call his people. All of his most powerful allies are also dead, all … but four. You three, you are the legacy of King Kev, alongside his spy who now feigns joy amongst the triumphant. And if you four are his legacy, let me call myself the universe's embodiment of his spirit. You know who I am, and what I am capable of.

"I believe that you are in the right, and those who now control Elementia are in the wrong. If you join me, I will command you, and together, we will create a new order in Elementia. An order in which the weak are subordinate, and there is nothing in their power they can do to change that. Whilst King Kev was tied down by his political bonds, I, being who I am, have no such petty restrictions forced upon my back. So I ask you now, Caesar894, and Leonidas300, and Minotaurus: Will you join me, and be the backbone of the effort to return Elementia to its full potential?"

416

Leonidas and Minotaurus looked at the figure for a moment, and then stared inquisitively at Caesar. He was the most powerful, after all; whatever he decided, they knew they would, too. And so it was Caesar who was the catalyst for the three players kneeling down, and paying respect to this unearthly being who was to return them to stature.

"Good, good. However, there is one more order of business. I ask you to pledge yourself to me, but not by my name that binds me with the universe, not the name that I am well known by, no. I ask you now to pledge yourself to me by a different name. Repeat after me: 'I pledge myself to you, Lord Tenebris.'"

And as the last rays of sunlight vanished over the horizon line, three players with nothing to lose looked into the face of their new master, and repeated the pledge.

Just as they did, a player appeared in the waning light of Spawnpoint hill. He looked around in wonder at the world around him, and then his eyes fixated on the four players standing at the base of the hill. His eyes widened in horror as the player closest to him raised a bow, pulled back an arrow, and let it fly. The new player was dead before he hit the ground.

Just as the Kingdom of Elementia had fallen, the New Order had begun.

TO BE CONTINUED...

PREVIEW OF BOOK 2 OF THE TRILOGY

Stan2012 may have defeated King Kev and restored balance to Elementia, but the journey is far from over. Stan now finds himself tasked with all of the struggles of transforming the ruined country of Elementia into the land that he promised, while still maintaining equality among his people in spite of the protests of King Kev's remaining followers. The problems intensify when an extremist group calling itself the Noctem Alliance emerges from the shadows of Element City, pledging to use fear and destruction to finish the work of their fallen King. Before long, Stan finds that his friendships are falling apart in the atmosphere of constant pressure generated by the shady Alliance. And without his friends to help him combat the terrorists, Stan may find that his rule in Elementia is over before it even begins.

MINECRAFT: THE ELEMENTIA CHRONICLES

BOOK 2: THE NOCTEM ASCENSION

About The Author

Sean Fay Wolfe was 16 years old when he finished the first book of the *Elementia Chronicles* in 2013. He is a Minecraft player and an author of action-adventure tales. Sean is an Eagle Scout in the Boy Scouts of America, a four-time all-state musician, a second degree Black Belt in Shidokan karate, and has created many popular online games in the Scratch programming environment. He lives in Rhode Island, USA with his mother, father, two brothers, three cats, and a little white dog named Lucky.

Connect With Sean

Website: www.sfaywolfe.com

Facebook: facebook.com/sean.faywolfe

Twitter: @sfaywolfe

Links to buy Sean's paperback and ebooks are on his web page.

Links to Sean's online games can also be found on his web page.

DEDICATION

When I first began writing *Quest for Justice* over a year ago, I never dreamed that it would ever amount to anything more than just a fan fiction. I am amazed and grateful that this book has been published, and there are a few people that I would like to thank.

I would like to thank Lexi, for being the first one to edit my book and for giving me words of encouragement.

I would like to thank Josh, Scott, and Celeste, my good friends, for reading the early drafts of the book and giving feedback and criticism.

I would like to thank my younger brother, Eric, who finally promised, as a Christmas gift to me, that he would read my book.

I would like to thank my youngest brother, Casey, the first one to read the entire book and give me much-appreciated praise.

I would like to thank my grandparents, who have always supported me, no matter what, in everything I do.

And last but not least, I would like to thank my mother and father, who have given me countless hours of devotion, editing and reviewing this book more times than I care to count, and helping me to make this book a reality. This book is as much theirs as it is mine.

Made in the USA
Middletown, DE
19 December 2014